JAIMIE ADMANS is a 32-year-old English-sounding Welsh girl with an awkward-to-spell name. She lives in South Wales and enjoys writing, gardening, watching horror movies and drinking tea, although she's seriously considering marrying her coffee machine. She loves autumn and winter, and singing songs from musicals despite the fact she's got the voice of a dying hyena. She hates spiders, hot weather and cheese & onion crisps. She spends far too much time on Twitter and owns too many pairs of boots. She will never have time to read all the books she wants to read.

Jaimie loves to hear from readers, you can visit her website at www.jaimieadmans.com or connect on Twitter @be_the_spark.

Also by Jaimie Admans

The Chateau of Happily-Ever-Afters
The Little Wedding Island
It's a Wonderful Night
The Little Vintage Carousel by the Sea

Snowflakes at the Little Christmas Tree Farm

JAIMIE ADMANS

ONE PLACE. MANY STORIES

This novel is entirely a work of fiction. The names, characters and incidents portrayed in it are the work of the author's imagination. Any resemblance to actual persons, living or dead, events or localities is entirely coincidental.

HQ
An imprint of HarperCollins*Publishers* Ltd
1 London Bridge Street
London SE1 9GF

This edition 2019

1
First published in Great Britain by
HQ, an imprint of HarperCollins*Publishers* Ltd 2019

A catalogue record for this book is available from the British Library.

ISBN: 978-0-00-833071-2

This book is produced from independently certified FSC™ paper to ensure responsible forest management.

For more information visit: www.harpercollins.co.uk/green

Printed and bound in Great Britain by
CPI Group (UK) Ltd, Melksham, SN12 6TR

For my Little Bruiser Dog.
Thank you for making me smile every day
for fifteen years.
I will miss you every day for the rest of my life.

Chapter 1

I am never drinking again.

Please tell me that pounding, throbbing sound is not coming from inside my own head. I peel one eye open and severely consider not bothering to open the other one.

I'm slumped on the living room floor and propped upright by the coffee table, with my face smooshed against the keyboard of my open laptop. My movement jogs the mouse and the dark screen comes back to life, and my eyes hurt at the sudden brightness. I wince and push myself away, instantly regretting it when my stomach rolls at the movement.

When I can bring myself to peer blearily at the screen, there are loads of new emails in my inbox – and most of the subject lines say 'congratulations'. More spam, no doubt. 'Congratulations, you're the sole benefactor of a millionaire Nigerian prince, give us your bank details and we'll pop a million dollars straight into your account. Totally legit, honest.'

There are three empty bottles of Prosecco beside me, and my phone is worryingly nearby. Why do I remember squealing 'thank you, luffly robot voice, we're moving to Scotland!' into the phone at some unmentionable hour of the night? While sitting on the living room floor? With my computer? And my phone? I glance at the empty bottles again.

Oh god, Steve. On the desk in his office. With Lucia from accounting. That's why I'd broken out the emergency Prosecco. And then the emergency emergency Prosecco. That bare bum thrusting in amongst the spreadsheets was enough to drive anyone to drink. I'd never seen it from that angle before. There in all its spotty, hairy glory. And all that grunting. Did he ever grunt like that with me? I'd always thought it was sexy, but when you walk into your boss's office and find him humping your colleague on the desk, it sounds more along the lines of 'stuck pig'. Which, conveniently, is exactly the way I described Steve yesterday, with a few choice swear words thrown in for good measure, as I clambered onto a filing cabinet and announced to the whole office what had been going on, quit my job, and stormed out with a satisfying door slam. I'd then sat in the fire escape stairwell and let the tears fall, hurt and annoyed at myself for trusting him. I hadn't, at first. I knew he flirted with everyone and didn't really believe he liked me, but he was so charming, so believable, and I'd let myself be taken in. Why did I ever think it would be a good idea to get into a relationship with my boss? Why did I ignore the rumours that circulated the office about him? Why did I drink three bottles of Prosecco last night? Why . . . wait, why does that email say 'receipt for your payment'? I must've gone on eBay and bought another pair of shoes that look pretty but, in retrospect, were obviously designed for women much younger than me and with much slimmer feet and more attractive legs than mine, who also possess some ability to walk in heels, which I do not.

I squint and move closer to the screen. That email's from an estate agent. Scottish Pine Properties. I recognise the name because I've been daydreaming about their listing for a Christmas tree farm all week . . .

I sit bolt upright, ignoring the spinning room and thumping head as I click on the email.

I didn't . . . did I?

Dear Miss Griffiths,

I'm pleased to congratulate you on your purchase of Peppermint Branches Christmas Tree Farm. Thank you for your fast payment. I look forward to meeting with you to show you around your new property and hand over the keys. Please give my office a ring at your earliest convenience to arrange a meeting.

I *did*, didn't I?

It suddenly comes back in a flood. Oh god, what have I done? Why did I think looking at the online auction for a Christmas tree farm that I've been fantasising about since the first moment I saw it was a good idea after so much Prosecco?

Why do I remember shouting 'Hah! Up yours R-five-hyphens-81, it's mine!' at some ungodly hour of the morning, probably scaring a passing cat?

R-five-hyphens-81. The other bidder in the online property auction – privacy maintained by the website only allowing you to see the first and last letters of your opponent's name. The buzz of the auction last night. Watching with bated breath as they put in a bid with ten minutes to go on the countdown timer. So I put in a bid. Then they put in another. And I added another. We went round in circles until there were four seconds left on the clock. I hit the button one last time. And I won it.

Now there's a multitude of emails in my inbox that say things like 'Congratulations on your purchase' and 'receipt for your payment.' The automated phone call from the bank, the robot voice asking me to confirm that it wasn't a fraudulent transaction, that it was really me requesting to transfer the small sum of fifty grand to Scottish Pine Properties in Aberdeen.

I've actually done it. I've spent almost all of Mum and Dad's money on a Christmas tree farm. In Scotland. What was I thinking?

I glance at the empty bottles again. That Prosecco has got a lot to answer for.

Note to self: change security questions. Must be something unable to answer when drunk. The origins of pi or long division or something. Unfortunately I still remember my mother's maiden name and my first school even after three bottles of fizzy wine.

You know how you get overexcited at eBay auctions and you only want that skirt if it doesn't go above £1.50 and you're there right at the end and people are bidding and suddenly you've won the thing for £29.77 and you're absolutely exhilarated until the invoice email comes through, and you realise you do actually have to pay £29.77 plus postage for someone's manky old skirt that's probably got moth-eaten holes in it and stitching coming out, and when you get it, it smells of stale cigarette smoke and clearly has never met a washing machine before? This is like that, but I've bought a Christmas tree farm. This is so far removed from anything I'd ever normally even consider doing. But somehow, it doesn't feel like a mistake. That money has been sitting in a savings account, waiting for something to happen to it. I wanted to make something of it, to use the money from the sale of Mum and Dad's house to honour their memory or make them proud or something. I've never known what. That's why I haven't touched it since it came through.

Dad grew up in Scotland and always talked about selling their house and buying a farm there in their retirement. He always wanted to return to his Scottish roots. He never got a chance to live that dream. And as I stared at my laptop last night, that auction suddenly seemed like the answer. It wasn't *just* because I was slightly worse for wear. It was because, without that Prosecco, I'd have talked myself out of it and convinced myself to do the sensible thing and *not* buy a Christmas tree farm in Scotland.

I should be terrified. I should be getting onto the estate agents and begging for a refund on the grounds of diminished capacity. Obviously, this is a mistake. Of course I don't actually want a Christmas tree farm in Scotland. I live in the tiniest flat known to mankind in the centre of London. What am I supposed to do with Peppermint Branches Christmas tree farm in the little village of Elffield in the northernmost corner of Aberdeenshire?

That's what I expect myself to be doing. But the very small part of me that doesn't feel completely sick from the hangover is fluttering with excitement. I *don't* want a refund. I don't want to back out. I saw that auction over a week ago and have daydreamed about it ever since. How amazing would it be to own a Christmas tree farm? I've spent hours picturing wide open fields, rows of lush green trees, snowy ground, sleigh rides, and the scent of pine needles hanging in the air. Subconsciously, I knew exactly what time that auction ended. I didn't inadvertently stumble across it just as it was ending, and accidentally enter a bidding war with the other anonymous bidder, driving the price up by a grand each time, until my final bid went in at £52,104. With estate agent fees and whatever other expenses will be added on, that leaves me with under £2000 left in my savings account for whatever investment the tree farm needs. The price was so close to the amount I got from the sale of Mum and Dad's house that it's almost like fate.

It wasn't a drunken mistake. I wanted it, and in the cold light of day, I still do.

And coffee. I definitely want coffee.

***

'A Christmas tree farm?' My best friend, Chelsea, says incredulously as I put two pumpkin spice lattes down on the table between us. She deserves that much for abandoning her Saturday morning plans with her husband, Lewis, and coming out for a coffee with me.

'I like Christmas and I like trees, so why not?' I say with a nonchalant shrug. I don't know why I'm trying to act like this *isn't* a monumentally big life-changing thing.

'Well, I like Easter eggs but I'm not going to go out and buy Cadbury's.'

'Now there's a thought,' I say, my mind drifting to daydreams of owning a chocolate factory. Now *that's* the kind of property auction I should have waited for.

'Leah . . .' Chelsea taps the table in front of me to get my attention. 'It's in Scotland. You're seriously going to move to Scotland?'

Like it's a question I haven't been asking myself all morning. It's a big thing, but without Steve, without a job and without Mum and Dad two hours' drive outside the city, what have I got to stay in London for? Chelsea is the only person I'd miss, and it's not like we'd lose touch. The more I think about it, the question changes from why I'd move to Scotland to why I'd stay here.

'I'm stagnating here,' I say eventually. 'Since my parents died, I've been standing still, waiting for something to happen. I thought that something was Steve, but it clearly wasn't. And now what? Back to the job centre to hunt for another mind-numbing data entry clerk role that gradually sucks the life out of me day by day? And let's face it, I'm not exactly going to get a glowing reference from my boss, am I? Not after I stood in front of the whole office and invited him to do unpleasant things to himself with a turnip. And definitely not after I poured a hot cup of coffee down his neck and probably scalded his willy which was still waving about all over the place, and then topped it off by storming out without formally handing in my notice. What's he going to say to my next potential employer? "Oh yeah, hire Leah, she's great for a quick fumble behind the photocopier but don't let her catch you humping the head accountant if you prefer your willy unscalded."'

Chelsea laughs and I sigh. 'After the initial shock of Mum and Dad, the weeks of paperwork and organising funerals and then probate and solicitors and clearing the house and everything . . . I've been motionless, waiting for the punchline to this terrible joke I'm trapped in while life moves on around me. I'm like one of those stagnant ponds full of dead reeds. There might actually be insects living in me.'

'If there's green slime, you *really* need to get that checked out by a doctor.'

'Ha ha,' I say, even though I'm trying not to smile. I'm pleasantly surprised that Chels hasn't told me I'm insane. She knows how I've been feeling, but I still expected her to tell me I'm mad for spending so much – literally my parents' legacy – on a drunken whim, and doing something that will change my life without thinking it through. But I had thought it through. I've been thinking of nothing but that auction since the moment I saw a quirky news story about a Christmas tree farm being up for sale last week.

'What happened with Steve? I thought you really liked him until that series of very drunken text messages you sent me in the middle of the night.'

I cringe.

'Don't worry, they were so badly misspelled that even autocorrect had given up. I thought things were going well with him?'

'Yeah. Turns out things were going well for him and Lucia in accounting too. And Amanda in customer service. And Linda in acquisitions. Even Penny in printing had photocopied their bum cheeks together.' I tell her the whole sorry story about walking into his office to find him giving the aforementioned Lucia a right good accounting to on his desk with his trousers round his ankles, complete with grotty underwear on show. Why did I never notice his ugly boxer shorts before? 'I was too trusting. I mean, who really falls for their boss and expects it to work out? It's a fantasy, isn't it? I should never have let myself believe it . . . but

I was so lonely that being with him was better than nothing.' I bite the inside of my cheek as tears threaten to fall again. I can't possibly cry over him any more than I did yesterday.

She makes a noise of sympathy and I wonder if I shouldn't have said it. She's been amazing since my parents died, she's stayed overnight at my flat on more than one occasion, she's offered to let me stay with her and Lewis, she's dropped plans just to sit in my living room and keep me company because I didn't know what to do. I tried to carry on with normal life while this gaping hole was still inside me, and then Steve got promoted into my department at work and flirted outrageously and it was nice to feel something again, *anything*. Harmless fun, innuendo in professional emails, the odd stolen snog in the stationery supplies cupboard, a cheeky raised eyebrow in a meeting that set off a round of giggles. Looking back, I see I wasn't the only one giggling. Other girls went to get a lot of supplies and it took them a mysteriously long time too. I *knew* that. And I still trusted him.

'You seem remarkably okay with it?' Chels ventures.

'What other options are there? After everything that's happened in the past couple of years, a man being so much of a pig that it's an insult to pigs to compare them is the least of my problems. The office is welcome to Steve, I've got more important things to think about.' She can probably hear the wobble in my voice, but there's nothing I can do but forget about Steve. He doesn't matter anymore because I bought a Christmas tree farm last night. Even thinking the words in my head seems unreal. It's like something out of a Christmas movie . . .

'What are you going to do with a Christmas tree farm?'

'I had this crazy idea about growing Christmas trees on it . . .'

She laughs. 'You know what I mean. I didn't know you had any interest whatsoever in plants. Do you know the first thing about growing Christmas trees?'

'Not really, but I can learn, can't I?' I sigh. 'I *know*, okay, Chels? I know it's crazy and I know I haven't thought it through completely and I know I shouldn't have done it, but . . .' I trail off, unsure of what comes after that 'but' or why it's there in the first place. Really the sentence should end at 'I know I shouldn't have done it'.

Whatever it is that I don't say, Chels hears it anyway. 'You know, when you called me earlier, I put my legal hat on and tried to remember everything I've learned from work about property law. I thought we'd spend this coffee picking through terms and conditions while you begged me to find a loophole to get you out of this contract, but I don't need to, do I?'

I think about it for a moment because it's what I expected too. Chels is an assistant at a big London law firm, she's the perfect person to ask for legal advice if I wanted to back out of this. 'I felt like I lit up last night,' I say eventually. 'I can't remember the last time I felt as alive as when I won that auction. I know it's crazy, but something drove me to stay online and not talk myself out of it. I expected to regret it in the morning, but I don't. I'm excited, and it's the first time I've been excited about anything in a really long time. Or maybe I'm just jittery from the six bucketfuls of coffee I had before I left the flat.'

'You do know how dodgy it is to buy a property without even seeing it? What about a surveyor? You don't know *anything* about this place.'

I shrug. Honestly, I've never bought a property before, I don't know the first thing about what I *should* have done before handing over that amount of cash, but it's a bit late now. 'There are pictures?' My voice sounds feeble and pitifully hopeful even to my own ears.

She holds her hand out for my phone, and I slide my thumb up the screen and go to my most visited browser tab. Over the past week, the auction listing for the Christmas tree farm has been at the top of my internet history. I had a look as soon as I heard about it and spent a few minutes fantasising about owning a Christmas tree farm, instantly dismissed it as a silly daydream and went back to real life. But since then, whenever things have been slow at work or I've been on my lunchbreak, I've found myself pulling out my phone and going back there, staring at the photos that show fields and fields of uniform green trees, tall ones that tower above the photographer, medium ones, and tiny saplings planted row by row in fields of grass and earth.

Chelsea scrolls through my phone, expanding the pictures and squinting at them, reading aloud from the closed listing. 'Twenty-five acres, five species of tree ready for harvesting, dwelling included that needs renovation . . . Don't you think "dwelling" is an odd way to describe a house?'

'Well, yeah,' I say because it's something that's been bothering me too, but by the time I'd decided I was going to go for it, it was too late to ask any questions. 'It was a once-in-a-lifetime opportunity, Chels. Someone else was bidding as well, and I was going to lose it if I didn't go for it then and there. How often do you see a Christmas tree farm up for sale *and* at a price you can afford? I made a split-second decision. It doesn't matter what state the farmhouse is in. My flat's not exactly posh, is it?' I think of the dark stairwells that always smell of pee, and you count yourself lucky if pee is the *only* stench. It's got to be better than that. 'All right, so maybe it needs a bit of cleaning and decorating, but I can do that. There's no point worrying about it now, I'm sure it'll be fine.'

'It's a bit odd that they haven't even included a picture of it . . .' She looks up at my face and trails off.

All right, it *is* an odd way to describe the cute country farmhouse nestled among a garden of Christmas trees that I'm imagining, and it *is* unusual that there isn't a picture of it. 'Maybe they thought the fact it needs renovation might put buyers off? Maybe it's got, like, boarded-up windows and stuff and they didn't think it added to the appeal so they left it out of the auction listing?'

'Yeah, maybe.' She sips her coffee in an attempt to hide the look of apprehension on her face. 'I'm sure it's not important. At least you know there's a dwelling of some sort there. It probably just needs a coat of paint. I've got some spare Dulux in the shed if you want to take it with you?'

I love her for being supportive even though she thinks I'm a maniac. Even *I* think I'm a maniac. But it *was* a once-in-a-lifetime opportunity and I'm not sorry I went for it. I just hope I feel the same once I actually get there.

'You might find your very own David Tennant!' She squeals out loud at the thought and then ducks her head when several other customers turn to look at us.

Chelsea's current sexuality could best be described as 'David Tennant in *Broadchurch*.' She and Lewis missed it on TV and have recently binge-watched the boxset. Their surname is actually Miller, and Chels has never found anything sexier than the way David Tennant says 'Miller' in the show, apart from the way he says 'murder'. Even poor Lewis has been forced into doing impressions. I imagine that all their neighbours hear most days is them shouting 'Miller' and 'murder' at each other in bad Scottish accents. It's a shame David Tennant isn't actually a policeman because I'm sure someone would've called him by now.

'Ooh, Richard Madden from *Bodyguard*. Now *there's* a hot Scot if ever there was one!'

'I'm not looking for a man, no matter how sexy or Scottish they may be. Steve was enough of a mistake for one year. I'm going to concentrate on Christmas trees for a while.' I give her a false grin that she knows is false. 'Seriously, Chels. Steve was the last straw for me when it comes to men. I need to learn the trade of Christmas tree farming, not lust after Scottish men. That's my mantra from now on: no men, just trees.' She goes to protest but I interrupt her. 'Not even if Richard Madden himself turns up.'

She sighs like I'm a lost cause. 'Just find me a sexy Scottish bloke who rolls his Rs and doesn't mind saying "murder" a lot.' She drags the R out like a cat's purr.

'If I find anyone who actually speaks like that, I'm going to call the local zoo to check for missing animals in heat. And you seem to have forgotten that you're married.'

'I only want him to speak! I don't want to sleep with the man or anything. Although I wouldn't mind if you found one with good thighs and a penchant for wearing kilts in the traditional way . . . you know, sans underwear. Purely for educational purposes, obviously. To learn about Scottish culture.'

'You can find him yourself when you come up to stay with me.'

'Hah!' She bursts into laughter, causing the customers who looked at us earlier to turn around and peer at us again. 'It's October. It's freezing and we're in London which has already got a good ten degrees on the rest of the UK. If you think I'm going to the back end of beyond in the middle of winter, you can guess again. Invite me next summer *if* the stars align and there's a heatwave, the rain stops, and all the Scottish midges go away. Does Scotland even get a summer? And you'd better check out this "dwelling" before you start inviting visitors, you might only have room for guests of the equine variety.'

'You're my best friend. You're meant to be supportive.'

'I am supportive. I'd just be a lot *more* supportive if you'd bought a vineyard on the French Riviera. *Then* I'd help you move and probably stay on as your employee to help you out. You could pay me in wine and French pastries. Do you think it's too late to exchange it for a French vineyard?'

'You should've bought a vineyard and I should've bought a chocolate factory and then we'd have been set for life. Wine and chocolate, who needs anything else?' I grin. 'Don't you think a Christmas tree farm sounds magical though? Even the name gives me little tingles of joy. It sounds so delightfully festive, and those photos make it look so pretty. All those trees blowing in the breeze . . . You can imagine it in the snow, reindeer grazing all around, Santa's elves dancing around the tree trunks while jingle bells ring in the distance . . .'

I can tell she's questioning my sanity. Maybe elves aren't quite the best thing to base your property-buying decisions on.

'Your mum and dad would be so proud,' she says eventually. 'Your dad used to love getting his Christmas tree every year, didn't he?'

'Yeah, and Mum always used to spend the whole of Christmas moaning about pine needles on the carpet, even though she loved Christmas more than any other time of year and always said it wouldn't be the same without Dad's tree making a mess in the middle of the room.' I tear up at the memory and Chelsea reaches over and squeezes my hand.

'They'd love this.'

I nod and try to will the tears away. They really, really would. Is that subconsciously what drew me to the listing? After they died, I was left their house, but apart from my job and flat being in London, I could never face moving back there with them gone. The best thing to do was to let it be a happy family home for another family, like it was for us when I was growing up. I wasn't sure what to do when the money from the sale came through. Chelsea's advice was to get on the property ladder because I've moved from rented flat with crappy landlord to rented flat with even crappier landlord for the past few years, but I've never found anywhere that felt like home.

'I can't believe you're leaving to become a Christmas tree farmer. Talk about random.' Chelsea sips her latte again. 'You hadn't even considered it twenty-four hours ago.'

I had. I just didn't realise that my hours of daydreaming about Peppermint Branches *were* considering it. 'That's the thing about fate. Sometimes things happen that you're not really in control of.'

'Also known as Prosecco? And the things that usually happen are drunken texts to exes and shoes you can't walk in, not Christmas tree farms.'

'You know what I mean,' I say, even though there are hazy memories of us having girls' nights out which ended in both messy texts and inadvisable shoes. 'I don't have any doubt about this. For the first time in years, I feel like I'm doing the right thing.'

'Do you have any idea how much I'm going to miss you?' She bangs her head down on her folded arms on the table and short blonde hair flops over her forehead. 'I don't even know what to say, other than good luck. I think you're going to need it.'

I grin at her. 'No, I'm not. It's going to be perfect, you'll see. Nothing could possibly go wrong.'

Chapter 2

Two weeks later, after handing in notice to my landlord, squeezing all my important belongings into every spare centimetre of my car, and leaving the rest in Chelsea's garden shed, I'm off up the M40 in my tiny blue Peugeot. Only six hundred miles to go. But the distance doesn't matter. Nothing has ever felt as right as this. I'm not someone who takes risks or does things without thinking them through, and in the fortnight it's taken me to pack up my tiny flat and give my keys back to the landlord, no modicum of doubt has crept in yet.

Even though Chelsea was very keen to let me know there'd always be a place for me on her sofa if it all goes horribly wrong.

It's the middle of October, but I'm moving to a Christmas tree farm, so it's only right to put on my Christmas playlist. The autumn weather is gorgeous as I drive north on a sunny Tuesday morning, listening to a carefully curated selection of Christmas classics. By the time I've detoured around Manchester, I've been on the road for six hours, and the afternoon light is fading fast. I stop for the night at a B&B before facing another five-ish hours on the motorway the next morning, singing along to Mariah Carey, Michael Bublé, and Cliff Richard, and everything feels different as I cross the border. I grin at the blue and white Scottish flag road sign declaring 'Welcome to Scotland' as I pass it.

Even the endless motorways seem prettier. There are green fields all around and wind turbines spinning in the distance, and the scenery gets even better as I join the traffic towards Aberdeenshire. The sea is far off to my right and the mid-afternoon sun reflects off the water, creating an almost blinding sunburst. As the motorways change into narrow roads, there are fields of lush green trees everywhere I look. The grassy verges at the roadside are a healthy shade of green even though it's nearly winter, and the farmland around me is all recently harvested fields full of bales of hay, interspersed with patches of uniform dark green fir trees. It gives me a little thrill every time I see them. The roads are lined with a fence of trees towering above the car, a perfect screen separating road and farmland, the remnants of yellow hay peeking through from the other side. I feel a flutter in my belly as I get nearer and nearer to the village of Elffield.

There are neat patches of evergreen trees in the distance and I keep glancing towards them and wondering if they're mine. Is Peppermint Branches that close? I have no idea how big the land is in reality. Twenty-five acres sounds like a lot, but how far does that actually stretch? How many trees will be growing in that kind of space? The satnav is beeping and telling me that I'm nearing my destination, but it's a bit weird because the nearer I get, the more the trees surrounding the road start to thin out. Instead of pretty patches of lush green, the car crawls up a narrow road surrounded by a forest of the skeleton branches of dead trees, fenced in by what looks like shredded chicken wire. Surely I've taken a wrong turn somewhere? I glance at the satnav but it still shows that Peppermint Branches should be straight ahead.

This must all be my neighbour's land. Whoever he is, he doesn't maintain his trees very well. Any minute now, I'm going to come out the other side and see rows of beautiful emerald Christmas trees.

But my satnav is repeatedly telling me that I've reached my destination, and in a big driveway set back from the road, there's a man in a smart suit leaning against the door of the shiniest black car I've ever seen. He pushes himself upright and steps forward as I approach, like he's waiting for someone. But it must be a mistake. He couldn't possibly be the estate agent I was supposed to meet here and there's no way he's waiting for me, because this is *not* Peppermint Branches.

Peppermint Branches was all green trees and Christmassy goodness. It looked like somewhere you'd sing Christmas carols and hear the jingling of Santa's elves. If you heard any jingling around this place, it would be because the elves were running away as fast as their jingling little feet could carry them.

And that . . . dwelling . . . behind him. It couldn't be *the* dwelling, could it? It's only got half a roof and its windows are a thing of history. There's green ivy scrambling up one side that looks like it's doing a better job of holding the building together than the crumbling bricks themselves.

I'm so distracted that I nearly mow the man down as he starts walking towards my car. He's definitely coming over with intent. Surely this is all some terrible mistake and whoever he's really waiting for will be along any second. My satnav must've made a mistake bringing me here. I can ask him for directions and be on my way.

I stop the car and don't bother to turn the engine off, I'm not staying. I roll my window down as he approaches.

'Miss Griffiths?'

I freeze. He knows my name. That's not a good sign. This can't actually be Peppermint Branches . . . can it?

The building was a cute farmhouse once, but not for many years. No wonder they described it as a dwelling, and that's pushing it a bit. I don't think even bats would fancy dwelling in it. And the trees. Where *are* the trees? There are fields of trees on both sides of the road, but not one of them looks like it's still living.

'Miss Griffiths?' The man in the smart suit leans down so his head appears in the car window, not looking too happy about having to repeat himself. 'Welcome to Peppermint Branches. Congratulations on your purchase.'

'Are you joking?' I turn the engine off and swing my legs out of the car door. One foot sinks immediately into a muddy puddle. Congratulations, indeed.

I squelch as I try to heave myself out of the mud and onto the weed-covered gravel driveway. God, it's grim. The sunlight from earlier has faded to a dull grey sky that looks like it's considering getting dark even though it's only half past three. The endless skeletons of dead trees rise up against the horizon. I glance behind me at the 'dwelling' and look away quickly in case I burst into tears, because tears seem like a distinct possibility. It was supposed to be a flourishing little Christmas tree farm. This looks more like someone's done the place up early for Halloween. 'Are you sure this is the right place?'

'Yes, of course.' He sounds like he doesn't understand why I'm questioning it. 'I'm from Scottish Pine Properties. We spoke on the phone.'

'This is nothing like it looked on the website.' I struggle to find words for how shocked I am.

'Well, it does say that we encourage viewings. We recommend all potential buyers pop by for a look around before making a decision.'

'Pop by? I live six hundred miles away!' I snap, feeling a bit guilty because he's not exactly wrong, is he? It's what Chelsea tried to say before I stopped her. Who would be stupid enough to spend their entire life's savings on a property that they'd never even seen?

'Yes, I'm glad you've arrived, I've been waiting for ages. Here's the paperwork.' He pushes a clipboard towards me with blue page markers at the places I need to sign.

'The photos made it look different.' I ignore the clipboard in his hand. 'What happened to the trees? They're all dead.'

He glances behind him like this is surprise news. 'Well, it's winter, isn't it? Trees drop their leaves at this time of year.'

'They're meant to be Christmas trees. They're evergreen by definition.'

'Not these ones.' He gives me a cheerful shrug and looks at the field of bare branches to our left again. 'I suppose the photos may have been a little outdated . . .'

'A *little* outdated?' I repeat. 'Judging by the state of the trees, it looks like they were taken centuries ago!'

'They were taken when the property went on the market, and it's been on the market for a *very* long time. No misrepresentation here.'

'How long?'

'I say, is that the time? It really is late, isn't it?' He feigns a look at his watch, completely ignoring my question.

Why has it been on the market for so long? It didn't say anything about that on the auction listing. I thought it would be in high demand. I thought there would be loads of bidders and that I was the luckiest person in the world when I won that auction. Who *wouldn't* want a Christmas tree farm, after all?

The estate agent taps the clipboard when I make no move to sign anything. 'You got an absolute bargain here, Miss Griffiths. Twenty-five acres of land, a viable business, an . . . er . . . residential property.' He glances at the building behind me and quickly looks away.

I've only been here for three minutes and I can already tell that it has that effect on people. It's not the kind of building you want to look at for too long.

'A viable business?' I say. 'It's a Christmas tree farm and there isn't one living Christmas tree on it.'

'Yes, but so much land.' He rubs his hands like he's trying to show me just how cold he is from waiting and his eyes flick to the clipboard again. 'And your main area of Christmas trees is down there.' He points down the lane between the house and the dead trees. 'Look, I can see some green bits in the distance. I'm *sure* plenty of them are still living that you can cut and sell.'

Cut them? I glance at the dead trees with peeling bark and broken branches. Most of them look like they're going to fall over at any moment and save me the trouble. 'This is a matter for trading standards. You're selling something that's nothing like it was advertised.'

'Everything's mentioned in the brochure.' He flicks up a page on the clipboard and taps it with his pen. 'PDFs were available on our website for all potential buyers to download, and if you'd checked the terms and conditions, you would've seen the disclaimer that all photographs are for guidance only.'

Another page full of tiny print held out to show me and I sigh. He's right again, isn't he? I got so caught up in a daydream and a bidding war that it didn't even cross my mind to check things like terms and conditions. Magical images of a Christmas tree farm and the possibility of owning one overruled the more menial things like common sense.

'It's all yours now, Miss Griffiths. To be honest, I'm glad to see the back of the place. I've been out here hundreds of times to do viewings, but no one's ever decided to make an offer for it. I've never understood why.'

I risk a glance at the house again. Even calling it a house is an insult to houses. To be honest, it's an insult to a garden shed. This guy must be over the moon that an idiot like me came along.

'The auction was the last shot before we gave up on it completely. Some properties aren't financially worth the trouble,' he continues. 'It's an unconventional property and we decided to try an unconventional way of selling it, and it certainly paid off in the end.'

'Right, and do you think the cashier at the supermarket is going to accept my unconventional way of paying for my next shop via IOU note?'

He laughs, even though I wasn't joking. What little is left in my savings *has* to be spent on the farm, and after looking at the place, it's clearly not enough. And I've emptied my current account to get up here. I doubt I could even afford the petrol to go back to London and sleep on Chelsea's sofa.

He flattens the papers on his clipboard again and pushes it towards me, back on the page with the markers showing where I have to sign.

I hesitate. Could I still get out of this? The agreement is made and the money exchanged. I signed something electronically, but this is the first time putting actual pen to actual paper.

He nods pointedly towards the pen that has somehow ended up in my hand and gives me what is probably supposed to be an encouraging smile. He's bouncing on the balls of his feet in his haste to get out of here with a signature.

I take a deep breath of fresh, fresh air, and already I can tell that it's so different from London. Even the air feels different as I look around again. We're on a big gravel driveway outside the house, and in front of us is a farm gate that leads down a wide lane, past fields of weeds which seem to be the only thing flourishing on this land. Beyond that, I can see the tops of some dark green trees. That's got to be a promising sign.

I take a few steps towards the wide wooden farm gate, peer at the trees in the distance and feel that little flutter in my stomach again. I thought the butterflies that I've been feeling since the auction had all dropped down dead the moment I pulled in, and if not, then one look at the house had certainly finished them off. But as I look out from the gate and survey the chaotic mess that is somehow my land, a little flutter comes again. It might not look like the pictures, but it did once. I could make it like that again, couldn't I?

'I don't mean to rush you but I really do have to get back. I've got a lot of work to do before we close tonight, and I've been waiting a while for you to arrive . . .'

He does mean to rush me, that's exactly what he's trying to do. He's probably terrified that I'm going to try to pull out of the contract and he's going to be lumbered with trying to find another idiot who doesn't read terms and conditions to offload this place onto. He'll likely get a handsome bonus for finally getting shot of such a problematic property.

This isn't what I expected, but I still don't want to pull out. A branch in one of the fields creaks ominously. I reconsider for a moment, and then I press the pen against the paper and sign my name on his dotted lines.

All right, it'll be more of a challenge than I thought it would, but I wanted a challenge. I wanted something completely different from what my life has been until now. It'll be fine. As long as I don't look at the house. If I look at it, I'll start crying.

'Phew.' The estate agent can't contain his relief as he skips across to whisk the clipboard out of my hands before I've even finished the *s* at the end of my surname. He unclips the papers and shuffles them, pulling some sheets out with a flourish and slipping them into his shiny briefcase. He taps the rest into a neat pile and hands them to me, then he removes a jangle of keys from his pocket and waves them in front of my face.

'Congratulations, Miss Griffiths. If you have any queries, feel free to get in touch with the office at any time.'

I can almost hear the unspoken 'but don't expect an answer, I never want to hear the words "Peppermint Branches" again' that he desperately wants to tack onto the end of that sentence.

'It's all yours now. Good luck.'

He rushes back to his shiny car and speeds out of the driveway faster than a rocket full of monkeys with extra jet fuel.

Surely it's not normal for estate agents to wish you luck?

Chapter 3

As the engine of his car echoes down the empty road, I stand in the driveway and look around, feeling a bit lost. I expected a friendly estate agent to show me around fields full of neat rows of trees like the ones I've passed on the way up here. I expected him to point out exactly what's mine and tell me something about Christmas tree farming, maybe stop for a cup of tea while we signed paperwork in my quaint farmhouse.

But that would be a Hallmark movie, not real life.

In reality, the 'quaint farmhouse' looks like it could be part of the set for a zombie apocalypse movie, and the neat rows of Christmas trees look like indistinct greenery in the distance, and the map that the estate agent has left me with may as well be written in ancient Greek because I can't work out how it translates into actual, real-life land.

I text Chelsea to tell her I've arrived safely and avoid mentioning the state of things. It seems a bit scary to venture down the lane towards the tall trees, and even scarier to face the farmhouse, so I lean into the car and grab a black bobble hat from the passenger seat and pull it down over my long hair. It's cold today, the kind of cold that creeps in and numbs your fingers before you even realise it, and I shove my hands into my pockets as I wander up towards the road.

I cross the tarmac and peer over the broken wire fence. There are loads of different trees in there. The bare branches of something that's already dropped its leaves for winter, the blaze of red, orange, and yellow of a few oak trees in their full autumn glory, and the first sign of a few Christmas trees. Unfortunately, they're all in shades of yellow to brown. The healthiest looking ones have a few sprigs of green in amongst the brown dead needles. I don't know much about trees, but I'm fairly positive that *that* is not what an ideal Christmas tree looks like.

I turn around and look back across the road towards the battered old farmhouse and the land stretching out behind it. It can't be that bad. All right, it's a bit neglected, but the map shows loads of land behind the house, the Christmas trees *must* be there, and they can't *all* be in this state . . . can they?

To my right is farmland that looks neatly maintained so obviously belongs to someone else, and adjacent to my house are fields and fields of pumpkins growing. I can see a farmer in one of them, crouching down by the large orange vegetables on the ground. In the distance is a picturesque farmhouse with smoke pouring from its chimney into the dull afternoon sky, looking cosy and perfect.

I go back across the road to my crumbling old house and have a look around outside. At the back is a little garden enclosed by what's left of a rotting fence. There's an abandoned caravan run aground in the overgrown grass, surrounded by the broken glass from its smashed windows. There are piles of roof tiles in such a state that I can't work out if they're to repair the broken roof or if they're the ones that have fallen off it. There are tools and cracked buckets and shards of wood, the bones of what was once a washing line, and unknown parts of unidentifiable machinery.

There's a noise inside the caravan and I edge a bit closer. You can guarantee there are rats or something living inside it, although given the state of it, I'm not sure even rats would deign to inhabit it – and maybe it says something about my day so far that rats are the least of my problems. Maybe it's not rats. Who knows what could be living up here outside of civilisation? Apart from the other farmhouse in the distance, there's nothing else around. It's been hours since I passed a garage or a shop. Species that don't exist further south could be thriving here. It's a different world to the city I'm used to.

Glass crunches under my boots as my weight presses it into the ground and I take a tentative step towards the caravan and look in through the jagged window frame. Inside, the caravan has been ransacked, everything is torn out of its fittings and upside down on the floor, and it's full of grime, mud, and god knows what else.

'Oi,' I say to the unseen occupant. 'When I find the nearest shop, I'm going to buy a nice big box of rat poison. I'm giving you a choice, mate, all right? If you pack up now and move out, we'll say no more about it. If you stay, I promise an untimely and probably painful death. You might have been living in comfort here, but I've bought the place now, and I don't know what you are, but I suspect you're the unwelcome kind of lodger.' I take another step and tap the side of the battered old caravan. 'And if buying a Christmas tree farm without thought was insane, god knows what a one-sided conversation with an unseen rodent about the ins and outs of squatters laws would be considered. So go on, matey, off you go.'

I whack the side of the caravan again with the flat of my hand, and there's a thunk and a scrabbling noise from inside. I peer into the window again to see what my squatter is, and a squirrel suddenly drops down from the ceiling and hits me square in the face.

I scream and stumble backwards as the end of a bushy tail flashes through the window, dashes onto the roof of the caravan, and hurls itself into the grass and scarpers to safety.

Bloody Nora. I expected rats scurrying around the floor, not a squirrel going for the World Gymnastics title.

At the sound of my scream, a dog starts barking, and there's a shout of 'Gizmo!'

My heart is pounding from the shock and I put a hand on my chest and try to catch my breath. Of all the things that have been a surprise about Peppermint Branches so far, a squirrel to the face was definitely the most unexpected of them.

There's still a dog barking, and I look up to see the farmer racing across the rows of pumpkins in the next field as a tiny white and brown dog dashes towards me.

The pumpkin field is fenced in by a short picket fence, but the dog leaps over it easily, and I back out of my garden and crouch down to intercept him before he reaches the road.

The Chihuahua barrels straight into my outstretched arms, barking and spinning in excited circles.

'Oh, aren't you adorable?' I hold my hand out and he licks all over my fingers with his tiny tongue, making me giggle as he puts both paws on my hand and stands up on his back legs, his whole body wagging with excitement. The farmer jumps the fence surrounding his pumpkin field and slows to a walk as he reaches the grassy verge that runs along the edge of the road. He lifts a hand in greeting and I do the same, and while I'm distracted, the dog paws at my trouser leg like he wants to be picked up.

'You're so friendly. You don't even know me and you want me to pick you up?' I glance behind – there's no traffic and doesn't look like there'll be any anytime soon, but better to be safe than sorry. The dog clearly runs a lot faster than his owner, and it's a good excuse for a doggy cuddle. It's been ages since I had a doggy cuddle.

I pick him up and carefully settle him under my right arm, and he licks my chin and his wagging tail tickles my arm, making me giggle again. 'You are just too cute, aren't you? Yes, you are, you are. What's a good boy like you doing out here all by yourself, hmm? Aren't you a lovely little boy?'

I rub his ears and coo at him, and he turns his head towards every ear rub. I don't realise I've degenerated into baby talk until someone clears their throat and I look up to see the farmer standing in front of me with his arms folded across his wide chest and a dark eyebrow raised.

And he is *way* hotter than he looked in the distance.

I take in the long dark hair in waves around his shoulders, the red plaid shirt and faded denim jeans that make his thighs look like they're made of solid steel. Since when are farmers this gorgeous? I thought farmers were all old scruffy types with bits of hay in their grey beards and a faint smell of cow dung. I catch a waft of juniper aftershave. Definitely not cow dung.

I climb to my feet with the dog still under my arm and look up into eyes halfway between blue and green, set off by the darkness of his almost-black hair and unshaven dark stubble. If I was interested in men right now, it would be enough to make me go weak at the knees, but I'm not, and my knees are completely steady. I stamp one foot against the ground because it's clearly uneven and that's what's causing any shakiness there happens to be.

'Sorry about that,' he says in a deep Scottish accent, and I can't take my eyes off the piercing in his lip. It's just one silver ball nestled in the dip of his upper lip, but it looks so out of place with the outdoorsy clothes that my eyes are drawn to it as he speaks. 'Usually I trust him to stay with me but he heard your scream and came to rescue you.'

His accent makes 'to' sound like 'tay'. I'm so fixated on the piercing that I forget he's standing there waiting for a response while I pet his dog's ears and stare vacantly at his upper lip.

I swallow a few times but my voice still comes out as a squeaky remnant of the baby talk. 'Yeah, sorry. There was a squirrel.'

'Utterly terrifying.' His voice is sarcastic but the expression on his face doesn't change.

'It made me jump. I'm not *scared* of squirrels, I just didn't expect it to hit me in the face.'

'If you're here for a viewing, the place is off the market, it was sold a couple of weeks ago.'

'Yeah, I know. I bought it.'

'You?' That eyebrow rises again. '*You* bought Peppermint Branches?'

I nod, wondering if he needs to sound quite so incredulous.

'Oh, right.' He sounds a bit taken aback. 'Are you in the Christmas tree industry?'

'No, I'm a data entry clerk. I worked for a company that analyses retail sales figures in London until a couple of weeks ago.'

He looks completely confused. 'So what are you doing here? Some sort of admin?'

'No. I'm going to run it.'

'Run it?' He scoffs. 'Run it as what?'

'As it is. As a Christmas tree farm.'

His eyes flick towards the patch of trees in the distance. 'But it *isn't* a Christmas tree farm. It *was*, once, but it's been abandoned for over four years now. As the owner of the adjoining land, I can tell you it's in a hell of a state. How on earth do you intend to sort it out?'

'Four years?' I say in surprise. 'It didn't mention that on the auction site either.' I avoid his question because I have absolutely no idea how I'm supposed to sort it out, and I try not to think about the little stone of dread that's settled in my stomach at his words. It confirms the niggling fear I've had since I arrived: that this *isn't* a viable business and it will need a hell of a lot of work and investment – work I know nothing about and money I don't have – to make it viable again.

He ignores my ignoring of his question. 'You're not what I expected at all.'

He runs his eyes down me from the cable-knit bobble hat weaved with sparkly thread to my black coat which I now realise is no match for the Scottish autumn air, and my muddy winter boots that were clean before I got out of the car.

'What did you expect?' I feel myself bristling, certain this conversation is going down some sort of sexist route.

'Well, I had this daft idea that someone buying a Christmas tree farm might know the first thing about Christmas trees.'

'How do you know I don't? I could be the world's leading expert on Christmas trees for all you know.'

'You could.' He gives a nod of agreement. 'But your pristinely sparkly car has clearly never seen a dirt track before, your shiny boots have clearly never stepped in a puddle before now, your nails are clean, and from the look of horror and confusion on your face, I'd guess that this place is not what you thought it was going to be.'

I try to arrange my face into a non-horrified, non-confused look, but it probably makes me look like I need an ambulance.

All right, I don't know the first thing about Christmas tree farming, but is it really that obvious? Between getting paperwork exchanged with the solicitors, getting hold of my landlord, and the small matter of packing everything I own, I figured I could learn when I got here.

'I'm Noel.' He holds out a hand and I stop rubbing his dog's ear long enough to shake it. His earth-blackened hand is warm despite the chill in the air, and his rough skin rubs against mine as I slip my hand into his huge one. 'That's Gizmo.'

I grin at the name. 'As in the Gremlin?' I pull my head back and look at the dog, who's got gorgeous markings – a white chest and brown sides, and around one eye is a big patch of white that extends over his head, making one side brown and one side white. 'That's such a perfect name, he looks just like Gizmo from the film.'

‘Ah, *Gremlins*. One of the most underrated Christmas films.’ He whistles the song Gizmo hums in the film, and the Gizmo in my arms turns his head to the side and his tail wags like he’s heard the tune many times before. I suppose if you have a dog named after Gizmo, why *wouldn’t* you whistle Gizmo’s song to him at every opportunity?

‘I’m Leah.’ I realise I haven’t let go of his hand yet and quickly extract my fingers and go back to rubbing Gizmo’s ears. ‘I asked Santa for a mogwai every year when I was little. Never got one though. Can’t imagine why.’

‘Probably because they’re not real?’

‘Oh, really? I had *no* idea that a race of animatronic fictional creatures from an Eighties’ Christmas film didn’t actually exist. You’re not going to tell me that Santa doesn’t exist next and that reindeer can’t really fly, are you? What about the tooth fairy? It’s not the parents all along, is it? And what of *Jurassic Park*? Are you trying to say that it *wasn’t* a documentary?’

‘Hah.’ He laughs but his face shows he has no idea if I’m being sarcastic or not. ‘I’m sorry. You’ve totally thrown me. I expected the person who’d won the auction to be a property developer intending to flatten the place and build something new, not someone turning up and intending to run it as a tree farm again. And you’re seriously telling me that you’re not in the industry and you haven’t got any experience? Do you have any idea how much of a state this place is in? What on earth were you thinking?’

‘I was a little bit drunk, okay?’ I snap, annoyance creeping in again. ‘What’s it got to do with you whether I have any experience or not? I’d just caught my boyfriend cheating with half the office and I wanted to change my life. All right, it needs a *bit* of work, but I wanted a challenge. What’s wrong with that?’

‘You were *drunk*?’ His voice goes high with indignation. ‘Didn’t you even come for a viewing?’

‘Look, with hindsight, I realise that not viewing it first was a bad decision, but it was on the spur of the moment; the auction was ending and I had to decide then and there whether to go for it or not. There was another bidder and I didn't even realise how much I wanted it until I put the very last bid in with four seconds to go.'

'Four seconds.' He shakes his head in disbelief. 'How do you even do that?'

'I buy a lot of shoes on eBay?' I offer, hoping it might make him laugh but no such luck.

'You bought a Christmas tree farm like it was a pair of shoes?'

'No, I used my experience of buying shoes to win an auction. Not that it has anything to do with you, obviously.'

His eyebrows rise and he has the decency to look a bit guilty. 'No, of course it doesn't. I was only trying to figure out how insane my new neighbour might be.'

'Well, I wouldn't accost a complete stranger on the road and start telling them what they're allowed to do with *their* money and make judgements about how they intend to run *their* property.'

'People around here are going to comment, you may as well get used to it.' He lets out an annoyed huff. 'You bought a Christmas tree farm, with no experience of the industry, because you were drunk? What did you expect? Did you think you could stand back and watch the trees fell themselves, net themselves, and toddle off to market on their own?'

'Maybe. Well, apart from the toddling bit. If Christmas trees were going to move independently, it would be more of a leaping sprint, don't you think?'

I can tell he's trying not to smile. His piercing shifts as his lip twitches. And then he shakes himself and frowns again. 'This could be someone's life, someone's livelihood. Peppermint Branches was important once, it really mattered to the community of Elffield, and you think you can snap it up on a drunken whim and lark about here until, what, the heels of your designer boots sink into the first cowpat, and then you can sell it on to the next idiot who comes along?'

'These are Primark, not designer.'

He looks down at my feet. 'I don't know what that means.'

I go to start explaining but stop myself. I don't think a Scottish pumpkin farmer is interested in the pros and cons of high-street brands. 'I don't want to sell it on,' I say instead. All right, it's not what I expected, but I wanted to do something that made me stop feeling like I was standing still waiting for the grief of my parents death to dissipate. 'Why can't I learn how to run a Christmas tree farm? When I started data inputting, I had no idea what I was doing, but I learnt. No one starts a job knowing exactly what's what. This is a job like any other.'

'This isn't just a job. This is a life. Living and working on a place like this is all-consuming. This isn't an office that you leave behind at 5 p.m. every night. You *live* it, day in, day out, 365 days a year, and no, you don't get Christmas off. You don't get holidays and pensions and medical insurance. You spend every day trying to keep these trees alive. You don't look like the kind of person who'd be very good at keeping things alive.'

'I think a séance might be the only way to help these. They're already dead, look at them.'

He glances towards the area of dead branches on the opposite side of the road. 'I wouldn't worry about those, they're the windbreaker fields. The northern fields are healthier. Marginally.'

'Northern fields?'

'Oh, for god's sake.' He gives me a withering look. 'You don't even know what you've bought, do you? You have a northern and southern patch of land. South.' He throws a hand out towards the patch of dead-to-dying trees in front of us like I'm an imbecile. 'Road.' He stamps his foot on the tarmac like I don't know what a road is. 'House. Beyond house, trees. Yours.'

'You Tarzan, me Jane?' I say in an attempt at humour.

It goes down like a lead brick with an elephant tied to it. Probably just as well. The image of him in nothing but a loincloth is a bit too much for me.

'You don't know the first thing about trees, do you?'

'Well, I . . .'

He points to a large green thing behind me, one of the only green trees in sight. 'What type of tree is that?'

I squint at it. Is this a trick question? I pluck a species name out of thin air and hope for the best. 'Fir?'

'Cedar.' He rolls his eyes. '*Cedrus Libani*, actually. But I'm sure you knew that.'

'Oh, right. Of course. I knew that, I was just making sure that *you* weren't bluffing.'

'And what's that tree dying of?' He points in the opposite direction towards a sad looking spindly thing that probably had leaves on *both* sides once.

It's another trick question. It doesn't look like there's any dy*ing* about it, it's almost certainly already completed the process. 'Creeping brown deadness?'

'Aye.' He gives me a scathing smile. 'Otherwise known as wind-burn. It happens when the wind pulls water out of the needles faster than the roots can replace it. I can see this is going to go really well.'

'But I can learn this stuff. You weren't born knowing this, you learnt it.'

'Over years of living here. I grew up on a farm. From the age of ten, I came over here every weekend to help Mr Evergreene. You're not going to pick it up after five minutes with a *How to Identify Trees* book. It takes more than *Trees For Dummies*.'

I make a mental note to check whether he's being sarcastic or if this book actually exists. *Trees For Dummies* sounds like just the ticket.

Also, Mr Evergreene – seriously? 'There's no way that was the previous owner's name. You're making that up. Who runs the local garage – Mr Petrol? How about the manager of the nearest supermarket – Mr Tesco, is it? If there's a bakery owned by Mr Croissant, I want to go there.'

'Peppermint Branches is an amazing place,' he continues, ignoring me. 'A special place, a beautiful tree farm that was once famous and could be again if it had someone to take care of it and restore it to its former glory.'

His green-blue eyes are fiery with passion. He must really love this place. 'I could do that. Why couldn't I do that?'

'You know what, rather than answering that question, I'm starting to think I should go home and let you figure it out for yourself. I predict it's going to be fun to watch.'

'You could give me some advice rather than trying to make me feel stupid,' I snap. 'I *want* to restore it to its former glory. I want to make it a functioning Christmas tree farm again. You seem to know so much about it, tell me where I need to go to learn how. Tell me what books I need to read, what websites I should visit. Tell me what its former glory was like and how I can restore it.'

'Why? So you can do two weeks here, realise it's too difficult, and swan off back to London?'

'I'm not going to do that. I'm committed to this. I want to make a go of it.'

'I've heard that before. It lasts until you spoilt city women get bored of not having the luxuries of designer shops and posh restaurants at your fingertips.'

I want to ask him where he's heard that before and why he sounds so bitter, but I get the feeling he doesn't like me very much and would tell me to mind my own business. 'Have you seen some of the things those posh restaurants serve up? The contents of a vacuum cleaner bag look more appetising. And given the amount of money I've spent on this place, even Primark will be out of my designer shopping budget for the next thirty years.'

His mouth twitches and I can tell that he's trying not to smile. I'm entranced by the little silver ball again as we stand there staring at each other.

'So, what do you grow?' I ask when I suddenly realise it's a bit weird to stand on the roadside with a stranger's dog under your arm while you stare at said stranger's upper lip. I tear my eyes away from his piercing and nod towards the field he came from. 'Pumpkins?'

'No, Brussels sprouts.'

I look over at the field and lift my hand to shade my eyes from a sun that isn't there in case it's distorting my vision. 'Those round orange things trailing along the ground? They're pumpkins . . . aren't they?'

He throws his hands up in despair. 'The fact you even had to question that . . .'

'Obviously I know they're pumpkins. I was being polite. It could've been a new variety or something.'

'When have there ever been round, orange, giant sprouts that grow along the ground on vines?' He sounds exasperated.

'That's not fair. That's like me showing you a designer handbag and expecting you to guess the designer and then laughing at you for not knowing.'

'But I haven't bought a business selling designer handbags. Forgive me for my mistaken assumption that someone who's just entered the Christmas tree farming business might know something about growing things.'

'I know plenty of things about Christmas trees.'

'What, that they're green and look pretty with lights and a fairy on top?'

'No,' I huff, racking my brains for something I might actually know about trees. Any tree would do at this point, not even a festive tree. *Come on, Leah, there are trees in London*. 'Antarctica is the only continent where trees don't grow.' Hah. That'll show him. And prove to my Year 7 geography teacher that I *was* paying attention in class all those years ago.

His dark eyebrow quirks at the perfect angle to show exactly how unimpressed he is. 'Oh, there you go then. My concerns are unfounded. I'm sure you'll be wowing hordes of early customers before the week is out. So dazzled will they be by your intrinsic knowledge of Christmas trees that they'll be queuing up to buy them six weeks early.'

'I'm glad you think so,' I mutter. I know he's being sarcastic, but I can't let him get to me, even though if I'm completely honest, he's kind of got a point. Meeting a real farmer who knows this land and thinks I'm a lunatic for taking it on . . . I'd be lying if I said it *hadn't* got me worried.

'Let me ask you something,' he says. 'I know how long this place has been up for sale and I know how much the price has dropped and I know they were trying of offload it in an auction as a last resort, so I've got a good idea of how much you paid – very, *very* cheap. Did that not start any alarm bells ringing?'

'I didn't know how much they cost. I've never bought one before. There's no price comparison site for Christmas tree farms.'

'No, but there's this weird, and obviously *miniscule* in your case, thing called common sense. I see it's a completely foreign concept to you, but did it not cross your mind that fifty grand was cheap for twenty-five acres? Have you not heard of the phrase "too good to be true"?'

I huff in annoyance. He might be gorgeous, but I'm starting to really dislike this bloke. He speaks sense that I should've realised *before* I ploughed all my money into a failing Christmas tree farm. 'Just how desperate were they to sell it?'

'It's been on the market for over four years. There must've been a couple of hundred viewings over those years, but it's worthless land because you can't do anything with it. The trees have gone wild. Pruning them back into shape and selling them is an almost impossible job, and cutting them all down and replanting means any potential buyer has got roughly ten years to wait for them to grow to a saleable size. No wonder no one's bought it, but an idiot had to come along sooner or later. It's the law of averages.'

I don't even bother to be offended. I haven't seen much further than the driveway so far and I'm inclined to believe that he's not being totally unfair in that description. 'Am I unreasonable to want something that even vaguely resembled the pictures on the auction site?'

'No, but you're unreasonable to buy a property without looking at it, without hiring a surveyor, doing any background research, or using the common sense that would tell most people that if they're getting something so big for such a ridiculously cheap price, it's probably not that much of a bargain after all.'

'I don't call fifty grand cheap.'

He does another sarcastic laugh. 'Cheap in relation to size. Thinking you were going to get a working, functional Christmas tree farm that you could simply step into and start raking in money for that kind of price.'

'I knew there would be work involved,' I say through gritted teeth. 'Did you see the auction listing?'

He scratches the back of his neck. 'No.'

'There were pictures of *living* trees on it. So far, that seems to be a complete misrepresentation.'

'This land hasn't been maintained in four years. It *would* resemble the pictures. *If* it had been maintained, which it hasn't. For four years. That's more than half a Christmas tree's lifespan to average selling age. It's a lot of work to get them back into shape *if* any of them are salvageable, but they're not *all* dead. Yet.'

I look at the brown to browner shades of the trees behind me. 'No, what are they then? Dressed up in their Halloween costumes? Performing a horticultural re-enactment of *Night of the Living Dead*?'

His lip twitches again. 'I wouldn't worry too much about these ones. These are your windbreaker fields.' He sighs at my blank look. 'They're to protect the Christmas trees from the worst of the Scottish weather. Strong winds can distort branches and desiccate needles, and that's if you get lucky and the wind doesn't take the trees down altogether. Good farmers plant windbreaker fields to take the full force of it instead of the Christmas trees.'

I look around for some sign of these Christmas trees, and he waves towards the land behind the farmhouse like he knows exactly what I'm looking for. 'They're that way.'

'Oh, brilliant,' I say, genuinely overjoyed by this news. Gizmo licks my chin in approval and his tail wagging amps up. 'When I was growing up, my mum and dad had a houseplant in the corner of the room, and once a month, my mum would drown the poor thing, and every time I'd fish it out, drain it off, and nurse it back to health. If anything on this farm is alive, it's better than I expected when I drove in. I'm going to go and have a look around.'

He doesn't say anything, but he turns his head upwards and looks pointedly at the darkening sky. It's gone 4 p.m. and it's well on the way to getting dark. I can't make sense of the estate agent's map in the daylight, never mind the dark, and the unseen forest of trees at the end of the lane beyond the farmhouse looks intimidating, but I don't want to let him know I'm bothered because he thinks I'm an idiot anyway, it'd make his day if he thought I was afraid of the dark too.

I decide to be brave and point towards the gate closed across the lane. 'There's not going to be anything out there, right?'

'Like what?' He's got that smug eyebrow quirked up again, waiting for me to say something stupid. 'Worried you might run into another big, scary squirrel?'

'No.' I wish I hadn't said anything now, but it looks remote and scary. Apart from him, there doesn't seem to be anyone around for miles. If no one's been on this land for years, anything could be lurking out there and no one would know. 'Didn't someone float an idea of reintroducing wolves to Scotland once? And what if I put my foot in a bear trap or something? I've seen wilderness films – there's always a bear trap when you least expect one.'

'Wolves and bear traps? Seriously?' He pushes a hand through his hair and shakes his head in despair. 'You do know that this is the United Kingdom, right? You may have driven a long way but you haven't actually left Great Britain. There are no wolves and no bears to require the use of a bear trap. Have you mistaken Scotland for northern Alaska?' He's using a saccharinely sweet voice and it kind of makes me want to punch him. And I'd had such high hopes given the gorgeous dog and love of *Gremlins.*

'Well, thanks for the warm welcome,' I snap, and spin on my heel to walk away. 'It was a *joy* to meet you.'

'Leah?' He calls after me.

Hah. One well-placed sarcastic comment is all you need to make someone realise what a miserable twat they are. He'll try to backtrack and apologise now, no doubt.

'Can I have my dog back?'

Oh. Bugger. I forgot I've still got Gizmo in my arms.

I pull my head back so I can look into Gizmo's big brown eyes. Would it be petty to say no? 'You'd come home with me, wouldn't you, lovely?' I murmur to him, pressing my mouth against the brown side of his head.

His tail wags against my side in agreement, but I stomp back towards Noel guiltily. Even though I think this lovely animal deserves a much nicer owner, I didn't mean to dognap him.

Noel holds his big, dirty hands out and I somehow manage to transfer the wagging, licky dog into his arms, my skin brushing the surprisingly soft sleeve of his red plaid shirt as Gizmo pushes himself up to start licking the dark scruff of Noel's neck, excited at being reunited with his owner. The dog must see a nicer side than I do. I've only known Noel for ten minutes and I'd happily never be reunited with him again.

'Thanks,' he mumbles, his voice muffled behind the dog trying to give him a facial. 'Feel free to give me a shout if you need anything. Cup of sugar, a pumpkin to carve for Halloween, help building a bonfire which is probably the best use you'll get out of most of the trees, the address of some local demolition companies . . .'

'Yes, thanks for the sterling, *solicited* advice you've given me so far,' I mutter, even though he's been more helpful than the estate agent was. 'I'm going to go and look around *my* farm now and figure out what's best to do with *my* Christmas trees for myself. Goodbye.'

I only get a few steps before he calls my name again. 'I wouldn't go out there in the dark.'

'Why not?' I say to the empty road, not giving him the satisfaction of turning around. I will retain the moral high ground here.

'Mountain lions.'

'What?' I turn to look at him in shock, all pretences of the moral high ground or any form of dignity disappearing, although I think the dignity was already lost when a Chihuahua came to rescue me from a squirrel.

He points towards the trees and nods knowingly. 'Mountain lions.'

I wait for his mouth to twitch up in a grin or for him to burst into that sarcastic laughter again, but he doesn't. 'You're winding me up.'

'Why would I do that?'

'Oh, come on. If there are no bears or wolves, there are no mountain lions. You're having a laugh.'

'Maybe I am and maybe I'm not. The only way to find out is to venture into those trees at night.'

We stare at each other in silence for a few long moments. I'm still waiting for him to continue the joke, but what's he waiting for? Me to run screaming to the car and zoom off back to London?

'Also because the fence between your property and mine is flimsy in places and I don't want you stumbling into my vegetable garden in the dark and destroying my livelihood. And there's a river running through your property that's not marked on the estate agent's map, and most of its banks are worn away. It's too cold to fall into a river at this time of year, so wait until it's light to go exploring, all right?'

'Do you think I'm incapable of using a torch?'

'No, but if you get lost and die from starvation or hypothermia or get eaten by mountain lions overnight, having to give a statement to the coroner is really going to delay my morning and I have a lot to do tomorrow.'

I gulp. There's no way he's serious about the mountain lions.

I don't give him the satisfaction of responding. I turn around and stalk along the grassy edge of the road until I turn into my driveway. I open the car door and lean in, pretending to hunt around for something on the passenger side so I don't have to see his smug face again, and I don't look up again until I see him and Gizmo walking back across the pumpkin field in the distance.

I sigh and stand up, stretching my back out and looking up at the rapidly darkening sky and then down the lane towards the trees in trepidation. I'm not going out there in the dark. Even though there are no mountain lions.

Probably.

Chapter 4

I'm annoyed enough by him to face the farmhouse. There's nothing more inspiring than someone implying I can't do something to get me motivated.

At the top of the three crumbling steps, I shove my key into the rusty lock and push aside a spider that crawls out, trying not to think about what it says for the house if even the spiders are trying to get *out*. The door creaks as I open it and peer in cautiously.

It's just a house, I tell myself. An old empty house that's been old and empty for many years. I stand in the doorway questioning the wisdom of watching *The Haunting of Hill House* on Netflix last week when I was meant to be packing.

Maybe it would be braver to face the mountain lions.

Inside, it's so dark that it's hard to tell what condition the farmhouse is in. I find a light switch near the door, but nothing happens when I flip it. Great. So there's no electricity either. I step inside and close the front door behind me, but it does nothing to alleviate the draught blowing through the place.

I stand still and wait for my eyes to adjust to the dark, half-expecting something to jump out at me, but nothing breaks the silence. It's quiet in a way things never are in London. In my flat, you can hear the neighbours shouting through the thin walls, the traffic, the general hustle and bustle of the street outside, and the ever-present sirens in the distance. Here, the only sound is the rustling of the breeze blowing through from the empty window frames and missing roof.

It's a small house, even smaller inside than it looked from the outside. I'm standing on a threadbare doormat that's still got the dried remnants of mud from someone else's boots on it. There's a wooden staircase in front of me, to the left is what looks like the kitchen, and to the right is a living room. I can see the outline of an upside-down sofa covered with dust sheets. I hold the banister of the staircase, my fingers leaving lines in layers of undisturbed dust as I walk up slowly, using my phone to light the way. Upstairs, circled around a narrow landing walkway, I find a storage room, a tiny bathroom, and a bedroom with a single bed on its side and the wardrobe knocked over with one door hanging off. Telltale stones lie among the broken glass reflecting from the floor, evidence of what happened to the empty window frames. No one's even bothered to board over the upstairs ones.

Half the landing and the storage room have brown stains of water running down the walls, a freezing wind is howling around my neck, and there's the constant flapping of tarpaulin sheets where someone's tried to repair the roof and the repair has fallen in too.

In the bathroom, there's still toilet roll unravelling from a rusty holder and when I try to flush the discoloured water in the loo, nothing happens. Great. No electricity *and* no water. The estate agent had plenty of warning that I was coming today, shouldn't they have got everything turned back on? I glance in the cracked mirror on the wall. Maybe they didn't think anyone would be stupid enough to live in it. It's not exactly inhabitable by any stretch of the imagination.

The stairs creak under my feet as I go back down them. There's a curtain of cobwebs blocking the living room door, and I pick up an old umbrella that's leaning against the wall by the door and use it to swipe them away. I scan my phone light across the room, aware that I won't be able to charge it again until I can get the electricity turned back on. The room looks like it's been ransacked. Apart from the upturned three-piece suite, there's a sideboard on one wall with an old-fashioned TV perched on it that was probably modern once but not this side of the Seventies. There's a bookshelf on its front on the Eighties-style damask patterned rug, surrounded by limp books that have fallen from it, and a table that's listing dangerously to one side with half a leg missing. There's an open hearth in the middle of the back wall, and two sets of windows, one at the front that looks out onto the driveway and another at the back that must look out to the garden behind the house. Both sets have got gaps in the wood boarding them up and look riddled with the holes of a woodworm infestation.

I turn away and trudge back through the hallway to the kitchen to see if that's any better. The upper hinge of the door has rusted away, and it leans dangerously into my hand when I go to move it. Just as I'm trying to prop it back into the frame, there's a knock on the front door behind me, which makes me jump out of my skin in the silence. Maybe it's the estate agent come back to tell me he's dreadfully sorry but he's made a huge mistake and taken me to the wrong property after all?

I cross my fingers as I open the door.

'Oh, hello,' I say in surprise at the sight of the little old lady on my doorstep in the darkness. There's a yellowed porch light above us, but it doesn't look like it'd work even if the electricity was on.

'Hello, flower. It's Leah, isn't it?' She thrusts an age-spotted hand out, but I'm too surprised to take it, so she reaches over and grabs mine, pumping it enthusiastically. 'I'm Glenna Roscoe. You met my son and his dog earlier.'

'Oh!' I say in realisation. No wonder the news travelled fast. Let's hope she's a bit nicer than her offspring. 'Yes, he came to rescue me when I screamed at an unexpected squirrel. He's so adorable, he spun in circles and let me give him a cuddle.'

'Noel does that sometimes, you'll have to excuse him.'

It takes my brain an embarrassing amount of time to realise she's joking, so I laugh hysterically to overcompensate and by the time I've finished, she's looking at me like I've got at least one screw in need of tightening.

'It's an easy mistake to make, they've both got barks that are worse than their bites.'

In Gizmo's case, I believe her. In Noel's case, not so much. Noel and biting makes my mind wander to that . . .For god's sake, I've got to *stop* thinking about that sodding lip piercing. It might've been hot, but the hotness is regulated by the twattishness.

In the hand that's not still shaking mine, she's holding a plate with a slice of pie on it, and I don't realise how much I wish it might be for me until she clears her throat and I realise I'm staring at it and probably drooling.

She extracts her hand and holds the plate wrapped in cellophane out to me. 'A slice of pumpkin pie freshly baked this afternoon. It's not much of a housewarming, but I didn't know you were coming or I'd have baked something for the occasion. Welcome to Elffield, Leah.'

The kindness of the gesture and the gentleness of her voice makes my eyes fill up involuntarily. 'Thank you,' I murmur as I take it from her.

The underneath of the plate is warm and I breathe a sigh of relief as my fingers touch it and heat spreads through them. I didn't realise how numb they've gone and how cold I am until this moment. There are airholes in the cellophane and cinnamon-spiced steam is rising through them, making my mouth water because I hadn't realised how hungry I was either. As if on cue, my stomach lets out the loudest growl of hunger I've ever heard, and Glenna giggles. 'Noel said you weren't local. You must've had a long day of travelling?'

'London,' I mumble, my cheeks burning with redness. First I nearly cry in front of her, and now my stomach is auditioning for the role of Pavarotti. And I bet her charming son told her exactly how much of an idiot I am, so I must've made a stonking first impression on my nearest neighbour so far. 'And I didn't bring any food with me. I can't tell you how grateful I am for this. A pumpkin pie from a pumpkin farmer – thank you.'

'Noel's the farmer, flower. I make use of the produce to save it going to waste. We have a *lot* of pumpkins.'

'Do you want to come in?' I look behind me into the dusty, dark hallway, but the look of distaste on my face is mirrored on hers. 'I mean, you're welcome to but I wouldn't recommend it . . .'

'Let me guess – no water, no electricity, and quite a lot of spiders?' She leans forward and peers in the door. 'You're not really staying here on your own, are you?'

'Well, I have nowhere else . . .' I start, before swallowing hard as I realise I really am alone up here. Tears threaten again so I paste on a smile. 'The sooner I get started on cleaning up, the better.'

Which is true, but my smile is so false that it actually hurts my cheeks to hold my face in that position.

'What a lovely positive attitude. You must be very brave.'

Am I? I don't feel brave. I feel cold and lonely and like the idiot her son thinks I am.

'Aren't you freezing?'

'I'm fine,' I say breezily, despite the fact I'm hugging the pumpkin pie to my chest in an attempt to absorb any residual warmth from it because I'm so cold that I genuinely can't feel my toes and I'm surprised she hasn't noticed my teeth chattering by now.

'Noel said you weren't in the farming industry?'

Oh, I bet he did. 'I've got a lot to learn,' I say, using the same cheerful voice and wondering if she can tell that my teeth are gritted.

'Have you had a chance to look around yet? Such a lot of land and an excellent bargain too.' Her Scottish accent isn't as deep as Noel's but it has a way of making things sound sincere, and she seems like she's making friendly conversation with a new neighbour rather than being judgemental and insulting like her son.

'I didn't have a chance,' I say. 'It got dark so early.'

'You'll have to get used to that, flower. I'm sure you'll have fun learning all the quirks of Peppermint Branches. It's such a special place, it deserves a special owner too.'

My body betrays me by letting my eyes fill up again. It's the first positive thing anyone's said about this place, and it's been a long time since anyone thought I was a special anything.

She gives me a sympathetic look and reaches over to pat my arm. 'It must seem overwhelming, but you've definitely got the right mindset.'

I get the feeling she knows that if she stands there being nice to me for much longer, I'm not going to be able to hold back the tears, and no one wants their new neighbour sobbing all over them.

'You've obviously got a lot to be getting on with so I won't keep you. I only wanted to say hello . . .' She hesitates and winds her finger in a lock of grey hair that's loose across her shoulders. 'You know where we are if you need anything? If you want any advice or help with moving in, Noel's a strong young chap, he'd be glad to help you with any furniture or anything you want shifted when you clean up and clear things out.'

Yeah, I'm sure. 'I'm good, thanks,' I say, hoping she doesn't notice the shudder at the thought of him *helping* me with anything. 'Thanks for the pie,' I add quickly, because I don't know what I would have eaten without it.

'You're very welcome. It was lovely to meet you, Leah. I have a feeling we'll be seeing a lot more of each other. Come by anytime. I've always got a hot kettle and a warm slice of pie for my only neighbour.'

'Are you okay getting home?' I say as she walks away.

'Oh yes, thank you. It's only across the field, I know every ridge like the back of my hand, don't you worry. Cheerio!'

'Give Gizmo an ear rub from me!' I call after her.

'Sorry, flower, I didn't quite catch that,' she calls back. 'Did you say Gizmo or Noel?'

'Gizmo!' I shout loud enough for astronauts on the International Space Station to hear me.

No response. Great. Sending Noel's mum home to give him an ear rub on my behalf would be the icing on the cake of this ridiculous day, wouldn't it? If I was going to ask her to give Noel anything, it'd be a swift whack with a broom, but I'd be worried she might take the pie back.

I take the plate into the kitchen and squeeze around the broken door, which is now hanging halfway between closed and open, and use my phone light again to survey the damage. Like the living room, it's got boarded up windows at the front and back, a sink and draining board built into an empty counter that runs along one wall and curves around the corner and underneath the front window. I use my sleeve to wipe part of the unit free of the muck and grime that's settled after years of not being cleaned and put the plate down. I'm starving and I could murder a cup of tea, but I settle for the bottle of water I've got in my bag and make do with giving my hands a good anti-bac wipe before I unwrap the slice of pie and take a bite. I've never had pumpkin pie before and the sweet creaminess of condensed milk and pumpkin, cinnamon, cloves, and ginger combine to make it taste like autumn in a mouthful. It's a good job the only neighbours are likely to be of the rodent variety because I'm definitely having a *When Harry Met Sally* moment. I hadn't even realised how hungry I was until the first mouthful filled my belly with warmth, and I stand there in the dark kitchen, taking bite after bite, washing it down with lukewarm water that's been in the car all day. There is *nothing* I wouldn't do for a cup of tea right now.

There isn't much to see in the kitchen. There's a rusty old fridge-freezer standing next to the passageway that goes under the stairs and straight through to the living room, past a back door that leads out into the garden where the caravan is. Cupboards line the upper walls, and it smells like someone never got around to throwing out whatever was left in them, because the kitchen is heavy with the smell of food that's been gradually rotting for years.

My phone pings on the unit where I've put it down and I look at the screen. Another text from Chelsea, asking me if it's a magical winter wonderland, following on from the one she sent earlier asking if I'd seen any elves yet, which I ignored because I couldn't face answering with the truth.

How do I tell her that my magical winter wonderland is full of spindly dead trees and fluffy-tailed rodents and the most elf-like thing I've seen since I got here is a Chihuahua called Gizmo who qualifies only on the basis of his pointy ears? How do I say that, far from a couple of coats of Dulux, the only thing likely to improve this 'dwelling' is the application of a wrecking ball, and that when we joked about it being a stable, it would actually be better if it was?

I put the phone back on the unit without replying. How can I do this? How can I stay here? How can someone who doesn't know the first thing about trees suddenly decide to run a Christmas tree farm? What was I thinking? I must've genuinely thought I was part of a made-for-TV Christmas movie and forgotten real life for a moment. I'd pictured stepping onto the set of a film, saving the gorgeous little tree farm from the edge of destruction with my annoyingly upbeat personality and perfect hair. Neither of which I possess in real life, so I'd definitely mistaken myself for a film character.

For the real me, this is overwhelming. I can't sort this mess out. How can I stay here with no water and no electric and nowhere to sleep? All the positivity I was feeling earlier has drained away in the cold dark of the night. I spent all of Mum and Dad's money because they would have loved a Christmas tree farm. And now I want to run away. I hate myself for wanting that.

My phone pings simultaneously with a low battery warning and yet another message from Chels.

Have you found David Tennant and run off with him and that's why you're not answering my texts?

I pick it up and try to formulate a reply that sounds more cheerful than I feel, but it beeps again before I can think of anything.

Are you buried under a vat of gorgeous-smelling pine needles? Are you building a snowman to welcome your first customers? Why do I imagine it's snowing there? Ooh, have Richard Madden AND David Tennant turned up and you're off having a naughty Scottish threesome under the Christmas trees?

The low battery warning gets more persistent as I stand there and stare at it.

I could go and charge it in the car. That's not a bad idea actually. I could even sleep there. There's too much stuff in the back to lower the seat, but I can sleep upright a lot more comfortably than I could sleep anywhere inside the house. And, more importantly than anything, it's got a heater.

It's nearly seven o'clock by the time I slide into the driver's seat. I plug my phone into the lighter socket and start the engine. I flip the light on above me and turn the heater up to full and hold my shivering hands over the air vents.

I reach into the back and snake my hand between boxes and bags until my fingers close around the soft edge of a Christmas blanket that Chelsea bought me last year. I pull it out inch by inch as the bag holds onto it tightly in the squashed space. I drape it over myself and wrap it around my face and breathe into it, trying to warm up my cold nose. I'm still unsure of what to say to Chelsea, so I let my phone charge for a bit and reach over to put the radio on instead. It's still tuned to my favourite

Christmas station, and the car is immediately filled with Mariah Carey singing 'Miss You Most At Christmas Time'. I wish I'd stuck to my playlist. The songs on there are safe. They won't remind me of my parents and how much I miss them.

I swallow hard. I should turn it off, but I sit and listen to it instead. It's a song I've successfully avoided since the first time I heard it after they died and ended up having a breakdown in the middle of Debenhams while Christmas shopping in my lunch hour.

As if the universe knows this, Mariah is immediately followed by 'Something About December' by Christina Perri, a song about childhood Christmases and memories feeling closer in December, and I don't even realise I'm crying until tears drip onto the blanket.

God, what am I doing here? How can I have made such an awful mistake?

I can feel panic creeping up my chest. I have nothing left and nowhere else to go. I look up at the dark house in front of me and the sight of its crumbling bricks and missing roof makes me cry harder. How can I have been so positive yesterday? Driving along sunny motorways, singing along to 'Carol of the Bells', glad no one could hear me because I haven't got a clue what the words actually are, to this – sitting outside what was supposed to be my dream home, sobbing because Elvis is on now. This probably wasn't what Elvis had in mind when he sang 'Blue Christmas'.

My phone beeps again.

LEAH! Will you answer a flipping text, please? I'm starting to get so worried that I broke out the capital letters. Send me a picture of the place or something! Is the dwelling better than we expected?

I hit reply and my fingers hover over the empty text box. *It's great*, I type and then delete it. I can't lie to her but how can I admit that I've made such a huge mistake? I know she'll try to help. I know she'll tell me to come back to London and sleep on her sofa, and she'll offer to help me find another job and probably get someone from the law firm to draft a letter to Scottish Pine Properties demanding my money returned because the pictures were inaccurate, and that would be great, but how much of a failure can one person be? I made this mistake, I should be the one to fix it.

More tears blur my eyes as I sit there staring at the screen of my phone, hating myself because I don't know what to say to my best friend. Chelsea and I text each other *all* day, even when we're in work and aren't supposed to have our phones on us. Thinking of something to say to her has never been a problem before.

I push the phone onto the dashboard and cry harder. I know she's going to ring in a minute because I haven't answered, but I'm crying so much that I can't even see the screen to type now.

I feel more alone than I've ever felt before. I just want my mum. What would she tell me to do? What would she and Dad do in this situation? I already know the answer. Mum would've found a mop and bucket and started cleaning the house and Dad would've gone out for a good look around to assess how bad things actually were before panicking about it. Mum would've whipped out a gigantic bar of chocolate and somehow produced a cup of tea, and promised that things would look better in the morning.

I don't know how long I sit there having a good cry. I miss them, and I don't allow myself to miss them very often, because I inevitably end up as a snot-drenched wreck, but none of this would've happened without their accident, their money, and their love of Christmas and the real Christmas tree that stood proudly in front of our living room window every December. I let the grief consume me in a way I haven't for many months now. In front of Chelsea and Lewis, Steve, work colleagues, and acquaintances who were friends once but have barely spoken to me for the past two years because they don't know what to say, I pretend I'm fine. The last time I sobbed in my own flat, a neighbour banged on the door and yelled at me to keep it down.

I look up at a glimpse of light coming towards me. It must be headlights on the road – the first car that's passed since the estate agent zoomed off. It's moving slowly for a car though, and as I blink tears away, I see it's only one beam of light, not two, and it's on the grassy verge, not the road.

Just a dog walker, I tell myself. Mountain lions wouldn't carry torches so it's nothing to worry about.

Until whoever it is stops at the edge of my driveway and the beam of the torch settles on the house, and then slides across the gravel to point directly at the car. Or, more specifically, my red, wet, snotty face *in* the car, and the owner of the torch moves towards me.

I recognise the faded jeans and the fall of dark hair across shoulders.

Oh, come *on*. It's like he's got radar to detect the worst possible moment and time his arrival accordingly. I've still got tears streaming down my face and I've been crying so hard that I can barely catch my hitching breath. I cannot deal with him right now.

If I stay still, maybe he won't see me, but I know it's hoping for too much. It's dark and the light is on inside the car – I'm literally a flame to a petulant moth. I sink down in the seat and pull the blanket up further over my face so I can barely see out, but it's no good, I can feel the beam of torchlight on me, coming closer.

I do the sensible, adult thing and stare stubbornly at the house, pretending I haven't seen him. Maybe he'll get the hint and go away? I stare resolutely ahead, even though I can sense the shadow outside the car window and see the beam of light disappear as he turns the torch off.

It still makes me jump when he knocks on the window.

Bugger. I sniff hard and turn away to swipe my hands over my face, trying to brush away the evidence. Maybe it's dark enough that he won't notice the red puffiness?

I paste a smile on my face and turn back to roll down the window just as he's about to knock on it again.

'Noel,' I say, my voice thick, the fake smile pulling painfully on the skin of my lips.

'What are you doing out here?' His voice has that same half-amused half-sarcastic tone that he had earlier. He rests his arm along the open window and his head appears in the gap, but he suddenly looks taken aback and his voice turns serious. 'Are you crying?'

Well, one point for observation, I suppose.

'No.' I don't know why I'm bothering to deny it; if the tears streaming down my face don't give it away then the snot definitely will.

'What's wrong?'

I *should* turn around and snap something at him, but his voice is soft and those two simple words sound so caring and genuine. No one has asked me that in months. I struggle to keep my emotions hidden in public, and when I hang out with Chels, if I slip up and look upset for a moment, she gives me a hug but she doesn't ask me what's wrong because it's obvious.

I go to say 'nothing', but it comes out as *noth-urrth* as another sob gurgles out of my throat and more tears fill my eyes and spill over. God, why am I like this? Why can't I even hold it together in front of this rude man? He's going to love this, isn't he? He already thinks I'm stupid, and now he finds me crying in the car. He'll have a field day with this. He'll probably go and tell all his mates about this silly girl who thought she could run a Christmas tree farm and make sure the whole town has a good laugh about it.

I turn away again and bury my face in the blanket. I can't even pretend not to be crying now. Maybe allergies?

My nose is running and I know there's a pack of tissues in the glovebox, but the passenger seat is so jam-packed that I can't open it fully. As I'm trying to snake my hand in the inch-wide gap and feel around for them, a packet appears in front of my face.

I take them from his hand and wrestle the packet open with wet fingers. They're soft and thick and large, and I pluck one out and hide my whole face in it. If I can't see him then he can't see me either, so maybe he'll go away? That's bound to work, right?

I breathe into the tissue for a few minutes but he doesn't go away.

I can feel the warmth of his presence beside the car, hear his breathing and the crunch of frozen gravel under his boots with every movement. Even the scent of juniper and dark cinnamon aftershave has wafted into the car and it's unfair that someone who is this much of a twat can smell so good.

I wipe my face on the tissue and blow my nose, managing to make the most undignified sound someone has ever made in front of a fellow human before. I take a deep breath, and force a smile onto my red, puffy, tear-stained face, and . . .well, I intend to turn to face him, but I lose my nerve at the last second and end up staring intently at the steering wheel instead.

'Are you okay?' He speaks before I have a chance to say anything. His Scottish accent sounds warm and gentle. It makes tears well up again because it's another question that people usually ask me when they know full well that the answer will always be a cheerful 'yep, thanks' no matter how I really am, but he says it so earnestly that I feel like I could tell him.

Not that I'm going to, obviously. Finding me like this has probably made his day, there's no need to make his month too.

'Fine, thanks.' My voice is thick and it shakes on both words. I swallow hard and try again. 'What was it you wanted?'

'I came to see if you were okay.' He's quiet for a moment, which gives my eyes plenty of time to start watering again because he's got a caring tone that he has no right to have. 'Which you're clearly not.'

'Well, there you go then,' I snap, betrayed by the sob that comes out instead. 'You've found out what you wanted to know. Goodbye.' I have to feel around for the window button, intending to roll it up, but I press the wrong direction and it makes a clunking noise because it can't go any further down.

'I'm not going anywhere until I know you're okay, Leah. I can't walk away and leave you sitting out here in the cold. What's wrong?'

Even if I wanted to, I can't answer him because I'm crying too hard. Snot is dripping from my nose again and tears are streaming down my face, dropping onto the blanket, and I wrestle another tissue from the packet on my lap and try to restore some semblance of dignity.

'Is this because of me?' He asks gently. 'Because of what I said earlier?'

'Hah. Don't flatter yourself.' I snort and a snot bubble escapes. I'm doing an *amazing* job of the dignity thing so far.

'I didn't mean it in an egotistical way. One of the reasons I came over was to apologise. I was too harsh earlier and I over-stepped the line, and I *am* sorry, really.'

I hate him because he sounds so genuine. Maybe it's the accent. He has a way of sounding sincere that leaves me unable to tell if he is or isn't.

I blow my nose again and scrub my hands over my face, telling myself that I need to tell him it's fine and say goodbye, but a really *really* microscopically tiny part of me doesn't want him to go yet. Before I've figured out how to say anything, he moves out of the window and the car door is pulled open from the outside, and he crouches down beside me.

The movement surprises me and I look at him without thinking. He looks even better tonight than he did earlier. He's got the same well-fitting jeans on, black welly boots halfway up his calves, a long waterproof coat with wooden toggles closing it diagonally across his chest, and his dark hair is sticking out from under an oversized bobble hat, looking windswept and touchable.

He nods towards the radio, where 'Fairytale of New York' is coming out of the dashboard. 'I've never been a fan of this song but is it really *that* bad?'

I reach over and switch it off.

'You can leave it on. It's never too early for Christmas music.'

'Finally, someone who understands,' I say, so surprised by someone who agrees with my stance on festive music in October that I forget about crying for a moment. 'I told my friend I'd dusted off the Christmas playlist for driving up here and she nearly disowned me because it's too early.'

'It's nearly the middle of the month. That makes it practically Christmas. If mince pies are in the shops, it's fine to play Christmas music.'

I can't take my eyes off that lip piercing again as he grins.

'So,' he starts, pressing one hand against the doorframe to balance himself, 'my mum came in earlier, rubbed my ears and said "that was from Leah." Would you happen to know anything about that?'

An unexpected laugh bursts out at the crystal-clear mental image. 'Oh, for god's sake, I said Gizmo, not you.'

'Yeah, he probably would've appreciated an ear rub more than I did.'

'Has she got problems with her hearing?'

'Aye, but it's undiagnosed because doctors can't do much about "selective" hearing.'

'I think all parents have that. My mum was the same . . .' I trail off and swallow past the lump in my throat. I've just about got the tears under control, I can't start crying again.

There's a charged silence. I know he's picked up the 'was' in that sentence, and I can almost hear him deciding on the best thing to say.

'At least you didn't tell her to give me a Bonio.'

That makes me laugh again but I can feel his eyes boring into the side of my head.

'Go on then,' he says eventually. 'Apart from having no water, no electricity, no heat, and no food, why are you outside crying in the car?'

It sounds as pathetic as it must look, but he doesn't seem as harsh and judgemental as he did earlier.

I take a few deep breaths and lean my head back and close my eyes. 'It's not because of what you said, it's because you were right. This place is a disaster and I have no idea what I'm doing. The house is cold and damp and broken, my phone ran out of battery because I had to use it as a torch, and my best friend has been texting all afternoon asking how wonderful it is, and I haven't replied because I don't know how to tell her the truth about what a stupid mistake I've made.'

His coat rustles as he shrugs. 'Tell her it needs work but you wanted a challenge. Here, give it to me, I'll write it for you.'

I don't know why, but I take the phone off the dashboard and put it in his open hand. I never trust *anyone* with my phone, but I don't think twice about handing it to him.

I'm almost hypnotised by his fingers as they fly across my screen. I watch him with a strange mix of gratitude and amusement, until he turns the phone around and shows me what he's written.

It's a great area and the neighbours are the most wonderful people I've ever met. Farm needs a bit of work but I wanted a challenge.

I laugh at the remark about the neighbours and give him the nod to press send.

It beeps with a reply before he's even had a chance to hand it back to me, and he laughs when he looks down at the screen.

Have you found a gorgeous, sexy farmer in a kilt yet?

Noel laughs. 'Please let me reply to that?'

I nod. In for a penny and all that. When he holds up the phone to show me what he's written before sending, it reads:

Yes, I have! The only thing missing is the kilt – too well-ventilated – but the wellies are sexy enough to make up for it! We might have a romp amongst the pumpkins next door!

I burst out laughing again, thankfully minus any snot bubbles this time. 'Romp? *Who* uses the word "romp" these days? Have you time-travelled from a Charles Dickens novel?'

He shrugs as he presses send again. 'Made you laugh though, didn't it?'

The skin of my face is taut where the tears have dried, but I can't deny it. 'Chelsea's going to know I didn't write that.'

'She'll probably think you're hanging out with your sexy new neighbour in his kilt and welly boots.' He winks at me, making the lip piercing shift and glint in the light of the car. 'And before you go getting any ideas, I would never defile the pumpkins like that.'

Before I can say that I'd rather snog a Jack O'Lantern than romp anywhere *near* him, Chels texts back again.

Romp? Bloody hell, are you in Scotland or the 1870s?

I take the phone back and quickly type a response.

That was Noel, he thinks he's clever, and also of the Victorian era, apparently.

She replies instantly.

Ooh, sexy name! Fittingly festive! Please tell me he sounds like David Tennant!

I hold the phone up to show him and he laughs. 'Do I?'

'No.' I don't tell him he sounds *better* than David Tennant. Instead, I type back to Chels:

No, but he looks like the sexiest version of Luke Evans you've ever seen.

I go to throw the phone back onto the dashboard without showing Noel my reply, but he plucks it out of my hand and reads it.

'Cheeky bugger,' I mutter, realising that talking about his looks while he's crouched next to me was probably not the best idea.

Chelsea sends back a series of drooling emojis and he laughs again. 'I don't know who that is. If I Google him, I'm going to find he looks like the back end of a mangled cow, aren't I?'

It makes me laugh again. 'No. Surprisingly, that wasn't an insult.' I take the phone back out of his hand and push it onto the dashboard. He leans heavier against the doorframe of the car and shuffles his feet with a wince. He's been crouched there for ages, his legs must be getting sore. And I need to stop thinking about his legs in those well-fitting jeans.

'It's not as bad as you think, you know.'

'What, this place?' I glance up at the tumbledown house looming over us. 'I think it's the biggest mistake I've ever made. The only way it could be worse was if I'd accidentally bought a slurry pit. Which, in some parts of the house, is actually not an unfair description.'

'What I said earlier . . . I *was* out of line. You took me by surprise and it's taken until now for my brain to catch up with my mouth. I shouldn't have been so blunt.'

'But you were right. I don't know the first thing about Christmas trees. The extent of my horticultural experience is pulling dead branches off a houseplant and putting some crocus bulbs in the lawn for Mum one winter. *How* did I ever think I could be a Christmas tree farmer? It would be bad enough if it was the working farm I'd imagined, but this . . . I can't do this.'

'But you were right too,' he says gently. 'You *can* learn. And it really isn't as bad as it seems. You'll see when you look around tomorrow. Your trees aren't all dead. Most of them are overgrown, but they can be sheared. Weeds can be pulled. You have fields full of saplings that didn't survive so you can dig the ground over and start again in the spring. There's so much potential here for someone who isn't afraid of a challenge.'

I didn't think I was, but I'm definitely having a wobble tonight.

'If you phone the electric and water companies in the morning, they'll have you back on by lunchtime. As for the house, it probably needs a few repairs but it's still structurally sound.'

'There's ivy holding it up.'

'Ah, but it's structurally sound ivy.' He looks towards it, nearly overbalancing with the movement and his hand grabs at the seat to stop himself falling, his arm brushing against my thigh. 'Can I tell you what I think?' He shifts his hand back to the doorframe, waiting for a response. He wasn't unforthcoming with his opinion earlier, but now I get the impression that if I told him to mind his own business, he would. 'I think you come from a flat in London which has always got hot water, electricity, and central heating, and whatever you expected Peppermint Branches to be like, it wasn't this. And now your fight or flight response has kicked in, and you're sitting here wanting to run away, and you're disappointed in yourself for wanting that, and you're also a bit embarrassed because you've built it up so much in your mind, and seeing the actual place has left you deflated and panicking about how you're going to deal with it.'

I try to muster up some indignation and tell him he's wrong, but he's hit the nail on the head with surprising accuracy. 'How do you know that?' I ask instead, my voice so quiet that he has to lean in to hear me.

'You're not the only one who's ever made a mistake.' His voice is just as quiet and he looks away for a moment and then turns back to me. 'I know this house well. I don't think there's anything that can't be fixed. Can I see inside?'

'What, now?'

'Well, mainly I've got to get up because my legs are killing me with cramp. I'm too old to be crouching like that for long, so I was just looking for an excuse not to admit I'm old and creaky and in agony here.'

I can't help watching as he stands up and stretches. He looks in his late thirties. I'm 36 and he can only be a couple of years older than me. I should look away, but I can't tear my eyes off him as he shifts from one foot to the other and stamps his feet, keeping his hands on the car for balance.

'I've not been inside since Mr Evergreene died, but the outside gives a good indication of the state of things. Maybe I can help?' He hesitates. 'And I've just realised that I'm a complete stranger and I didn't make the greatest of first impressions earlier and you probably don't want to be alone in a dark house with me, so don't worry about it. I didn't mean to be pushy.'

The fact that he's aware of that makes me trust him a lot more. And honestly, the thought of going back into that house by myself is a much scarier option. He seems knowledgeable and if he could give me even an indication of where to start . . . 'That'd be great.'

He looks surprised that I've agreed and moves away from the car to give me space as I swing my legs out and groan when I stand up because I've been sitting still for too long.

He's still trying to get feeling back in his legs with some demented version of the Hokey Cokey.

'Why are you being so nice?'

'I don't know whether to be offended that you think I'm such a horrible person or just to apologise for being such a twat earlier.' He sighs. 'Because I can't bear seeing people cry. No one with a heart could watch someone else cry and not try to help in any way they can.'

The way he speaks is so gentle that it's a war with myself not to start welling up again.

'If you're anything like me, you just needed to let out a bit of frustration before you pick yourself up and get on with it.' He leans across and pushes his torch into my hand. 'Here. Let me go and grab some supplies and I'll be back in a minute.'

'Supplies? At this time of night?' I call after him because he's already started walking off across the driveway, his shoulders hunched and his hands shoved into his pockets.

‘You’ll see,’ he replies without turning back.

‘Watch out for those mountain lions,’ I call before he reaches the road.

He laughs, and this time he does turn back, the wind blowing his wavy hair across his face. ‘There aren’t any mountain lions.’

‘I knew that,’ I mutter, but I don’t think he hears me.

Obviously there are no mountain lions. I knew that all along. Mountain lions in Scotland. Hah. *No one* would’ve fallen for that.

Chapter 5

It's not long before there's a knock and I open the front door to find Noel at the top of the three steps, laden with stuff. 'What's all this?'

'Supplies.' He hands me a folded-up air mattress and a foot pump, and then pushes a sleeping bag at me. Then he bends down to collect something else from the ground by his feet while adjusting the rucksack on his back.

'Are you moving in?' I look at the array of things in bewilderment. How did he manage to carry all this at once? His arm muscles are obviously as strong as they looked through his shirt earlier.

'No, you are.' He shoos me out of the way while he drags a little heater and bottle of paraffin in with him and closes the door behind us.

I watch as he stomps his boots on the remainder of the doormat and looks around. The smell of his autumnal woody aftershave and the chemical hint of paraffin from the bottle he's carrying have almost obliterated the cloying smell of damp emptiness that permeates the entire building. His eyes fall on the half open kitchen door and he shakes his head. 'Evergreene had been meaning to fix that for years.' He glances between that and the living room and then up the stairs before looking back at the kitchen. 'That'll be the cosiest room. Let's take everything in there.'

He watches in amusement as I squeeze through the gap, pushing the air mattress through first, tossing the pump after it, then squishing myself through, getting my boobs unpleasantly squashed, and pulling the sleeping bag in behind me. When I'm finally in the kitchen and panting for breath from the exertion, his hand slots around the edge of the door and he lifts it easily, pulling it fully open. He gives the hinge a good smack with the flat of his hand and it stands upright, making me feel like a bit of a fool. Why didn't I think of that?

He looks around by torchlight. 'If I set up this heater and pump up the mattress, you'll be nice and cosy in here. You can "camp out" until you've got the bedroom sorted.' Before I have a chance to say anything, he shrugs the backpack off his shoulders and holds it out to me. 'Mum sent this over for you.'

I put the bag on the unit I wiped clean earlier. It's warm to the touch, and when I undo the zip, the most gorgeous spicy cinnamon smell wafts out.

'Thermos of hot pumpkin soup, pumpkin bread just out of the oven, another slice of pumpkin pie, and a flask of tea,' he says before I can question what's inside.

'And if you don't like pumpkin?'

'You're stumped.' He laughs at his own joke. 'Stumped, get it? You know, tree farm, et cetera?'

It does actually make me laugh, mainly at how pleased he sounds with himself for such a good pun. 'Anyone would think you were a pumpkin farmer.'

'Well, I think we've proved that I'm not a comedian.'

This time my laugh is genuine as I unload the bag and set the lovely things Glenna has sent out on the unit. The sight of a flask of tea makes my eyes sting again. I knew I was desperate for a cuppa, but I had no idea quite *how* desperate until this moment.

I force myself to swallow and bite my lip until I'm certain I won't cry again. 'Thank—' I go to thank him but my voice breaks on the first word.

I can't believe I didn't even think to bring any food with me. I just thought I'd pop down the street to one of the many shops or takeaways, like I do in London. I didn't even consider how remote this place is and how vast the countryside seems.

I can feel his eyes on the back of my head, and he seems to know that I'm barely holding it together in the face of warm, pumpkiny food and PG Tips.

'And yeah, don't ever eat with us if you don't like pumpkin. I grow eight thousand pumpkins a year, we have a lot to use up afterwards.'

'Eight *thousand*?' I say in surprise. 'Your farm must be massive.'

'So's yours.' He sounds nonchalant. 'Bigger than mine, even. You've got about six thousand Christmas trees.'

'*Six* thousand?' My voice has risen to a pitch only audible to whales. He's got to be joking. 'And they're not all dead?'

'Of course they're not. But don't go getting too excited, they're not in sellable condition either.'

'What am I supposed to do with six thousand Christmas trees?'

'Origami?'

It makes me laugh again. I can hear him doing something behind me, so I turn around and watch as he goes to a cupboard under the stairs and comes back with a mop. He takes the keys the estate agent gave me off the unit and lets himself out the back door. Outside there's a bucket of steaming soapy water waiting, which he must've left there on his way over. He plunges the mop in, squeezes it out, and comes back inside to start swiping over the floor.

'Are you seriously mopping my kitchen floor for me?'

'There's no point in putting clean things down in this mess. It won't take a second.' His eyes are twinkling in the low light and there's something in his smile that makes me smile. 'Have a cup of tea, you look like you need one.'

I can't argue with him there. I gratefully guzzle tea from one of the plastic flask cups. Within minutes, the kitchen floor is a totally different colour than it was before, and Noel's unfolding the air mattress and spreading it out. He inserts the nozzle of the foot pump into the hole and starts pressing his foot up and down on it.

'I can do that,' I say, thinking I should probably start doing something to prove I'm not *completely* useless at fending for myself. I've pumped up a few paddling pools and inflatable flamingos over the years, when the summer's hot and Chelsea decides to put a kid's pool in her miniscule back garden and sit in it drinking wine.

I go over to where he's standing and try to take over without losing any of the air he's already pumped in, but the process of me standing on one leg was never going to be a neat one – what I actually do is stamp on his foot and nearly overbalance. I flail around like a drunken great white shark trying to perform the Bolero routine and clutch the sleeve of his flannel shirt to stay upright. When did he take his coat off? I glance through the open kitchen door and see it hanging on the rack in the hallway, along with the hat he was wearing earlier. He's wasted no time in making himself at home.

Once we've established that I'm not going to fall over and I've got a rhythm going with the foot pump, he goes back to the collection of things he dumped by the refrigerator and takes the heater outside to fill it. When he comes back in, he sets it on the floor, lights it and puts the safety guards in place, and sits back on his knees to show me the knobs to operate it. It makes the room smell like a Saturday morning at the garage. 'This can burn quietly all night to give you a bit of light and warmth. The fumes will burn off in a minute, and you've got no roof or upstairs windows so there's plenty of ventilation.'

I can feel the heat emanating from the little heater already, and it makes something that's been tight in my chest since the moment I set foot in this house start to loosen.

He nods towards the pump. 'Are you all right carrying on with that? Can I go and have a look around?'

'Do you need a tour guide?'

'This was my second home growing up, I know my way around.' He takes a few steps across the kitchen but stops before he reaches the door. 'Unless you want to give me the grand tour, that is? This is your house now, I have no right to walk around uninvited.'

I wave a hand dismissively and nearly overbalance again. 'Be my guest.'

He adopts a French accent, which doesn't work at all with his deep Scottish tone, and sings a few lines of 'Be Our Guest' from *Beauty and the Beast*. It makes me laugh so much that I nearly overbalance yet again. Disney songs and imitating singing candlesticks are the last things I expected from him, and his French accent gets progressively worse as he goes up the stairs and strains of the song filter down through the floorboards.

The mattress is starting to take shape, and I manage to switch legs without falling over when my thighs start to burn. I listen to the creaking floorboards as he crosses the landing and goes into the rooms above me. I like that he thought to ask if I wanted to show him around, even though he undoubtedly knows this house better than I do, and I'm strangely comforted by the sound of his footsteps upstairs.

'So, what do you think?' I ask when he comes back into the kitchen.

He cocks his head to the side. 'It's not that bad.'

'Not that bad? There are more bits of the house missing than still in existence.'

'Your main problems are the roof and the windows. Everything else is superficial. Things will look better once you have electricity, water, and some cleaning products, but the windows all need replacing.'

Considering there are no windows left *to* replace, even I could've guessed that. 'How much is that likely to cost?'

'I don't know. A few thousand, at a guess. You haven't got one whole bit of glass in the house.'

My eyes widen in shock. 'I can't afford that.'

'You could afford this place,' he says with a shrug.

'Yeah, exactly. That was it. I put everything I had into buying it.'

'And you didn't think you might need to set aside some of your budget for essential repairs?'

'Well, yeah, but I have a very limited amount left and it has to be prioritised.'

'And there was me thinking you were just another rich city girl with more cash than sense and enough money to wake up one morning and say "I think I'll be a Christmas tree farmer today" while dear old Daddy pours money into your trust fund.' He must clock the look on my face because he looks suitably guilty. 'Sorry. That wasn't meant to be as offensive as it sounded. I've met people like you who come up here thinking it'll be an easy get-rich-quick scheme in a film-worthy setting. They've seen the size of the land and dollar signs appear in their eyes. I assumed you were the same.'

'The last thing I thought about was getting rich. I bought it because my parents would've loved it.'

'Would have?' he asks gently.

'They died. Just over two years ago. I had the money from the sale of their house. I didn't know what to do with it, only that I wanted to keep it for something important, and then I saw the auction and . . . I don't know. It spoke to me. My dad always wanted to move back to Scotland. He *loved* Christmas trees and my mum loved Christmas, and I knew they'd love it. It seemed magical from the pictures.'

'It was, once upon a time. A real winter wonderland.' He looks around the dingy kitchen. 'But that was a long time ago.'

There's emotion in his words that makes me look at him, *really* look at him. I take in the slump of his wide shoulders and the sadness in his voice, and he realises it too because he shakes himself. 'You could replace the windows one at a time to spread the cost. If you want me to, I can come over tomorrow and board up the remaining ones upstairs. And Evergreene had been intending to fix the roof for years, so there's new roofing felt in the barn. I don't mind nailing that over the hole as a temporary fix until you can afford to get it repaired properly. It's a priority because the more water that gets into this place, the more damage is being done.'

My stomach drops like I've just got into a lift. How many Christmas trees will I have to sell to afford this sort of thing?

'And I've got a builder who does all my building repairs. If you want his number, he'll give you a decent price on the roof. Most of the materials are already here. The replacement tiles are stacked in the garden. You probably came across them when you were running from the monster squirrel earlier.'

'It wasn't the squirrel, it was the shock of the squirrel,' I say, knowing that I'm never going to live it down, no matter what I say in my defence. 'I've never been confronted face to face by an unexpected squirrel before, okay?'

He raises both eyebrows with a look of scepticism on his face. 'From a spectator's point of view, it was hilarious. I only wish I'd had my phone out to record it. Millions of views on YouTube beckoned. I've never heard such a bloodcurdling, ear-piercing scream over something so small and cute before. I thought you'd found Theresa May doing a dance or something equally horrifying.'

His ability to create the most random mental images is impossible not to laugh at.

'Thank you,' I say when the mattress starts letting out squeals of air because it's full. I watch as he gathers up the pump and puts it back with the pile of other things, and sort of hovers next to it, paused halfway between helping with something else and picking up his stuff and leaving.

'How about a cup of tea?' I ask, because I don't want him to leave yet. 'I'm knackered after all that pumping.'

He is, of course, not even slightly knackered. He hasn't broken a sweat and he isn't gasping for breath or anything. 'That bodes well for the amount of Christmas trees you'll have to lug around if you really are going to get this place up and running again.'

'Thanks for pointing out my complete lack of fitness. I'm so glad you noticed,' I wheeze as I unscrew the flask to refill my empty cup and the other one for him.

Instead of replying, he gets the sleeping bag out and lays it on top of the mattress. Finally, he throws a camping pillow next to it, and sits down cross-legged on the floor next to the heater.

I take the two cups of tea across the room and hand him one, his fingers brushing against the back of my hand as he takes it. I wonder how his skin can be so warm when it's still chilly in here, even with the heater going. I go back and collect the tin with a loaf of pumpkin bread in it. It's still warm from the oven and the smell of cinnamon and spice that wafts up is mouthwatering. I sit down opposite him on the clean patch of floor, surprised to see the tiles are actually cream and have delicate beige leaf patterns along each edge. Patterns and colours are something that was lost under the grime earlier. I put the bread between us and push the tin towards him, and the way he hesitates before pulling the crust off is quite sweet.

We eat in silence for a few minutes. I want to look at him, to watch that lip piercing because I can see it out of the corner of my eye, catching the glow from the heater as he eats, but I tell myself to stop being weird. I concentrate on the chunk of pumpkin bread in my hand instead.

'Do you think I can?' I ask when the silence is almost as cloying as the smell of paraffin the heater is giving off. 'Get this place up and running, that is?'

'If you're willing to put the work in. You've got a good six weeks to prepare for the Christmas rush. It won't be easy, but if you get out there and shear the trees and dig up the weeds, you could be ready to open to the public in December – assuming you're planning to run it as a choose-your-own tree farm?'

'As opposed to what?'

'There's a Christmas market in Elffield. It's a wee craft market all year round, but in September, it becomes a gorgeous Christmas market. Villagers gather there to sell their local produce, and there are people selling handmade gifts, crafts, and festive food and drink. It's a real hub for the local community, and it's popular with tourists too. Evergreene used to cut the trees himself and take them there to sell. When he was older and the work got too much for him, he opened Peppermint Branches up as a cut-your-own farm, but I'd never trust people to walk around my farm unattended with sharp blades. Choose-your-own is great, but you need staff on hand to do the cutting.'

'What do you do with your pumpkins?'

'I do both. I have a stall at the Christmas market so I'm there every morning from September onwards, and then in October, I open as a pick-your-own pumpkin patch. No one needs sharp weapons to pick a pumpkin, and I've invested in good fences to keep people out of the growing areas I don't want them stamping across, so you can generally leave people to their own devices. It's different to letting people run around a tree farm with saws. Evergreene had all kinds of trouble with it – people would start cutting one down and find it too difficult, or their kid would run off and find one they liked better, and he'd have a load of half-cut trees, and I mean with damaged trunks, not drunk.'

I once again start giggling at the mental image of drunken trees swaying in the wind, and he laughs too. 'The funny part is that I know exactly what you're thinking, and I *knew* you were going to think it as soon as I said that.'

'Well, I don't know what trees get up to in their spare time, do I?' I try to compose myself. I've already cried in front of him tonight, I can't start a giggling fit too. 'They could be right old lushes for all I know, off down the pub every night to get blootered.'

'They do that leaping sprint on the way and the wobbly crawl on the way back. Haven't you ever been to a Christmas tree farm at night? They all disappear down the local and stumble home in the early hours, and by the time you get up, they're all leaning over groaning and there are pine needles thrown up everywhere.'

The fit of laughter takes over and I let out a snort even more embarrassing than the snot bubble earlier. 'Are you still trying to make me feel better or are you naturally this funny?'

This time, his cheeks definitely turn red, and his hair falls across his face as he looks down. I have a sudden and unexpected urge to tuck it back, and I've never had the urge to touch a complete stranger's hair before.

'This place means a lot to me. To everyone in Elffield.' His words are quiet and directed at the floor. 'And it can't be brought back to life by someone who doesn't understand that. And I didn't think you did.'

'But you do now?'

'It's . . .' He pulls his sleeve up and looks at his watch. 'Nine o'clock and you're still here. That's better than I expected.' He looks up and grins at me, his eyes flashing with the reflection of the red glow from the heater. 'We both want the same thing. I'd love nothing more than to see Peppermint Branches up and running as a Christmas tree farm again. So would every villager in Elffield. Judging by tonight, so would you.'

I've got to admit, there is something about this place. The way I felt when I saw that auction listing for the first time . . . that feeling I got when I leant on the gate and looked out at the trees in the distance . . . I kind of understand what he's talking about.

'How come you have so much camping gear?' I ask in an attempt to change the subject because the idea of every villager in Elffield being invested in what I do here is a bit unsettling. 'Do you go camping a lot?'

'Nah, I had some problems with teenagers getting into my land and lighting fires over the summer. They burned down half my sweetcorn so I decided to play them at their own game and sleep out there for a few nights.' He waves a hand in the general direction of the fields across the road. 'Caught them red-handed, and they didn't come back.'

'Sounds terrifying.'

'Aye, for them. You've never caught sight of me in the middle of the night without a coffee in me. Believe me, they thought they'd found the three-way lovechild of Nessie, a sasquatch, and a scarecrow.'

'Okay, another question. The last owner . . . his name wasn't seriously Evergreene, was it?'

He snorts like he didn't expect that question. 'It was. I'm not sure what came first, the name or the tree farm though. The first trees were planted by his great-great grandfather. I think there was some controversy along the line when his great-grandmother married and refused to take her husband's name, unheard of in those days, but you can't own a Christmas tree farm and give up the name Evergreene, can you?'

'You knew him well?'

He looks at me with a raised eyebrow, like he knows I'm prodding for information and he isn't sure he trusts me yet. 'Yeah,' he says eventually. 'I spent my weekends over here from when I was old enough to hold a shearing knife and a saw – not together, that's a recipe for disaster. My mum and dad were *extremely* impressed to find out I often cut school so I could come back here and cut Christmas trees instead. Our farm was more of a regular farm back then, livestock and all sorts of produce, but the Christmas trees were so much more exciting. Evergreene was like a grandfather to me, you know, the naughty one who encourages you to do things your parents would never allow you to, and then gives you a cheeky wink, puts on an innocent face and denies all knowledge when caught?' He puts on a shaky, elderly voice. '"*What do you mean Noel was in the back cutting Christmas trees when he was supposed to be in maths class? Really? I had no idea. I thought it was an overgrown elf running around with that chainsaw.*" Only to be followed be piercing shrieks of "*You let him use a CHAINSAW?*"' He looks down at the tiles again and I can feel the sadness settle over him. 'But many years have passed since then.'

'What happened to him?'

'He never recovered after a stroke and died a few months later. Over four years ago now.'

'No family to inherit this place?'

'Just one absolute git of a son who was never interested in Christmas trees. When we were younger, he got his jollies off by zooming around the village on his motorbike, deliberately frightening livestock and old ladies. He only saw this place in pound signs, and I *hope* he's extremely disappointed with the fifty grand you paid, but I gather the estate agents were at their wits end with trying to sell it. They must've been over the moon that an idiot who doesn't know anything about Christmas trees turned up.' He looks over with a teasing grin. 'I bet you don't even know what type of tree you get every year, do you?'

'Oi. I know *exactly* what type my tree is – a plastic one.'

He doesn't hide the look of horror on his face, and I hold up a hand to stop him. 'I know, I know, it's an affront to all of Scotland. I sent it to the tip before I left London. We used to have a real one growing up but not since . . .' I swallow hard, unable to tell him that I only had a plastic one in the flat because I spent Christmas at my parents' house, and since they died, I haven't felt much like celebrating Christmas. 'Well, a plastic one's easier, isn't it?'

'I'm going to pretend you didn't say that. What kind did you have when you were younger?'

'A green one.'

'Oh, come on. Blue spruce? Fraser fir? Nordmann fir? Balsam? Pine?'

'I don't know, my dad always chose it.'

The look on his face leaves me in no doubt about what he thinks of me.

I drop my head into my hands. 'I *know*, okay? I'm fooling myself here, aren't I?'

'Oh, I don't know. If Mr Blobby can have a fanbase . . . anything's possible.'

'Now there's a vote of confidence if ever there was one . . .' I struggle to take my eyes off that lip piercing as a smile spreads slowly across his face, laughter lines crinkling up around his eyes and replacing the tautness.

'What do you do after Halloween? Is the pumpkin market big year-round?' I ask because *something* has to distract me from his upper lip, and I'm already thinking about seasons and how in-demand Christmas trees are between January and October. I suspect the answer is 'not very'.

'I keep my market stall. In December I dig up the winter veg that people want for their Christmas dinner, and then in January, I sell cut winter flowers like snowdrops and primroses. In spring I sell the first earlies that have overwintered in my polytunnels, and in summer I sell whatever's ripe. Then in autumn, I sell the corn ears that haven't been cut, I raid the apple trees and wrestle my hazelnuts from the squirrels, and then it's pumpkin season again. Pumpkins are my main crop. I have loads of varieties spread across many acres. Everything else is kind of a "whatever fits in around them" crop. The business is seasonal so you have to fill every available space to keep yourself ticking over throughout the year.'

'I hadn't thought about that aspect of Christmas tree

farming . . .' I say, because let's face it, it's one of *many* aspects I hadn't thought about.

He looks towards the front door like he can somehow see the farm through it. 'You're going to get one income a year and you've got to make sure it's big enough to last until next Christmas. For now, you've got more than a year's worth of work to get this place back up to standard. The trees need a lot of looking after during the year. They need herbicide and fertiliser put down, you'll have to inspect them all the time for diseases and insects, they all need some serious shearing, arrangements need to be made for however you're going to sell them, seeds need to be collected from between the scales of pinecones, and saplings need to be planted, and if things were up and running as they should be, then cutting should begin in November . . .' He must notice the blank look on my face because he trails off. 'Too much for the first night, aye?'

I pull my ponytail around and pick a stray dust-bunny from it. 'I only understand approximately 38.5 per cent of what you just said.' I sigh and flip it back in frustration. 'What have I got myself into here, Noel? Seriously. Does someone with no experience have a hope in hell of making this work or should I give up now and go home with my tail between my legs?'

He glances over at me. 'Where's the annoyingly perky made-for-TV movie character who tried to kidnap my dog earlier?'

'That's twice now you've referenced those made-for-TV rom coms. Don't tell me you watch them?'

'My mum watches them. If I'm in the room, I try my best to ignore them, but the main characters are usually so annoyingly shrill that their voices penetrate even the most industrial of headphones, and then I end up getting sucked into them. There you go, judge me.'

'I would never judge you for that. In fact, I think that might be the most adorable thing I've ever heard.' The harder I try to stop myself smiling at him, the more he makes me smile. 'I love them too. I record them when I'm at work and watch them in the evenings and weekends. I can get through five on a Sunday if I try really hard.'

He bursts out laughing. 'I don't have weekends off, but I try to marathon a couple in the evenings. One of my guilty pleasures is lying in bed with a tin of Christmas chocolates and watching them.' He's gone so beetroot red that even the semi-darkness of the kitchen doesn't disguise it. 'And I can't believe I just admitted that. Even my mum doesn't know that.'

'Nothing to be embarrassed about. In December, I turn down invitations to go out for Christmas drinks with work colleagues in favour of curling up on the sofa with a hot chocolate and as many romantic comedies as can reasonably be fitted into a weekend. I like escaping into the perfect fantasy life that none of us can ever hope to live. You can believe the world is a better place for a couple of hours.'

'Maybe that's why you bought a Christmas tree farm? That's exactly the kind of thing one of the annoyingly squeaky main characters would do. Or inherit one. The busy marketing executives usually inherit unexpected things, don't they?'

I grin because I've never met a guy who likes these films before. 'And of course they meet the gruff but sensitive, slightly grumpy and disapproving guy who rescues them and shows them the ropes, and you know they're going to fall in love from the moment he steps onscreen in some adorable accident where she pours coffee all over him or something.'

'Hah.' He scoffs. 'Well, we can be certain that's not going to happen here. Unless there's a sheep in a nearby field you fancy.'

'I did pass some very handsome cows on the drive up . . . '

'And on that note, I'd better go.' He gets to his feet and gathers up his stuff.

'Thank you for everything.'

'You're welcome,' he says as I hover in the hallway, watching him shrug his coat back on and pull the hat down over his thick hair.

He must sense my sudden nervousness at being alone again, because he looks up in the middle of pulling his boots on. 'Don't worry too much. Things will look better in the daylight.'

It's exactly what my mum used to say and a lump forms instantly in my throat and I have to swallow it down. I can't possibly cry any more tonight. But somehow hearing it makes me feel better too. A little reminder that life goes on tomorrow, even without my parents here. Peppermint Branches is mine now, and I owe it to them to be brave and do the best I can with it, come what may.

Even if it's mountain lions.

Chapter 6

I might not know much about Christmas trees, but for the past few years, I've been inputting sales figures from retail shops so someone more qualified than me can analyse them and present the retailers with facts and figures for maximising profit. I've spent most of the night lying on the air mattress, formulating a sort of business plan on the back of the estate agent's map and when I wake up after a couple of hours of disturbed sleep, I'm feeling a lot more positive about things. This is a business, a retail establishment like any other. To make enough profit to live on, I have to bring in more money than I fork out. Simple.

I've been studying the map too, trying to work out how many fields there are and divide the six thousand trees Noel mentioned into some kind of number that makes sense. This is simply a matter of numbers. Trees grown per square acre versus trees sold. I don't feel as out of my depth when I think about it like that.

I sit up and look around the darkened kitchen, wrapping the sleeping bag around my shoulders because the heater has burnt itself out overnight and the chill in the air is back with a vengeance. I'm excited to get out there. It doesn't feel as overwhelming as it did last night. It feels like the first day of the rest of my life, and I feel like I can face anything as I pull on some clothes and run upstairs to wash my face and clean my teeth, using only the two-litre bottle of water that Noel brought last night. I eat the last of the pumpkin bread for breakfast and pretend that yesterday's water is my usual coffee. I promise myself several cups of tea later when the water and electric are back on and I've got the kitchen box out of the car.

I've got a plan. Noel's right in that I have absolutely no idea what I've bought, so the sensible way forward is to start by making a full inventory of everything I've got and everything I'm going to need, and prioritising the budget for it.

Outside, the sky is blue and bright, and I take a picture and send it to Chelsea to prove that we get sun in Scotland. There's a patch of land behind the farmhouse that's home to several outbuildings – a huge barn and a handful of tin sheds in varying states of decay, and I decide to start there. The grass is a grey-ish brown and overgrown to knee-height, tangled and flopping over, and there's an unsteady stone wall separating my land from Noel's, with half the top fallen away and stones missing, leaving gaps of weeds poking through. It's mostly shaded by the buildings and a tall hedge, and even I can tell that nothing but the couch grass is going to grow here.

At least I understand why there are so many keys on the keyring the estate agent gave me now. I start with the big barn first, trying different keys in the rusty padlock until finally one turns.

The double doors are so heavy that it takes all my strength to haul them open, then I realise that I need the light from outside, so I have to let them close, find a stone fallen from the wall and kick it across to use as a prop when I've dragged them open again. As I stand in the doorway, panting from that tiny bit of effort, I'm surprised that a swarm of bats don't swoop out. It looks like the kind of building that would have bats hibernating in it. The stench that hits me is damp rotting wood, rusty metal, and leaking petrol. It's definitely a machine graveyard, because there's a tractor and trailer parked in the middle, surrounded by other bits of metal machinery, none of which I can identify.

There are tools too – an array of shovels, spades, forks, rakes, and a huge pile of saws in all shapes and sizes. There are wooden holders nailed to the brick wall with long knives hanging from them in sheaths. A rusty push-along lawnmower. Shears, strimmers, hedge trimmers, and all manner of equipment that I don't recognise.

I feel my confidence ebbing away as I step inside and wander around the damp barn. How the heck am I supposed to take an inventory if I don't have a clue what half of this stuff is or what it's used for?

My eyes fall on the tractor. I know what that is. And it doesn't look like it's in bad condition, apart from a few cobwebs. I imagine myself bouncing along on the red tractor, cheerfully waving to passersby as I drive it around the farm. I wonder if it starts? At least it'd be one thing I could tick off the list. I give it a wary glance. The spiders have certainly had a field day with it. I brush cobwebs away as I climb up onto the seat, find the ignition key on my keyring and push it in. It's going to be like the manual car I learnt to drive in. It won't be a problem. I use my feet to press down on the clutch and the brake as I turn the key, and the tractor rumbles underneath me. Just as I think it's about to start chugging merrily, it lets out a huge bang and the engine cuts out as the barn fills with smoke.

Perfect. I cough and cover my mouth to avoid breathing in the fumes.

'That went as well as I expected.'

I jump and spin around in the seat to see Noel standing in the open door, waving smoke away from his face. Gizmo is on a lead beside him, peering worriedly in from a safe distance.

Perfect. Again. He's definitely got radar for the worst possible timing. Couldn't he have come five minutes later when I'd tried it again and it miraculously worked this time? Which it is definitely going to, because I can *not* afford a new tractor.

I clamber off the tractor and duck past him in the doorway to get outside into the fresh air. Gizmo looks up at me and wags his tail, and I kneel down on the concrete ramp to the barn door and give him a scritch. He's wearing a hand-knitted blue hoodie with a paw print pattern around the edges and the hood tucked back under his harness. Just when I thought he couldn't possibly be any *more* adorable.

I squint up at Noel in the morning sun. His hair is loose again, and the sunlight is picking out strands of golden brown that I hadn't noticed yesterday amongst his mass of dark hair. His soft flannel shirt is red and grey plaid today, and he's wearing black cargo trousers tucked into brown work boots laced up above his ankles. 'What are you doing here?'

'I was walking Gizmo and I heard the distinct rumbling of some idiot trying to fumigate themselves by starting a tractor that hasn't been started for over four years indoors.'

'How was I supposed to know it was going to do that?'

'Common sense? It's been sat there for years. At the very least it needs an oil change and checking over by someone who knows what they're doing. You don't just ram the key in and try it. And you need *some* instruction on how to drive it. They're dangerous things to operate and you've clearly never seen one before in your life.'

I mentally add *Tractors For Dummies* to my list of books I need to order the moment I can get a Wi-Fi signal. 'I was trying to be proactive. I can't do much unless I know exactly what the situation is here.'

'Killing the tractor is not going to help.'

I glare up at him without taking my hands out of Gizmo's short fur, and he leans against the doorframe and hooks one leg over the other and nods into the barn. 'I'm impressed with your progress. So far you've managed to open the barn door. Even that would prove too much for some city girls.'

'What have you got against people from cities?' I say in baby talk as I make faces at Gizmo.

'Nothing. I just don't believe in worlds colliding. You're a . . .' He gestures towards me, waving his hand around like he can't find the right word. 'You're a shopper. No matter how good your intentions might be, you don't even own a pair of wellies. How can you attempt to be a farmer when you don't own a good pair of stomping boots?'

'Did you come out of the womb wearing welly boots? Which would've been really weird. And really uncomfortable for your poor mother,' I snap because he seems to have completely missed the fact that these things can be bought.

He lets out an unexpected burst of laughter and hands Gizmo's lead to me, then he strides into the smoky barn and comes back out with the notebook I was using. 'Your inventory-taking skills are enviable. *Tractor. Lots of tools. Metal thingies. Long sharp knives.*' He reads aloud from what I've scribbled down so far. 'Otherwise known as shearing knives – your most important tools during shearing season. *Lots of saws. Strimmer. Hedge cutter. Chainsaws. Big metal frame thingy with wheels and blades.*' He's laughing to himself as he reads it.

'It's not funny,' I say to Gizmo, who leans up to lick my nose.

'No, it's hilarious that someone who wants to be a Christmas tree farmer can't identify a plough.'

So *that's* what it is. 'I knew that.'

'Aye.' He rolls his eyes. 'It's a chisel plough. In January, you hire a stump grinder and pull out the stumps of the trees previously cut. Then you hook the plough up to the tractor and plough the empty fields, and put down pre-emergence weedkiller, then in March and April, you can plant saplings out, but you have to be vigilant with the weeds. Larger trees can handle them but saplings will be overpowered and you'll lose the whole spring's worth of work and fields of stock for future years. That's what the strimmer and the lawnmowers are for, and the . . .' He runs his finger down the list until he finds my entry. 'Gallons of unknown chemicals.'

'Have you just come to make fun of me or do you actually want something?' I get to my feet, pull my notebook out of his hand, and thrust the plastic handle of Gizmo's extending lead back towards him.

Our fingers brush as he takes the lead, and instead of leaving, he reaches into his shirt pocket and hands me a piece of paper covered in his calligraphy-like handwriting. 'I came to give you these. Phone numbers for the electricity and water companies. If you give them a ring, they'll probably have you back on in a couple of hours. I've also put down the name and number of that builder I mentioned, and my Wi-Fi password if you need it. Reception's patchy up here and I know you don't have a landline, so hop onto mine anytime you want to.'

'Wi-Fi! I could kiss you!' I clear my throat. 'But I won't. Obviously.'

Despite his harsh words, he's kind and thoughtful too, like last night. Never mind builders, electric, or water, I pull my phone out and type the password in, and squeal in delight when it connects to his WiFi, even at this distance.

I know my face has lit up because when I look up from my notifications, he's looking at me with one of those dark eyebrows raised. 'Has anyone ever told you that there's more to life than the internet?'

'Yeah, but, like . . . what? I mean, if you've got Amazon, what more do you need?'

The other eyebrow joins the first.

'I'm joking, Noel. But now I can buy books on growing Christmas trees.' I can hear the glee in my own voice when I glance back into the barn. 'And identifying farmyard machinery.'

If his eyebrows go up any further, they're going to pop off and go on a minibreak to the Outer Hebrides. 'And you think this is the kind of industry you can learn from a book.' He sighs. 'I have nothing to say to you but good luck – good luck in finding another buyer when you decide to give up on your drunken whim and realise this is a difficult job and you need some level of natural aptitude and passion for it.'

'I have passion,' I say as he tugs Gizmo to walk away but the little dog stays wagging his tail at me. 'And I have a plan. Assuming that aptitude as a Christmas tree farmer isn't based solely on rubber footwear.'

'A plan?' He turns back and folds his arms. 'This should be good.'

It does not sound like a compliment.

I get the page of scribbled notes out of my pocket and unfold it as I hand it to him and watch his light eyes scan over my scribblings. I get a bit self-conscious when he doesn't say anything but lines start creasing his forehead.

'It's a bit rough. It's scrawled on the back of a map in semi-darkness and I was shivering with the cold so I couldn't hold the pen steady.'

'Well, either you've invented a whole new language, or you're fluent in Ancient Egyptian Hieroglyphs.' He looks up at me and then looks down at it again. 'And cave wall paintings.'

I step closer and try to point out what I've drawn. 'Look, this is the field to the left of the lane. It's empty so has to be replanted. From the scale on the estate agent's map, I've worked out that it's about two acres. If each tree takes up a few feet each, I reckon I could get three thousand trees per acre. That's a lot of trees. I've had a guess at expenditure, and I'd only need to sell a couple of hundred at £40 each to break even.'

'Yeah, but this is in seven to ten years' time when they're fully grown. It doesn't help you now.' He thrusts the paper back at me like it's contaminated. 'Unless you've got money to burn for the next ten years, you need to concentrate on the trees you have *now.* And these figures are way off. Your expenses will be *so* much more than that, and to sell a tree at £40, it's got to be a *perfect* specimen. The ones you have here are far from perfect and never will be again. And it's great that you're already thinking about replanting, but nothing will grow crammed that tightly into a field. They'll all get cut down by disease or destroyed by pests if you're going to try to plant them that close together. Christmas trees need space around them. They need light and air, and room to walk between each one to shear them, and if one dies, you can remove it before whatever killed it spreads to the rest of the plot. These figures are great for someone sat in front of a computer screen, but absolutely useless in the real world.'

God, he's *so* knowledgeable. He seems to know everything there is to know about Christmas tree farming and he *isn't* a Christmas tree farmer. It makes me realise just how much there is to learn, and how little time there is to do it in if I want to sell anything this year. I also wish he was a bit more approachable and a little less condescending so that I could ask him for advice without being ridiculed.

'You need to concentrate on the trees you already have for *this* season. In January, you think about saving seed, preparing the soil, and planting up saplings, but your farm is a ridiculously overgrown mess that needs a lot of real-world physical work right *now* if you want to get it even halfway up to scratch before December.'

I gulp.

'This business isn't about sales figures,' he continues. 'It's not like putting a neatly boxed product on a shelf and waiting for people to buy it. A business plan isn't going to help with the real-life physical work that doesn't take place behind a computer screen.'

'I know figures. All businesses succeed or fail based on figures.'

'Well, I don't know figures, but I do know Christmas trees, and this—' he pokes the crinkled piece of paper in my hand '—is worthless.'

We hold each other's gaze for a long moment, and then he jerks his head towards my fields. 'Let me show you what I mean. Want to come for a walk around with me? Maybe I can stop the next inventory consisting of "green trees, tall green trees, and taller green trees" so you've at least got some clue about what you've bought.'

I give him a scathing look because he's nowhere near as funny as he thinks he is. I'm going to go on Amazon and order every book on Christmas tree farming I can find *and* fork out for next-day delivery, but he's been more helpful than anything else so far and he clearly knows his stuff. He might think I'm an idiot, but I really need his advice. 'That'd be great. As long as you're bringing Gizmo.'

The little dog stands on my foot and I reach down to rub his ears as he wags his tail.

'Of course. You're honoured to see him at this time of day. Gizmo doesn't *do* mornings, but he couldn't wait to come over and see you.' We hold each other's gaze again, until Noel shakes his head and turns away. 'He was probably worried that the squirrel might've come back and terrorised you overnight, or that you might've terrorised it.'

I narrow my eyes to show him just how unfunny I think he is, and he and Gizmo wait while I phone the two numbers he gave me and set up accounts with the water and electricity companies, who assure me the supply of both will be restored this morning. I'm not sure what I'm more excited about – light and water or the prospect of finally seeing some Christmas trees on this Christmas tree farm.

***

'Welcome to Peppermint Branches.' Noel unlatches a wooden gate at the end of the lane past the house and holds it open for me to go through. We disappear into a line of tall conifer trees, and in front of us is a wooden sign with directional arrows bearing names of tree species. *Nordmann fir, Norway spruce, Peppermint fir, Blue spruce, Balsam fir.* I reach out to touch the arrow signs, the words burnt into the wood in fancy writing. We're in a grassy central area behind the conifers where wide tracks meet, one from the left and one from the right, and one back through the gate to the lane we've just come down. Through the tree trunks, I can see the first hint of a Christmas tree farm. I squeal in delight and that starts Gizmo off barking, and he pulls on his lead to chase after whatever unseen thing he thinks I'm squealing at.

'I guess we're going this way.' Noel laughs as he lets himself be pulled along by the tiny dog. 'Nordmann firs coming up.'

The path is wide enough for a tractor and the earth is dry and solid underfoot, hedged in by a row of holly bushes on either side. They haven't been trimmed for a few years, with wild tops and branches shooting off in all directions, covered in green berries showing the first flush of red, and they've obviously outgrown their intended height because I can barely see over them.

'Festive,' Noel says when he sees me looking. 'You should see it in the snow when the berries turn red and the robins go bob-bob-bobbing along the hedges. It looks like a scene from a Christmas card.'

I can picture it easily and I get a little flutter at the thought that this is mine. Somehow, I own this incredible place. It doesn't seem real yet.

'These are beautiful.' I run my fingers carefully through the hedge, avoiding the thorns. The usual dark green glossy leaves are interspersed with different varieties of holly, some of the bushes have lighter green leaves with cream edges, and some are variegated leaves splashed with yellow. 'Sprigs of these would look amazing as a table centrepiece. Or in wreaths.' I reach up and pluck one of the overgrown bits from the top of the hedge, twisting the thick green stem around my fingers. I pick another branch of the darker green holly and wind them together, holding it up to show him. 'Twist that with a few branches of cedar and some pine cones and it'd make a beautiful fresh wreath.'

'My mum makes autumn wreaths. We sell them at the market from September onwards. Living wreaths are getting more popular every year. Already thinking about diversifying, eh? Maybe you're not quite as terrible as you seem.'

I can't hide my smile and the hint of pride that creeps in. I never thought twirling branches of holly together would be an enviable talent, but anything that makes me feel slightly less clueless is welcome at this point.

'The track runs right the way around the farm so you can get the tractor out to every field, and each field has wide lanes to let you drive between them to collect the trees.'

The holly hedges break for a wooden gate with a faded 'Nordmann fir' sign hanging over it. He unhooks the gate and lets Gizmo go through first as we walk into a field full of Christmas trees, and even though I'm trying to contain it, a squeak of excitement slips out. Now *this* is a Christmas tree farm. In front of us is a never-ending field full of trees. Real, green, Christmas trees. *This* is what I'd pictured. *This* bears some resemblance to the photos on the auction site.

'Why is this all hidden away back here?' I say the first thing that comes into my head. 'If it had looked like this when I drove in yesterday, I'd have been a lot happier.'

His laugh is quiet. 'It's not hidden away, it's the fall of the harvest years.' I must look at him blankly because he rolls his eyes. 'You know the fields out front that are empty? Usually they're full of Christmas trees too, but it just happens that Evergreene's last harvest was from those fields. You cycle year on year. You plant a field one year and that'll be mature in seven years' time. The one you planted the previous year will be mature in six years' time, and so on, until you've got a rolling stock of Christmas trees with a new batch ready every year. That system has got lost to the years of no maintenance and it'll take a while to get it back into place again. One of the last things Evergreene did was replant those fields with saplings, but with no one looking after them, they were strangled by the weeds that have taken over. In the spring, your first job should be to dig over those fields and replant them. You'll have to collect seed from your pinecones this winter, but the seedlings will be too small to plant direct. Evergreene prided himself on always growing from scratch and all his trees being of proper Peppermint Branches heritage, but the missing years have really set things back. A tree farm turns over year by year. One year relies on the next. Losing so many makes it almost like starting from scratch again.'

'Tree heritage.' I shake my head. I had no idea there was such a thing. 'Do they have DNA tests? Ancestry.com for trees? Roots.com?'

'Trees would be nothing without their roots.'

His voice is deadpan and his face doesn't give anything away. I wait for him to start laughing, and when he doesn't, I narrow my eyes at him. 'Was that another tree pun?'

Finally, his mouth twitches at one side. 'I don't know, maybe I'm just *branching* out.'

I can't stop myself giggling. He's rugged and handsome, a typical broad-shouldered farmer, but some of the things that come out of his mouth are ridiculously adorable.

He stomps his boots into the grassy ground. 'These are the Nordmann firs. Broad needles that retain water so they don't drop, strong branches and soft foliage, and the needles have got a waxy coating so it's the best tree for allergy sufferers.'

I'm kind of awed by the way he talks. His voice is deep and rough, but there's a lightness to it when he talks like this. His eyes shine with passion, the colour of the trees reflecting to make them look closer to green than blue. I go over to the nearest tree and touch one of the lower branches. 'Can I sell these this year?'

He casts his eyes across the field. 'It's not ideal, but you can. Thing is, and you have to understand this, everything you do for the next few years will be a way of trying to fix what's happened to the farm in the years of being abandoned. These trees are overgrown and their roots are suffocated by weeds. You can dig up the weeds, but the damage is already done. They would've taken what they needed from the soil and prevented the trees from having it. They haven't been fed so they're missing the nutrients that make a healthy tree. The branches are thick and woody and growing haywire because they haven't been sheared, and the optimum time to shear them is in the spring so they form new growth tips, and the summer gives the wounds a chance to heal without disease getting in.'

'How about a nice Elastoplast?'

He laughs and then looks annoyed with himself for laughing. 'I'm serious, Lee.'

Even Chelsea doesn't call me Lee. I go to protest about him shortening my name, but he carries on before I have a chance.

'You now have to prune them at the beginning of winter and they won't have time to heal before cutting for sale – but you can't sell them like this, look at the state of them, the poor buggers.'

They obviously look all right to Gizmo because he's got his extending lead wrapped in some form of complicated bowline knot around several of the trunks and is now cocking his leg up one. 'There you go, Gizmo's helping with the nutrient situation.'

We're both laughing as he finishes his business and walks around another tree, further entangling the lead. I look at the trees as Noel follows him, walking around trunks in an attempt to untangle the knot, like some kind of giant, forestial cat's cradle game. Gizmo takes this as part of the fun and woofs at Noel, running off every time he gets close to him, circling through the weeds around each trunk, until the lead reaches its maximum length and Noel starts reeling him in.

I realise I'm just standing there smiling at them both, this giant man and his tiny dog. You'd expect a guy like Noel to have a big dog, not a Chihuahua wearing a hand-knitted paw-print hoodie. I can think of a few guys at work who'd scoff at the idea of having a little dog and probably make fun of anyone who did, but I like that Noel doesn't care about stereotypes. I force myself to concentrate on the trees instead. The whole field looks like a wild forest. The trees themselves are standing at all different heights, and the branches have sprung out in every direction. None of them look anything like the traditional Christmas tree. None of them look like something you'd want standing in your home, although some of them could make decent Halloween decorations given the bare branches and gnarled twiggy ends. The once-uniform rows have been swallowed by weeds, and the ground is squelchy underfoot and the air smells of damp forest and rotting vegetation.

'That'll teach me to use the extending lead.' The field is on a slight hill which I only realise when Noel stomps back up it with Gizmo safely in his arms. 'So what do you think? Feel like you've bought a Christmas tree farm yet?'

'I'm starting to,' I say, because last night, it really did feel doubtful.

He holds the gate open and lets me go through first. The wooden sign bangs against it as he closes it behind us and deposits Gizmo on the track, locking the extending lead in place with a determined click. Gizmo ignores him and trots off down the path, expecting Noel to follow, and I lag behind as I watch him get pulled along.

Gizmo seems to know exactly where he's going. He doesn't look at Noel for direction or wait to see where we're heading. It seems like a walk he's done many times before, and it makes me wonder how much time Noel's spent here over the years because I get the feeling it's much more than he's letting on.

The land slopes downhill and I run to catch up with my guide and his human, falling into step next to Noel as the burbling of a stream somewhere starts to filter into the silence created by the trees. All I've been able to hear until now is the occasional chirping of birds. It's quiet in Elffield anyway, nothing like the city noises I'm used to, but being in the trees like this blocks out all other sounds and makes me feel isolated . . . no, not isolated. Quiet and still. Peaceful. It's something I haven't felt for a long time.

The hedges are lower as we walk around the bend of the track and I can see more trees, the fields we've yet to explore, and I'm sure my heart stops beating for a moment. I take a step nearer the hedge and duck to see under the lowest branches of a tall conifer. Between trunks, I can see how the path curves around the farm, the green of the low holly hedges fencing in fields of trees like the one we've just come from, and it really does take my breath away.

When I turn back, Gizmo and Noel are waiting for me.

'Impressive, isn't it?' he says as I walk towards him. 'There's a spot on one of the bridges that gives you an even better view. I was going to show you on the way back.'

'*One* of the bridges?' I say. 'Just how big is this place?'

'Big enough to require two bridges?' he says with a laugh as we wander off down the track again. 'Like I said, you've got an unmarked river running through the middle, and this path runs around the farm in a circle, so it crosses the river in two places. The track was dug by Evergreene's grandfather and the bridges were hand-built by him and his son – Evergreene's father. You should see them in the winter when the icicles form. Another Christmas-card-worthy scene.'

'This whole place is like something from a Christmas card.' I look behind me even though the hedge has risen up again now, blocking the trees from view. 'I didn't think places like this existed in real life. I thought they were only made by movie set decorators.'

'They don't make them as good as this,' he says, and there's such genuine affection in his voice that it makes me feel warm inside despite the chill in the October morning. 'You'll love it when it snows. We get quite a bit here and it's brilliant for business. It makes people want to come to a Christmas tree farm. There's something special about so many trees in one place. One acre of trees produces enough oxygen for eighteen people, so maybe there's something chemical in the theory. Inhaling all that oxygen makes your body produce extra serotonin or something. Did you know that opera singers used to walk among Christmas trees before a performance because they believed that breathing in pine would lubricate the larynx?'

I can tell he's trying to redirect the conversation. I think about the way his voice sounds different when he talks about Peppermint Branches and how even Gizmo knows his way around. 'You've spent a lot of time here, haven't you?'

'Yeah, my dad always loved this place. We used to come over every day when I was little. In the summer, we'd bring picnics and Evergreene would join us, him and my dad would sit on the riverbank while I paddled in the stream, and then in the winter, it was pure magic. The trees were like a maze and I'd run through them with Dad chasing me. We were always here early in the morning, before it was open to other people, and you know how snow blankets every other sound and makes everything seem soft? Those snowy winter mornings in the Christmas trees, making the first footprints in acres of pure white fluffiness . . . they're my favourite memories. If it wasn't snow, then the whole place would be sparkling with frost. Evergreene used to tell visiting kids there were elves here, that they'd dash in and out of the trees and report back to Santa on who was being naughty and nice and whenever you saw the frost sparkling, it meant he'd been down from the North Pole for an update. I was far too old to believe in any of that stuff, but when I was here, even I started to wonder . . . This place makes it easy to believe in magic.'

'It sounds perfect.'

He nods. 'My dad always said that if Evergreene decided to sell, he'd buy him out and run both farms side by side. It wasn't meant to be, but . . .' He trails off and gives himself a shake. 'Sorry, I'm being a sentimental sod. But that magic . . . that feeling that makes all the Christmas stories seem like they could be real . . . I've been to other Christmas tree farms, but *that* is something that's unique to Peppermint Branches. You need to recreate that.'

Recreating magic. That sounds easy. But there's something about the way Noel talks that makes me believe it could be like that again. I wish I could've seen it back then, because it sounds like such a special place, and I don't feel worthy of trying to make it that special again.

There's another gate hidden in the hedgerow and Gizmo stops in front of it and wags his tail, waiting for us to catch up and let him in. He's probably excited by the prospect of some more tree trunks to get tangled up in.

'Peppermint fir.' I run my fingers over the wood-burned sign. 'Another tree name I've never heard of.'

'Yeah, there's a reason for that. Lee, wait. This field . . . there's something I need to tell you . . . '

'Let me guess, it's overrun with weeds that have leeched all the nutrients from the soil, the trees have grown wild, and I haven't got a hope in hell of getting anything back right again before Christmas?' I unlatch the gate and Gizmo rushes through before I've got it fully open.

I stop in surprise and Noel crashes right into me when Gizmo reaches the end of his leash and yanks Noel with him.

'Sorry,' he murmurs, backing away.

This field is different. There are no weeds. Instead, the perfectly cone-shaped trees are planted in tidy rows on a bed of neat moss. Each one has a circular shape of bare earth underneath it, and the sharp, sweet and refreshing scent of Christmas trees fills the air.

'Someone's been taking care of these,' I say, although it's blatantly obvious who that is.

He bends down to unhook Gizmo's lead and the Chihuahua bounces across the moss like he's done it many times before. 'This is Evergreene's life's work. He was attempting to create the perfect Christmas tree by making a hybrid of all the best. They've got the shape of a Norway spruce, the needle retention of a Fraser fir, the branch strength of a Nordmann fir, the colour of a cross between a Blue spruce and a White spruce, and the scent of a Balsam fir, the most desirable and traditional Christmas tree scent.'

'He bred these?' My feet press into the spongy moss as I walk across to the nearest tree and run my fingers over one of its stiff branches, surprised by the softness of the needles.

He nods. 'From years and years of grafts, splicing seeds, and cross-pollinating.' I feel his eyes on me as I look at the tree. 'Strong branches for holding ornaments but needles that are soft to the touch and won't fall out.'

I inhale the scent from the branch and close my eyes, instantly transported back to Christmas in my parents' living room, sitting next to a tree that smelled like this, tearing wrapping paper off Barbie dolls and Polly Pockets that I'd been wanting for months. Lying on the floor beside it in the afternoon, full from Mum's Christmas dinner, playing Monopoly with cousins while grandparents from both sides of the family dozed in front of the Queen's speech.

'It's got a lot of water retained in its trunk, so it won't die if people forget to water it. Its roots are neat so it transplants easily. It won't grow beyond eight foot so it remains manageable. We did surveys for years asking everyone what they wanted in a Christmas tree, what annoyed them most about the ones they'd had, what they'd liked, what they hadn't, and what they'd like to be different.'

'They're beautiful.' I run my fingers over the soft needles even though I can't take my eyes off Noel. He lights up when he talks about trees.

He walks over to the one I'm stroking, pulls a pair of secateurs from the pocket of his cargo trousers and deposits them in my hand. He nods to the tree in front of us. 'There are a couple of strays that need to come off.'

'What are you – an exam invigilator?' I use my thumb to turn the metal catch on the handle and open the secateurs, snipping them in the air a few times before I attack the tree.

I surprise myself because I can actually see what he means. There are a few slim branches of fresh growth – soft, brighter green needles that have sprung out from the neat lines of the shaped tree, and I clip them off, feeling his eyes on me as I walk around the tree to ensure I haven't missed any. 'So is this part of the coursework and does it count towards my final grade?'

He laughs. 'And that's your first lesson as a Christmas tree farmer – never go anywhere without secateurs in your pocket, you *will* find strays that need to come off and you'll never find them again if you walk away.'

I twist the two branches I snipped off with the sprigs of holly that are still in my hand. The colours are gorgeous together, the greens intertwining to make the red berries pop. It would make a perfect wreath with some pinecones and a couple of silver bells added.

'You can keep those,' he says when I go to hand the secateurs back to him. 'They were Evergreene's anyway, a long time ago. And I'm sorry about the trees. I know they weren't mine to take care of. I've been trespassing onto your land for years.' He winds his fingers in his hair and tugs at a dark lock. 'This field backs onto one of mine so it's been easy to slip through the hedge. I shouldn't have, I know that, but I couldn't sit back and watch them die when I knew how much they meant to Evergreene. He'd spent the last twenty years of his life working on them.'

His tongue must be twiddling the piercing because it's turning in his lip, and I find that I don't really care about anything else. Maybe it has some kind of hypnotic power. 'You keep saying "we" – you were involved too?'

'Just the leg work, the planting, the heavy lifting. It was his science and his knowledge of Christmas trees. I'm not that clever.'

I watch him as he chews on his lip. He's definitely being modest there.

'I never thought Peppermint Branches would run as a Christmas tree farm again. I was certain it would go to a property developer who would flatten it and re-use the land. I intended to make a deal with the new owner to buy this field in exchange for a good chunk of cash or a different part of my adjoining land. Anything to stop these trees being destroyed.'

'Oh. Okay, I suppose we can still do that . . .' I start, trying not to sound as disappointed as I feel.

'No way,' he says quickly. 'That was only my plan if it sold to someone who was going to destroy it. You're running this place as a tree farm, so these are yours now. I was only an interim caretaker. Just try not to kill them.'

I laugh at his offhand tone. 'No pressure then.'

He doesn't laugh. 'I'm sorry about the trespassing. It's terrible, and if anyone had known I was doing it, or caught me in here, they wouldn't have been so understanding.'

Either I'm missing something or I just don't get what the big deal is. 'The land wasn't mine then. It wasn't anybody's. These trees are beautiful, and obviously important, you weren't doing anything wrong by keeping them alive.'

His shoulders drop as relief visibly floods through him, and he smiles for the first time since I opened the gate.

The tree I'm standing next to must be roughly seven foot high because I have to look up to see the tip. 'How old are these?'

'This one is six years,' he says without needing to read the label that's tied around a low branch. 'But they vary. Each row was planted at a different time. The oldest ones are eight and the youngest ones are toddlers at three.'

'Do they scream a lot and refuse to eat their vegetables?'

This time he does laugh, a warm rumbling sound that makes me grin as he points out the younger trees, each row shorter than the one before. It looks organised and professional. The moss is green and plush and the trees themselves have an unusual eye-catching colour, the traditional dark green but with an underside of a lighter greyish-blue that makes you want to stop for a closer look, and it's all about a million miles from the hotchpotch of dead trees I saw when I drove in. In comparison, the Nordmann fir fields look like an overgrown forest, and it makes me realise how much work I've got to do to get the rest of the fields looking anything like this, and I haven't even seen the balsams and spruces yet.

'There's something else,' Noel says in a rush. 'When they reach about six feet, they're mature enough to start producing cones, so I've been collecting the seeds and growing them. It sounds like stealing but I was only trying to protect them and make sure the species would live on, no matter what. I have a polytunnel full of seedlings that are rightfully yours.'

'What's a polytunnel?'

'You haven't . . . You don't *know* what a polytunnel is?' Him being able to make fun of my horticultural knowledge eases the weird atmosphere in the air between us. 'It's a bit like a greenhouse but much bigger and covered by polythene rather than glass. It's for frost protection, cover and warmth for starting vegetables off early. Pumpkins need a long growing season, so I start hundreds of seeds early in the year, so they're well-established plants by the time the risk of frost has passed and I can plant them outside. Christmas trees are much hardier, but the little seedlings need a bit of protection in the first couple of years.'

I try not to think about how complicated it all sounds. God knows how he remembers all this stuff.

Gizmo runs back up to us, woofs and dodges around our legs, then runs off again. I can't help grinning at his happy tail wagging as I follow him to get a better look at the rows of trees. There must be at least five hundred of them spread throughout the field, and I can't believe how amazing it looks.

'At least with the saplings I've got, you'll have enough stock to replant in the spring without interrupting the Peppermint Branches ancestral line.'

His words make me feel more excited than it's reasonable to be over a tree, but maybe it says something about my life lately that tree heritage is currently the best thing in it.

When Noel's finally captured Gizmo, we leave the Peppermint firs and I can't help leaning on the gate as I close it and looking at them for a moment longer. They really are beautiful, like sentries in their rows, making me feel optimistic and bright again.

'Thanks for taking care of them,' I say as we walk further down the track and cross a little stone bridge across a gently flowing stream. 'I feel guilty for selling them when they're not mine to sell. You're the one who's raised them. I shouldn't be earning a profit from something that had nothing to do with me.'

'You're missing the point of a Christmas tree farm. They were raised for the farm. Whatever money you earn from them will go back into the farm – believe me, you have a *lot* of work to do here, and every bit of your income will go towards that for the next infinite amount of years. The only reason I took care of them is because those particular trees are special, but they were never mine to begin with. They're yours now, everything on this land is yours, and every bit of money you make from it will be returned to make it better. Farming is an endless circle. It takes a lot of years to make a disposable income – Evergreene was doing well for himself, but those missing years have been a huge setback. You've lost a lot of his crop, and a lot of what's left might be unsalvageable, and you only have a few weeks to learn everything you can about Christmas trees and how to shear them, cut them, and make people buy them.'

'Is that as impossible as it sounds?'

He shrugs. 'Depends how dedicated you are and how much you want this. If it's too difficult, are you going to hop back in your car and leave in January?'

We've stopped at the edge of the bridge and there's a little pebble beach leading down to the shore of the river and Gizmo is pulling to go onto it. Noel bends down to unhook his lead and I can't help watching as his big hands give the tiny dog a scruffle before letting him go, his bright eyes watching him potter around in the stones. This isn't the first time he's mentioned leaving when things are difficult. It's obviously what he expects. Instead of answering, I look around. The mixed scent of all the different species of Christmas trees is heavy in the air, the little stream is burbling away beside us, a trickle of water that looks like something that should be in a country park and it's unimaginable that this is literally my garden. For the first time since my parents died, I feel like I could live again.

I look back at Noel. 'There's something about these trees that makes life seem better. It's unreal that I own this place. *You* make it sound so special. I was terrified last night, I thought it was a huge mistake, but talking to you and now walking around it . . . how could this ever be a mistake? I'm not going to run away because somewhere as special as this is worth any amount of work I have to put in.'

When I pluck up the courage to look at his face, his smile is obscenely wide in a way it hasn't been before. There's nothing tight or sarcastic about it. He seems totally uninhibited, and the silver ball in his lip catches the light every time he shifts, making me forget what I was thinking about in the first place.

Suddenly there's a woof from the beach below us and we both look down to see the plop of a frightened fish as it flops back into the stream, and Gizmo on a rock in the middle of the water, having jumped there from the shore.

'Giz, no!' Noel shouts and flies off down the shallow slope after him. 'Don't you dare chase that poor little fishy, it's October, you'll freeze if you fall in.' He stops short at the edge of the water and leans over, trying to reach the dog, but the rock is far enough out that he can't get there.

The fish makes the mistake of jumping again and Gizmo yaps and crouches down on his haunches and wiggles his back end, readying himself for launch.

I see Noel resign himself as he wades into the river and lets out a yell as cold water seeps into his work boots. He scoops the dog up easily with one huge hand. 'Oh, no, you don't, matey. Not at this time of year. Leave the poor salmon be.'

Gizmo grumbles his disapproval.

'How did you manage that jump?' Noel grumbles back at him. 'Leah's pet squirrel must've been giving you athletics training.'

I can't help giggling as Gizmo tries to squirm over Noel's shoulder to get back to the fish.

'Yeah, yeah, I know it's my own fault for letting you off your lead near a river at salmon migration time. But don't worry about it, it's not like I'll have frostbite or gangrene in my toes by the time we get back or anything.'

Gizmo is still grumbling about it.

I'm laughing so hard at the conversation between them that I have to sit down on one of the large, flat stones behind me. 'Do you think he's going to multiply if he gets wet?'

'Like the mogwai in *Gremlins*?' He trudges up the bank, leaving a wet trail through the pebbles behind him. 'I wouldn't mind that. I love him so much, I'd happily have ten of him.' He stops to look up and give me a wide smile. 'And I'm glad you find my misery so funny.'

'Actually I was laughing at how much he's telling you off.'

Noel grins down at the little dog in his arm and drops a kiss onto his brown and white head. 'No way is he going in the river at this time of year. His fur is really thick and takes hours to dry, and he doesn't realise there's a difference in water temperature between now and when he was happily splashing about in there in July.'

I barely have time to register the hot flush at the huge man being so openly affectionate with the little dog, before Noel's in front of me. He leans over and deposits Gizmo onto my lap and my arms automatically encircle him to prevent him jumping off and giving chase to the fish again. As soon as he realises he's on me, he turns in a circle and licks my arm before standing up to lick my chin. Noel sinks down on another rock to my left with a groan and leans over to unlace his boots.

'I think he's mistaken himself for a grizzly bear. You know how you see them in the shallows catching salmon as they swim upstream? It's my fault for letting him watch *Countryfile* unsupervised.'

I stroke his tiny head as he turns in a circle to get comfortable and curls up on my lap. 'Oh, bless him. Butter wouldn't melt.'

'Not now his dad's got wet feet, it wouldn't.' Noel grouches.

'You're being a big baby, you know that, don't you? It's a lovely day, you'll dry out quick enough.'

He glances over his shoulder at me with a raised eyebrow and a look of indignation. 'I will, my boots won't.'

Noel unlaces his boots and pulls them off one at a time. He tips the first one upside down, looking unreasonably forlorn as a trickle of water splashes onto the stones at his feet. He pulls the sock off and wrings it out, then does the same with the other foot.

I try to concentrate on stroking Gizmo, but it only gets more difficult when I catch sight of a flash of colour on his ankle and make a noise of surprise. 'Is that a Truffula tree?'

He glances down at his foot and then back at me. 'So, let me get this straight, you can identify a fictional tree tattooed on my ankle but you can't identify a cedar standing right in front of you?'

'I love Dr Seuss.' I hold my hand out and scrunch my fingers together. He turns to the side and holds his leg out behind him, letting me see the tattoo.

I lean over Gizmo, who huffs at being squashed, to clamp my hand around his wet trousers and pull his leg closer until I can see the back of his foot.

'I can't believe you have a *Lorax* tattoo. That's amazing.'

Without even thinking, I run my fingers across the red cotton candy tree and down the striped trunk that extends from a patch of grass at the back of his heel and leans over the outside of his ankle bone. 'Unless,' I say aloud, reading the word that's written underneath it, an echo of the final stone-carved message The Lorax leaves behind when all the trees are gone. 'I *love* that quote. I had it pinned on the noticeboard above my desk in my old job.'

He's gone from laughing to very still as I've been touching his foot and he murmurs the full quote.

'That's the most amazing tattoo I've ever seen,' I whisper, feeling like talking in a normal voice will ruin the peace that's settled over us. It feels special, like he's trusting me with something by showing it to me. It's hidden in a place that probably not many people get to see, and he's gone so quiet that I get the impression he didn't intend for me to see it. It feels too personal.

'Thanks.' He's whispering too. 'You're the first person who's ever understood that. My ex couldn't understand why I had a "pretend tree from a Danny DeVito children's film" tattooed on me. She thought it was a drunken dare or something. Didn't even know it was a book first.'

'Good clue as to where the "ex" part comes in.'

He laughs, looking as surprised by it as I am. It didn't seem like a laughing moment. 'I love the quote, I love the meaning of the story, and I love trees. Dad used to read it to me when I was little. One of my most vivid memories is snuggling up in bed with him and reading *The Lorax* together. When I was older and he was ill, I got into bed with him and read it aloud and neither of us could stop giggling. It was the last time I ever heard him laugh. He never approved of tattoos but I think he'd approve of that one.'

'It's beautiful,' I murmur, my fingers stroking the skin of his ankle.

He sighs, looking lost in memories for a moment, until he suddenly shakes his head and yanks his foot out of my grasp. He starts straightening the socks on the sunny rock like they need the concentration of a chess game, and I struggle to take my eyes off him. He tucks his right foot behind his left leg so the tattoo is hidden again then smooths the wet bottoms of his trousers out, trying to squeeze river water from the material.

It obviously means a lot to him, and I want to ask about his father, but he definitely doesn't want to talk about it anymore. 'I didn't think you got this much sun in Scotland.'

He looks over his shoulder at me with a dark eyebrow quirked, like he knows I'm offering a much-needed subject change. He holds my gaze for a long moment, before he shakes his head again and looks determinedly back out towards the river. 'A common misconception. All right, we get more than our fair share of drizzle, but we're generally treated to gorgeous autumns and a good bit of winter snow. It's not for everyone but I think it's perfect here.'

I make noises of agreement as he starts talking about the Scottish weather because I'm as grateful for the neutral conversation topic as he is. There's something about him that makes me want to say too much, makes me want to *know* too much, and it can't be good, because he obviously isn't interested in sharing it with me. Besides, I definitely don't want another man in my life – Steve was more than enough for one year. 'What do you do with all your pumpkins?'

'My goal is to sell as many to the public as possible, but it's impossible to predict how many will realistically sell each year so I end up with loads left over. I sell some to restaurants around the county, and there's a local produce shop in Peterhead that I supply throughout October. I sell a lot at the market too, and then at the very end of the season, there's a farmer a couple of miles away who buys whatever's left in bulk and uses them as cattle feed. But pumpkins are a fussy crop and need a lot of care to grow in this climate. You won't have to worry about stuff like that with Christmas trees though – trees never expire. Whatever you don't sell will still be here next year. Any trees that are dead, you can cut down and replant with saplings in the spring, and any trees that are okay but unsellable, you can use the branches for your wreaths, and anything that's beyond saving, you cut up and poke the smaller bits through the woodchipper and use the chippings as mulch around next spring's saplings, and dry out the trunks to use as firewood.'

'You make it sound so straightforward.' I try not to sound as nervous as I feel. I really hadn't a clue what I was taking on here, and the huge number of things to do, learn, and keep track of, is beyond overwhelming.

'You'll get the hang of it.' He looks up and meets my eyes. 'Once you've done it a few times, you'll get used to it. Give it a few weeks and you'll be telling me what to do.'

I let out a laugh. 'I can't imagine anyone telling you what to do.'

'You have met my mother, right?' He pulls a face of pure terror and it sets me off giggling again.

I think he can hear that my laughter is covering my nerves, because he turns serious again. 'Have you thought about taking on seasonal workers?'

The idea of employing people, of being responsible for other people's livelihood, even for a few short months makes the hairs on the back of my neck stand up, and it must show on my face because he chuckles.

'It's not that terrifying. Evergreene and I used to share seasonal workers, because your season begins just as mine ends. The same two blokes still work for me every autumn, they're trustworthy and hard-working and they know what they're doing on a Christmas tree farm. If you get in quick before they find festive work elsewhere, I'm sure they'd be overjoyed to stay on and work for you too. I *guarantree* it. Get it? Guaran-tree?'

I laugh, mainly at how pleased he is with himself for such an excellent pun. And it makes sense, I know that. It's becoming increasingly obvious that I can't manage this on my own.

'One of the guys at the market used to be a groundsman for

Evergreene. Keeping the weeds down, path maintenance, gritting in winter, that sort of thing, and I happen to know he's between jobs at the moment. He helps out with his dad's gingerbread stall across the aisle from mine, if you wanted to have a word. I'm going in the morning if you fancy tagging along? Meet some of the locals? You'll love Fergus and Fiona. They'll never admit it, but they've got a little flirtation going on between them, that's always fun to watch. And believe me, once they get wind of this, *everyone* in Elffield will know about Peppermint Branches reopening, and it's never too early to start getting the word out.'

'Right. Er, okay,' I say, wondering what exactly I've got myself into here. Then again, where would I be now if I was still in London? Staring at the wall behind my desk, inputting data that starts to blur because it's so boring that it all looks the same. Pumpkins, gingerbread, and flirty pensioners have got to be more fun than that.

Eventually he puts his wet socks and boots back on and stands up. I pick Gizmo up off my lap and tuck him under my arm without giving him another chance to escape and chase after the fish. Noel jumps up the bank and holds his hand out, and I slip my left hand into it. My hand feels small in his huge one, his fingers completely encasing it as he pulls me back onto the path and drops it quickly.

'Will you tell me more about what it used to be like?' I ask as we walk past another gate in the holly hedge, the sign on this one reading 'Norway spruce', the trees inside just as overgrown as the Nordmann firs and the ground just as overrun with weeds.

'It's a great place to come in the winter. You should open in December even if the farm isn't ready and you just select the trees yourself, cut them, net them, and stack them on the driveway to be sold as pre-cuts. People came for dog walks when it was open and picnics by the river if it wasn't too cold. Evergreene used to give kids tractor rides around the track when he went to pick up trees.'

'Oh, that would be so much fun. If the tractor starts.'

'It will. You'll see. These things are built to last. It just needs a bit of care and attention before you make the poor thing explode again.'

I lean on the next gate and look over. A wide, overgrown tractor path is the only thing separating this field of trees from the next, which Noel informs me are Balsam firs and Blue spruces, the colour making it easy to differentiate between them. It looks magical. I can see why Noel was convinced there were elves here when he was a kid. I think back to when I was younger. I would have *loved* to come to a place like this. 'Has there ever been a Santa here for kids to visit?'

He shakes his head. 'Evergreene wore a Santa hat throughout December, but that's as far as it goes.'

'I could hire a Santa. Set up a little Santa's grotto for kids to meet him. And you thought elves used to scamper between the trees . . . I could hang some elf hats around like they've been snagged on trunks, and I could make stencils to put down some glittery footprints. All I'd have to do is get a couple of sheets of thin bendy plastic and cut out some little footprints and sprinkle glitter through them onto the ground. There could be some bells hidden in the highest branches so they'd jingle whenever the wind blew.'

Even Gizmo is watching me with his head on one side, his big ears twitching.

I close my eyes and think of all the films I've seen where the characters go to buy a Christmas tree. 'We need loads of lights and some carollers. People are always walking around *fa-la-la-la-ing* in festive movies. At the very least, we could play Christmas music. Some of the trees need to be transplanted to the outer fields so it looks attractive from the road. I can string them with lights all along the driveway and the lane down to the fields. And hot chocolate! I could set up a stall outside the house. Hot chocolate is pretty much a requirement on a Christmas tree farm.'

He's smiling as he looks at me with a sort of proud smile, his eyes twinkling as the morning sun reaches its peak in the sky.

'What about the caravan?' I ask, trying not to think about what that smile means.

'I think it'll take more than a cup of hot chocolate to fix that.'

'No, I mean, it's wrecked anyway. What if I drag it out of the garden and clean it up and paint it festively red. I could use it as a hot chocolate stand. It'd give me a little kitchen area to work in, everything would stay dry, and the back window could act as a serving hatch . . . ' I know I'm talking too fast as my excitement builds.

'You don't have a license to serve food to the public. And it'll take longer than six weeks to get one.'

'Oh.' I try not to show how disappointed I am.

His smile goes from playing around his mouth to spreading all the way across his face and making his eyes dance. 'But I do.'

I narrow my eyes at him, trying to ignore the fluttering in my belly at the sight of that smile. It's just excitement about the tree farm. Nothing more.

'If you take out the garden fence, which is rotted away anyway and shift the caravan about three feet to the right, it'll be on my property, and I have all the necessary licenses. You can shift it back and get your own by next year, but it would do for this season.'

'And you'd let me do that?'

He shrugs. 'Sure. It sounds like a lovely idea. We do hot drinks when the pumpkin patch is open and they go down like, well, hot drinks on a cold day.'

We stand together looking out at the rows of silent trees until Gizmo starts pulling to chase a dried up oak leaf that's had the audacity to flutter by.

'Ideas.' Noel nudges his shoulder into mine as the little dog catches the leaf and tears it apart with teeth and paws. 'Maybe you're not *quite* as "not cut out for this" as I thought you were.'

'Was that a compliment?' I grin at him. 'You weren't kidding about these trees, were you? What kind of magical powers are they hiding if they can even coax a compliment out of you?'

His laugh rumbles around the farm and my chest is fluttering with festive joy as we carry on walking. I can imagine it as he describes it, and I'm suddenly brimming with ideas to make it a reality again.

Chapter 7

Noel promised to pick me up bright and early, although I didn't bother asking what constituted 'bright and early' because I didn't expect to get any sleep at all. I'd planned to spend the night lying on the air mattress and scribbling down ideas, but by the time I'd retrieved more essentials from the car and snuggled into the fabric conditioner scent of the sleeping bag . . . the next thing I know, there's a car horn blasting outside the boarded up window, and I wake up with a leap.

Screech. Screeeech. Screeeeeeeeech. Screech. Screeeeeeeeeech. I think it's Morse code for 'I'm a loud and annoying twat'.

I stumble blearily upright, squinting like a mole emerging from its burrow for the first time under the harsh kitchen lightbulb that's still on from last night.

Screeeeech. Screech. Screech. Screeeeeeeech.

I stumble into the dark hallway and fumble around for the key. I shove it in the lock and twist it harshly – anything to stop that awful noise as quickly as humanly possible – and burst out the front door, only to be greeted by . . . nighttime.

Screeeeeeeee— 'Oh good, I was about to start knocking. Good morning, sunshine!'

'Sunshine?' I mutter, blinking at the shock of the damp

morning air and the darkness. From the noise he's making, I'd assumed it was about midday. 'You said bright and early, there's nothing bright about this, it's still dark.'

Noel's leaning out of the driver's side window of a battered old truck that looks like it might have been yellow once, but is now distinctly patterned by rust and peeling paint. 'It's 6 a.m. The sun doesn't rise until eight o'clock at this time of year. Are you ready?'

'Ready?' I ask, realising that I've just vaulted out of bed, my hair must be smooshed up in all directions and I've probably got crusts in my eyes and drool dried on my chin, but he looks ridiculously good for this time of day. There's a tuft of a ponytail sticking out under a red and white snowflake patterned beanie hat, a navy flannel shirt covering his arms, and a body warmer which would probably look ridiculous on anyone else, but he manages to make it look sexy.

'For the market. I have to get there early to set up.'

'*This* early?'

'Yup.' The grin he gives me is totally smug and a little bit sultry. 'Look on the bright side – at least you got some sleep.'

'And I could do with a lot more of it.'

He grins again. 'Go and get ready. I'll wait.'

I mumble something unrepeatable about what he can do with his pumpkins, and he gives me another grin that says he heard every word. I turn around to go back inside, ridiculously grateful that the water and electricity came back on yesterday, but before I've got the door closed, he screeches the horn again.

'What is *wrong* with you? You'll wake the neigh . . . oh.' When I look back at him, he's got a travel mug in his hand and a grin on his face.

'I *am* the neighbour. It's not bothering me.' He holds the cup up in an imaginary toast and winks at me.

I close the door with a resounding slam, and I can still hear his laughter from outside.

Inside, I do an excellent impression of a flapping fish as I run up the stairs with a change of clothes and my toothbrush and toothpaste. I will never take running water and electricity for granted again, even though the light shows up how badly the bathroom needs a proper clean. I promise it I'll get onto it later as I manage to get ready in record time and fly back out the door.

Noel has still got his window wound down and his arm across the gap. He grins over the top of the mug as I close the door behind me and slip the key into my pocket.

'Nice hair.'

'I couldn't find my hairbrush, okay? I'll put it up now, I didn't want to keep you waiting any longer in case you started screeching that blasted horn again.'

'It looks fine. Maybe you could stop in one of my fields on the way and scare off a few crows for me.'

I must give him a look that says I want to kill him because he starts laughing. 'It wasn't an insult. You'd be the prettiest scarecrow I've ever had.'

I try to glare at him as I walk around the truck, but I'm fighting with myself not to smile because no one has ever called me pretty before, even in a scarecrow context.

Faded paint comes off in my hand as I touch the door handle on the passenger side, and the door lets out a groan when I pull it open. The smell of fresh coffee fills the truck and I close my eyes and breathe it in for a moment.

Then I remember that I'm about to get into a death-trap and I haven't really woken up yet. 'Is this thing roadworthy?'

'Define roadworthy.'

'Has it had an MOT this side of the Eighties?'

'It's *had* one . . . I can't promise it passed.'

'Noel!'

He laughs. 'I'm joking. Of course it passed. It's fine, just a bit of superficial damage, doesn't affect the running of it. None of us would be roadworthy if that was the case.' He rolls his eyes. 'Are you coming or are you going to stand there all day? You're letting the cold air in.'

'Your window . . .' I go to protest that his window's open so the cold air has come in anyway, but I give up before I can finish the sentence and climb into the truck.

A festive radio station is playing quietly from the dashboard, Bing Crosby singing 'Silver Bells', a real old-fashioned Christmas song that makes me shiver with nostalgia. The brown leather of the front is one long bench rather than individual seats, and in the space between us is another travel mug and a paper bag with 'Roscoe Farm' printed on it.

'I brought coffee and breakfast,' he says as I pull the fraying seatbelt over my chest and snap it into the buckle beside me. 'Homemade pumpkin spice latte and a pumpkin spice muffin fresh from the oven.'

'Oh my god, you are my favourite person in the universe right now.' The blue travel cup has got foxes and autumn leaves on it, and I grab it and sip it.

I feel every part of me relax as that first sip of caffeine hits my system and Noel starts the engine again and backs slowly out of my driveway. 'God, this is *amazing*,' I say, making an orgasmic noise as I take a second sip. 'And surprisingly strong.'

'I firmly believe that people who don't need a strong caffeine hit at this time of day are some species of pod person.'

I sip from the mug again, enjoying every hot mouthful as it warms me up from the inside out. This is literally the best coffee I've ever tasted. And Chelsea and I go out for a *lot* of coffee in London. 'You make your own pumpkin spice for coffee? In big chains, they use syrup, right?'

'That's exactly why the homemade version is better.' We back onto the main road and drive in the opposite direction from the way I came in, towards his farm. 'And yeah, you mix up ginger, cinnamon, cloves, nutmeg, and allspice, add fresh pumpkin puree and a touch of vanilla extract, and add it to any drink. It's amazing in hot chocolate too.'

I sip it again. 'You're a genius.'

He laughs. 'With eight thousand pumpkins a year, I've learnt how to make the best of them. But thank you, no one's ever called me that before.'

I go to say that I'm sure he's being modest, but he interrupts me, and I get the impression he's embarrassed by the compliment. 'Try a muffin, my mum's the baking genius in the family.'

I unscrew the twist in the paper bag and take an orange-coloured muffin out. It's in a black case with tiny orange Jack O'Lanterns all over it and 'Roscoe Farm' emblazoned on the bottom. 'Branded bags and cake cases too?'

'We sell this stuff on the market stall along with the pumpkins, and we have a huge bakery stand outside the pumpkin patch when it's open to the public. My mum's amazing in the kitchen, her goodies are very popular.'

I can see why. The top of the muffin is all cracked and sprinkled with powdered sugar. It looks like an artisan creation in a fancy bakery, and I almost feel guilty for pulling a lump off and popping it into my mouth. It tastes as good as it looks. The perfect blend of sweet and savoury, buttery, spicy, and warm, the case underneath heating my hand as I hold it. 'Oh my god.' I let out another orgasmic noise. Actually, that's an unfair comparison because I've never enjoyed an orgasm as much as I'm enjoying this. It was worth the six-hundred-mile drive just for this muffin.

We're coming up to his farm and I can see a light on outside, flooding the front with brightness. I can't help pressing my forehead against the window for a closer look. Glenna is in the huge open driveway outside the farmhouse, and I can see signs leaning against walls and pumpkins piled everywhere. Noel honks the horn again and she stops what she's doing and gives us a wave. The farmhouse looks as picturesque from up close as it looked in the distance, all old stone bricks and window boxes that were undoubtedly filled with flowers in the summer. There are double wooden gates open wide, and their tarmac driveway is a huge empty space, surrounded on the edges by freestanding stalls covered by orange and white striped awning and decorated with huge vases of brightly coloured autumn leaves.

Glenna is still waving as we pass by and leave her behind. 'No Gizmo?'

'You are joking, right? Gizmo doesn't get out of bed at this time of day for *anyone*. He'll saunter out when he's ready, have some breakfast, a gentle walk, and then snuggle under his duvet on the sofa until lunchtime, and after that he'll be dragged out to the fields with me while I work, and then snuggle on the sofa until teatime.'

'Oh, bless him,' I say. 'I can't wait to see him again.'

'Yeah, he woofed about you all night too. He thought there might have been some really big spiders he needed to protect you from, or maybe a giant ant or something.'

'They don't exist, do they?'

'Dunno. I suppose half the fun is in finding out.'

'Your definition of fun and mine are quite different.'

His tongue must twiddle the piercing from the inside because the ball starts moving in his lip and my eyes are drawn to it again as the song changes. 'It's the Most Wonderful Time of the Year' by Andy Williams starts playing, and I wonder if he's put a festive station on because of what I said on Tuesday night or if he'd usually drive to work listening to Christmas music in October. I don't think he would, somehow.

At the edge of their farm, as we pass a hand-drawn chalk sign that says 'Pick-your-own pumpkin patch' in swirly lettering, there's a giant pumpkin. It must be at least six foot tall and almost as wide, it's surrounded by loads of smaller pumpkins, real ones in all shades of orange, yellow, and white. They're arranged so it looks like they're pouring out of its mouth in a wave. It's so striking that I actually gasp at the sight. 'Did you make that?'

He nods. 'Wood and plaster and a *lot* of sandpapering. But it's stood the test of a few autumns now and everyone comments on it. It's brilliant for visibility from the road. People love stopping for selfies with it.'

'Wow.' I look over my shoulder as we drive past. It's an incredible sight and I can't believe anyone could make it. 'You're incredibly talented, do you know that? Is there anything you *can't* do?'

'Maintain a relationship? Greet new neighbours in a reasonable way? Crochet?'

It makes me laugh again, and I want to carry on the conversation, but his face is as red as the shirt he was wearing yesterday, and he's got a look about him that says he'd very much like to hide.

Luckily, I'm distracted by a sign coming up on the right-hand side of the road and I lean forward to see it. It looks like another hand-lettered chalk board, permanently printed on weather-resistant plastic this time, but instead of a nice and friendly pumpkin, there's a cartoon sweetcorn cob with red eyes and the words 'GET LOST' in big capital letters. The sign is positioned outside a field of tall green plants with thick silver chains criss-crossing the entrance. 'Oh, that's nice and welcoming,' I say. It might not even be Noel's land, but the chalk writing is the same as the sign we passed earlier.

I don't expect him to start laughing, like proper belly-laughing, so hard that the seat shakes. 'It's a maize maze, Leah. Maize with an *i*. It's *ah-maze-ing* fun! The sign is an invitation, not an insult.'

'It's a maze . . . made of sweetcorn?' He nods and I lean forward then back to get a better view around him. 'Wow, I've never seen anything like that before. It looks . . . ah-maze-ing.' I try to see through the back window as it disappears behind us. Green ears of corn that must be taller than me line the edges along the road, and I get the feeling that you'd need to see it from above to get a clearer picture. 'Are you sure that's a good idea? I've seen the horror films, Noel. Bad things happen in fields of corn.'

He laughs again. 'Just another way to maximise revenue. I was growing corn anyway, so I thought why not grow it with proper paths between it to create a maze and let kids run around in there. The corn's tall enough by late July so I open it seven days a week in the summer holidays, then weekends only until the October half-term when it's open all the time and the corn's much taller, and of course the pumpkin patch is open too so people can come for a real family fun day out. At the end of the season, I cut the corn and sell it, and in the spring, I dig over the field and replant it in a different formation so it's never the same maze twice if people come back year after year. One of my favourite jobs is designing the maze each year.'

'Wow,' I say, struggling for any other words. There really does seem to be nothing he can't do. He's creative and outdoorsy, and he seems to do so much to stay in business year-round.

I can sense his eyes on me and he must be able to tell how impressed I am, because he says, 'There are a few around the UK, it's nothing original before you tell me I'm a genius again.'

I poke another bit of pumpkin spice muffin into my mouth to avoid replying. I do think he must be a bit of a genius when it comes to farm stuff, but he obviously doesn't like hearing it. 'You're really busy, aren't you?'

'Aye, but I like it that way. The seasonal growing business isn't for everyone. It takes a lot of year-round maintenance, but you only get an income generally once a year. It can be a shock at first, especially when you're used to the nine-to-five guaranteed monthly paycheque. Personally I'm lucky because my dad started Roscoe Farm long before I was born, so it's had over forty years to build up a reputation. I also got lucky because I made the call to give a few fields over to pumpkins at exactly the time when Halloween started to get as popular here as it is in America, and British people started wanting to visit pumpkin patches like Americans always have. Sometimes in this business you make calls that are wrong, and sometimes you get it right. I've taken plenty of wrong turns along the way too.' He glances over at me and his eyes flick quickly back to the road.

It makes me think about what I'll have to do to stay in business. Noel obviously works hard to make sure things tick over throughout the year. What on earth am I going to do to make Christmas trees earn a living in any month outside of December? 'What did Evergreene do to survive all year round?'

'I hate to say it but he didn't need to. Peppermint Branches was loved far and wide, it was extraordinarily profitable in the later years. He had a massive wholesale contract that was worth a fortune and turned over a huge amount of stock each year, and he spent the non-Christmas season looking after the trees.' He taps his nose and puts on the deep, strongly accented voice of an elderly Scottish gent. 'The more you put into a crop, the more you get out of it, my boy.'

I smile at the impression but it doesn't ease the knot in my stomach. The wholesale contract is obviously long gone and my current crop of trees wouldn't have a hope in hell of getting anything similar. 'What about growing something else? You grow and sell other things outside of pumpkin season, right?' He nods but my mind's already whirring. 'Strawberries? They could grow in the shade between the trees, and they'd be long gone by the time the farm opens.'

'Depends how much time you've got to waste planting and caring for a crop that aren't Christmas trees, and how many you'd have to grow to make a profit.'

'If there were enough, I could open the farm as a pick-your-own in the summer too . . . Oh! Opening the farm in the summer!' I nearly spill my coffee as I sit up straighter and the idea bubbles into life. 'Christmas in July is a thing, right? I could do something festive at that time of year. Meet Santa in the summer for a riverside picnic or something?'

'Drown Santa? Send a few Santas white-water-rafting down the river and have a race to see which one makes it back by December?'

'I was thinking more along the lines of meet Santa by the river for an afternoon tea of candycane cupcakes and gingerbread houses and get a mid-year update on his preparations for Christmas? There could be festive-themed games and presents, and a theme of keeping the spirit of Christmas alive all year through, like Scrooge says at the end of *A Christmas Carol* when the last ghost leaves.'

I expect him to laugh at me, but when I pluck up the courage to look at him, he's still watching the road but his lips are tucked together and both his eyebrows are raised. He doesn't look completely unimpressed.

It gives me the courage to continue. 'There could be scavenger hunts to find presents hidden under the trees and elf hide-and-seek. Don't you think it would be nice for kids who love Christmas to get to celebrate it in the middle of the year too?'

'You're planning on sticking around that long then?'

I flinch at the harshness of his words but he continues before I have a chance to snap something back at him.

'In my experience, when things get tough, people usually don't.'

'I didn't come here thinking this was going to be easy.' I don't mention that I expected it to be *marginally* easier than it is, but that's beside the point. 'I wanted something to completely change my life. Something my parents would've been proud of. I'm not going to give up at the first hurdle. That would defeat the object.'

'Well, summer Santa and elves and scavenger hunts sound great. You're not going to make Santa wear his summer uniform of tiny red Speedos with a white furry trim, are you? I don't think my eyeballs could take all the bleach they'd need after that sight.'

The thought makes me giggle even though I'm annoyed at him for thinking that I'm going to leave *or* that I'd dress Santa in swimming trunks that don't look good on *anyone*, especially a man of Santa's traditional age, body type, and hirsuteness.

'Maybe we can team up and do some co-advertising next year, your festive summer picnics and my corn maze. They're close enough that people can easily visit both, and we could think of a way to incorporate each other's produce and extend both the Christmas and Halloween season.'

'I'd like that.' I accept it for the concession it is. He must've been hurt by someone leaving, and he hasn't got a high opinion of anyone from a city, and he obviously doesn't like me enough to tell me about it, so there's no point in pushing it.

I finish my muffin and slurp the last of my coffee, then pull my hair over my shoulder and try to finger-comb it into resembling something other than a rats' nest. I push my fingers through the top and flatten it down, trying to work it into a plait without a mirror.

I can feel him watching me and it makes me blush even though there's no reason to. When I tie the end with the spare band that's always on my wrist and flip it back over my shoulder, I feel fluttery for no reason at all.

'Welcome to the lively, buzzing centre of Elffield.' Noel slows down when we eventually reach a more built-up area. I've lost track of how long we've been driving. The distance between things seems so wide here, and everything seems so far away from everything else.

I realise he's being sarcastic as we turn down a narrow street with houses on both sides. Among them is a post office on one side and a convenience shop on the other. That's it.

'We're a village that relies solely on our market, but there's a good community here. We support our own.' He lifts a hand and points directly ahead of us. 'That's the market.'

I look towards a large set of pillars ahead of us. They look like columns from ancient Rome, holding up the sharp angled roof of a covered market building. The lights are on inside, making it look warm and inviting, and the area in front of the entrance is paved with slabs in shades of grey. Noel drives around it and takes a narrow side street that winds around the back of the huge building and eventually opens up to another set of pillars wide enough to let vehicles through. 'Trade entrance,' he says. 'If you sell trees here, get customers to drive round this way to load their car, it's much easier than dragging an eight-foot spruce between all the stallholders.'

I nod, wishing I'd brought a notebook and pen to jot all his tips down. I'm never going to remember all of this. Also, just how heavy are eight-foot trees?

I've never seen anyone drive as slowly as Noel creeps through the wide market lane, already buzzing with people setting up their stalls. There are people on stepladders stringing up bunting and fairy lights across their awning, people carrying crates of goods to and from their cars, and people merrily chatting away with cups of coffee in hand.

Noel stops at a covered stall, a series of long trestle tables in a backwards L-shape with a wide space in front of it, bright orange awning emblazoned with a big Roscoe Farm logo and 'Pumpkins' in swirly calligraphy doodled underneath. I stand on the flagstone floor and have a look around while Noel shouts good morning to other traders in our lane and greets them with a wave and a smile.

It's a good spot. One lane back from the front entrance, just enough for a bit of protection from the elements, easily visible from both side entrances, and on the corner before the market opens out into a much larger space with many more stalls. In the chaos of set-up time, I catch sight of a Scottish souvenir stall, a used bookseller, a baker whose scent of freshly baked bread has wafted through the building, a handmade jewellery stall, and a cheese seller offering chutneys and crackers along with a selection of locally made cheeses.

Noel pulls the cover off the bed of his truck, uncovering wooden crates which are so packed with pumpkins that they're spilling over the edges. 'Do you think you brought enough?'

'It would be a good day if I didn't,' he says, completely missing the sarcasm.

'Can I help?'

He grunts as he sets the first crate down in front of the back table. 'Pick the best ones and display them along the back of the stall. The side area is for baked goods.'

I crouch down beside the crate and wonder what on earth constitutes a 'best' pumpkin. He unloads another two crates and puts them next to the one I'm still poring over. He stops on the way to get a fourth one and leans down beside me, plucking one I'd already rejected from the crate with one hand and plonking it onto the table with a thud. '*That's* a good one. It's not a nuclear chemistry exam, just grab anything. All defects make interesting features to a pumpkin carver's eye. People like the dodgiest-looking ones.'

He hefts yet another crate from the truck and dumps it on the ground next to the others. I pick a random pumpkin from the second crate, examine it for anything that could be defined as an interesting feature, and plonk it quickly onto the table to show him that I'm not completely useless.

The fourth crate of pumpkins seems to be the last, because he moves onto another crate, and this one smells so good that I can tell what it is before he's even pulled the cover back. It's full of pumpkin spice muffins packed in boxes of two, individually boxed pumpkin cupcakes with buttercream swirls, wrapped sugar cookies in the shape of pumpkins and iced with orange icing, bags of roasted, salted pumpkin seeds, and jars of pumpkin ginger jam and pumpkin orange marmalade with handwritten labels and gingham tops.

'Your mum made all these?' I ask, impressed with the many uses Glenna can find for a pumpkin and how delicious everything looks. I had no idea pumpkins were so versatile.

'Yep.' He retrieves a large sandwich board from the truck, sets it down in front of the stall and crouches in front of it. He pulls a pack of chalk from his pocket and starts sketching on it. When he stands up, it's got orange pumpkins and green vines decorating the edges and in the middle, in neater handwriting than I've got on lined paper in biro, is written 'Pumpkins: 75p each or two for £1' in swirly, fancy white writing, complete with green leaves sprawling from each letter. It's a work of art and it's only taken him three minutes.

'Two for a pound?' I say in surprise. 'They're, like, three quid each in the supermarket.'

'Exactly. If a busy mum with a family of four goes to the supermarket, that's quite an outlay – she's probably only going to buy one pumpkin for all the family – but if she comes past here, at fifty pence each, it's easier and cheaper to say, 'oh, you can all have one'. I sell more pumpkins, her family gets to enjoy themselves for minimal cost. It might seem counterproductive to someone who's used to paying over the odds for everything in the city, but here we sell cheap and we sell more.' He lays out a handful of Roscoe Farm branded carving kits beside the pumpkins. 'Remember that.'

I clearly have a lot to learn about the pricing of Christmas trees.

'Oh, look, there's Fergus and Iain now.' His hands touch my back and push me across the aisle to where a car has pulled up next to a little wooden stall covered by red and white striped awning. 'This is Leah. She's just bought Peppermint Branches,' he shouts across as a white-haired man leaning on a walking stick gets out of the passenger door and a man in his fifties emerges from the driver's side.

'Could you shout a bit louder?' I turn back to hiss at him. 'I think there's a deaf chap in Cornwall who didn't quite hear.'

'I was telling her you used to work there, Iain . . .' he calls over as I shake both their hands.

I don't know how it happens, but I start telling Iain about the state of the trees and the overgrown hedges while Fergus hands me a tray of neatly wrapped gingerbread . . . llamas. Llamas in biscuit form. I have to blink a few times to make sure I'm not mistaken as he directs me to put it on the stall. While I help them unload the car, Iain talks about cutting trees and keeping the weeds down, and the heady scent of all the gingerbread makes me take leave of my senses, because before I know it, I've offered him a job and he's starting on Monday.

'There you go, that wasn't so difficult,' Noel says when I go back across to the pumpkin stall. 'You've got your first employee. And if you come and talk to my seasonal workers this afternoon, you'll easily have two more.'

'And suddenly I'm an employer.' I feel a bit shellshocked. 'I wasn't expecting this. I intended to plod along by myself, learning as I went. I didn't expect to be employing three people. That's quite a responsibility. Don't I need some kind of insurance? What if I can't pay them?'

'You need employers' liability insurance, and public liability when you open to the public. It's easy enough to sort out. And whatever you've got left of the budget *has* to go on the workers' salaries. It's going to be a vicious circle otherwise. Without help, you won't be able to get the trees anywhere near sellable or the farm anywhere close to opening standard, so you won't sell any trees and you'll be in an even worse position next year. This is great. You're off to the right start.'

I wish I felt as confident as he sounds. Instead, I feel overwhelmed again. I glance back towards Iain, who is now giving his father an animated demonstration of shearing Christmas trees. He was *so* happy about the prospect of working there again, and Noel has made it sound so magical and loved by so many people . . . I can feel the pressure building on me. What if I let everyone down?

'You should go and introduce yourself to everyone, start getting the word out that Peppermint Branches is opening again.'

'Talk to strangers? Just, like, randomly go up to people and tell them I bought the tree farm?' My heart jumps into my throat and my palms start sweating. 'You are joking, right? People don't actually do that, do they?'

He laughs, not realising that I'm *not* joking. 'Everyone's very friendly. And Peppermint Branches was really popular around here, people will be overjoyed to hear it's opening again.'

'I can't just go up to people I don't know and tell them I'm opening a tree farm!'

His eyes cast over me with a contemplative look. 'You had no trouble giving me a piece of your mind the other day and I was a stranger. Where's this lack of confidence come from?'

'Yeah, but you're infuriating. There's a difference.' I don't give him an answer to the confidence question. If I had time to think about it, I'd tell him about Steve taking advantage of my vulnerability after my parents' deaths, and that discovering I was one of a handful of women he was sleeping with was enough to make me want to hide away and never speak to another human again.

Except I wouldn't, because that would be oversharing, obviously.

'Elffield survives on its community. If you're going to live here, you're a part of that. Just go and say hello, tell them you've moved into Peppermint Branches and the conversation will flow from there, I guaran—'

'Don't do the *guarantree* thing again, it wasn't funny the first time.'

'I know. That's why you laughed.' He gives me a wink. 'And I wasn't going to say that. I was going to tell you to go out on a *limb*.'

Despite my best efforts, it makes me laugh and eases some of the nerves as he shoos me away.

The market is quiet at this time of day. Most people have finished setting up their stalls and are standing next to them, chatting to other stallholders over cups of takeaway coffee from the hot drinks counter. It's almost light outside and there's a cold breeze blowing in through the open front. As I pass Fergus and Iain, Fergus calls across to the man selling hats and scarves at the next stall and tells him that I've bought Peppermint Branches, and it makes it surprisingly easy to start a conversation. As the hat and scarf seller asks me where I'm from and what I was doing before, the lady selling Scottish souvenirs catches wind of the conversation and comes over to join in, and then she drags me across to her stall, gives me a fittingly pine-scented air freshener of the Scottish flag, and introduces me to the woman who sells handmade candles on the stall behind her. Before I know it, I've been given a sampler candle, a loaf of bread from the breadmaker, the souvenir woman has weaved a string of tiny paper flags into my plait, the bookseller has gone through his stall and handed me a book about Britain's native trees, and if anyone pays me another compliment on my hair, which I haven't even *brushed* this morning, I might burst into tears.

People are so *nice* here. Customers have started wandering around the undercover part of the market and are joining in the conversations. I lose track of how many people ask me about Peppermint Branches reopening and tell me how much they've missed it and that they're looking forward to getting their tree there again this year.

There's an artist who sells framed prints of his work and does bespoke sketches of children and beloved pets while customers wait, who pulls out his phone and shows me a painting he did at Peppermint Branches years ago, and a lady who sells intricate glass art, from jewellery and ornaments to wind chimes and suncatchers, who tells me she used to get inspiration from walking through the Christmas trees.

I feel a fizzle of glee when I spot a shoe seller with a pair of wellies on display, and thankfully he has them in my size. The black rubber boots come up almost to my knee and are comfier than any of the shoes I currently own, even though I'm only buying them as a figurative two-fingered gesture at Noel. As I'm paying, I spot something else. Tucked away right at the back is a little booth with a twenty-something lad and his laptop sat behind it, advertising custom printing, logo design, postcards, flyers, banners, business cards, and other promotional materials. Like a tiny Scottish Vistaprint.

I stand there and stare at him for a moment. I could get business cards and flyers made up, couldn't I? It's all very well and good to concentrate on reopening the farm, but it'll all be for nothing if no one *knows* it's reopening. On one hand, it's bound to be a big expenditure, and I might fail. What if I *can't* learn everything I need to learn? What if I can't shear Christmas trees? What if I don't manage to cut them and carry them and the tractor doesn't start and the wreaths fall apart? What if the insurance is rejected or the seasonal farmhands refuse to work for such a newbie, and it just gets nearer and nearer to December and I can't open on time?

In my head, I can hear my mum's voice saying, 'what if you *can*?'

I should ask Noel where he advertises, but he's already been so helpful, and has promised to come over and board up my empty window frames and roof this afternoon. I can't rely on him to tell me what to do at every turn. I have to stand on my own – I look down at the bag from the shoeseller in my hand – welly booted feet.

I approach the guy in the booth with caution, but he greets me with such a wide smile that it makes me think he doesn't get much business. I tell him about Peppermint Branches, and he suggests designing a logo and getting flyers made up, along with postcards to advertise the grand reopening, and a set of normal business cards. I sit behind his booth and watch as he pulls up software on his laptop and throws together some logo ideas. It doesn't take long for me to settle on a red-bordered one with a few simple Christmas trees in shades of green, that he manages to make look like they're growing out of the word Peppermint Branches in an earthy font. His prices aren't too unreasonable, even on my budget, and he tells me they'll be ready to collect from next Friday onwards.

I feel quite proud of myself as I say hello to owners at a few more stalls on the way back to Noel's pumpkin stand, my bag gradually getting heavier because I can't resist buying some of the locally made cheeses, shortbread biscuits, and homemade fudge from the sweet stall.

When I get back, Noel's wearing the black cargo trousers and navy plaid shirt that he was earlier, but his sleeves are rolled up around his elbows now. He's taken the bodywarmer off, gone are the hat and ponytail, and in their place is a headband. A black headband with four plastic pumpkins spread across the width of it, standing out on springs and bobbing around with every movement.

'Wow,' I say, at a bit of a loss for any other words in the face of a springy pumpkin headband.

He grins and reaches up to a little battery pack behind his ear to flick a switch, and the pumpkins start flashing so brightly that I can see the reflection of the pulsing orange lights in the concrete floor.

'Amazing, right? They can be seen from right across the market.'

He makes this sound like a good thing. 'Well, of all the things I expected when I got back, battery-operated headgear wasn't one of them. You *seriously* wear that every day?'

'Every day I'm here, aye. If my farmhands cover the market shift then they wear it. I can get you a Christmas tree one, if you want?'

'Oh, I think I've got enough challenges ahead without adding flashing neon hairbands to the list, but thanks.'

The pumpkins jump around centimetres above his head on their springy stalks. It's like some sort of demented tiara from Tim Burton's *The Nightmare Before Christmas*, and his whole face breaks into a grin as he shakes his long hair back, which shouldn't be nearly as sexy as it is. He dips his head towards me, amusement dancing in his blue-green eyes that never leave mine as the flashing pumpkins rattle around. How does he still manage to look gorgeous? I never believed that someone as rugged and effortlessly sexy as Noel would wear neon flashing headgear, but he manages to pull it off *and* still look hot.

All thoughts are cut off by a squeal from the bath bomb stall next to us, and a lilac-haired lady in her seventies appears at my side and clamps her hands around my arm.

'This is Fiona,' Noel says to me and then turns to her. 'And this is—'

'Leah's coming for a coffee with me and Fergus!' Her hands tighten around my arm and she drags me away, surprisingly strong for her age. I can't help smiling as I follow her in all her pastel-coloured glory, complete with bright lilac bob cut, a lemon blouse and pale pink skirt, and neon plastic jewellery.

Iain has left and Fergus has disappeared from his stall as she pulls me across to the far end of hers. It smells like the best Lush shop I've ever walked past, and is full of rows of gorgeous-smelling bath bombs, fizzers, butters, and bubble bars.

Fiona sits down on one of her stools and starts filling me in on every bit of gossip about every person in the market, despite the fact I don't know any of them. She manages to cram an impressive amount into the few minutes before Fergus appears behind us and makes me jump with his sprightliness because I hadn't heard him approach. Despite the walking stick, he's managing to carry a tray of three cardboard cups and a biscuit from his stall. 'Hello, lass. I'm so glad my Iain's going to be working for you. He missed that place so much when it closed.'

Before I have a chance to reply, he pushes one of the cups into my hand and bashes his own against it like he's making a toast. 'A coffee to welcome you to Elffield Christmas market.' He also hands me the gingerbread biscuit, wrapped in a paper bag and covered by cellophane, and I try to work out what it might be without showing my surprise at the sight of a gingerbread . . . trombone? It might be a trombone. I've never seen biscuits in the form of brass instruments before.

He hands Fiona a coffee cup and a biscuit too, and I focus on the way he touches her elbow and turns towards her as he sits down. She gives him a shy smile that's completely at odds with her loud voice and outfit.

'Noel certainly kept you quiet,' Fergus says. 'I didn't realise he was seeing anybody.'

'Oh, we're not—'

'Oooh!' Fiona squeaks. 'He didn't tell me you were his girlfriend! What a lovely couple you make!'

Fiona's squeak has attracted Noel's attention and now he's looking over at us.

'We're really not—'

'About time too,' Fergus interrupts. 'He's such a good chap, he deserves someone to take care of him after he does so much for everyone else, and he's been alone for so long now, we were starting to think he wouldn't find anyone after that evil woman broke his poor heart.'

'We're not . . .What evil woman?' My curiosity gets the better of me. I can set them straight in a minute.

'That horrible stuck-up one who came back from the city with him years ago. A right hoity-toity cow who thought she was so much better than all of us, and Noel's so down to earth, we could never work out what he saw in her. All she did was take advantage of him. Still, the poor bugger was destroyed when she left. No wonder he hates city-types now.'

Oh, great. What the heck does he think I am then? 'Which city?'

'London,' they say in unison, like there's only one city in the whole of the UK.

'Noel was in London?' I ask in surprise. I look over at him and he raises a questioning eyebrow. He knows he's being talked about.

'He lived there for quite a while, a good few years ago now mind, but he wouldn't go back again – he's got nothing but contempt for the place now.'

'Well, that might explain his grumpiness,' I mutter to myself, surprised by this revelation. Noel doesn't seem like a city dweller at all. He seems to fit so well in the countryside that I assumed he'd been here all his life.

They both laugh at the mention of Noel's grumpiness. 'You

mustn't take him seriously. He's so busy at this time of year that he barely has time to breathe, he forgets to eat most days because he's so busy helping everyone else.'

'You'll be good for him,' Fergus says. 'He needs someone to share the burden with.'

Fergus seems to have a knack for saying things that are impossible to ignore. 'Burden?'

'Well, how hard he works for the farm, and looking after his mum, and everything he does for the community. It takes its toll on him but he'll never let it show. It'll do him good to have someone to open up to.'

That doesn't sound like Noel at all, at least not the Noel I've seen so far. I look over at him as he takes money from a customer and puts two pumpkins into a bag for her. 'We're not together.'

'Are you single?' Fiona demands.

'Yeah, but . . .'

Her face lights up like she's just connected to the National Grid. 'There you go, then. You won't find a better man than Noel.'

I can't help the laugh. 'Even if I was looking, which I'm *not*, he's not . . . I mean, I'm sure he's a nice bloke. He makes me laugh, and he's kind, but he's made it very clear what he thinks of me and I've just got out of a relationship that wasn't a relationship at all, and . . .' I stop myself quickly because I've said too much. I don't want to give these two any more gossip. No doubt my relationship status will be all round the market by eleven o'clock at the latest.

That little hint of personal information sets Fiona off and she starts gossiping again. Fergus hobbles across to serve someone who starts poking through his gingerbread ukuleles, and I start edging slowly back towards the pumpkin stall, feeling a bit uncomfortable with how quickly gossip spreads.

As the hours move on, I can't believe how busy it is. One crate of pumpkins is empty, and a second one is well on its way there. Of the edible goodies that Glenna made, only a couple of jars of jam are left, and I've lost track of how many customers have heard the news about Peppermint Branches and come over to tell me how much they miss it being there on the outskirts of Elffield and how much they're looking forward to visiting again this year. A little thrill starts burning inside me. If even half of these people really do come to buy their Christmas tree from me this year, that's a good twenty sales I've made already. It's not a lot, but it's a start.

I actually get quite into serving customers, watching as Noel carves pumpkins for display and puts battery-operated tealights inside them, enjoying the way people pore over the crates of pumpkins to select the perfect specimen. I wonder about selling Christmas trees here. It's a gorgeous place, the atmosphere is laidback and cheerful, and there's Christmas music pumping quietly from a speaker near the back. I'm quite disappointed when Noel's full-time employee turns up to take over at ten o'clock.

'Hold on, you two!'

We turn to see Fergus hobbling across the market lane on his walking stick, somehow managing to carry two pies. 'Have either of you eaten a mince pie yet this year?'

Noel and I both shake our heads.

'Oh, thank god.' Fergus lets out a sigh of relief as he thrusts a mince pie at us both. 'Here, your first one of the season. You have to make a wish as you bite into it. It's tradition.'

'Isn't that birthday cakes?' I ask in confusion.

Noel laughs. 'This is an old mince pie tradition and Fergus won't rest until he's provided all of Elffield with his magical mince pies.'

The idea of magical mince pies makes me start giggling and the serious expression on both Noel and Fergus's faces only makes it funnier, until Noel elbows me in the arm. 'Well, wish or no wish, one of Fergus's mince pies is a miracle in itself. Thanks, mate.'

He takes a deep breath, closes his eyes, and hesitates for a second like he's making a wish, then he seems to steel himself before biting into it. 'Mmm, this is *so* good,' he says around a mouthful. 'So rich and decadent, Fergus, you've outdone yourself this year. In fact, it's so good that I'm going to save the rest for later. I'm still full from breakfast so I can't fully appreciate it.' He wraps the pie back up in its paper bag and stuffs it into his pocket. 'Thank you, I'm going to savour that with a cuppa when I get home.'

I narrow my eyes as I look at him. He's overcompensating and I can't work out what for. Fergus's gingerbread trombone that I had earlier was delicious. Maybe Noel just doesn't believe in magic.

He nudges me. 'Go on, Lee, make a wish.'

I know he knows something I don't know, but Fergus is looking at me with that same expectant look he had when he gave me the gingerbread trombone earlier, so I close my eyes, silently make my wish, and take a bite of . . . unusually hard pastry, and . . . good lord, *what* is that in the middle? Surely that's not the usual fruit and spice mix? It's very . . . chewy, and not in a good way. Was that a raisin? I nearly lost a filling to that. I suddenly know exactly why Noel was overacting.

'Oh, wow, that's *really* good, Fergus.' It just sort of sits there in my mouth, impossible to chew, impossible to swallow, and impossible to spit out with Fergus watching. 'I've never had a mince pie quite like it.'

A beam lights up his face. He genuinely can't realise how bad these mince pies are, can he? Maybe he's trying to re-enact the *Friends* episode where Rachel got the pages of her recipe book stuck together and put beef in a trifle?

I'm regretting taking such a big bite. Fergus is still watching me with a proud look, and it's almost impossible not to shudder as my teeth crunch on something that might once have been a cranberry. Or some form of animal defecation.

'It's certainly busy here.' I look around the market as I try to swallow without Fergus realising how difficult it is.

'Didn't expect that, did you, Londoner?' Noel says.

'It's a real hub here,' Fergus says. 'Our market is known country-wide. People even come over from Europe closer to Christmas. We're on a list of best markets in the UK and it brings in so many tourists. Of course, it used to be so much better . . .'

'Budget cuts.' Fiona suddenly pops up behind me, making me jump with her sudden appearance. I hope she didn't notice the grimace as I turned away to swallow the last of that pastry or the way my eyes are watering because a particularly sharp bit caught my throat on the way down.

'We used to have lights all over the building and the most gorgeous tree right there in the entranceway.' She points to an elevated platform in the centre of the walkway inside the main entrance. 'But the council cut funding a few years ago so we haven't had one for a while, and it makes such a difference to the festive spirit. Last year, the handbag stall owner was kind enough to bring in a moth-eaten plastic tree that had been in his loft for a few years. It was okay after we got the dust off it, but it fell apart before the end of the season.'

'Do you want a real tree?' I ask as the idea comes to me. 'I'd be happy to donate one. It's definitely a good cause – the market is gorgeous.'

'Oh, would you really?' Fergus says.

'The darling Mr Evergreene used to donate one every year, but we didn't expect you to carry on the tradition,' Fiona adds. 'And it's ever such good advertising. We'd put a big sign up saying where it came from, and the tree stands right in the entrance so *everyone* would see it . . .'

I can't help giggling at their mischievous faces, leaving me in no doubt that this was exactly the way they'd hoped the conversation would go. 'How about one of the Peppermint firs?' I turn to Noel. 'They're so striking, that would be an ideal place for one.'

'And some smaller ones for the corners of the market?' Fiona says.

'Of course.' I had no idea that Evergreene used to provide trees to the market. Maybe it's a good omen that I thought of it too.

Noel rolls his eyes. 'You two are incorrigible, you know that, don't you? Leah hasn't been here forty-eight hours yet and you've wheedled god knows how many trees out of her.'

'Sounds painful. Here, have a gingerbread fire extinguisher to make up for it.' Fergus produces two wrapped biscuits from his cardigan pocket and hands us one each.

'It'll be a great way to spread the word,' Fiona says. 'And will you be selling your trees here too? What a brilliant way of advertising, we can put a sign out telling everyone exactly where your stall is.'

'And we all know the market's in trouble. If we're going out, at least we're going out with a Christmas tree-scented bang. That artificial thing was a mess last year. It dropped more shiny plastic pieces than a real tree would drop needles.'

'I think we'd better be going before you two talk Leah into giving you a tree stand and a tree skirt too,' Noel says, putting a big hand on my shoulder and extracting me from the circle Fergus and Fiona have formed around us.

'A tree stand would be wonderful!' Fiona calls as we back away. 'I can make a pretty skirt for it, don't you worry about that!'

At the pumpkin stall, Noel picks up the stack of two empty wooden crates and carries it with one hand, swinging it along beside him like it weighs nothing as we walk towards the side entrance of the market where his truck is parked.

'You got totally taken advantage of there, you know that, right?'

'What, for the tree?' He nods and I shrug. 'I don't mind. It'd be nice to get off on the right foot with the locals. Besides, the market *is* gorgeous, it deserves a real tree, and I can easily spare one.'

'And some little ones for the corners. You'd be surprised how many "corners" Fiona can find in this market.'

'It's fine. I have thousands. I don't need them all.'

'The generous spirit of a terrible businesswoman.'

'You can talk. I've lost count of how many times I've heard

about you doing things for the community this morning. I think they're petitioning to get you a knighthood.'

His cheeks redden as we walk along in the middle of the lane, dodging shoppers at the stalls on either side, but he doesn't say anything else.

'So, magical mince pies, huh?'

'Aye, and the only thing magical about them is that no one's died after eating one.' He glances at me. 'Yet.'

He looks behind us to check no one's listening and gives Fergus a wave over his shoulder. 'Every year, he gives 'em away to anyone who comes past because he's long since given up on finding any poor unsuspecting soul gullible enough to actually *pay* for them. His wife used to do all the cooking and he ran the stall, but she passed away eight years ago, and he took over doing both jobs. He got her gingerbread recipe right, but god knows where he's gone wrong with the mince pie recipe because each year they're systematically worse than the year before, bless him. He was thinking of quitting a couple of years ago but then Fiona came along and gave him something to stay for.'

I look behind me to see Fergus and Fiona deep in conversation by the bath bomb stall. 'Why do I get the feeling you have a little something to do with that?'

'Me? Meddle in pensioners' love lives?' He does a gasp of mock indignation. His truck is on the pavement outside the trade entrance, and he swings the crates up into the empty bed and walks round to the driver's side. 'I don't know where you'd get an idea like that.'

'Yeah, who knows.' I hop into the passenger side and grin at the way a smile creeps onto his face while he crawls down the main street in Elffield, which is full of people on the pavements, all heading towards the market.

'What did you wish for?' he says, out of the blue as we turn onto a country lane surrounded by green fields.

'Am I allowed to tell you or will that mean it won't come true?'

'Do you really think any wish on *that* mince pie is going to come true?'

'For things to get better,' I say without really thinking about it.

'What things?' He pauses. 'Sorry, that was intrusive and insensitive. It's nothing to do with me. Most people wish for avoiding a trip to the dentist after one of Fergus's mince pies. Not getting food poisoning is also a useful wish.'

I grin at the joke, but there's something about him that makes me feel like I could share anything and he'd understand. 'I feel like things haven't been . . . *right* . . . for a couple of years now.' I struggle to find the right word. 'It's why I'm here, why I bought the tree farm. Because I was desperately searching for a way to make things feel right again.'

'I know that feeling,' he says quietly.

I wait for him to expand, but he doesn't, and I'm not sure what else to say without breaking down in tears, and Noel's seen me cry enough for one forty-eight-hour period.

'So,' he says after a long silence, and I realise I've just been staring at his hands and the way his forearms flex every time they tighten on the steering wheel. 'I know why Fiona drags people off for cups of coffee. What strands of gossip do I have to clear up?'

'Well, the woman who runs the children's clothing stall's guinea pig has just had babies but they aren't sure which male guinea pig is the father, and someone's hairdresser saw one of her client's husbands out with another woman, and he said it was his sister but no one believes him.'

He laughs. 'Yes, and?'

I give him an innocent look.

'I know Fergus and Fiona. What did they tell you about me?'

'You were a Londoner once.'

He doesn't react. 'Yes, once. And I'm 38, single, my shoe size, the results of my last blood test, the date of my last haircut, the brand of bathroom cleaner I buy every week . . . I know what they're like.'

'You buy bathroom cleaner every week? Who cleans their bathroom *that* often?'

He bursts out laughing. 'It was a metaphor for their pushy oversharing. I promise I don't buy bathroom cleaner *every* week.'

I laugh too. 'Oh, thank god. I'd started to get worried there for a minute.'

His tongue twiddles the lip piercing because it moves, glinting in the autumn sun shining through the window, and I suddenly feel hot and flushed. Thinking about Noel's tongue is seriously hazardous to health.

I force myself to look away and think of something else. 'What Fergus said earlier – is the market really in trouble?'

'Yeah, kind of. It's great at this time of year because it's a buzzing Christmas market. It's on a couple of "best of" lists online so tourists come, people come to the UK and do tours of all the best Christmas markets, and that's great, but from January to September, it's not like that. It's quiet, the only people who shop there are loyal locals and the other traders. It's a big space and it's only profitable for four months a year, so the council have been making noises about relocating the traders and flattening it to build a new bus interchange. There's one in Peterhead that's being demolished and local councils are competing to be the new location.'

'Bus interchange?' I say in surprise. 'Aren't the roads too narrow? Your truck barely fitted down the main street. How would that work?'

'Exactly. How do you widen roads without taking down the houses on either side? There's already talk of compulsory purchase orders on the people who live there. If we lose the market, Elffield as we know it will literally be flattened.'

'That's terrible.' There's a pang in my stomach and my heart speeds up. Surely it's not normal to feel this attached to somewhere you've only been once?

'Funding has been cut further every year, to the point where there's no money for anything now, not even the most basic of repairs. We have to club together and pay for essential maintenance ourselves, which is another chunk out of our earnings that most of us can't afford to lose, and people are seriously starting to consider giving up. Lots of them have been there since the early days and are long past retirement age, and there comes a point when the work on their products, the setting up every day, the early mornings, the cold weather . . . it's not worth it anymore. I've had a feeling for a while now that this will probably be the last year that Elffield market exists as we know it.' His voice breaks and I look over at him, but he keeps his eyes resolutely on the road.

'What about the relocation?'

'There's nowhere to relocate to. If they relocate us, it's going to be to some industrial estate a couple of miles away, somewhere that no one walks past and little old ladies can't toddle down to with their shopping trolleys. The whole point is that the market is local and convenient, anyone who pops to the post office or needs a pint of milk wanders in because it's on the doorstep. If they make it a car journey, a parking fee, or a bus ride away, who's going to bother?'

'I'm sorry.' I bite my lip. 'Is there anything we can do?'

'It's been coming for a long time now. If we have an amazing Christmas season, we might be able to delay it for another year, but we've all been trying to figure out how to add year-round interest and none of us have managed it yet. We'd need sponsors or local businesses advertising or something, and that's fine when you've got Christmas tourists coming in, but impossible during the months that you haven't.'

'People keep mentioning me selling trees there . . . I was surprised by how many pumpkins went this morning, but are people really going to buy trees like that?'

'You'll be surprised. Peppermint Branches is the only tree farm for miles. People have got to drive a heck of a long way to get a real tree since Evergreene died. Most don't bother. You've already got more of a fanbase than you realise, and Fiona *is* right that having a huge tree right in the entrance of the market with a Peppermint Branches sign next to it will be amazing advertising.' He looks over at me and quickly swivels his eyes back to the road. 'And half the stall is yours from mid-November.'

'What?'

'No one buys pumpkins once Halloween is over. From mid-November, I use the stall only to sell my mum's baked goods and a crate or two of culinary pumpkins and a bit of winter veg. You're far too late to get a stall of your own now, they're in high demand and the last space for rent had sold out by March, so you and your trees can take the space of the pumpkins until after Christmas. I've got a good spot and I don't need it all. Why shouldn't we share it?'

'Why?' I say, so surprised by such a kind gesture that I can't find the words. 'Why would you do that? I mean, I'll pay you whatever the rent is, but I don't . . .I didn't know they were in such demand—'

'Lee, it's fine.' He reaches over and touches my hand where it's resting on my thigh, and I wish the warmth of his fingers would linger before he quickly pulls them away. 'And I'm paying the rent anyway because it's too good a spot to give up, so don't worry about it.'

'Why?'

'Can I tell you something?' He looks at me and quickly back at the road again. 'My wish on the mince pie was that Peppermint Branches would be a success. I've thought for years that the place would be demolished, and if you're not going to do that, then I'm going to do everything in my power to help you, because Evergreene was like family to me. It's what he would've wanted, and it'll be good for Elffield.'

We're coming up to the first of his pumpkin fields and I can't take my eyes off them as we pass. They look like someone's about to sing 'Bibbidi-Bobbidi-Boo' and turn them all into fairytale carriages, and it makes me feel more positive than I have in years. 'Then you know what? Let's make this the best Christmas that market has ever seen, even if it's the last one. Let's make it a Christmas to remember.'

'To a Christmas to remember.'

I'm grinning wider than I have for months as we drive towards the sun twinkling in the sky, making the trees in the distance look dark green and perfect.

Chapter 8

'And you had the nerve to insult my neon flashing pumpkin headband,' Noel says as I open the door.

'I'm cleaning.' I become the epitome of sophistication by poking my tongue out at him as he stands on the doorstep.

'I see that.' He reaches over and plucks a dust bunny from my hair, which has started to tumble down from the knot I tied it in.

I pull away but I don't know why. He saw me first thing this morning; Marigolds up to my elbows and messy hair aren't any worse than that sight, which was terrifying enough to send even the most haphazard of scarecrows running for cover.

He's got boards of wood under his arm, a huge toolcase in his hand, and a holdall slung over his shoulder. Glenna appears behind him with Gizmo under her arm, carrying her own bucket of cleaning products and rubber gloves. 'Come to help, flower.'

'Gizmo's going to help too,' Noel says. 'Assuming a vital job is keeping a Chihuahua-sized spot on your sofa warm.'

'Giz!' I pull the gloves off with my teeth and push past Noel on the step to get to the little dog when he starts wagging his tail so hard that it looks like Glenna's having trouble keeping hold of him. I offer him my hand, which he sniffs and licks, and then I give him a double ear rub when he moves from sniffing to trying to nudge my hand onto his head. He strains in Glenna's arms to get closer, and I can't resist his happy little brown and white face. I bend down to rub my nose against his, but accidentally get a bit too close and a slimy doggy tongue swipes across my mouth.

As I splutter, Noel's laughing so hard he has to lean against the doorframe. 'I know which member of the Roscoe family I'd rather kiss too.'

I follow him and Glenna inside, glad the farmhouse is looking marginally better than it did on the first night. After coming back from the walk with Noel and Gizmo yesterday, I found my way to the nearest supermarket to buy food and just about every product in the cleaning aisle. I spent the rest of the evening scrubbing, mopping, turning furniture the right way up, hoovering with a vacuum cleaner I found in the cupboard under the stairs, washing out the fridge and kitchen cupboards so I could actually put my food away, cleaning the bath so I could wash after such a sweaty day, and not worrying about how much water and electricity I was using until the bills come in next month.

I didn't expect any help with cleaning, but seeing Glenna and Noel come to help touches me in a way I've never known before, and I have to turn away for a moment and blink furiously to stop tears forming.

They both have their own work to do – Noel has made no secret of how busy he is in October more than any other month – but they've both come to help me because some people are just that kind.

Even though this farm is more isolated than I've ever been, and I've left all my friends and colleagues six hundred miles away, for the first time in the two years since my parents died, I feel like I'm not alone.

***

While Noel's upstairs hammering boards across the window frames, Glenna and I tackle the rest of the kitchen, and it turns out she's an expert cleaner with tips and tricks for everything, and between us we make fairly quick work of the kitchen and bathroom, to the soundtrack of Gizmo's adorable snores as he sleeps on the sofa with Noel's jacket covering him.

Noel's moved onto the roof when Glenna and Gizmo leave. I'm on a roll with cleaning now and want to keep up the momentum because I know I'll probably fall asleep if I sit down. I tell Noel to shout loudly if he falls off, slip my welly boots on and grab one of the garden forks and a scythe from the barn, and head out to tackle some weeding, pulling on gardening gloves as I walk.

One of the books I bought says that Nordmann firs and Norway spruces are the most popular trees sold in Britain, so I decide they're the two fields I need to get ready to open first. If that's all I can do, then it'll be better than nothing for this year. With Iain starting next week and the seasonal workers in November, if we can get all of them sheared and the two fields weeded between us, that'll be a good enough start for this year, especially with the Peppermint firs as well. The balsams and the spruces will have to wait.

I try not to acknowledge how daunted I feel as I open the gate and look out at the vast forest that greets me. It looks so much bigger now than it did with Noel explaining things and Gizmo running around tree trunks. Now it looks like there are at least a thousand firs spread out in front of me, the staggered planting making them all different ages and heights, branches so overgrown that they're tangling with the branches of the next tree, and so many weeds that I can barely get near some of them.

I knew it would be a challenge. I *wanted* it to be.

I just didn't expect it to be such a jungle that I half-expect Ant and Dec to pop out looking for some celebrities.

I take the scythe out of its sheath and start where I stand inside the gate, slashing away at the taller weeds, knowing I can't even begin to start digging their roots up when they're at this height. I've never used a scythe before, but I've watched the topless scything scene in *Poldark* many times, and that's pretty much the same thing. Who says television isn't educational? Aidan Turner looks a lot better topless than I do though, and he doesn't have to worry about boobs getting in the way. I'm not going to try it, but I suspect boobs would be hazardous to topless scything.

After I've cut down a huge patch along the edge of the field, I gather up the limp weeds and pile them in a heap beside the gate. I'll get a wheelbarrow later and take everything to the composter between two of the tin sheds on the scrubland. I get the fork and push it into the earth, driving it down with my foot, and levering a huge clump of roots out of the soil. I shake the loose mud off and then toss the roots onto the pile too. I move over and heave out another clump, and another, and another, until there's a space of fresh sandy soil and I've freed a couple of metres of the holly hedge from weeds.

I try not to look at how far I've got versus how much there still is to do, and this is only one field. If I think of it as a whole, it's too much. One step at a time. One patch of weeds and then the next. One tree and then another.

I run my arm across my forehead to wipe sweat away and stop for a minute to get my breath back. I've barely stopped moving all day. It also feels quite . . . good? My lungs feel full of fresh air and greenery, a healthy feeling, as opposed to the body odour and pollution they feel full of when I get off another crammed train in London. I know I'll ache tomorrow but I ache at five o'clock when I get up from my desk after a long day of sitting still, and this feels like a much better ache, if aches can be divided into categories of desirable and non-desirable. A much healthier ache.

I tell myself that as I swish the scythe through another load of stalks and dig up their roots, and another, and another. I know this isn't the end of it. I know I'll need to put down herbicide to stop them coming back, and flatten the newly-dug ground enough for customers to walk on it when the farm opens, but for now, it feels good to be outside and doing something productive – something towards making the dream of this farm a reality.

I don't know how long I work for. It's late in the afternoon judging by the grey tone the sky has taken on, but I jump so much when Noel clears his throat that I nearly take out half the holly bushes with the scythe.

'Well, aren't you a regular *Poldark*?'

'Oh ha ha, I hadn't thought about that once.' I stop and swipe an arm across my forehead again. My hair's falling down despite already putting it up again twice. How many times in one day can you look an absolute mess in front of one of the hottest men you've ever seen?

He flips a bottle of water in his hand and holds it out to me. 'Second rule of farming: dehydration isn't fun. Bring a bottle of water every time, even at this time of year. This work is hard and I wouldn't mind betting that you aren't used to it.'

Is it that obvious? 'Actually, I do plenty of scything and digging at home. You barely see me indoors for all the scything and digging I do.'

'That'll be why you asked me if The Grim Reaper had left his "thingy" behind when you saw it in the barn?'

I glare at him. 'I was winding you up. I knew it was a scythe.'

'From *Poldark*?'

I huff and he nods towards the bare soil in front of me. 'Got to admit I'm impressed.'

I can't hear any sarcasm in his tone, and I wait for him to follow up with a snarky comment, but he doesn't. I look around at the patch I've cleared. It isn't a lot, but it's a start. And I feel better for it. For actually getting out and getting my hands dirty. Literally. I pull off the gloves and look down at my nails. Three are broken and all of them have got mud ingrained underneath them, even through the gloves.

'The roof's done temporarily,' he says. 'But it's not going to hold up under a storm, and there are a few due this winter. All I've done is nail felt across the broken bits. You need to get onto that builder as soon as you can.'

'I know.' The roof is already on my endless list of things that need repairing or replacing. 'But I have to pay the workers and fork out for insurance. The roof can wait. Opening this place in December can't.'

'I agree, but living in a warm, dry house is also important. But your priorities are admirable. I thought you'd be all about the cosy home comforts and the trees would be an afterthought.'

I'm sure there's an insult in there somewhere. It's no secret that he thinks very little of me, but he doesn't sound insulting. 'Thanks for everything you've done, Noel.'

'Ah, I'm not finished yet. I came for your help. I've hooked the caravan onto my truck to get it across the fence and into position, but I could do with someone to guide me in.'

'I didn't expect you to do that,' I say in surprise. 'I could've done it.'

'Because you've got a towbar on your pretty little car that's never seen a mud splash in its life?'

Okay, fair point. I take another gulp of water to avoid answering.

I like how kind and helpful he is, even though it's pretty clear he still disapproves of me. I didn't expect him to do any of the things he's done to help me today, and I know he's got plenty of his own work he needs to be doing, but he hasn't made a big deal out of it at all.

He's much different than I thought he was.

***

There are a variety of crunching and grinding noises as Noel reverses the truck diagonally across my little back garden at the pace of geriatric snail, trying to slide the caravan onto the wide grass path at the side of his pumpkin patch. I've swept up the broken glass and kicked down the remains of the rotting fence, and now I'm trying to guide him incrementally left or right in an attempt to stop the caravan veering off, feeling a bit like a Chuckle Brother with all the 'to me, to you-ing'. He seems to be doing a better job without my help.

Once the caravan is on his land, he straightens up easily and guides it neatly into perfectly parallel place. As he gets out of the truck and detaches it from his towbar, I climb inside, and discover it's not as bad as I first thought. It needs a deep clean, and the upper cabinets that are dangling off need to be removed completely, but the units installed around the kitchen area are still sturdy. If I replace the broken window with a wooden shutter it can act as the rustic serving hatch I'd imagined and keep the squirrel out if colliding with my face didn't give it enough of a fright to prevent it ever returning.

'What's it like?' Noel pokes his head round the door and leans in.

'It could be worse.' I kick my foot through some of the debris on the floor, and then walk to the seating area at the other end. The cushions and soft furnishings have been chewed to bits by the previous bushy-tailed resident, but I get my hands under one and rip it off, and the wooden benches underneath are still undamaged.

The caravan dips under Noel's weight as he climbs in too and treads through the rubble to poke around the kitchen area and prod at the window frame.

'What do you think?' I bite my lip as I wait for his verdict. I'm assessing it like I know the first thing about caravans when the nearest I've ever got to one before is being stuck behind them on the motorway.

'It could be worse.' He deliberately repeats my words. 'Pull an extension lead out from the house and you'll have a power supply, a folding shutter on this window, and a really good clean inside and out. I think it's a cracking idea. I looked into getting a hot chocolate machine a couple of years ago, so I know that's going to set you back about three hundred quid. It's kind of an investment, but it's going to be better quality and easier than trying to do it with a kettle, and if you can imagine a cold, snowy day after walking around a Christmas tree farm in December . . . there's nothing people will want more than a hot chocolate.'

It does seem like a good idea. All right, it's another expenditure I hadn't planned on – and something tells me there are a lot more of those to come – but I can't think of anything nicer than walking around the farm and then coming back to the entrance for a cup of hot chocolate to stave off Jack Frost nipping at your nose. There will be waiting time while trees are netted and paid for and fitted into cars, and there's nowhere else nearby for people to get refreshments. It's the festive equivalent of the ice cream van in the beach car park.

I duck around a hanging cabinet as I go back towards the kitchen area, trying to assess how much work the caravan will need and how much time I'll have to do it in. I bump into Noel as we move around each other in the small space and he leans over to test the under-unit storage cupboard doors. It's so nice of him to get as involved as he has, and I wish I could do something in return.

'If I sort out the caravan and get a hot chocolate machine, you could borrow it next year, if you want. Just as a thank you for letting me use your land this time around. I mean, why shouldn't we help each other out, if we can?' I say, fully aware that there's pretty much nothing I could help him with because he's an expert who seems to have everything under control and running like the well-oiled machine it should be. Clearly, I need his help a lot more than he needs mine.

'I don't expect anything in return, but that'd be great.' He turns around to speak and jumps as we bump into each other again. 'We usually make drinks from the kitchen when the patch is open, but it gets busier every year and running back and forth and passing drinks out through the kitchen window is getting increasingly unprofessional. You can be the guinea pig and see how it goes this year. It might fail miserably for all you know.'

'Yeah.' I roll my eyes. 'Thanks for that vote of confidence.'

'Just being realistic. You've got all these grand plans, but . . .' He trails off, deliberately not finishing the sentence.

He doesn't need to because I can finish it for him. *But you're a city girl and this world isn't for you.* He might be helping me, but he's clearly still in no doubt that I'll leave whenever things get tough. I decide not to push it. I can't tell him he's wrong about me – I can only prove it. 'How is it possible that you're this grumpy on a lovely sunny evening, but at six o'clock in the morning, you're as chirpy as a cheerful canary who's had frosted cereal for breakfast?'

He raises an eyebrow that gradually goes higher and it takes a ridiculously long time for him to start laughing. 'I'm a morning person, all right? By this time of day, the caffeine hit has worn off and I turn back into a yeti. Like a hairier Cinderella in reverse.'

The mental image washes away all the lingering annoyance. 'You'd never suit a ballgown.' I don't mention that his shoulders are so wide and his arm muscles are so defined that they'd never find a ballgown large enough for him *to* suit.

He laughs. 'But at least I've got plenty of pumpkin carriages and a terrible sense of timekeeping, and the prince wouldn't have any trouble remembering my giant feet in glass slippers.' He rubs his fingers over his chin. 'The stubble might give it away too.'

I'm giggling so hard that I have to lean against the caravan wall for support, and the more I laugh, the more it makes him laugh too, until the lines around his eyes are crinkled up and tears of joy are forming in the corners.

He suddenly seems to realise that we're just standing here laughing at each other, because he jolts upright. 'Pumpkin spice!'

'What?' I say in confusion, wondering how you go from Cinderella to pumpkin spice.

He looks really pleased with himself. 'It goes brilliantly in hot chocolate, and you look like you could use a drink. Stay there, I'll prove it.'

He squeezes past me in the narrowest part of the caravan and our bodies drag against each other as we both breathe in and I try to flatten myself against the wall to let him pass.

I get the feeling it's an excuse to get out of this cramped space and away from whatever that was that sparked between us, but a hot chocolate sounds absolutely perfect right now, and I find myself watching from the doorway as he walks through the rows of pumpkins towards his house.

The sun is setting in the distance, making the clouds around it look pink and gold. It's too late to start cleaning up the caravan tonight, and now I've stopped moving for a few minutes, I realise that I'm as knackered as I must look. I grab the long, flat cushion I've just pulled off the bench and put it on the grass outside. I turn it upside down and sit on the least damaged part, facing the setting sun.

Noel grins as he comes back, a Roscoe-Farm-branded recyclable cup in each hand and a paper bag between his teeth, containing two pumpkin cupcakes with orange butter icing and sprinkles of sugared pumpkin seeds.

'I like your thinking.' He sits beside me on the cushion and hands me one of the cups. 'Pumpkin spice hot chocolate. Roscoe Farm's finest. If you like it, I've got plenty of pumpkin spice you can have for the caravan. And you'll have to get some peppermint flavouring as well, because you can't run a place called Peppermint Branches without offering peppermint hot chocolates. A couple of different options will help too. If you don't make them too expensive, people are likely to try a plain hot chocolate when they arrive and then a flavoured one when they leave.'

'You're really good at this sort of thing, aren't you?'

His cheeks go red as he sips his hot chocolate and flinches because it's too hot.

I set mine down on the grass beside me and start on the pumpkin cupcake instead, swiping my finger through the sweet icing and taking a bite of fluffy and lightly spiced orange-coloured cake. As arrogant and harsh as Noel can be sometimes, he's actually quite humble, and in the few days I've known him, I can already tell that he's terrible at taking compliments.

'I'm fascinated by the number of things your mum can pumpkin-ise. Is there anything she doesn't put pumpkin in?'

'Hmm.' The look of concentration on his face makes me smile as he seriously considers it. 'Toothpaste?' he says eventually with a grin.

The sky above us is almost completely pink as the sun drops to the west, the pumpkins sprawling out on Noel's side, and Christmas trees waving in the gentle breeze on mine.

'It's been ages since I stopped to watch a sunset.'

'The sunsets in autumn are always the most spectacular.' I nod towards the sky. 'It's my favourite time of year.'

'And yet you bought a Christmas tree farm . . .'

'Ah, but my favourite thing about it is the lead up to Christmas. Autumn and the part of winter before Christmas blend together for me. This is my ideal place. Literally sitting right in the middle of autumn and winter.'

'Something else I totally agree on. Festive music in October *and* September to December being the best months of the year. You never know, we might start getting along at this rate.' He nudges his shoulder into mine, and it makes me grin because we definitely seem to be getting along, despite the occasional grumpy hitch.

I pick up my cup, not quite sure how I feel about the prospect of pumpkin spice working in hot chocolate. Coffee, fair enough, but hot chocolate seems a bit of a stretch. His other pumpkin goodies have been delicious so far, so I breathe in the steam for a moment and brace myself to take a sip.

'Oh my god, that's *incredible*.' The smooth chocolate liquid feels thicker, rounded out by the taste of pumpkin and just a hint of warming spice that only comes out after you swallow it. Chelsea and I have always had a thing for pumpkin spice lattes in the autumn, but this puts them all to shame. It's the perfect level of sweet, warm, and chocolatey – a blend of autumn and winter. 'You're going to have to teach me how to make it.'

He hides his face behind his own cup. 'With pleasure.'

I concentrate on the darkening pink sky, thinking about what would go well with hot chocolate. 'What about roasted chestnuts?' I speak before I even realise I'm going to say anything out loud.

He laughs. 'You're going to have to elaborate.'

'I could offer food of some sort. Something festive and fun to eat while people are walking around . . . I went to a Christmas fair with Chelsea last year and we got little paper bags of hot roasted chestnuts from a stall selling them straight from a tabletop cooker. Do you think it'd be worth it?'

I really appreciate the amount of serious thought he gives it. 'I can't think of anything nicer. Or anything more Christmassy. It's perfect.'

It'll be yet another unexpected expense, but I can't get the grin off my face as I sip my hot chocolate again. A bag of freshly roasted chestnuts would go down perfectly with it. Nothing has ever sounded more tempting on a cold winter's day.

Noel stretches his legs out straight in front of him, setting the cup between his knees and leaning back on his hands. I sip my hot chocolate and try not to show I'm watching him as his eyes scan from the pumpkins, to the sun disappearing below the horizon, to the Christmas trees.

'Do you think your parents would like it?' he asks softly, and I know from the gentle tone in his voice that I don't have to answer if I don't want to.

'They'd *love* the hot chocolate.' I know full well that he meant it in a much bigger sense, but I'm not sure whether I want to talk to him about it or whether I *can* talk about it without crying.

'They'd love it,' I say eventually. 'Running off to Scotland and buying a Christmas tree farm was exactly the crazy sort of thing my dad dreamed about doing in his retirement. He never got that far, but . . .' I swallow and bite the inside of my cheek to stop myself welling up again. 'It's exactly what I wanted the money from their house to be spent on. It's what I was waiting for without realising I was waiting for it.'

'I thought you were drunk and good at buying shoes?'

'Well, yeah, that too. But it was an answer to a question I didn't know I'd asked. My whole life has been covered by a blanket of grief, and that auction was the first sparkle of hope I'd felt in two years.'

'I want to ask you what happened to them, but I don't want to pry, or push, or make you talk about something you don't want to talk about. I'm going to leave that sentence there and if you don't want to talk about it, just stay silent and I'll start talking about rainbows and fluffy kittens or something.'

It makes an unexpected laugh burst out of my throat. He has a knack for making me laugh when it's the last thing I feel like doing, and he has no idea how much I appreciate it in moments like this.

'It was a car accident.' I close my eyes so I don't have to see anything. 'Dad died at the scene, Mum died from her injuries two days later in hospital. No one's fault. An accident. Wrong time, wrong place, wrong patch of black ice on a September evening two years ago.'

He nudges his shoulder against mine again and holds it there for a long moment. I don't open my eyes, just let myself appreciate the silent gesture of warmth and strength.

'I think the correct thing to say is I'm sorry, and that's terrible, and that must've been so hard to cope with, but I also get the feeling that you're sick of mindless platitudes, so I'm just going to say that life is unfair and cruel and leave it there. Because it is. Cruel things happen and somehow you have to keep standing up and carrying on, even though it doesn't feel worth it some days, because horrible things keep happening and there's nothing you can do to change them.'

I concentrate on my breathing. In and out. In and out. There's something about his bluntness that's so real, and so open and honest – I can't stop myself pushing it. 'You know, don't you?'

'I was 16 when my dad died. Cancer. Months of watching him gradually deteriorate. Being told by well-meaning family how much my mum would need me to be strong. The distance from friends because teenage boys don't know what to say to other teenage boys whose fathers are dying. The way people don't understand that sometimes there's nothing *to* say and that's okay. The awkward silences with relatives terrified of saying the wrong thing because they aren't sure if you want to reminisce or if you want to pretend nothing's different. The sheer terror that something might make you cry, and the overwhelming fear that if you start crying, you might never be able to stop.'

'The way it makes you want to pull out of life and pull away from everything?' My eyes are still closed and his shoulder has left mine now, but the hairs on my arms stand on end from the closeness of the brushed cotton shirt covering his arm. His hand is resting right next to mine, and if I reached my fingers out, I could probably touch his.

But I don't, obviously.

'Exactly. And you wonder what the point in getting close to anyone ever again is because everyone's going to leave you anyway, it's better to protect yourself and be alone?' He finishes the sentence for me in much more eloquent words than I could ever have chosen.

I lean my head back and look up to catch his eyes and he gives me a gentle smile, and a little fizzle of something sparks between us. If I tilted my head just a bit, it would be so easy to kiss him.

He must feel something too because he clears his throat and turns away, looking intently back towards the pumpkin fields.

'So you were 16 when you took over the farm?'

'Are you kidding? No. I ran away.'

I look up at him in surprise and he closes his eyes with a sigh. 'I was determined that my father dying wouldn't affect my life. I pushed the grief away and pretended I was fine. The only time I let myself grieve was when I hid in the trees on summer nights and no one knew where I was. I spent that summer helping Evergreene out, isolated with just the trees for company because I could pick up a shearing knife and disappear into those fields. Then, in September, I went to college, pushed away friends and did nothing but schoolwork. I got into a university in London, then I got a job and stayed there. It took until I was 28 to stop running and acknowledge the fact my father had died and it had changed me.'

I clench my fingers to stop myself slipping an arm around him and squeezing tight. There's an edge of disbelief to his voice even as he's speaking, like he's surprised at himself for being so open with a virtual stranger.

I look over, and like he can feel my eyes on him, he slowly opens his until our gaze locks again and his mouth quirks up, giving me a tiny smile that looks soft and vulnerable, and I think it's a smile that not many people get to see under his grumpy exterior.

Chapter 9

'Now, we'll have one here and one there.' Fiona points to a pillar on either side of the entrance to the market building. 'Oh, and we could do with a couple outside too to draw attention. Not quite as big as the one in the main entrance, but big enough to see. Seven foot should do it.'

Noel laughs at how thorough she is with her commands as we both follow her around the market and I scribble down notes about her list of tree demands. It's early and we've left Fergus watching the pumpkin stall while he sets out his biscuits, although all he seemed to be watching when we left was his fingers in the jar of Glenna's pumpkin marmalade that Noel gave him.

'One could go here.' She points to a space between the used bookseller and a stall that's reserved for handmade decorations closer to Christmas. 'And another over there by the craft beers, and one there by the festive food from around the world stall . . .'

'We're going to have more trees than stallholders soon,' Noel says.

It's a quiet Tuesday morning and there will definitely be more trees than customers at this rate. 'Maybe the trees can take over the stalls and give the workers a break.'

'As long as they haven't been out on the lash the night before.

You can never get trees with hangovers to turn up on time, and no one wants them puking pine needles over the produce and snaffling up fried breakfasts all morning.'

It makes me giggle and me giggling sets him off too, and we don't realise we've missed Fiona's latest instruction until she stops in her tracks and turns to face us with her arms folded and a pinched look on her face.

'Sorry, Fiona.' Noel tries so hard to adopt a serious face that it makes me laugh even more.

'Sorry, Fiona.' I giggle and it makes him start up again too.

Fiona raises an eyebrow, but her face changes from annoyed to knowing, and she gets the same look she always gets when she hears a bit of gossip.

Suitably scolded, I take more notes as she walks us through the market, pointing out where she wants the smaller trees, and saying hello to all the stallholders as we pass.

Fiona stops for a chat with her friend at the candle stall, and I take the opportunity to dash towards the back of the market and collect my business cards, flyers, and postcards from the printing stall. They were ready to collect last week, but I've been so busy with the farm that this is the first chance I've had to get back here and pick them up. Weeding has been top of the agenda. I reasoned that the seasonal workers who have started now will be experts at shearing trees, but it would help if they could actually get to them first.

I squeak in delight when the lad hands me a box and inside is the most beautiful set of marketing materials I've ever seen. They're perfect. The background is so bright white it almost glistens and the dark green of the trees make the red of the border pop. They look simple and professional and make me feel like a proper tree farmer. If I picked up one of these, I'd want to go there.

'Whatcha got there, love?' the candlemaker asks when I get back to where Fiona is still gossiping.

'I got some postcards and flyers printed up and they're

amazing.' I know I'm sporting a gleeful smile, and the lad at the stall designed them, not me, but it feels good to be taking steps to make Peppermint Branches work, even small ones.

The candlemaker clears a space on her stall so I can put the box down, and all three of them gather round and ooh and ahh as I open the box. She plunges her hand in and pulls out a handful of flyers. 'I'll tuck one of these in with every candle I sell. Lots of people come here to buy their Christmas gifts, no doubt they'll be wanting a tree come December too.'

'Oh, you don't have to do—'

She interrupts my protest. 'Nonsense. We help our own here. And Fiona was telling me you're going to be festifying our market with lots of trees, so it's the least I can do.'

'Thank you. That's really kind.' I hadn't got as far as figuring out what I was actually going to do with these yet, but I'm genuinely touched by how welcoming the stallholders are here and how quickly they've accepted me.

'Leave me some postcards too. I'll pop a little stack of them on the stall for people to take. Ask the other stalls too. I'm sure everyone will be more than willing to help you out.'

I thank her and we move on to the baker's stall, where Fiona shuffles round the back with a stack of flyers and asks him to hand them out too, getting a similarly enthusiastic response.

'I've been getting my tree there every Christmas since I was a boy,' he says to me. ''Twas devastated when it closed. I'll be your first customer this year, you mark my words. And let me know if you need anything else.'

Fiona shows him the postcards and he asks for some of them to display on his stall too, and honestly, I have to turn away for a minute because everyone's kindness is enough to make my eyes start filling up.

'You okay?' Noel steps nearer and ducks his head to whisper as Fiona hands out business cards and postcards to the bookseller, stopping for a well-earned gossip.

I swallow and paste a smile on, and turn back just in time to catch Fiona furtively pointing a finger towards the two of us.

I elbow Noel in the ribs even though he was watching anyway. 'We're being talked about.'

'You're new round here. What I've learned is that there will always be gossip in a place like this, and the more you try to fight it, the more you make everyone think you've got something to hide. Don't worry about it. Someone's budgie will escape tomorrow and go and mug some parakeets and it'll all be forgotten about.'

I snort and we get raised eyebrows from both Fiona and the bookseller.

'You're not helping,' I hiss at Noel.

'Nah, if I wasn't helping, I'd do this.' He strides across the aisle to the flower seller, picks up a bunch of pink roses and makes a loud clang of change as he hands the bloke a few coins, ensuring every eye in the vicinity has turned in our direction. He comes back and presents them to me with a flourish and ends with a bow. 'To brighten up the stall,' he says close to my ear. 'You can carry them.'

'You know no one heard that, right? They just think you bought me flowers.'

'Why'd you think I said it so quietly?' His eyes are dancing with mischief, but he makes up for it by talking the florist into popping a postcard inside the wrapping of every bouquet.

'So you want them to gossip about us?' I shift the flowers to my other arm so I can still hold the notebook and pen when Fiona's finished her chat.

'People are going to gossip about us no matter what we do. If a feminine-looking pigeon comes in twice, Fiona thinks it wants to ask me on a date and Fergus starts asking around for bird-friendly restaurants.'

It makes me laugh again. 'Will you stop being so funny?'

He grins. 'Ah, let 'em talk. You're way out of my league. I'm honoured if they think you'd look twice at me.'

I don't hide the double-take. 'Are you jok—'

Of course, Fiona chooses that moment to finish her conversation and point out the location of another tree. I hastily mark it on my scribbled map of the market, but she's already hurried onwards and we both rush to follow her. It stops me thinking about what he's just said and how he could possibly think that. He's literally the most gorgeous man I've ever seen in my life. His shoulder-length dark hair is ridiculously sexy, soft and touchable but just scruffy enough to look rugged and handsome as well, blue eyes that look closer to green when he's outdoors, with the dark shadows of a thousand early mornings that make it look like he's wearing natural eyeliner, that lip piercing nestled in the deep dip of his Cupid's bow that I can still barely tear my eyes away from. More importantly than any of that, he's hilarious and kind. He's literally the most thoughtful person I've ever met. He's been popping over to help fix remaining things in the house and we've been working on the caravan together. He's even managed to get a pane of double-glazing from somewhere and replace the kitchen window. How he could think anyone was out of his league is beyond me. Even the Queen would be lucky to have him. If she was into dating 38-year-old Scottish pumpkin farmers. She's probably not.

It's early November now, and Halloween passed in a blur of carving pumpkins, helping kids craft their own scary masks at a workstation outside Roscoe Farm, and watching Noel chase people around the maize maze while dressed as a scarecrow.

Admittedly, the sexiest scarecrow ever. Including Fiyero from *Wicked*. And *he* takes some beating in the sexy scarecrow stakes.

'Do you have decorations for all these trees?' I ask as we complete a full circle of the market and return to the pumpkin stall, where Fergus has moved onto dipping a gingerbread piano into his marmalade.

'No budget.' Fiona isn't really paying attention, she's still scouting around for any spare inch where we could squeeze in another Christmas tree. 'We'll ask the stallholders to bring in their own decs from home, maybe even ask the customers to donate any old ones that they don't want. I bet loads of people have got boxes of decorations gathering dust in their attics and would be glad of a way to get shot of them.'

'Oh, that's terrible.' I picture those gorgeous trees decked out in faded foil lamettas, fire-hazard lights with half the bulbs missing, and moth-eaten paperchains that had seen better days before the Nineties, let alone now.

Noel meets my eyes like he can tell what I'm thinking. 'The trees deserve better than that.'

'You say this is a popular tourist market for the festive season?' I look around, my eyes wandering to all the empty spots where Fiona's demanded a tree. 'Why don't we ask local businesses to decorate them for the free advertising?'

Noel makes a noise of interest, Fiona's head whips round faster than a flash of lightning, and even Fergus has looked up from the marmalade.

'They could do, like, themed decorations for their products, with a couple of big signs saying who they are and where to get their stuff. For example, you . . .' I point at Noel. 'You know those miniature clay pumpkins you were selling as Halloween decorations? You could make more of those with a ribbon through the top and a bit of glitter and hang them like baubles. You could use white tinsel with sparkly orange bits, garlands of green vines, a couple of Cinderella pumpkin carriages, maybe some glass slippers too. Your mum was telling me about her knitting, she could knit Roscoe Farm bunting to string around it, that sort of thing. And you . . .' I turn to Fiona. 'You could hang up some miniature bath bombs and string up chains of bath pearls, pastel coloured tinsel to match your products, with a sparkly bath puff on top instead of a star. Fergus could have strings of gingerbread men, baubles of . . . well, knowing Fergus it'll be baubles of donkeys and Mary and Joseph and—'

'Nutcrackers!' Fergus shouts. 'I've never made a gingerbread nutcracker before.'

'But not just the market traders. We pitch the idea properly to big businesses, preferably local, who have products to sell and don't already have a presence in the Christmas market. It's a great way to get their products in front of customers who wouldn't otherwise see them and show that they have a bit of Christmas cheer and community spirit too.'

'This is brilliant.' Noel is almost bouncing on the spot. 'Why have we never thought of this before?'

'Because we've never had a wonderful newcomer willing to donate lots of Christmas trees before!' Fiona comes over and pulls me into a hug. 'You're brilliant, you are!'

I blush because it's been a long time since anyone thought that.

'I'll start work on a list of businesses to pitch to right away.' She releases me and goes to hug Noel and then Fergus. Fergus's hug is a lot longer than either of ours and Noel meets my eyes and raises an eyebrow at the sight.

'We could make it a competition.' I feel a bit more confident in the idea now that they haven't laughed me out of the building. 'We could ask them to decorate the smaller trees, and then get local schoolkids to judge them, and whoever wins will . . . I don't know. Win something. We have to make it worthwhile for businesses to want to get involved. You said there used to be a big tree at the other end of Elffield, right?'

Noel nods. 'Yeah, but the council cut it from the budget years ago.'

'And there's a motorway over there . . .' I point in the general direction of where I think the motorway passes, and Noel touches my hand and moves my arm around to the opposite direction. 'So the tree would've been visible from it?'

He gives me another nod of confirmation.

'So what if we put it back? What if we take one of the biggest Peppermint firs and put it there, and whoever wins this little market competition will get to decorate it. If it's visible from the motorway, that's incredibly good advertising, and something a bit different for Christmas. Local businesses would be interested in that, right?'

'And the motorway exit is just past that spot, so people could pull right off and come in if they fancied it,' Fiona says.

'You're happy to give away all these trees for nothing?' Noel raises a cynical eyebrow.

'It's not for nothing.' I think of how light the box of postcards and flyers under my arm is now, how happy the stallholders have been to hand them out to their customers, how welcoming everyone has been and how many people have told me how much they loved Peppermint Branches and how happy they are to see it reopening. 'We help our own round here.'

He laughs at the repetition of words that have been said to me a few times this morning.

'I know someone on the council, I could have a word, see if they'd support it?' Fergus says. 'It'd bring loads of extra people into the market. The businesses could pay something towards it, either an entry fee into the competition or a rental fee for their individual trees, so that would bring in revenue that the market sorely needs, and it would be fun for the whole town with the kids getting involved too. Kids would love judging something like that. I'll make gingerbread Christmas trees to bribe them into picking mine . . .' Fergus lets out a giggle. 'Oops, did I say that out loud?'

'Do you do any kind of co-incentives here?'

'I don't even know what they are,' Noel says.

'Co-ordinated shopping. Like, if you buy a tree here, you get 20 per cent off at the decorations stall. If someone buys a bath bomb, you could give them a coupon for the candle stall and vice versa. If someone buys two loaves of bread from the baker, they could have a free gingerbread biscuit from Fergus.'

'I could make gingerbread in the shape of loaves!' Fergus says.

'We've never done that.' Noel looks around the market and then back at me. 'Why have we never done that? That's genius.'

I blush again. The Noel I've got to know over the last couple of weeks is a creative genius, so hearing that from him is a real compliment. I barrel on because I don't want to think about how fluttery it makes me feel. 'We need to give people a reason to visit the whole market, to look at every stall, to buy things that they didn't know they wanted before stepping foot in here. If we have any chance of saving this place, we have to do it together.'

'Do you think we can?' Fiona looks between me and Noel. 'There's been an underlying current between traders that it's as good as gone. There's no saving it.'

'I think a good season could delay it.' Noel sounds like he's being careful not to get their hopes up. 'If businesses take up the Christmas tree idea – and if we can get a good bit of publicity going online and in the local area then I think they will – it could be a game-changer. If we can get people talking about it, encourage kids from all around to come and vote for their favourite, the trees would be the sort of thing that people would visit specifically to see. And with this wee genius on board, who knows what the year could bring?' His arm drops around my shoulder and he squeezes me tight into his side.

The surface of the sun is currently cooler than my burning cheeks. I reach up with the intention of smacking his hand where his warm fingers are curled into my upper arm, but as soon as I touch his skin, my hand sort of ends up staying there, closing over his. I don't make any attempt to move, despite the fact Fiona's eyes have swivelled to our joined hands and even Fergus is craning his neck for a better look.

'Were you in marketing before?' Fiona asks, her eyes alternating between my shoulder and Noel's face. 'We should take you on as a market manager permanently. You're wasted as a tree farmer.'

'Not as wasted as the trees are most days,' Noel replies quickly.

My face contorts as I try to stop myself chuckling but fail magnificently. This time I do smack his hand. 'Will you stop it?'

His other hand comes up and brushes my long hair aside so

he can lean down and whisper in my ear. 'Every time you say that, it makes me want to make you laugh even more.'

If my grip on his hand tightens with that delicious Scottish accent so close that every word moves my hair against my skin then it's completely coincidental, and it's absolutely not connected to the way I close my eyes and lean into him for a moment.

I can feel Fergus and Fiona's eyes analysing every movement we make. I know I should move away from him, but he's solid and his body heat is warm through his olive plaid shirt and I can feel the flex of his forearms against my back.

'Fiona's right, you know,' he says loudly. 'Every time you speak, I find myself saying 'why have we never done that?' You're exactly what Elffield needs.'

'Exactly what someone else needs too, hmm?' Fergus waggles his eyebrows.

This time, Noel steps away and his cheeks are as red as mine when I glance up at him, and I try not to think about how much I liked that arm around my shoulders.

'You two should pool your ideas for the Christmas tree campaign. Why don't you both pop off for a cuppa and we'll watch the stalls before we leave for the day?' Noel offers.

Fergus and Fiona don't need telling twice.

'Don't forget to talk to the other traders and see what they make of the idea,' he calls after them as Fiona slips her arm through Fergus's and they hobble away.

'You're meddling again.' I point an accusatory finger in his direction once they've disappeared around the corner towards the hot drinks counter and seating area.

'Me? Meddle?' He manages to look so simultaneously innocent and affronted that it makes me grin again. 'Oh, come on. They're head-over-heels. I know you see it too.'

'Yeah, of course. They're adorable together. They spend most of their time making eyes at each other across the aisle. I've never seen someone put away as much gingerbread as Fiona gets through from all the times she wanders over to see Fergus, and he must be the nicest smelling man in all of Elffield with the amount of bath bombs and bubble bath he buys.'

That soft smile plays across his face again. 'Let me put it this way – I've been to Fergus's house and he doesn't own a bath, only a shower. He has no need for bath products.'

'Aww.' I can't help the noise that comes out of my mouth. 'That's so sweet.'

'And you wonder why I meddle.'

'Speaking of meddling . . .' I start. 'The main thing they're head-over-heels for is village gossip, and you're only making it worse.'

'I'm not doing anything!' He holds up both hands with a grin, and even though I'm trying to be annoyed, I can't help grinning at the cheeky glint in his eyes.

'Are you *trying* to get them to talk about us so they stop trying to set you up with pigeons or something?'

'Yes. On my list of possible matches, you are marginally above a pigeon. Only marginally, mind. And only because I think you're slightly more likely to share your chips.'

He makes it impossible for me to frown at him.

He must notice the expression because he sighs. 'Look, they're romantic old sods who believe people need a relationship to be happy. I've told them I'm not interested about fifty million times and it doesn't make any difference. They're determined to see something that isn't there. If we have a laugh together, they think it's the start of something, but equally, if I ignored you and we didn't speak to each other, they'd convince themselves that we were playing hard to get *because* we liked each other.' He winks at me. 'And where would be the fun in that when there are the drunken antics of trees to discuss?'

'Maybe they're trying to get you back for all the meddling you do?'

'I don't meddle. That makes me sound like a crotchety old bat twitching the net curtains all day. I don't even have net curtains.

I'm just trying to help two elderly singles enjoy their twilight years together before the pair of them bankrupt themselves by buying each other's gingerbread and bath bombs that they don't use.'

I raise an eyebrow. 'So it's retaliatory meddling then?'

'They're always worried that I'm lonely. A beautiful girl moving in next door to me is the nosy pensioner's equivalent of all their Christmases coming at once.'

I ignore that. He's seen me snotty-nosed and mid-ugly-cry, as well as first thing in the morning having vaulted out of bed at 6 a.m, and up to my elbows in rubber gloves, cleaning products, mud, and then the facepaints at his farm on Halloween. *No one* could think I was beautiful after that. I'm plain and forgettable at the best of times. The only thing anyone's likely to remember about me is that my hair's so long I can almost sit on it. In his case, the snot bubble has undoubtedly made me unforgettable for all the wrong reasons.

'So I'm sorry, but you've unwittingly walked into the middle of a powder keg of gossip. It'll fizzle itself out next time someone accidentally eats tinsel or gets their head stuck in a Christmas stocking.'

'*Are* you lonely?'

'You're never lonely with a Chihuahua,' he says without missing a beat. It sounds like a line he's said many times before.

Instead of giving me a chance to push any further, he takes an empty jar from the bakery crate, fills it with water from a bottle, and picks up the bouquet of roses from the table where I'd put them down.

I decide it's best to end this conversation here like he so clearly wants to do. 'How do you *accidentally* eat tinsel?'

He lets out a bark of laughter without looking up from the paper wrap he's trying to wrestle from the roses. 'I love how you say that like *intentionally* eating tinsel is completely normal.'

I watch as he slices the bottom off the stems with a penknife on his keyring and puts an abnormal amount of effort into arranging the flowers.

'You're going to do it, right?' I say quietly. 'The tree thing, I mean. If it works out like we hope and other businesses go for it, you'd have a great chance of winning. Kids love Halloween and fairytales, and pumpkins are inherently fairytale-esque, and you're so creative, and—'

'Of course I'm going to,' he cuts me off before I have time to turn that into a compliment. 'And if I didn't, then Mum would never let a chance to knit a pumpkin pass by. It's a great idea. Genuinely.'

It makes me blush again because he sounds so impressed and for the first time in a long while, it makes me feel like something I do could actually make a difference.

I can't help smiling when he looks up at me. His bright eyes twinkle as he holds my gaze, the corners of his mouth tipping up more with every second until he lets out a full laugh and ducks his head. It's enough to make me forget about everything else.

The back table is still full of pumpkins, but instead of traditional Jack O'Lantern faces cut into them, they're carved with swirl patterns and snowflakes now it's November, their tealights blinking inside them. He walks over to sit against it, stretches his legs out and shakes his hair back, using his fingers to pull it out of his shirt collar and detangle it. He whips a black hairband from around his wrist and puts it up in a short ponytail, his forearm muscles moving as he works, and I think I might've accidentally started drooling.

I've never watched a man tie up his hair before, but I'm used to doing it with my long mane and generally I just get into a mess and spend most of my time trying to detach hair from my bra straps and untrap it from where it inexplicably gets caught in my armpit, but my breathing has sped up involuntarily at how insanely sexy he looks. I think porn companies should give up on all the sweaty nakedness stuff and just concentrate on men putting their hair up from now on. His dark lashes fall across his cheeks as he looks down and bites his lip in concentration.

He knows I'm watching him without looking up. 'What?'

'I like it,' I say. I don't know what else *to* say, because 'you are the hottest man on the planet' probably wouldn't go down too well. 'You don't see many guys with long hair, but it suits you.'

'Even though I'm not a hipster with skinny jeans and a man-bun?'

I smile at the thought. There's no way his muscular legs could be vacuumed into skinny jeans, and a man bun would never work. His hair is so thick that it doesn't sit nicely in a ponytail and a couple of the shorter bits have already sprung out, and there's something questionable about my sanity given how much I want to go over and tuck them back.

Thankfully he speaks again before I have a chance to do anything that stupid. 'Thank you. My mum thinks I'm an unkempt slob.'

My breath catches in my throat because there's something in his voice that I haven't heard before, a flatness, a resignation. A vulnerability.

Like he can sense how much it makes me want to go over and sit next to him, he looks up at me and our gazes lock and the air suddenly feels charged with expectation, like we're both waiting for something to happen.

I take a step towards him and he suddenly launches himself off the table, making one of the pumpkins roll off and thud onto the floor. The flickering tealight inside it goes dark as he makes a show of checking his watch like it was the reason he got up so fast.

I bend down to pick the pumpkin up, turn the tealight back on, and replace its lid as I set it back on the table.

I can feel his eyes on me, and I'm blushing again for no reason. When I turn around, he's got that soft smile on his face again and he's shifting awkwardly from one foot to the other.

Thankfully Fergus and Fiona choose that moment to re-appear, and we watch them tottering down the aisle towards us arm in arm.

'We're going to catch them snogging behind the bike sheds one day.' Noel leans down to whisper like he can read my mind. 'They nip off for coffee every morning and they always return ten minutes later, all giggly and clinging onto each other.'

It's probably a good thing that we don't have any bike sheds. Because I could easily imagine myself kissing Noel behind them.

I shake my head at myself. Lingering gazes, desires to touch, and kissing men behind sheds or in any other place . . . I don't know what's got into me lately.

Chapter 10

'Not like that, like this.'

It must be the fortieth time Noel's said it so far this morning, and I still haven't got the hang of it. We're out in the Balsam fir field below the stream, Gizmo's safely at home with Glenna due to the proximity of sharp knives, and Noel's trying to teach me how to shear a Christmas tree.

'Did that tree drunkenly catcall you or something?' He looks sorrowfully at the overgrown thing I've just wielded my knife at. 'It's obviously done something to make you hate it.'

I'd never seen a shearing knife up close until I spent an hour in the barn this morning trying to work out how to sharpen them and polish them. They're like a cross between a sword and a massive knife, and I'd feel a bit like a swashbuckling pirate if it wasn't for the fact he's insisted I wear leg and arm protectors and goggles. I actually feel like a foam-covered *Transformer* off to a welding class, with protective plates covering my jeans from foot to knee, knee to upper thigh, and again from wrist to elbow. I'm not sure if they're to stop me getting injured or just because he wants to see me look like an idiot.

Noel, of course, swishes two knives around like a cross between a master swordsman and Jack Sparrow. He walks around each tree, cocking his head to the side and looking along the edge of the knife to judge the angle, and then swish, swish, swish, like a better-looking Edward Scissorhands, and the tree in front of him has gone from an overgrown jumble of branches to a perfectly conical tree that would look good in anyone's living room.

'*How* are you doing that?' I haven't even got to grips with the one-handed method yet and he's twirling both two-foot long blades around like a demented hairdresser.

'Like this.' He executes another perfect swish and unwanted branches spray from the tree in a snowstorm of green needles that make the balsam scent even stronger and drop to the ground in a perfect circle.

'You're just showing off now.'

He grins. 'I'm not. But I've been doing this for twenty-something years, and *you* thought Christmas trees naturally grew in a perfectly symmetrical cone shape.'

I watch as he demonstrates again, but watching Noel is never conducive for concentration, and what I find myself watching is the way his biceps move, straining against the cream and brown flannel shirt with every flick of his knife. He's wearing faded, holey work jeans and that navy padded bodywarmer again, and his shirt sleeves are rolled up to his elbows, despite the fact there's a fine mist of drizzle in the air.

He gestures towards the tree in front of me, indicating that I should try again, so I point the knife at the Christmas tree.

'My name is Inigo Montoya . . .'

I burst out laughing so hard that I have to drop the knife for safety reasons.

'Will you *stop* doing that?' I rasp at him. It's not the first *The Princess Bride* reference he's made today and I have no doubt that it won't be the last. 'Are you trying to make sure I'm terrible at this so I have to beg you for help or what? Are you secretly looking for another job?'

'I love doing this.' He shrugs. 'This is not work to me. You have a *lot* of trees to prune and, no matter how quickly you learn and how many workers you employ, you're not going to get them all done with less than three weeks until December. Although, like I said, it's completely the wrong time of year for pruning. We need to do only the ones you intend to sell this year and the rest can be tackled in the spring. The spruces and firs can survive being pruned now, but the new growth becomes harder and more difficult to shape in the future, so you're setting yourself up for problems down the line, but it's a choice between that or absolutely no trees for sale this year, apart from the Peppermint firs, and with only those to offer, the crop will be decimated too quickly.'

I pick up the knife again and aim it at the tree, holding it sideways on. I try to mimic the downwards slicing motion he makes look so effortless. There are plenty of branches sticking out from the dense body of the five-foot tall tree in front of me. It cannot be that difficult.

'Aaargh!' I decide a battlecry will help as I swoosh the knife down the edge, determined to nip at least a few surplus bits off, unlike the last attempt in which I took a huge chunk out of the poor undeserving tree but somehow managed to avoid all the bits that *should* have come off. This time, what actually happens is that I miss the tree completely, and the knife slices down and thwacks blade-first into my shin pad. Maybe they weren't such a bad idea after all.

When I look up, Noel's bent double with laughter. I raise an eyebrow because it's not *that* funny, and eventually he stands up and throws both of his knives onto the ground. 'Come on, we're going to have to do the *Ghost* thing.'

'I don't think pottery is going to help in this situation.'

'I don't think anything's going to help in this situation.' His boots make imprints in the freshly weeded earth as he walks towards me. 'It's no wonder these trees need to drown their sorrows. Poor buggers. Look what you've done to that one.'

He points out my first attempt from earlier, in which I aimed the knife the wrong way and embedded it directly into the heart of the unsuspecting tree's trunk.

'Right, c'mere.' He steps up behind me and the closeness sends a shiver through me that has nothing to do with Christmas tree shearing. 'Okay to touch you?'

I nod, afraid that if I try to talk, it'll come out as 'ahrumgu-urrgh' or something that makes equal sense.

His chest presses against my back and his hands slide over the protective pads on my arms until his skin touches mine and his fingers cover my hands. He squeezes gently in a way that I'm sure has nothing to do with tree cutting as his elbows fit underneath mine and he somehow uses the strength of his arms to pull me closer. Every inch of his body wraps around me and his chin lands on my shoulder, his barely-there stubble brushing against the side of my neck, and I wish that his bodywarmer wasn't there because it provides a padded barrier between us.

And that aftershave. I have *never* met a man who smells so good. An earthy mix of juniper and dark patchouli, with a hint of cinnamon that smells different depending on whether he's warm or cold.

He's murmuring something about the knife in my ear but I haven't heard a word of it, and it strikes me that maybe I shouldn't spend *quite* so much time thinking about his aftershave.

His fingers curl around mine and he angles my hand, pressing his head against the side of mine to tilt it sideways. He picks up my second knife and holds it up so both blades touch at the tip, forming a triangle. 'The branches need to come out in a conical shape from the leader, hold your knives like this as a guide at first, but eventually it'll be second nature and you can easily eyeball it.'

He lets his knife drop and uses his hand to move mine, pointing out a rough line to follow and the branches that need to come off. 'Usually there's much less than this to take off, but you should only have a year's worth of growth. This time round, you've got four years' worth.'

His voice is barely above a rumble in my ear, and I'm thinking about doing it wrong just so he stays there.

He guides my hand softly until his fingers tighten and he shows me how to angle the knife against the tree and how to judge what needs to come off. All I can think about is the feel of his warm and deliciously solid body pressing against mine.

Come *on*, Leah. Christmas trees. Knives. Not hot Scottish pumpkin farmers. I think he must wear that aftershave to make sure it's impossible to concentrate on *anything* around him.

'You've really got to swing it.' He manoeuvres my hand in the direction I need to cut. 'Strong, firm strokes from left to right across your body. Don't be afraid of getting it wrong. This is something that can't be taught from a book. The only way you can learn is by doing it. Yes, you'll lose a couple of trees in the process but that's part of it. You ready?'

I nod and feel his chin shift against my shoulder. His fingers tighten around mine and raise the knife, bringing it down in a smooth, swift motion, and the tips of the unwanted growth drop to the ground like fallen limbs. He does it again and again, using his feet on either side of mine to gradually shuffle us around the tree, swooshing the knife in downwards strokes, over and over until the overgrown tangle of branches begins to look like a nicely shaped Christmas tree.

Once I've got the motion going, his fingers loosen and although his hand stays on mine, he's no longer guiding the knife, and I'm not sure what feels better – to be doing something worthwhile or to have him standing so close.

When Noel's satisfied that the tree looks reasonable, he murmurs in my ear again. 'Now pick your leader and chop the other top branches off. It encourages the tree to grow up nice and straight, and you only need one for the star to go on, so choose the sturdiest and then lop off the rest.'

Even to me, it's easy to see which one is the best growing tip. I don't need the support, but his hands splay across my back as

I lean up with one knife to hold the top sprig aside, and I bring the other knife up to slash the smaller ones away.

'Yeah!' He lets out a whoop. 'Congratulations, you've successfully pruned your first tree!'

I cheer too and turn around in his embrace, expecting him to move, but he doesn't and his lips are *right there* in front of mine. I feel him swallow and his arms tighten around me. 'See, it's easy really.'

I'm starting to think that running a marathon might be easy if I had his arms around me. And that I might agree to something that crazy if his cologne blocked out all my other senses.

I feel completely lost in his arms. Our mouths are barely a breath away from touching, and when he wets his lips with his tongue, we're so close that I can feel the heat from it. His stubble is rough against my face, his hair tickling my neck, and his hands tighten where they're still holding onto mine, and we stand still, neither of us daring to move for a long few seconds.

He suddenly swivels his head towards the tree, his chin pressing so tightly against my shoulder than I can feel the little cleft in it. 'Only another 5999 to go.'

His words are abrupt, and I expect him to do his usual thing of jumping away and putting as much distance between us as possible, so I'm surprised when he doesn't move. Instead, he stays where he is, his arms around me from behind so I'm sort of leaning back against him. There's a giant knife somewhere that we shouldn't lose track of, but none of it seems to matter as I stand here in his arms looking at the tree we've sheared together.

He rests the side of his head against mine and I *know* he's lingering this time, and I wonder if he really needed to show me that way or if he wanted an excuse to stand close. It makes another shiver go through me as I try not to think about what it means if he does.

Like he can sense what I'm thinking, this time he jumps and takes a step back. 'Sorry. Trees release pheromones when they're cut, I think they're getting to me.'

'Yeah, me too,' I murmur. Because I don't know what the hell I'm thinking in getting this close to Noel or wanting to kiss him *quite* this badly. The *last* thing I need at the moment is a relationship, particularly with someone who so plainly isn't interested either.

'Go on then, try one,' he says before I can think anything else about it.

I shuffle over to the next tree and he comes close again, lifting my hand and positioning the knife in the right place before stepping back. Somehow I force myself to think about what I'm doing instead of how close he is. I feel the weight of the knife, hold it up and look along it to judge the angle. This time when I swish the knife down, I actually manage to lop a few branches off, and after a couple of strokes, the tree starts to look better for it, and I can kind of work out what needs to be trimmed and what doesn't, and I manage not to cause any injuries to myself or the shin pads.

I also notice with a bit of smug glee that Noel has stopped laughing now, and *The Princess Bride* pirate references have dried up. He watches silently as I slice branches off all the way around. When I lop the top off the growing tip, I turn and do a bow with the knife, grinning at him, but I nearly overbalance and narrowly miss impaling myself.

I can tell he's trying not to smile as he walks around inspecting the tree, stroking his chin with his fingers, giving it the severe deliberation of grading an exam, and I suddenly feel ridiculously nervous.

It's not perfect. I've taken a couple of chunks out and been a bit overzealous with trimming the top leader, and it's taken me ages despite only being a small tree, whereas Noel does even the eight-footers in thirty seconds flat, but it's better than I thought I could do this morning, and I feel positive about it, like it's something I can learn and get better at. And I have a *lot* of trees to practice on.

Eventually Noel reappears from behind the tree and I can tell he's struggling to keep a straight face – but he gives up far too easily and a smile spreads, making his eyes dance. 'This is good. You should've seen the first one I ever did. It looked like the lovechild of *Spongebob Squarepants* and *Peppa Pig* had been in a terrible accident.'

I try not to show how happy his verdict makes me. I don't need his approval, but his smile and the way he looks genuinely proud makes it impossible not to grin.

Maybe I am cut out for this after all.

Chapter 11

'Nice, tight wiring. Now place another bunch just below so it overlaps, and wrap the wire around three times to hold it in place.' Glenna nods in approval at my wreath-making skills or lack thereof. 'You've got it.'

I don't feel like I've got it at all, but I understand her instructions and can see how the wreath will take shape. It's too early to make fresh wreaths and garlands for sale yet, so I'm practising with a pile of shearing offcuts, the overgrown tops of the holly hedges, sprigs of berries, pinecones, and some ferns that were growing wild. I'm pulling them all together in little bunches and tying them to the metal wreath ring with floral wire, alternately tilting each bunch inwards and outwards so it fills the ring and maintains a nice round shape.

Glenna is an absolute expert wreath-maker. Noel sells the autumn wreaths she makes at the market, and they are so incredible that you think they must be artificial, but they're not – she's just that good. They're laden with orange, yellow, red, and brown leaves, which I see her out gathering around the farm every morning. She's got cinnamon sticks, pinecones, the crisp orange cases of Physalis lanterns, twigs of Alder cones, bunches of winged sycamore seeds, and miniature pumpkins and apples, and they practically fly off the stall even though they're one of the most expensive things Noel sells.

She whizzes through a festive one with my supplies and finishes it off with a big red bow from a spool of ribbon she brought over.

'Wow.' I don't try to hide how impressed I am as I get my own wire tangled and snap a fir branch by mistake.

'You'll get there with a bit more practice, flower. You're already getting the hang of it.' She reaches down to stroke Gizmo who's pottering around our feet in the barn. 'You're a natural. You chose all these greens, and even thought of the ferns. I wouldn't have thought of using them but they work well.'

I blush even though I don't believe her.

I was lucky to find one of Mr Evergreene's old stone outbuildings contained nothing but Christmas decorations. Boxes of outdoor lights, tinsel, now-faded festive signs, and tons and tons of supplies, from a box full of wreath rings and wire, to elf hats, bags of jingling bells, boxes of baubles, and hanging snowflakes. It was like everything I've thought of to make this place better was already there waiting for me, in the building with the least leaky roof.

'If I can make enough of these, I could display them on my fence that runs alongside the road, it'd be a great way to show them off.' I tie my last little bundle of greenery onto the ring and poke the ends underneath the brush of the first bundle to hide them, then I get a bunch of holly berries and slot that in too. I check my watch to see how long it's taken me.

'The trick is always to work in the same direction around the wreath so it becomes a habit,' Glenna says when she sees the face I make because it's taken me far too long. 'Pretty soon you'll be able to do it with your eyes shut. Lots of tree farmers find things like wreaths and garlands are actually more profitable than the trees themselves, because it doesn't take much time to make them, and you're using the bits you've already cut from around the farm anyway. It's a great sideline, and displaying them along the fence is bound to attract people driving past with their kids. Lots of Noel's trade comes from people driving by with little kids in the car and their faces light up at the sight of all those pumpkins and they beg their parents to go in because it's such a magical sight.'

I make a bow from Glenna's ribbon, tie three bells together and wire them all onto the bottom of the wreath.

'See, you've got a knack for this. It must be very different from your last job?'

'Yeah, but that's not a bad thing. I love doing creative things like this. Before I was sitting at a desk all day, staring at the wall. Being outside all the time makes me feel like I'm *living* again for the first time in years. My old job was something I left behind at five o'clock every night, so it's a bit daunting when I think about the next few years and how much work and responsibility this is. There's so much to keep track of. Collecting seeds from the pinecones in the autumn, sowing them in the spring, and growing them until they're big enough to be planted out. Preparing the fields, tree fertiliser, weed killer, and nothing's been planted for four years, so in a few years' time, there's going to be a shortage. I know Noel's looking after some saplings for me, but who knows if it'll be enough.' I cut myself off there, suddenly aware that I'm rambling. I've tried to appear bright and breezy whenever anyone asks how things are going, but inside, I *am* scared that I haven't got the knowledge to pull this off. Christmas tree farming is a lot more complicated than I thought it was. I didn't intend to tell Glenna any of that, but she's such a warm and friendly motherly figure. She reminds me of my own mum, and it's easy to be open with her in a way I wouldn't with anyone else.

'You've been brave enough to take this huge step – the kind of thing that most people dream about doing but never have the courage to actually do. Don't underestimate how much courage it takes to throw yourself headfirst into a completely different life. If you can do that, you can overcome whatever else is thrown at you.'

Gizmo stands up on his back feet and paws at my leg, so I put my wreath down and pick him up. I rest my chin on his head and rub his brown ear while his white ear twitches in Glenna's direction and his nose sniffs for any hint of food he might be able to snaffle.

'For what it's worth, I think you're doing an excellent job so far.' She gives me a wide smile and nods at the little dog in my arms. 'And so does Gizmo.'

'Thank you.' I don't try to hide the surprise in my voice. 'I think I'm floundering around in the dark. I've been reading the books I bought and my head is so full. I don't know how I'm going to remember any of it, and I'm never sure if I'm doing it right.'

'You could always ask Noel.'

'I've already been asking Noel too much. I don't know what I'd have done without his expertise and advice, but he's got his own farm to run and his own business to take care of. I can't keep asking him all these questions and expecting him to help me with everything.'

'You came to help us on Halloween night.'

'But that was just a bit of fun. Who *wouldn't* want to spend Halloween on a pumpkin farm when they live next door to one?' I try not to think about my disastrous pumpkin carving attempts that night – from the hedgehog that looked like Simon Cowell to the bat that everyone thought was a fried egg. 'I can't keep relying on him. I need to be able to do this stuff by myself. I didn't come here so my gorgeous neighbour could run a Christmas tree farm *for* me.'

I only realise what I've said when Glenna's face lights up like I've given her next week's winning lottery numbers. I did *not* just admit how gorgeous I think he is to his own mother. I've never wished for a sinkhole before, but I certainly wouldn't be opposed to one popping up to swallow me whole anytime now.

'He's one of the best, you know?' She says after a few minutes of cringingly awkward silence.

She would say that, she's his mum.

'I know you're probably thinking I would say that because I'm his mum, but he'd help you out with anything. Noel's a true gent. He'd be the perfect man if you could get him to cut his hair and take that piercing out . . .'

I know *exactly* what she's hinting at, but I think she's about to tell me he's wormed, defleaed, housetrained, and comes with a puppy pack in a minute, and I haven't got the heart to tell her that his lip piercing is probably the sexiest thing about him, and his hair is a close second.

She looks at me like she can tell I'm staying silent for a reason. 'You're right. Your love lives are none of my business. It's just that he can be a bit abrasive on the surface, and he pushes people away when he really wants to let them in. I didn't want you to see the way he protects himself and think it's the way he is deep down inside. He's been single for *so* long now, I think he's forgotten how to act around women he likes.'

I feel a bit sorry for him with the emphasis she puts on the '*so*'. Before Steve, I'd been single for a long time too – I only wish I'd stayed that way. Good on him for staying by himself rather than settling for someone who wasn't right.

'So, how's the plan coming along for the Christmas tree competition?'

'It's okay, flower, we can change the subject.' She's smiling when she looks up at me. 'It's going well. We've gone with your idea of a Cinderella theme. I've been buying up all the glass slipper ornaments I can get my hands on, and I'm knitting strings of tiny pumpkins. Noel's doing something with model train tracks for a moving fairytale carriage. It's going to look miraculous.'

'It's the talk of the market. Fergus and Fiona have made themselves heads of the Christmas tree committee, and all the traders have got involved and started swapping ideas. Apparently, the uptake from nearby businesses has been great too, better than Fergus and Fiona expected. They're really pleased.' I can't help the sigh that escapes. 'I just want it to help. I love it there. I don't want to see it disappear. It would change the whole town.'

Glenna's crinkled face mirrors my sadness.

'I was thinking about trying to get the media involved,' I say cautiously. 'Chelsea's got a lot of contacts in that area. If we could get some coverage in local papers about the competition and what we're trying to do . . . it could really help.'

'The publicity might encourage more businesses to get involved,' she agrees. 'People are already talking about it, and there's a real buzz in the air that Peppermint Branches is reopening. It was here for a long time and so many people made it a Christmas tradition to come up with their families and choose their Christmas tree. Even us Roscoes when Noel's father was still alive, and dear Mr Evergreene always let us have the first choice before the farm opened in December. It will be lovely to see it running again.'

'Noel talks about how magical it used to be a lot. I only hope I can recreate that.'

'I think you're on the right track.' She nods towards the wreath. 'And I'd be happy to help when you open. I don't get out much these days and Noel's always telling me I need more fresh air. I've seen you two cleaning and painting the caravan, and he's told me about the hot chocolate and the chestnuts, and I was thinking maybe I could serve for you, and have a little sideline in my pumpkin jams and marmalades. I've always got so many pumpkins to make use of, and it would be wonderful to have an extra opportunity to sell some of my goodies, and I make an excellent hot chocolate if I do say so myself.'

The caravan is now painted with enamel paint I found in the barn, a festive shade of red, and so are my hands, my face, a vast majority of my clothes, half of Gizmo who came to 'help', and a bit of the grass outside that escaped the tarpaulin we'd put down to cover it. There's fake snow draped across the roof, and inside there are twinkly lights around the window, and the broken glass has been removed and replaced with a serving hatch shutter. I'd been wondering whether to hire someone to run it, but time is short, and I can't justify employing yet another person when I can probably manage it myself between tree customers.

'I could also make little goodies for your own sales,' Glenna says like I need further persuasion. 'Peppermint bark in the shape of trees and some candycane sugar cookies would go down a treat with hot chocolate.'

'That would be amazing. Noel's always saying he wishes he could extend pumpkin season, and I've been trying to figure out a way we could join forces and help each other out. He's helped me so much, so if the tree farm being open can help you guys out in any way, let me know. And you'd be doing me a huge favour too. The seasonal workers are still going to be here, so I was just going to put whoever isn't busy with customers in charge of it.'

'The seasonal workers will be needed in the fields to advise customers and cut and carry their trees for them. I think you're going to be a lot busier than you think you are. You saw the pumpkin patch at Halloween.'

I did. I watched the pumpkin patch throughout the last two weeks of October, and Noel was *busy*. Cars coming and going all day and children running around enjoying themselves, even the shouts of joy from his corn maze filtered across to me as I weeded the driveway and dug over the edges of the lane for display trees, but he sells his pumpkins at fifty pence each. Christmas trees are much more expensive, and much bigger and more difficult to transport and recycle afterwards. But on the other hand, almost all of my postcards and flyers have gone and the stallholders at the market have requested more, so I just hope she's right.

It feels like it's all starting to come together, but none of it will matter if customers don't come. It needs to be a good season. Because I don't know what I'm going to do if it's not.

Chapter 12

'Not like that, like this.'

'Are those your favourite words or what?' I snap, standing upright to wipe the sweat dripping off my forehead again. It's three weeks into November now, it's far too cold to be sweating this much.

Noel grins, his forehead not glistening even slightly, the fit bugger. Another Norway spruce falls effortlessly into his hand and he lays it down gently.

I crouch down and wriggle around the saw that I've got stuck in the trunk. Again. My hands stick to the handle because I'm covered in sap. Again.

He stomps over, picks up my gloves from the ground and hands them to me, then he kneels and removes my saw with ease and pats the earth beside him.

It's drizzling again and the earth is damp, but I reluctantly kneel down and silently apologise to yet another pair of jeans for ruining them. He hands the saw back to me and taps the trunk above the awful hacking half-cut I've just made. 'Try again here, above the damaged bit so you cut it off.'

We're heading to the market with the first trees this weekend, so it's my first opportunity to attempt to cut them down.

Peppermint Branches opens to the public next weekend, and things are starting to take shape. Between us, we've pruned almost two thousand of the spruces and firs, and Iain and the two workers have done a huge amount of the rest. There are only a few hundred overgrown trees left now, and the ground around them is weed-free and solid. We've dug up loads and planted them along either side of the lane, and each one is strung with the twinkling outdoor lights I found. The hot chocolate machine and chestnut roaster are installed in the caravan, and Noel and I have been testing them both to ensure quality. Vigorous testing. Multiple times.

But this is the real groundwork – the actual cutting of Christmas trees. Like the shearing, if I can't do this, I'm going to be a pretty rubbish Christmas tree farmer.

It's one of the younger spruces I'm trying to cut, but the bow saw grinds to a halt a quarter of the way the through the slim trunk. Again.

Noel rolls his eyes and wriggles the stuck saw until he can get it free.

'What am I doing wrong?' This is the third tree I've tried to cut this morning and the third one that Noel's had to rescue from my terrible attempts.

'No idea. I'm stumped.' He looks up at me and grins. 'Stumped, get it?'

'Your tree puns would be a lot funnier if you didn't point them out immediately after making them.'

'You've obviously *twigged* that my sense of humour is just too sophisticated . . .'

I do an exaggerated groan. 'At least that's a new one. I've lost track of how many times you've used the stumped one.'

'Oh, come on. There are prime times for the stumped pun and this is clearly one of them.' He gestures animatedly at the stumps in front of us and mischief flashes across his blueish-green eyes. 'At least I'm not making acorn-y joke.'

It should be illegal to laugh at something so terrible, but the look of earnestness on his face makes me guffaw so hard that it takes a few minutes to recover.

He puts the saw back into my gloved hand. 'Try again. In a straight line. I don't know why you're so determined to cut it at an angle. You're trying to slice it, not hack at it like a chisel. Long smooth strokes. As close to the ground as possible while still giving yourself room to work.'

'I know,' I say, because he's told me ten times, and I'm still cutting too high up, and the saw still inserts itself at a downward angle.

His hand closes around mine. 'I'd better help. We're going to run out of trees at this rate. There are only another five-thousand-odd for you to practise on.'

'Oh, ha ha, almost as funny as the tree puns,' I murmur as he uses his other hand to push back the lower branches and give me better access to the trunk.

His head is close to mine and his leg is pressed against my thigh as his hand guides mine back to the tree, his fingers covering mine as he makes me hold the saw against the trunk at the correct angle and starts moving it back and forth in strokes much longer and smoother than the ones I was managing. With him in charge, the saw doesn't catch once, and the narrow trunk is sliced nearly all the way through in seconds.

Noel holds onto a low branch to hold the tree upright. 'Don't push it when it starts to lean, that'll make the bark splinter.'

He jumps to his feet to catch it, and I slide the saw through the last centimetre until the tree falls into his waiting arms and he lays it down.

The tractor is at the edge of the field with the trailer attached for the trees to be piled on and taken back to the barn for netting, before being loaded into Noel's truck and taken to the market stall on Friday.

I'm quite proud of myself as I stand up and look at the tree lying on the ground. All right, Noel did most of the work, but still. Small victories.

With the next one, he stands at the back to support it and reaches around to hold the lower branches out of the way as I kneel down again and attempt to replicate the sawing movement he's just shown me. The tree makes some ominous creaking noises, and the saw catches a few times, but after the longest few minutes in history, the blade finally comes out the other side and the tree falls.

Noel lays it down and gives it a not-entirely-disapproving nod.

It's not quite the sixty seconds he can get through a tree trunk in, but it's a start, and I move onto the next tree before he has a chance to direct me.

I'm going to have to do this on my own. I love that he's helping me, but he's got his own farm to run, he can't be here all the time.

It's fine, I tell myself. A few weeks ago, I never thought I'd get the hang of shearing trees, but now I feel like I've been doing it all my life.

One thing I've learnt is that you don't have time for doubt in this job. You jump in and learn as you go while treading water in the deep end and hoping there are no sharks circling down below.

'You're keen.' Noel supports the next tree, peering around it to watch the cut I'm making.

'You're not always going to be here to help me. I can't tell you how much I appreciate you teaching me stuff like this, but I have to get the hang of it myself.'

'I know, but my season is over for the moment so I've got time, and I love this place. I love being here again. I even love watching you grow into this role and the way you pick things up and have ideas that I would never have thought of. It's inspiring to see it all through the eyes of a newbie again.'

Inspiring. Something I never thought anyone would say about me, ever.

‘You keep thanking me for helping you, but I’m enjoying it too. I loved fixing up the caravan with you and seeing it take shape into something fantastic before our eyes. Even Gizmo is enjoying his new red markings.’ He gives me a grin. ‘And yeah, my season starts again in January with digging over the land and planting seeds in propagators, but until then I’m only running the market stall and the corn maze at the weekends until the corn dies back. I’m happy to help.’

He makes an ‘oof’ sound as the tree I’ve just cut down falls into him, and I can’t help the grin of glee. He was so distracted that he didn’t even notice me slicing through another trunk.

I run my gloved fingers across the fresh stump. It’s not as smooth as Noel’s, but it’s better than my earlier cuts. For the first time since he knocked on the door this morning with a backpack over his shoulders, two bow saws in one hand and coffee and muffins in the other, I feel like it’s actually something I’ll be able to do.

I grin up at him as he sets the tree on the ground and walks around it to assess the trunk and gives an approving nod.

‘And we haven’t even started on the chainsaw cutting yet. And yes, you *do* need to learn how to use a chainsaw,’ he says, pre-empting what I was going to say. ‘If you’re harvesting a lot of trees in one go for wholesale or something then you need the speed, and mainly, if any customers cut their own trees down with wonky cuts then you have to straighten them up before they leave, otherwise the tree won’t stand right in their house and they’ll blame you even though they did the wonky cut themselves.’

‘Oh, great. Problem customers.’ I hadn’t even thought about that aspect of the job. ‘There’s always one, isn’t there?’

‘Actually, there are usually two, just to make a really good job of ruining someone’s day.’

It makes me smile as Noel leaves me cutting and starts carrying the trees up to the waiting trailer and loading them in. I watch for a moment as he starts moving them, lifting the smaller ones with one hand around the trunk at the bottom, and rolling the larger ones up onto his shoulder to carry them up to the nearest tractor path. He moves them quickly but gently, stacking them into the trailer with care, looking like he's been doing it for most of his life. It makes me wonder again just how much he used to do for Mr Evergreene because there doesn't seem to be a thing he doesn't know about Christmas trees.

When I've cut some more down, I start loading too. I've already hauled a few dead trees – ones that I've been able to hack up with an axe and drag around because they can't get much more damaged when they're already dead – but this is my first time picking up a living Christmas tree that still has to be in a good enough condition to sell by the time I'm finished with it.

I go for one of the younger spruces and follow Noel's lead, one hand around the base of the trunk, one hand carefully around the slimmer width of the top, and lift it, expecting it to be much heavier than it actually is. I carry it up to the trailer and lean it against the side until the bigger trees are loaded in underneath the smaller ones to save them being crushed. After a couple more, I go for a bigger one, hoisting it up over my shoulder. I turn around and complete the classic cartoon character move of decapitating everything in a circle around me, spraying needles around as the tree crashes into several of the ones still standing.

Noel hooks one ankle over the other and leans against the trailer, not hiding the amusement on his face.

All right, I'm not an expert at it yet, and lifting the heavier tree has made me realise how much I'm aching from all sawing and carrying. I've used muscles I've never used before in my life, and every part of my upper body is hurting, from my wrists, forearms, and upper arms, to my shoulders, neck, and right the way down my chest.

'These are surprisingly easy to move,' I pant as I stagger towards

Noel, sweat dripping off my forehead again. All right, the larger ones are a bit on the heavy side, but I didn't mean that in a fully sarcastic way. It's easier than I imagined when I thought about what lugging trees around would be like. I look at the rows and rows of neatly sheared trees standing around me. Maybe I'll reconsider that after I've cut, carried, netted, and transported a few hundred more.

'That's because you've gained some muscles since you started here. Believe me, I can tell.'

I think my entire body flushes from my toes to the tips of my hair at the implication he's been looking.

'That wasn't supposed to sound anywhere near as pervy as it did.' His face colours too, and he rushes off to collect the last of the trees. 'Genuinely, Lee,' he says without looking up when he comes back and starts loading them into the trailer. 'You're better at this than I thought you'd be.'

My hands and arms are still shaky from the exertion of carrying. 'You're a good teacher.'

'Nah.' He blushes and looks away, intently concentrating on laying trees one on top of the other.

'You really don't like compliments, do you?'

'Shall we have a break for lunch?' He doesn't acknowledge the question, and I didn't expect him to. He never accepts a compliment but he gives them freely. 'There's something I want to show you, but it's right on the other side of the farm, we'll be hungry by the time we get there.'

I don't tell him that I'm famished now. All this tree cutting is hard work, and it's nearly midday. Even Noel's muffin and pumpkin spice latte haven't sustained me this long, but I still feel like I haven't seen every corner of Peppermint Branches, and he's by far the best tour guide I could've wished for.

He covers the trailer to prevent the trees drying out while I collect both the bow saws and put the protective covers back on the blades. We pull our gloves off, and he shrugs his rucksack onto his shoulders and holds his hand out to me. 'The ground might be uneven, and we've got to cross the stream.'

I'm quite capable of walking on uneven ground, and could easily cross the stream without assistance, but there's something about his tone that's so warm and his open hand looks inviting. Against my better judgement, I slip my hand into his and his fingers close around mine, making another little shiver go through me which has nothing to do with the unending drizzle that's been gradually soaking through my clothes all morning.

We walk carefully through the rows of Norway spruces and across the wide tractor lane between those and the Blue spruces, and the scent becomes sweeter. Noel's been talking about the different scents of each species, and I've always thought they all smelt the same, the generic pine smell of all disinfectants, but walking among them, stroking my fingers down different branches as we pass – I'm starting to notice each individual scent.

The stream weaves along a jagged line between the Blue spruces and the Balsam firs, much shallower here than at the spot where Gizmo tried to jump in the other day. Noel puts a foot on the crumbling bank and steps across the trickle of water, tightening his hold on my hand and then turning to offer me his other one too. I step across the water easily, and even though I don't need the support of either hand, I still don't let go as he pulls me up the bank on the opposite side.

'Does it ever get deeper than this?' I ask. 'The river that ran through the village where I grew up was always bursting its banks.'

'It fills up when we've had a bit of rain, but you know Scotland, we're usually treated to constant drizzle rather than heavy downpours. The banks could probably do with a bit of maintenance because they're crumbling away, but generally it's always been shallow enough no matter how much rain we've had. A river's not the best idea for a Christmas tree farm, but years ago, back when Evergreene's father was still running the place, the local council decided to put a main road through and had to re-route the river, and he was forced to let it run through his land. That's why it's sometimes not marked on maps.'

I nod, still surprised by how knowledgeable he is. He seems to know *everything* about this place, and every tree, plant, soil, moss, or type of weed. I learn something every time he speaks. 'Does it cause problems?'

'It would be a disaster if it flooded. The land slopes downhill, so you'd lose everything below it. And you wouldn't even know at first because trees can look like they've survived periods of stress, but months down the line, they'll chuck all their needles off and fall over, and only then do you realise that the roots drowned and they've been standing there gradually dying ever since. Even if they did survive, they'd be weakened and more susceptible to diseases and insect attacks.' He glances at me. 'But don't worry about it. It hasn't happened yet, and it's been decades since the re-route. If you're that concerned, you could get someone in to dig it out and reinforce the banks, line a load of sandbags along the side, but given the state of the farmland and the trees themselves, I think the river is the last of your problems.'

We leave the trickling stream behind us as we walk through rows and rows of imposing spruces of differing sizes, across another tractor lane. Eventually we get to the hedge that runs along the line where Peppermint Branches meets Roscoe Farm. He brushes a hand along it until he obviously feels some give, because he moves the branches aside. 'This is the spot. You go first.'

He holds the branches back and our hands drop so I can climb through the gap in the hedge, getting stabbed and prickled by only a few hundred holly thorns. Of all the things you voluntarily climb through, holly is *not* one of them.

'Welcome to my favourite place on the farm.' He clambers through after me and sets the hedge branches back into position.

'Wow.' I can't help the intake of breath as I look around. We're in a clearing surrounded by hedge, the ground under out feet is covered with lush green moss, and in the centre is a tree I'd seen on the horizon but hadn't realised was quite so close. A huge, gnarled old tree, with a trunk so thick it takes a few minutes to walk around its ginormous perimeter. The bare branches are twisted and curled together but there are still patches of greenery in them, the bark is silvery and flaky as it towers above us, so tall that I can't see the top from down here. If magic exists in the world, this is the kind of place it would be hiding, and I half-expect to see pixies sitting on toadstools and goblins chasing after gnomes as they dash out of sight.

I can feel Noel watching me as I look around in awe. 'The middle line of this clearing is exactly the spot where our farms meet. It's the only spot that doesn't have a fence, wall, hedge, or border between us. Half of this clearing is yours and half is mine.'

It feels like a magical little hideaway, far removed from the rest of the farm. I follow the invisible line he points out. If it was there, it would run directly through the centre of the tree, cutting it in half.

'Legend has it that a few hundred years ago, long before any of Evergreene's ancestors owned this land, a boy from this farm was in love with a girl from my farm, but their warring parents forbade anything from happening between them. They secretly met here one autumn, at the point where the properties connect, each bringing a piece of fruit from their respective farms, and both had chosen an apple. They swapped and ate by the light of the moon, and plunged the cores into the earth, where they grew combined, two seedlings sharing their lives to become one huge tree, the only form of togetherness the lovers could ever share.'

'Aww. You seem like the last person on the planet who'd believe romantic old fairytales like that.'

'I was just telling you the story behind it. I didn't say I believed it.'

'Yeah, but you do. I can tell.'

A grin lights up his face. 'It's a nice story. I think if you find a tree that's stood here for as many years as this one, it's got to have some history behind it. Why shouldn't it be a nice fairytale? Evergreene used to say that the apples were poisoned and they died out here, and the tree grew from the seeds in their stomachs when their corpses finally rotted into the earth.'

I laugh at the way his eyes light up. 'Now that's more like it.'

'But my dad always told me the nicer version, so that's what I'll stick with. Life is miserable enough without taking the joy out of fairytales too.' He walks over to the tree, dumps his rucksack on the ground, and sits down on the moss next to the trunk, his back against the aged bark. He looks up at me through his eyelashes and pats the ground beside him.

I don't hesitate to go and sit there, surprised to find the moss is dry underneath me, the deformed branches and patches of greenery above giving it protection from the drizzle. The trunk is so thick that two of us can easily sit against one side, and Noel wriggles back until he's leaning on it completely. He lets out a long sigh and tension drains from his body as he relaxes. His eyes drift closed and he inhales and exhales for a few long moments, and my eyes are drawn to him. The way he drops his head back to lean against the trunk, tiny droplets of drizzle coat his dark hair, and the straggly bits blow in the gentle wind, making my desire to tuck them back stronger than ever. I settle back against the trunk, the moss and bark combining to make a surprisingly comfortable seat, and try to follow his lead. I concentrate on my breathing, trying to keep it slow and steady despite the fact that now we're sitting so close, his aftershave has taken over my senses again. Even the damp green scent of the moss is not as strong as the spicy juniper and patchouli, and the temptation to press my nose into his neck is definitely one better left unexplored.

'Look up,' he murmurs.

I tilt my head back and from this angle, I can see that the

patches of greenery growing in the knotted old branches have elongated lined leaves with rounded ends and are covered in smooth white berries. 'Is this a mistletoe tree?'

'No. Mistletoe doesn't . . .' He shakes his head fondly. 'Oh, you have so much to learn. Mistletoe doesn't grow in trees of its own. It's a parasite that leeches off the nutrients of other trees. This big old thing hasn't got the energy to produce apples anymore, so the mistletoe grows in it instead. It's pretty rare in Scotland, but it's widespread further south.'

'Wow,' I mumble, stunned by his knowledge and feeling a bit fluttery at sitting in this beautiful place with this beautiful man who has somehow shared this with me. There's a sense of magic in the air, a feeling that fairies might flit past our toes at any moment, and I can tell how special this is to Noel.

'The ancient druids believed mistletoe grew from heaven because it doesn't have any roots.' He's so relaxed that his voice is almost slurring. His hands are limp in his lap, and I wish I could pluck up the courage to trail my fingers down his arm until my hand touches his, but I can't.

'Thank you for showing me this,' I whisper, because speaking normally will break whatever spell we're under and we're definitely under some kind of spell because there's no way I'm *really* contemplating holding his hand or that he'd contemplate letting me.

'It's half yours.' He shifts his head and looks over at me. 'And just so you know, the only other person I've brought here is Gizmo. Well, not person, canine. You know what I mean. Although to be fair, Gizmo's a better person than most of the humans I know.'

'Same,' I mumble, wondering why he *has* brought me here. Surely we both know what you're supposed to do under mistletoe . . .

'There's plenty of it if you want to cut some and sell fresh bunches this year.'

It takes me a moment to realise he's gone back to the mistletoe. 'I could use it in the wreaths too. It would look amazing twirled up with some red holly berries.'

'It's easy enough to propagate if you want a crop of it. You make a nick in the branches and press the seeds into it. It takes a couple of years to get established and then it takes off. It won't do well in the Christmas trees, but it will enjoy itself out front in your windbreaker trees, and it'll provide a point of interest from the road when all the leaves are gone in the winter and only the mistletoe remains.'

How much better would this place have looked on the first day if all those skeletal trees had been full of glossy mistletoe? Just the thought makes me smile. It would look like the entrance to a winter wonderland. 'It's perfect. I've never seen mistletoe growing before.'

He reaches over and lifts my hand to his mouth, touching his lips to the back of it. The cold metal of his piercing presses against my skin, at odds with the burning heat coming from his touch, and I let out a completely involuntary whimper that wasn't supposed to be audible.

'Sorry, just a peace offering to the ancient druids given what you're usually supposed to do under the mistletoe.'

I genuinely would not have minded *at all* if he'd done it in the traditional way.

Either he can tell what I'm thinking or he's thinking the same thing. 'I could sit here all day but we should eat.' He drops my hand and pulls himself upright, leaning over and tugging the backpack towards him. 'Hope you're not sick of pumpkin yet.'

I sit forward too and give myself a shake. ''Course not. But I'm going to get a bit worried if there are any apples in that picnic . . .'

He laughs as he starts unpacking the bag, setting out Tupperware containers and a flask along with packages of various things. 'Pumpkin biscuits sprinkled with sea-salted roasted pumpkin seeds, sliced local cheese with pumpkin dip on the side, and tea. Not pumpkin-flavoured.'

He hands me a paper bag containing a fresh loaf of pumpkin and hazelnut tear-off bread, which he knows is my favourite. He's been feeding me often, probably too often. No takeaways deliver this far out in the countryside, but I'm not even missing them because he usually pops over in the evenings with Gizmo and something Glenna's made.

It doesn't even seem weird to be having a picnic in November. It's cold, but my feet are warm in layers of fluffy socks inside my boots, and my coat is snuggly, and I think there's some sort of heat-by-osmosis science behind sitting so close to someone as hot as Noel. This beautiful big tree protects us from the drizzle, the moss is soft underneath us, and the world around us is peaceful as we eat in comfortable silence, smiling every time we look up and catch each other's eyes.

He leans back when he's done and I can feel the heaviness of his body as he relaxes against the tree trunk again. I expected him to jump up and carry on with cutting, but he's clearly happy to sit here a bit longer.

I settle back too. My hair is in a loose plait that's gradually fallen down over the course of the morning, and I can feel it catching on the peeling bark at my back. I lean forward and drag it over my shoulder. My hair is straight and super thick, it doesn't allow bands to hold it for long before they slip out and I'm used to having to put it back up multiple times a day.

I can feel his eyes on me as I pull the band off the bottom of the plait and fingercomb it, splaying it across my shoulder. Before I have a chance to get any further, his hand comes up and tangles in it, the backs of his fingers unintentionally brushing against my chest.

'Love your hair,' he says quietly, sounding completely entranced. He leans his head down to rest on my shoulder and his relaxation spreads through me as well, and I slouch against the tree with him leaning against me.

His fingers keep stroking through the lengths of my hair, and it's so weird, so innocent – he's completely unguarded and vulnerable. I've never seen him like this before.

'Love yours,' I find the courage to whisper back. It takes everything I have not to press my lips to his forehead. Instead, I tilt my head until it rests against his, and the only sound is the rustle of needles blowing in the breeze in the nearest Christmas trees.

I'm not sure if mutual hair compliments are the strangest thing I've ever done with a guy, but I'm definitely the most contented I've ever been, sitting here leaning against a tree to the back and a gorgeous Scotsman to the left, so relaxed it would be easy to fall asleep – unless that's just exhaustion from all the saw-wielding – and his fingers are still weaving themselves through my hair.

'Tell me about London,' I blurt out.

'Capital of England, UK's largest city, population of about eight million . . .'

'Ha ha.' I reach over and whack his thigh. 'I meant tell me about what happened to you there. You obviously hate the place.'

'I don't hate it.' He sighs. 'I hate the person I became there. It wasn't the city's fault, it was my own.'

I nudge his arm with my elbow where he's still leaning against me. 'You know you have to elaborate on that, right?'

Without moving his head from my shoulder, his eyes shift up and catch mine. 'Somehow I don't mind that with you.' He closes his eyes and settles his head until it's more comfortable. 'I was slowly killing myself there. I got a job straight out of university, and I drowned myself in it so I didn't have to think about the farm and the family I'd left behind. If I was there, working, I could pretend that my dad was still alive and well up here, and if I just didn't come back, it wouldn't be real.'

'What did you do there?'

'Investment banker.'

'*You*?' I say in surprise. I want to see his face so I can work out if he's joking or not, but nothing in the world could persuade me to dislodge the way we're leaning against each other. I settle for my voice rising to a pitch usually reserved for the dolphin species. '*You* were an investment banker? That's the furthest thing away from anything I can ever imagine you doing.'

'I think that's what attracted me to it in the first place. I wanted something that was a million miles from the farm I was supposed to take over after my dad died.'

The hand that's not tangled in my hair has gradually crept across his lap until it's resting against my thigh, and I find myself automatically rubbing my fingers over his palm as he talks, my nails catching on the grooves in his work-rough skin.

'I thought I had my life all under control, but looking back now, I can see I was a total mess. I was working literally every hour in the day. I was existing on energy drinks and scotch from bottles that cost more than my car that we used to impress clients and celebrate good deals. We had a lot of international clients and conference calls and Skype meetings had to be done on their time, so I was often in the office until three or four in the morning. I had the most incredible flat in Canary Wharf and I barely saw it. I'd get in and pass out facedown on the bed, come round a couple of hours later, take off yesterday's clothes and have a cold shower to wake myself up. Then I'd throw a couple of energy drinks down my throat and start all over again. The only thing I ate was maybe a salad if we had a meeting when a salad cart came round. I was a really horrible person. I was angry all the time, I yelled at people who didn't deserve it, I was grouchy, skinny, drunk, and so constantly exhausted that I couldn't think straight. No one in London ever saw me smile.'

I can't imagine him like that. He seems so strong, solid, and dependable. He's good-natured and fun to be around even when he's being grumpy. 'What made you come back?'

'Mum had a fall and needed help with the farm. She called me at work, and I was having a really bad day. I was in such a flap that I seriously thought the stress was going to kill me, and she said she'd fallen out in the fields and broken her hip and ankle. Evergreene had found her and got her to hospital, and was sending his workers over because she couldn't do the physical farm work while she recuperated. It hit me like a ton of bricks. I couldn't work out what the hell I was doing there, playing with money for people who *clearly* didn't need any more of it, and hating every second. I suddenly realised my mum was old, alone, and in need of help, and I hadn't been home in over ten years.'

'Is this where the girl you brought back comes in?'

He lets out a laugh. 'I'm glad to see Fergus and Fiona *don't* gossip about me at every chance they get.'

I can't help giggling too. 'They may have mentioned it. Once or twice.'

I'm too close to see him blush, but I can feel the heat emanating from his face. 'And yeah, there was a girl. I thought she was in love with me, and that I wasn't so closed off and cold that I was capable of loving someone too. With hindsight, I basically paid her to love me. I had money to spare because it was a well-paid job and I never had a chance to spend anything other than the rent. I hardly ever saw her because I was working so much and so bone-crushingly exhausted the rest of the time. I'd give her a call whenever I had an hour free, and then make the mistake of sitting down for a minute, and I'd be unconscious on the sofa by the time she arrived. I was handing her money to make up for it. It would be like, "You've come all this way and I can barely open my eyes. Pay for a cab home and here's a little extra to treat yourself to something nice because you've got such a crap boyfriend." Sometimes I'd have a Sunday afternoon out of the office and we'd go for a walk, but I *never* put my phone away. I'd constantly be online, watching the stock market, emailing clients, taking calls, and she'd be waiting for me outside a shop with a pretty dress in the window, and I'd feel so bad that I'd send her in to buy it and whatever else she wanted.'

'Fergus and Fiona said she took advantage of you.'

'Oh, to be a fly on the wall in that market.' He laughs again. 'Looking back now, I can see that I was an emotional wreck and it wasn't really love, but at the time, I was head-over-heels, and I could somehow convince myself I was normal because I had a girlfriend.'

My fingers rub the fleshy part at the base of his thumb. I love that he trusts me enough to open up, because I get the feeling it's not something he does very often.

'I don't know what I was thinking asking her to come back here with me. She thought it was a joke at first. I made the decision in an instant. Within five minutes of hanging up the phone to Mum, I'd put my resignation letter on my boss's desk and walked out. I hadn't shared any part of my life with her before then, she'd had no idea that I'd grown up on a farm or that my dad was dead, it came as quite a shock. And yes, I do *now* see how unhealthy the relationship was, but I thought we were in love. I knew I hadn't treated her right in London, and this was going to be a fresh start for us, a new life away from the distractions of the city. I thought that was what she wanted. I thought *I* was what she wanted.'

I move from stroking his palm to playing with his slack fingers, trying to be bold enough to slot mine between his and properly hold his hand.

'Once we got here, I changed instantly. The invisible weight I'd been struggling under lifted the moment we crossed the border into Scotland. I'd been running away for years. I'd always felt like I was trying to outrun something in London, a crushing steel fist of the grief I'd never acknowledged. Here, everything felt right for the first time in years. I slotted back in like I'd never been away, but all she wanted to do was go shopping. She didn't seem to realise that I wasn't earning the money I'd had before or that there wasn't a Harvey Nicks five minutes down the road. I kept trying to get her involved, but she hated every inch of it. It was like she was humouring me, waiting for me to come to my senses and go back to London. I see how it looked like she was taking advantage, but I felt like I'd ruined her life by bringing her here. I tried to make up for it by paying for treats and days out shopping and spa days, but the farm needed investment and what was left of what I'd earned in London had to go on that. When the money ran out, she realised that it was the only thing she'd ever liked about me and left. Turns out that everlasting true love is about as deep as the bottom of my bank balance.'

This time I do slot my fingers between his and his hand closes around mine. 'I'm sorry, Noel. That's horrible.'

He shrugs. 'The only surprising thing was how hurt I was. Somehow I never saw it coming. I'd fooled myself into thinking I was okay because someone loved me, and then I had to face the fact that I'd got so lost along the way that my bank balance was the only thing anyone could possibly like about me.'

I squeeze his hand so tightly that I'm sure I hear a few bones crick. 'Either you're seeing something that I'm not or you're very different now.'

I feel his face move against my shoulder as he grins. 'It was ten years ago. I've had a lot of time to straighten myself out. You know how people pay for therapists and stuff?'

I nod, my cheek moving against his hair.

'Trees are surprisingly good listeners and digging over fields is therapeutic work. Evergreene was ten years older than when I'd left, so was my mum, they both needed help, and it's good outdoor, fresh air, physical work. It helped. Also, Chihuahuas. Chihuahuas are good.'

I can't help chuckling at the sentiment. Gizmo would approve.

'Peppermint Branches is a strange place. You can hide from the world here, but at the same time, you can't escape the world here. There's a whole other life that exists only in our Elffield bubble, and you have no choice about being part of it.'

'Because if you back away, Fergus and Fiona will come along and ply you with gingerbread rhinoceroses and village gossip?'

His entire body shakes as he laughs.

'The weird part is that I understand what you mean, and in a strange way, I think it might be exactly what I need. I've definitely been hiding from the world.'

He looks up at me but I close my eyes and keep my head pressed against his to avoid eye contact.

'Maybe you need a different world,' he says eventually. 'I think when someone you love dies, it changes you. Not on the surface, but deep down inside, there's a part of you that will never be the same again. What you know doesn't "fit" anymore. I can't pretend to know how it feels to lose both parents in the way you did. I'd guess that you do whatever you have to do to get from one day to the next, and the only thing you have to cling onto is the hope that one day it will get better.'

I swallow around the lump that has suddenly leapt into my throat. 'You've got to stop being so nice, you're going to make me cry again in a minute.'

His fingers curl around mine and his grip on my hand tightens. I expect him to suddenly realise we're holding hands and do the abruptly jumping up thing, but he doesn't. 'Fiona happened to mention you'd been in a relationship with someone who didn't treat you right.'

'Oh, she did, did she? I never said that. Her and Fergus have put two and two together and got a mince pie there.'

'Have they?' He looks up, forcing me to catch his eyes. His tongue wets his lips, and I have never wanted to cup someone's face and kiss them so badly, no matter how impossible the angle. 'Go on, your turn. Tell me about you.'

I groan, even though I'm kind of touched that he wants to know, and honestly, I'd listen to a three-hour seminar on the history of waiting rooms if it meant we didn't have to move from this spot. 'I got into a thing with my boss. It wasn't even a relationship, not really, it was just nice to feel wanted again. It was nice to feel *anything* again, and he knew that. I was so lonely, and secret clandestine meetings with him gave me something in my life, no matter how pathetic. Everyone in the office knew what had happened to my parents and everyone treated me like I was fragile and liable to burst into tears at any moment.'

'Yeah, that's not like you at all.'

I snort even though he's teasing me, grateful for the unexpected giggle.

'No one knew what to say or how to act. If there was a joke in the office, no one would share it with me because people felt guilty for getting on with life, like treating me normally was somehow downplaying this monumentally awful thing that had happened. I felt like an outsider. Everyone was scared to talk to me because I was in a permanent state of being four seconds away from a complete emotional breakdown. I didn't want to be there, but I knew I needed to keep busy. A couple of months later, Steve transferred in as the new head of department, and with hindsight, I can see that he wormed his way into everyone's affections. He'd take everyone into his office individually and sit down for a cup of tea and a chat, and it seemed like a nice way of getting to know us, but looking back now, I can see that he was very cleverly finding out everything he could about everyone who worked there, their strengths and weaknesses, so he knew exactly what buttons to push when he needed to. He chose the women he knew were vulnerable. I can't believe I didn't see it at the time. He made each of us feel special and important, when all he really cared about was what he was going to get from us.'

'It's amazing how the most predatory men can spot the most emotionally vulnerable person in their vicinity and home in on them like a penis-driven missile, isn't it?'

Tears sting my eyes and I turn my head away, determined to

blink them back. Steve doesn't deserve any more tears.

'So, what happened?' he asks gently. I know he knows I'm trying not to cry and is keeping me talking as a distraction.

'Walked in on him shagging one of the other girls on his desk. Called him every name under the sun, poured hot coffee down his naked front, quit the job, vowed never to let a man take advantage of my weakness again, and sat crying in the stairwell for half an hour.'

'And then drowned your sorrows, had a tipsy peek at an auction for a Christmas tree farm, and the rest is history?'

I nod, quite impressed by how much he's paid attention to the throwaway comments I've made over the weeks we've known each other. 'It was exactly what I needed. Packing and getting ready to come up here took my mind off Steve. It stopped me feeling used, and stupid and weak, because I was taking back control of my life and doing something I never imagined I'd have the courage to do.' My voice is still shaky, but I realise the words are true as I say them. Buying Peppermint Branches empowered me. It gave me a chance to break the cycle of grief and guilt and move on with life on my own terms.

'Well, I'm glad you did. Come up here, that is.'

I look down at the dark head of hair which is still resting on my shoulder. 'I'm starting to think it might not be the *worst* mistake of my life.'

'Starting to?' He finally lifts his head and pushes himself upright, shifting around to face me as stray bits of hair fall across his face. 'And you say that before you've cut hundreds of Christmas trees, learned how to grade every single one with colour-coded ribbon, and sold enough to replant another few thousand in the spring.'

'What, that little job?' I say with a grin. 'Oh, that's eas—'

He kisses me. His hand slides along my jaw and cups my face as he draws me to him and presses his lips to mine. It's soft and gentle at first, just a chaste touch of lips on lips. I can feel the outline of his piercing against my skin and it makes me shiver in the most delicious way. I've been desperate to kiss him since the moment I caught sight of that silver ball glinting in his lip. My fingers come up and wind in his gorgeous hair and tug him closer and he takes the hint and kisses me harder, his thumb rubbing gently along my jaw, his stubble dragging against my chin. I let out a little moan of desire and he echoes it, and then he's gone.

He scrambles back onto his knees and runs a hand over his face. 'I'm so sorry. I think all those berries must've got to me. They probably release a mind-altering poison or something in such vast amounts. Hallucinogenic properties in those mistletoe berries, I'm telling you. It's the only explanation. Or maybe this moss has got some dodgy mushrooms growing in it.' He runs his fingers through the tufted greenery, looking for evidence.

He's right, of course. Well, maybe not about the mushrooms, but kissing him is the last thing I intended to do. If mistletoe berries aren't known for their psychedelic properties, then his aftershave might be.

He yanks the backpack over and starts clearing up the debris from our picnic, his fingers shaking so much that he keeps dropping things, his cheeks flaring so adorably red that I want to throw my arms around him, but I force myself to be sensible. I swore no men, only trees. Just because he's got a tattoo of a tree, it doesn't count.

'Well, you're supposed to kiss under a sprig of mistletoe, you certainly have to kiss when you find a whole tree of the stuff, don't you?' I say, desperate to ease the weird tension that's shot through the clearing. It's not like he did anything wrong because I wanted to kiss him too. But running a Christmas tree farm is complicated enough without adding Noel to the mix, and I can't make another mistake like I did with Steve.

'Aye. Wouldn't want to anger any ancient druids.'

It makes me giggle and he looks up and meets my eyes with a

grin that looks forced, but it does ease the atmosphere between us. It's just because we were both a bit raw and exposed after talking so openly. It didn't mean anything.

On the plus side, if there are any ancient druids looking down on us, we definitely made them blush.

Chapter 13

I open my eyes and groan when I see 01:03 blinking from my alarm clock on the cabinet. It's Thursday night, and we're taking the first of the cut Christmas trees to the market tomorrow, alongside the Christmas tree competition, which is being judged at lunchtime. Market traders and people from local businesses have been rushing around all week putting the finishing touches to their trees, and tomorrow is the day that local schools have arranged trips to the market so the children can pick their favourite tree. The winner will get the new town Christmas tree decorated with their winning design. The council came to collect the tallest Peppermint fir and have installed it on one of the hills between the market and the road, clearly visible from the busy dual carriageway. It's something a bit different when it comes to exposure and advertising, and most local businesses have jumped at the chance to get involved in the festive fun at the market, even if they don't win.

It's the right time to start stocking pre-cut trees on the stall. After all the cutting practice yesterday, today Noel and I left the farmhands shearing and weeding, and went to cut a selection of trees, brought them back to the barn, tagged them with species and size, and netted them with a big tunnel-type machine that

Evergreene had in one of the outbuildings. It's a metal contraption that you thread net around the edge of and pull the cut tree through by its trunk so it picks up the net on its way out, covering its branches and holding them in tight to make the tree stackable and easier for transporting. A pile of trees is waiting in the driveway to load into Noel's truck in the morning, a few of each variety – the Norway spruces, the Nordmann firs, the Blue spruces, the Balsams, and the Peppermint firs.

We didn't talk about the mistletoe kiss.

I'm *exhausted* after such a long day of cutting, hauling, heaving, pushing, pulling, and stacking. I never thought I'd be able to say that driving a tractor was the easiest part of my day, but with so much cutting practice, my tree stumps no longer look like they've been chewed off by a hyperactive beaver, and I've found bones in my shoulders that I didn't know existed before because every inch of them aches. I should be asleep by now, but the excitement of actually selling a tree tomorrow is keeping me awake. This will be the first time I find out if strangers think my trees are good enough to buy, and it's a scary prospect. In the past few weeks, I've worked harder than I ever have before in my life, but none of it will matter if no one buys.

After a few more minutes of tossing and turning, I give up and go downstairs for a cup of tea. Sleep is clearly not happening anytime soon. As I reach the bottom of the stairs, I hear a noise coming from outside. I stand inside the door and listen for a moment, just to be *absolutely* certain that it's not the growling of mountain lions, then I open the door and go down the three steps to the driveway.

It sounds like the whirr of an electric sander on wood. It's intermittent, like someone is stopping and starting again, and it's coming from somewhere behind the house. I go across the garden, past the caravan, and walk down the narrow path towards the patch of wasteland where nothing grows. On my side there's the barn and Evergreene's collection of stone outbuildings and tin sheds, and on Noel's side there's one huge barn and a couple of old stables that he uses for storage.

The main double doors at the front of the barn are closed, but the side door is cracked open and there's light spilling from under it, and I step over the short wall dividing the land to get a bit nearer.

When the sanding noise stops for a moment, there's the low hum of Christmas music coming from inside. I stand still and listen to the dulcet tones of Cliff Richard's 'Mistletoe and Wine' before the sander starts up again. It can only be Noel.

Somewhere in the trees, an owl is hooting persistently. He obviously appreciates Cliff's Christmas classic too.

I go to invite myself in, but a shiver makes me realise how cold I am. I didn't think to put a jacket on over my pyjamas, and it's freezing tonight, and I know that if Noel's got any heat in there, it'll only be the little heater he brought me on the first night. Instead of going straight in, I go back to the house and pull on the coat that's hanging by the door and wrap it around myself, freezing after only a few short minutes outside on such a cold night. In the kitchen, I make two large mugs of tea and grab a packet of biscuits. If he's outside working on a sub-zero night like this, you can guarantee he needs a cuppa and a chocolate digestive.

I'm purposely quiet as I carry the two mugs back to the barn, the packet of biscuits leaning precariously out of my jacket pocket as I slide the door open with my foot and freeze in shock.

Inside the barn, Gizmo is wearing a purple knitted hoody and sitting on the bench of a huge wooden sleigh while Noel sands the side. Neither of them have heard me come in above the noise of the sander, and it gives me a chance to look it over in awe. It's huge. Plain, unfinished wood, with a bench at the front easily big enough for two people, and another two benches facing each other in the back. There's metal glinting from the wide ski-like runners, and smoothly curved edges all around that make you want to run your hand over them. The barn is heavy with the scent of freshly sawn wood, and above the noise of the sander, I can hear a hint of Paul McCartney singing 'Mull of Kintyre'. I can't tear my eyes away from the sleigh. I can instantly imagine it painted red with gold edges and sparkly snowflakes, happy families sitting on the benches, drinking hot chocolate with their chosen Christmas tree propped up nearby. He must have built the whole thing from scratch . . . but why? Why is he making a sleigh?

I wait until he stops sanding the rounded side before I speak. 'Wow.'

Gizmo barks and jumps up, instantly diving off the bench and down the step from the sleigh to the floor. 'Hello, lovely,' I say as he rushes over, his tail wagging like a propeller. My hands are full so I balance on one leg and gently pet him with my foot.

When I look up, Noel's put the sander down and is pulling his gloves off. 'Sorry, I was trying to be quiet. I didn't mean to wake you.'

'You didn't.' There's a metal tool cabinet near the door so I put the teas and biscuits on that, and crouch down to give Gizmo a proper rub. When I stand back up, he dashes across to the sleigh, jumps up the step and back onto the bench, and I follow him for a closer look at the festive masterpiece.

Noel steps away while I walk around it, running my fingers over silky curves and edges carved into smooth swirls. The lines and knots in the wood make it look rustic and pretty, and beautiful in an imperfect way. 'How can you be so talented that you can *make* a sleigh?'

He picks up a mug of tea and hides his face behind it. 'I hope one of these was for me because I've just hijacked it if it wasn't.'

'You're allowed take a compliment, Noel.'

'I was making it for Evergreene. The wood is from his own fallen Christmas trees. I didn't get it completed before he died, but now it looks like you're staying, I thought you might like it instead. I've been out here for the past few nights to see if I can get it finished by December. It's really nothing.'

I look over the top of the sleigh at him but he just stands there breathing in the steam from the hot tea without looking up. Building a sleigh from scratch is *not* nothing.

'How did you know these were my favourite biscuits?' He opens the packet of biscuits and stuffs a whole one into his mouth.

I roll my eyes at his determination to never take a compliment. 'They're chocolate digestives – they're everyone's favourite biscuit.'

Gizmo is sitting in the sleigh with his nose twitching in the direction of said biscuits, so I reach over and rub his ears again and he turns into my hand. 'What are you two doing out here at this time of night when I know how early your start is?'

He checks his watch like he's got no idea what the time is. 'Well, it was much earlier when I started, and I've just carried on.'

I watch the way he's mainlining chocolate digestives like they're going out of fashion. 'Have you had anything to eat or drink?'

'No, that's why I love you.' Panic flashes across his face and he frantically nods to the tea and biscuits. 'For these, obviously. Not for anything else. I didn't mean . . .'

I blush almost as much as he is, but I don't know why I'm blushing. Obviously he didn't mean anything else by it. 'Can I get in?' I gesture to the sleigh to stop myself thinking about why either of us are blushing so fiercely.

'Of course. That's what it's designed for. If I can get it finished in time, I thought it would make a great place for the Santa you've hired to sit and meet kids, a cool backdrop for photographs taken with him. I know you were thinking of hiring a grotto, but I think it's too late in the year for that.'

I've managed to book a man to play Santa through an agency, and Glenna suggested either hiring a grotto or putting up a little shed myself, but I ran out of time to do either. And now he's made me a sleigh. 'Noel, this is . . .' I trail off as tears fill my eyes. This is *unreal*.

'Evergreene was intending to take on a herd of reindeer. There are a lot of concerns about reindeer being used for entertainment purposes now so it's probably not such a good idea, but if you ever wanted to keep horses in the future, it's light enough to be pulled by a working horse. You could offer sleigh rides around the farm in a real "one horse open sleigh".'

'God, that would be . . . magical.' I sit down beside Gizmo, who gets up and turns around, getting comfortable on his blanket until he's leaning against my thigh. I scritch along the line between brown and white patches on his head while Noel picks up both mugs of tea and somehow manages to snag what's left of the biscuit packet with his little finger and carry the whole lot across. He hands me my tea and flops down on the opposite side of Gizmo, leaning back against the bench and exhaling like it's the first time he's sat down in hours.

The song changes to Lady Antebellum's cover of 'Let It Snow' and he holds the biscuit packet out to me. I take one, and he takes another one and puts the packet down on his other side, out of Gizmo's reach. Gizmo thinks all food is meant for him and tries to clamber across Noel's lap to get to the biscuits. When that fails, he climbs up his chest and tries to take the digestive right out of his mouth, his tail wagging like it's the best game ever.

Noel's laughing as he turns away from him, clamping his lips shut and swallowing quickly. 'You can't have that, my love, it's got chocolate on it.'

Gizmo sits back down on his blanket with an annoyed huff. I've never seen a dog sulk before, but he may as well have folded his arms and stuck his bottom lip out. If he was a teenager, he'd have shouted 'it's not fair!' and flounced out with a door slam.

Noel laughs when he tries to stroke him and he huffs and turns away, and I nearly choke on my own biscuit when he looks at me beseechingly and stands up again, wagging his tail as he puts a tentative paw on my thigh like he can have a bit of mine instead.

'Giz, look.' Noel whistles Gizmo's tune from *Gremlins* to get his attention, and then digs around in his pocket. I watch the wide pointy Chihuahua ears go up and down at every movement of his fingers in the pocket of his slate-grey hoodie until he produces a tiny dog biscuit with a flourish and presents it to the little dog, who gets so excited about it that he nearly wags himself right off the bench.

He puts a paw on Noel's fingers and pulls his hand towards him, taking the biscuit delicately and crunching it up.

'Are you sure you're supposed to feed him after midnight?'

'What, because of *Gremlins*?' Noel laughs and when he looks up at me, there's something soft in his eyes that look closer to blue than green in the harsh light of the bare bulb above us. 'You're the only person I've ever met who loves that film as much as I do.'

'It's a Christmas classic. I used to watch it every year.' I reach over and give Gizmo's back a rub but he turns away from me, protecting his biscuit in case I want to steal it. 'They turn into little monsters if they eat after twelve.'

'Well, Giz is already a wee monster, aren't you?' He rubs the back of the dog's neck and the affection in his voice is palpable as he hands him a few more biscuits and Gizmo returns the look of love as he munches them happily.

When he's finished and checked us both over for signs of crumbs, he resigns himself to both his and our biscuits being gone and gets down from the sleigh to trot across the barn for a few laps from his water bowl. There's a soft-looking basket filled with cushions and he climbs into it, turns in a few circles and then curls up. Noel puts his mug down on the bench, takes the fleece blanket that was between us, and goes over to cover Gizmo up with it. 'He'll have to have a lie in tomorrow to make up for the late night. He'd stay in bed all day if he could.'

'I know the feeling,' I mutter.

'Oh, me too.' He groans as he stands upright again and walks back over to the sleigh.

'Don't you have too early a start to be up this late?'

'Yep, so do you.' He jumps into the sleigh and settles back against the bench again.

I can't help the nervous flitter at the thought. Or maybe it's how close he's sitting now that Gizmo's not between us, or maybe it's the fact that 'All I Want For Christmas Is You' comes on the radio and he's humming along under his breath without realising it, or how the scent of sawn wood mixes with the charred cinnamon of his aftershave, and the proximity makes it even sexier. I suddenly want nothing more than to rest my head on his shoulder and breathe him in.

'C'mere, you've got wood dust in your hair.' I have to swallow a few times before the words come out without a wobble in them.

Instead of getting up and shaking it out like I thought he might, he shifts closer and turns slightly to the left so I can reach the back of his head.

His hair is thick and full of volume, with straight bits that stick out before they hang down and thicker wavy bits that give it its length. It always looks the perfect mix between scruffy and styled, and the temptation is too much to resist.

I slide one hand into the dark strands and brush away the little patch of dust from the wood he's been sanding. It's only a few grains and it disappears easily enough, but running my fingers through his hair feels surprisingly nice. Even when the wood dust is long gone and I should stop, I keep doing it. He's cradling the mug of tea on his lap and he lifts it for another sip and his piercing clinks against the china, and if my fingers tighten in his hair, it's a completely involuntary reaction. His eyes drift shut and he breathes out slowly, putting the mug down on the bench beside him. One hand drifts across until the back of his knuckles is resting on my thigh, and I take it as a sign that he doesn't want me to stop yet.

I stroke his hair a bit harder, making it obvious that I'm

stroking it rather than brushing out wood dust that was gone at least five minutes ago, and he sinks down against the bench and lets out the most ridiculously sexy moan that sends a tingle right the way through me.

'What are you doing to me?' he mumbles under his breath, his voice sounding ragged. 'I don't know what's wrong with me. I keep losing myself around you, and it's so unlike me, but I don't want it to stop.'

I know exactly what he means. Everything is so easy with him, just being with him, spending time with him . . . When I'm close to him like this, when his walls aren't up and he lets himself go a little bit, it *is* easy to get lost in the moment, to believe that whatever *this* is . . . it's something that could be more.

His palm is facing up, open and inviting, and I let the index finger of the hand that's not in his hair trail across it. His fingers close around it, entwining with mine. It makes me smile, and when I risk a glance at his relaxed face, the same smile has crept across his mouth too.

I realise I'm sitting here smiling at him for no reason, which is probably weirder than having one hand tangled in his hair and the other held in his fingers, and no matter how much I try to tell myself how weird it is, I can't stop myself letting my fingers drift through his hair and shifting nearer to him every time he leans a bit heavier against me.

'We should get together and watch *Gremlins* sometime.' His voice sounds distant, like an ethereal whisper.

'You could always come over one evening. Bring Gizmo and some of those pumpkin spice popcorn kernels you've been selling at the market. I haven't seen it for a few years now and Gizmo makes me want to watch it again.'

He lets out a guttural groan of longing. 'That sounds perfect. On your twelve-inch CRT TV. In black and white.'

I stretch out the fingers that are linked with his and use them to whack his leg. 'It's not black and white.'

He lets out a low, contented laugh. 'How can you tell with all the lines and static you get?'

I nudge his leg with my knee. 'The TV isn't my priority. I need to read books about Christmas tree farming, not watch TV.'

'It's good you have books, but you can ask me anything. I'll always be happy to help, no matter what. It's nice to feel needed.' He rolls his head along the back of the bench until he's looking up at me and his hair flops over his face. 'Even if you only want me for my Christmas tree knowledge. I know when I'm being taken advantage of.'

I know he was taken advantage of before, no matter how much he blames himself for it, and there's something underneath his playful tone of voice, a hurt that still hasn't gone away, a silent plea that his knowledge isn't the only thing I want him for.

I disentangle my fingers from his and reach up to tuck his hair back from where it's fallen across his face. He lets out a breath and closes his eyes again, and my fingers go from tucking the same bit of hair back over and over again, to stroking across his earlobe, and trailing down the side of his face, my thumb brushing his stubble. I let the backs of my fingers dust across his cheeks, draw a line down his nose, my little finger tracing the outline of his lips, grazing across his piercing, and he shivers, but it's definitely not in a bad way.

His lips part as he lets out a breath, his tongue wetting them, shifting the piercing, making it press against the skin of my fingers as I dance them across the curve of his upper lip again and again.

'Please kiss me.' His voice is barely a breath. I feel the words against my skin rather than hear them. It's the most raw, vulnerable, unguarded thing anyone has ever said to me, and it makes my chest ache with longing.

I lean over and press my lips gently to his. My long hair falls across his face, surrounding him, and his hand comes up and tangles in it, pulling it back and using the grip on it to tug me closer as the kiss deepens. He sits up straighter and pulls me tighter against him without breaking the connection between us, urging me over until I'm straddling his lap, my knees pressing into the wooden bench on either side of his thighs. Both my hands are so tangled in his thick hair that I might never get them out, one of his is still holding my hair aside, the other is curled into my jacket like he can't hold on tight enough, his fingers rubbing my back where they touch, constantly pulling me closer than it's possible to get. I know my whimpers of pleasure are mixing with his moans as we kiss for what seems like ever.

I'm panting by the time we pull back, and he releases his hand from my hair so it falls in a messy curtain around us again, caging us in as I lean my forehead against his and we both try to get our breath back.

I untangle my hands from his hair, fully expecting to come away with a few handfuls given how tightly I've been holding it. I go back to stroking it gently, unwilling to remove my hands from him or move from where I'm still straddling his legs. His hands are running up and down my back, his fingers gentle but his wrists are pressing tight, holding me there.

'I bet a sleigh has never been used for this sort of thing before,' he murmurs.

'Oh, I don't know. Santa and Mrs Claus must have feelings too. Certain . . . desires . . . that they feel the urge to act upon. When the reindeer aren't looking.'

He lets out such a burst of laughter that it reverberates through me too. 'Ooh, yeah, can you imagine kissing Santa? I bet there are crusty bits of mince pie in his beard and sticky chunks of half-sucked candy cane . . .'

'You can't say that about Santa!' I kiss him again to shut him up. 'He smells of sugarplums and washes his beard with the sparkly tears of elves every day.'

'He probably bathes in reindeer droppings. That's why no one's ever seen him – because the stench makes everyone's eyes water so much that they're blinded whenever he approaches.'

You'd think it would be hard to laugh and kiss at the same time, but somehow we manage it, and when we pull back to pant for breath this time, I force myself to shift off his lap before this doesn't end at kissing. Even so, I *love* the noise of disappointment he makes, and the way his hand clamps onto my thigh, like he can somehow hold onto me for a little longer.

I sink down on the bench, the whole side of my body pressing against his, and he lifts an arm and drops it around me with a heavy thud, tugging me into his side. I drop my head onto his shoulder, feeling lighter than I have in months. Everything feels so *right* here, whether it's Noel or Peppermint Branches or Scotland in general, or just having a completely fresh start away from the rut I was in back in London.

'What are you thinking about?' he asks when we've both got our breath back.

'About fate. About the auction. About my mum and dad and you, and if there was some external influence driving me to win that auction because I was somehow supposed to come here.'

He presses a kiss to my forehead, which makes me melt so much that I nearly slide off the wooden bench. His arm tightens around me and his head dips down to rest against mine.

'I can't describe the fog of grief I've been living in for the past two years, and the way you talked about it, the way you normalised it and made me feel understood . . . Having someone that I'm not afraid to talk to makes so much difference. Everything feels different. I love it here. And I'd have run away that first night if you hadn't found me and made me stay.'

'Nah, you wouldn't. You had to stay just to prove how much of a twat I was on that first day.' He shifts his head and looks down at me. 'That was my plan all along, you know.'

I reach over and rub along the fraying seam of his butter-soft jeans that are so worn and faded they look like they could fall off at any moment. And *there's* a thought for another day.

'You gave me something back too, you know.' He reaches over with his other arm and lifts my hand, his fingers playing with mine.

'A second job that you don't get paid for?' I ask, because he's been helping me out *so* much.

'My heart.'

I try to look up at him but he doesn't budge so I can't make eye contact.

'I've been dead for ten years.'

I almost laugh at the deadpan tone in his voice. 'Well, you're looking remarkably good on it. Sexiest zombie I've ever seen. Do brains taste nice?'

He bursts out laughing again. 'See? I laugh now. I didn't laugh before. And I know people around here will tell you that I'm pleasant and friendly and I help them out where I can, but all of my interactions have been superficial. Every time I give them a smile, it's surface only, inside I've felt nothing. I always picture my heart as cold, dark, and hard, like a lump of coal, and the only thing that's made it glow again in the last few years was getting Gizmo, and then you came along and made me laugh about drunken trees and something lit up inside me.'

'When did you get him?' I ask, mainly to distract myself because the idea that I could make anyone's heart glow when I've felt so cold and detached for the past couple of years is making me feel so fluttery and overheated that I might actually be in danger of throwing up, passing out, or both. And that's really *not* the way to end this amazing night, with this amazing man who makes something inside of me glow too.

'I didn't get Gizmo, Gizmo got me. He picked me out as his new dad the moment we saw each other. Evergreene always donated a tree to the nearest animal shelter, and I went to deliver it. Walked into reception and one of the volunteers was about to take this little Chihuahua out for a walk. I had the tree over my shoulder so she stopped to let me through the door, and he ran over and put his paws up on my leg. It was love at first sight.' He's getting choked up as he speaks. 'I had *no* intention of getting a dog, and if I had then it would've been a working farm dog, not a toy handbag dog. I used to laugh at little dogs like him walking along the road in their jumpers and coats. But the moment I saw him, I dropped the tree and picked him up, and there was never a moment of doubt that he was coming home with me. I made the woman wait while I registered and reserved him and then went out for the walk with them, and honestly, I was in tears most of the way. It was this wave of emotion that I never thought I'd be capable of feeling again. That was seven years ago and he still makes my life better every day.'

There's something about a man who isn't afraid to admit how much he loves his dog that makes him seem like a genuinely good person. And completely irresistible. I squeeze his hand and move until I can get my lips somewhere near his, but I just end up smashing my mouth against the side of his face, halfway between his eye and ear.

He laughs and moves until we can kiss properly again. Time fades away to his mouth, the occasional extra sensation of the cold silver of his lip piercing, his stubble, his hands, how good he makes me feel, and I quickly realise we could sit here all night, completely lost in kissing, and we'll both regret it when the alarm goes off tomorrow morning.

It must come across in my body language because he pulls back with a reluctant noise. 'Why do I know what you're thinking?'

'Because you helped me stack all those trees on the driveway earlier and you know as well as I do that they've got to be loaded into the back of your truck at silly o'clock in the morning, and you've got a competition to win, and I care about you too much to not let you get any sleep tonight.'

He sinks back against the bench and lets out a groan. 'You think I can *sleep* after that?'

I giggle nervously because sleep is the last thing on my mind too. But given how much I want to straddle him again and pick up where we left off, I force myself to be the sensible adult that I supposedly am, and tear myself away. 'Come on. I can see how tired you are and it's well past two o'clock now. My alarm's set for five and I know you well enough to know that yours will be even earlier.'

He grunts as I disentangle our hands and place his gently back on his lap before I push myself upright and step out of the sleigh.

'I'm not sure if I love you more for making me feel like this or for taking care of me.' His head is still resting on the back of the bench, his eyes are closed and his voice is slurred and sleepy.

The empty mugs clang together as I gather them up, the noise making me jump as much as the words do. Obviously it's just a figure of speech. He doesn't love me at all, not for either reason. We've only known each other for a few weeks. I chew my lip as I stand there watching him, waiting for him to jump up and frantically backpedal, but he doesn't move.

He's too tired to have his defences up and it makes me smile to myself because Noel not constantly guarding himself and second-guessing his every word is as rare as a red banana.

I put the empty mugs back on the tool cupboard by the door and pick up the empty biscuit packet, loving that between us we've polished off the whole lot and thought nothing of it. There's nothing better than a man who can appreciate a good biscuit.

I crouch down to give Gizmo a head scruffle because he's heard the clang and is watching me move around the barn from the comfort of his warm basket. I go over and stand on the right-hand side of the sleigh and lean over to push Noel's thigh. 'Come on, you. You're asleep already. Do I need to take you home and tuck you into bed?'

His eyes shoot open and he blinks in the light from the barn's single bare bulb. 'That shouldn't be such a sexy prospect.' He gets to his feet and jumps down the step onto solid ground, and runs a hand over the edge he was sanding when I came in. 'This was supposed to be a surprise. Sorry I woke you and made you come out here and see it early.'

'Well, I'm glad I did, because otherwise you'd *still* be working on it, hungry and dehydrated, and you'd be exhausted in the morning.' I step closer to him and bump my shoulder against his upper arm. 'And you're making me a *sleigh*, Noel. That's . . .' There are no suitable words for how amazing that is or how touched I am. 'That's unfathomable. I can't imagine how anyone could make this. You are so incredibly talented, and—'

He wraps both arms around me and pulls me tight against his chest. His grey hoodie is open and the black cable-knit jumper underneath is soft against my skin and smells of fabric conditioner and wood dust. His chest is wide and strong and as solid as it's always looked. It should be illegal to be this gorgeous, warm, funny, and kind-hearted to boot.

'You'd even hug me to get out of hearing a compliment,' I say into his chest.

'I can stop if you're complaining,' he murmurs against my hair, not sounding like he has any intention of stopping.

I wrap my arms around him and squeeze him too, just in case he has any doubts about how I'd happily stand here hugging him for the rest of the week.

Without breaking the hug, he starts carefully manoeuvring us towards the door, one step at a time, until his leg bumps against the tool cabinet and knocks the mugs together again.

He turns his head to the side and calls, 'Giz, bedtime!' I look over my shoulder to see Gizmo give him a doggy glare, huff, and then reluctantly step out of his basket and have a lazy stretch like he's got all the time in the world.

Noel turns us again, and I can feel him fumbling for the door, but we stumble and it swings open under our weight, and we fall out of it and into . . . snow.

'Well, that woke me up.' He's trying to sound grumpy but his eyes are bright as he looks around.

I push myself up from where I've landed on top of him and get to my feet. 'It's snowing!'

He sits up on the quickly whitening grass and looks at me, a smile playing around his lips. 'You act like you've never seen snow before.'

'I lived in the centre of London, Noel. It's a rare sight. We don't even get it when the rest of the UK does.' I reach out my hand and haul him up. 'I knew there'd be snow here!'

'Well, this is Scotland, we do get snow.'

'Oh, stop trying to be grumpy. It's the first snow on a Christmas tree farm. Anyone would be excited.' My feet crunch into the thin layer of freshly fallen white stuff covering the short grass outside the barn, and the few pumpkins that remain on the vines in Noel's fields are stark orange against their white carpets and the increasing white hats atop their green leaves.

I skip around him, kicking up what little snow has settled so it looks like he's standing in a summoning circle before I turn my head to the sky and stick my tongue out, trying to catch a few snowflakes.

'How could anyone be grumpy around you?' he murmurs, and the affection in his voice makes me stop and look at him. He shakes himself. 'Apart from Gizmo, obviously. He hates getting his feet cold.'

We both look over at the barn, where Gizmo is sitting in the doorway shivering, looking between us and then longingly back at his basket. The expression on his face leaves no doubt that he thinks we're a pair of complete lunatics.

I hear Noel move behind me, and I really should have realised what he's doing, but I don't until a snowball hits me in the back.

I squeal in surprise. 'You didn't!'

His eyes are watering with laughter and I immediately start scraping snow up to make my own, lobbing it at him and giggling when he ducks easily. I grab another handful and throw that one in his general direction and miss, until he stands still, letting me get a hit in, and laughing harder as it *still* sails past him. He's laughing so hard he almost can't see to gather another handful of snow, compacting it properly into a ball and holding it up, giving me a chance to prepare myself, and this time, I manage to duck at the right moment and it hits the side of the barn, breaking apart and sending snow scattering in all directions. Some of it lands near Gizmo's feet, and he looks at it disdainfully and plods back inside to the safety of his cosy basket.

The snow has barely started and there's not enough for a snowball fight – we've already exhausted our supply and fighting with Noel is nowhere near as appealing as hugging him again. I reach up to brush snowflakes out of his hair and he scrubs a hand over his face. 'You must've put something in that tea. That's the only explanation for any of this.'

'Or there's another patch of those dodgy mushrooms around here somewhere?'

'Aye, exactly!'

'You keep telling yourself that.'

Both of our hands are cold and wet, but when he reaches out to take mine, the sensation starts to come back into my fingers, numb from the snow. He leans down and presses his lips to my cheek, his nose icy cold where it touches my skin, his lips like a burning hot brand in the best way possible. 'Nothing I tell myself makes any sense when I'm with you.'

I know the feeling. I watch as he goes back into the barn and picks the whole dog basket up, including Gizmo, and carries it under one arm, his other hand holding Giz secure. 'Goodnight, Lee. See you in the morning. Bright and early.'

I smile at the throwback to one of my first days here, even though 'bright and early' doesn't seem to be a specific time with Noel, and I have a feeling that tomorrow will be even brighter and earlier than usual.

He nods a goodbye and I watch as he crunches his way back through the undisturbed snow of the pumpkin field, growing thicker by the second as large flakes fall down. I look up at the black sky and twirl around a few times.

This is nothing like what I expected when I won that auction – it's a million times better.

Chapter 14

By the time I get myself up and dressed the next morning, Noel is already outside in the dark with his truck, slinging trees into the back of it like they weigh nothing, and whistling 'Rockin' Around the Christmas Tree'.

'How can you be so ridiculously chirpy?' I can't help smiling at the sight of him as I open the door and walk down the steps.

He's obviously had a shower and changed because his hair is still wet. He's wearing black cargo trousers and a navy long-sleeved top with a blue and grey flannel shirt over it, the puffy bodywarmer over the top of that, and knitted fingerless gloves. It's not right that anyone can look this good at five-thirty in the morning.

He stops in the middle of picking up another tree when I get close to him and looks up to grin at me. 'I'm chirpy because I get to do this.'

In one swift move, he slides his arms around me, lifts me up and sits me on the bed of his truck, then stands on his tiptoes and presses his lips against mine.

'It's way too early for that sort of display,' I murmur against his mouth, holding onto his shoulder for support.

Even so, it's nice to be taller than him for once, and I slide my arms over his shoulders and cross my hands behind his neck, my fingers automatically winding in his dark hair as he kisses me again. As usual when his lips are involved, I lose track of time, but when we pull back, the sky looks lighter and birds have started chirping their morning chorus.

I tighten the loop of my arms around his neck and rest my forehead against his because I don't want to lose this yet even though I know we need to get going.

'Are we going to keep this to ourselves?' I whisper. 'It's just that I like Fiona and I suspect she might burst if she finds out, and I'd quite like her to *not* burst.'

He laughs, panting for breath, and I try not to think about the fact that he can chop down and lug around a few hundred Christmas trees without breaking a sweat, but kissing me makes him pant.

'Are you kidding? It's our duty to avert the mild coronary event that will occur if she finds out. Besides, you're my wee secret and I want you all . . . to . . . myself.' He punctuates every word with a brief kiss, and I can feel the butterflies in my belly taking flight again because being 'his' anything is all right by me.

I pull back and smooth his hair down where I've had my hand tangled in it, and he closes his eyes and actually looks like his knees are going to buckle for a moment. 'As much as I hate being the sensible adult – you've got to stop doing that or we're going to be late on the one day that we *really* need to be early.'

His arms slide around my waist and he lifts me down, setting me safely back on the snowy ground. 'Breakfast and coffee's in the front. I'll finish loading.'

I gratefully retrieve the travel cup of pumpkin spice latte and stand in the open passenger door while I watch him shake his hair out and tie it up, his bicep muscles straining against his shirtsleeves as his hands move behind his head. More paint flakes off as my hands tighten involuntarily on the truck door, and I know he knows the affect that has on me and he's doing it on purpose. And I really don't mind.

When I've had enough sips of caffeine to feel like a functioning human again, I put the cup down and go over to the small pile of Norway spruces that he hasn't already loaded, pick one up, and follow his footsteps through the snow to heft it up onto the bed of the truck. It's surprising how quickly you get used to handling trees, but with all the cutting practice, pulling them through the netting machine, shearing, and everything else, it's hard to remember a time when I *wasn't* flinging around Christmas trees.

He jumps up onto the bed of the truck and lets me pass the trees up to him while he stacks them safely.

The snow has stopped for the moment, although it carried on falling for a long while after we went to bed judging by the depth of the drifts around the side of the house and along the grassy verges of the road. Footprints and tyre tracks where Noel's reversed in are all that's visible of the driveway. Even the few pumpkins left in his fields are lost under a blanket of white.

'Did you sleep okay?' I ask as I hoist the last tree up to him and he jumps out of the truck and closes the tailgate.

He makes an incomprehensible grunting noise, jangles the keys out of his pocket and walks around the side towards the driver's door, then he stops and comes back. 'I don't know why I said that. I slept better than I have in months because of how you made me feel.' Even in the dark morning, I can see his cheeks are burning red. 'Sorry, I don't know why I said that either. I'm delirious from spruce needle inhalation. Come on, we should go. Fergus has promised gingerbread trees to mark the occasion, which will probably be the most normal thing he's baked all year. Of course, knowing him, they'll be pink dragonfruit trees.'

He's in the truck before I can even blink, with the engine revving and the exhaust pipe puffing warm fumes out into the cold morning air. I sigh and walk around to the passenger's side.

When I get in, his hand is on the gear stick ready to move, and I cover it with mine, stopping him. I reach across, slide my hand up his jaw and deliberately pull his face down and press my lips to his cheek. I don't say anything, because he obviously doesn't want to talk about it, but I see him doing what I've done every day before work for the past two years – you gather yourself, steel yourself, prepare yourself to face the day while outrunning the wave of emotion inside you. You prevent yourself from *feeling* anything in case something as mundane as the bus driver asking you for your ticket is enough to set off a complete emotional breakdown. You live in constant fear of crying in front of someone. Of letting someone see your weakness and somehow use it against you.

I pull away to shift back across the bench seat and busy myself with putting my seatbelt on. His hand leaves the stick and slides across until it touches my thigh. He squeezes gently. 'Thank you.' His voice catches and he shakes himself, yanking his hand back and pulling out of the driveway with a sharp jolt.

And I smile to myself because I think I understand him a bit more than he thinks I do.

***

Even before six in the morning, the market is buzzing. It's busier today than any other time I've been here. I've noticed a huge increase in customers recently, and there are more traders too – stalls that have been reserved but empty until now are starting to open up, selling Christmas decorations, handmade gifts and cards, and traditional festive food from different countries.

Today, there are cars and vans parked all the way along the country lanes that take us into Elffield, and the main road to the market is choc-a-block with people parked up on either side. Noel performs some impressive driving manoeuvres to squeeze past.

The market looks amazing in the dark. Everyone who works there has clubbed together and bought numerous decorations for the building, and Noel and the others have put in a good few hours of stapling up lights and garlands. The pillars on either side of the main entrance are wrapped with twinkling fairy-lights, the trees that Fiona requested for the outside are against the walls, laden with multicoloured baubles and sparkling lights. The sparkling continues along each edge of the building and up to the roof. Inside, through the open entranceway, the welcoming main lights of the market give us a glimpse of the Peppermint fir – an impressively symmetrical seven-foot tall specimen that Noel selected as the best – currently standing in the centre of the market, decorated with input and help from all the traders.

Noel made up a gorgeous double-sided chalkboard sign, with 'Peppermint Branches' written in big, swirling letters with holly leaf swashes, directing people to the tree stall on one side and advertising the opening next weekend on the other side, and I've been reassured by the fact that the tree has elicited a gasp of admiration from everyone who's seen it so far.

Noel knocks his knee into mine. 'Doesn't it look amazing?'

'Mmm.' My knuckles have turned white where they're gripping the door as Noel skirts the truck around yet another van parked on a diagonal outside the post office.

'I'm not that bad a driver, am I?' he asks, thankfully without taking his eyes off the road.

'No. I just think this truck is so old that if you knock it even slightly, it will disintegrate around us.'

There's no way he should be laughing that hard while trying to navigate this crowded street.

'They came!' I forget all about road safety when my eyes fall on a group of vans and cars parked near the entrance of the market, and one of the vans has the local news channel logo emblazoned across the side of it.

'Local news?' Noel asks.

'Hopefully more than just them. Chelsea's boss is in media law so I asked her to get in touch with some of their contacts, but I didn't expect it to lead anywhere, and I've been emailing and tweeting every news site I could think of to tell them about trying to save the market and asking if they'd cover the competition. I didn't get any confirmation, I was just hoping they'd turn up.' My hand suddenly flies to my head in horror, where my hair is tied in a loose knot on top. 'Why didn't I at least use a mirror to put my hair up this morning?'

He laughs. 'You could use a porcupine to brush it, it would still look gorgeous.'

It makes me laugh and blush at the same time. He never takes compliments but there's something about the way he gives them that seems so genuine. I've always thought people only flatter you because they want something, but there's something about the way he speaks that makes him impossible not to believe. I just wish I could get him to take a compliment once in a while too.

Thankfully, once we turn the corner behind the market, the trade entrance is clear of cars because the florist is outside in a hi-vis jacket stopping anyone who tries to park there. He waves us through the side entrance, giving us a thumbs up, the delight clear on his face. Most of the stalls are already set up as we edge through the buzzing lanes of Elffield market, and workers from the various businesses are crowded around their respective trees, making last-minute adjustments. Even Fiona is looking more colourful than usual as she sits on a stool next to Fergus, and they're having a giggly conversation which involves lots of good body language. He keeps reaching over to touch her leg, her foot is hooked over her knee towards him and she keeps twirling a lock of lilac hair, and if they lean any closer to each other, they're likely to crash together and fall off their stools.

'Adorable, aren't they?' Noel says as he pulls up at the pumpkin stall and we sit and watch them in silence for a minute.

A minute is all we get before Fiona sees us and gets so excited that she spills her coffee, leaving Fergus to clean it up as she rushes over to the truck.

She's waiting at the door before Noel's even got it open. She takes his arm and drags him around to my side as I slam the door behind me, where she practically throws us together and embraces us both at the same time.

'Good morning to you too, Fiona,' he says, the tone of confusion in his voice making me giggle.

'I know why you two are late!' She squeals at a pitch that I haven't heard since that time my grandfather sat on his hearing aid when I was little.

'We're much earlier than usual,' he protests.

'Traffic,' I say.

'Kissing!' She chirps so loudly that several people nearby stop what they're doing and look at us.

Noel chokes and extracts himself from the hug. 'I assure you the only creature I've kissed lately is Gizmo. Who, admittedly, *is* a very good kisser. It's only when he starts using tongue that you run into problems.' He meets my eyes over the top of Fiona's head and winks at me, and it doesn't help the giggling situation.

'And on that note, I'm going to start unloading seeing as we're *so* late.' Noel pats her shoulder and excuses himself, giving Fergus a wave as he walks round to the back of the truck.

'I should help,' I start but Fiona stops me.

She beckons me nearer like she wants to whisper something. 'You have stubble rash.'

My hand flies to my face in a panic. Is she serious? I know I kissed him a *lot* last night, but I've never had stubble rash in my life. No wonder she knows there's something going on between us. Why didn't I look in the mirror this morning? It doesn't feel sore or raised, but I rub my fingers over my chin worriedly, and she produces a handheld mirror from her pocket and hands it to me.

I open it gratefully and turn it this way and that, tilting my chin towards both the normal side and the magnifying side. There's nothing there. 'I don't have stubble rash.'

'Ah, but you wouldn't have even questioned it unless you'd been doing something that might've *given* you stubble rash.' She beams as she whisks her mirror back out of my hand, looking extremely pleased with herself.

'People your age are supposed to be above such sorcery,' I say, even though I'm kind of impressed by her innovativeness in her quest to get us to admit to something we *might* not have done.

'You don't get stubble rash from kissing Chihuahuas,' Noel says as he walks past with a tree over his shoulder. 'I've just heard there's a bath pearl gone wonky on your tree, Fiona, you should go and double-check it before the kids get here.'

She falls for it and rushes off even though the schoolchildren who are judging won't be here for hours yet, and I thank him for rescuing me.

He laughs. 'I don't know how she knows, but she knows. She'll try to catch you out again, believe me. I was late one morning last year, and she's *still* trying to get me to admit where I really was, even though it was nothing more interesting than oversleeping.' He holds his hand out to help me up into the truck bed. 'C'mon, make sure you're busy before she comes back. You can pass me trees and pumpkins down and I'll get the stall set up.'

In the bed of his truck, there are still a couple of crates of pumpkins – although they're culinary pumpkins rather than ones for carving now – and a few crates full of Glenna's goodies. She's really gone overboard in preparation for the extra customers the competition will bring in today. Apart from trees, I've got some bunches of mistletoe and a few wreaths I've made from the branches of unsellable Christmas trees, fronds of fern, with twists of mistletoe, pine cones, and holly leaves and berries.

I hand him down the crates of pumpkins first, followed by Glenna's goodies, and then haul trees over the side one by one, absolutely *not* appreciating the sight of his arms as he shoulders two at a time and makes it look easy when he leans them against the stall in neat piles organised by species.

We've also got one of each species to decorate for display, not for sale but to attract customers like the carved pumpkins he displays in Halloween season. I jump down from the truck to set them up in stands and give them some water, while Noel carries on arranging the table full of Glenna's pumpkin muffins, pumpkin loaves sprinkled with rosemary, jars of pumpkin jam, marmalade, and pumpkin spice mix for lattes.

We're going for a peppermint decoration theme, and while he's still stringing red and white peppermint-striped tinsel and strings of red and white lights around my display trees, I have an idea for the finishing touch to his competition entry before all the local schools arrive on a multi-school trip for the judging at lunchtime. I grab a pumpkin carving kit, help myself to a bag from his belt and load six small pumpkins into it, aware of Noel's curious eyes on me along with Fergus's watchful gaze.

The trees for the competition are spread throughout the market. Noel's stands in a corner between the bookseller and the baker, and I really think it's got the magical fairytale quality to appeal to kids. He and Glenna have gone with the Cinderella theme; the tree is laden with glass slipper ornaments and sparkly pumpkins, and surrounded by a horse-drawn glittered glass carriage running around the base of the tree like a model railway. Instead of a star on top, there's a knitted fairy godmother, complete with magic wand, sitting on a wooden sign that reads 'you shall go to the ball'. The fairylights give out a warm orange glow, the tinsel is white with iridescent orange bits which catch the twinkling lights and make it look like it's moving, and the knitted bunting is wrapped around the tree with glittery green leaves and tiny pumpkins dangling from it. If I had a vote, it would be my winning tree. Not that I'm biased or anything, but it's a truly special tree, and it stands out from the others in the market because of Noel's creativity and attention to detail. It's an immersive experience to stand and look at the Roscoe Farm tree – something that makes you feel festive and simultaneously like you're standing in the middle of a pumpkin field where a fairy godmother could pop out at any moment.

A lot of the businesses have simply decorated with baubles made from their own logos. Some have gone for the excessive fairylight approach – if you can see it from Jupiter, it must be a winner. Some have been a bit more creative, like the way Fiona's tree is decorated with strings of bath pearls, mini bath bombs hanging up like baubles, and tiny festive soaps tied to the end of each branch, the amazing scent being her crowning glory. Fergus has put so much effort into helping Fiona with hers that his biscuit-themed tree looks a little lacklustre in comparison, decorated with lots of lights, tinsel and hanging gingerbread depictions of every festive thing you could ever imagine, from nutcrackers, sleighs, Santa's boots, and brightly-iced presents, to every conceivable character in the nativity scene, including the donkey, the cattle, the inn keeper, various shepherds and their sheep, some fleas that were probably on the sheep, some of the earthworms that might've been living in the grass, and a gingerbread recreation of Mr Bean on the theory that *everyone* watches *Merry Christmas, Mr Bean* at least once a year.

I kneel down in front of the green fluffy blanket that Glenna put in to hide the tree stand and start cutting lids in the top of each pumpkin and scooping the guts into the empty carrier bag, enjoying the quiet in this little corner as I watch the market waking up for what everyone knows will be an important day. There's even someone wandering around playing Christmas tunes on the bagpipes today.

I love how easygoing things are here. Everyone trusts their neighbours to look after their stall when they need to pop out for a few minutes. The used bookseller has already learnt that I love reading romantic comedies and started putting them aside for me when he gets them in. The baker brings a fresh loaf of bread over whenever he sees me. If the flower seller has an influx of bouquets, he brings one over to decorate the stall. Noel does the same with Glenna's goodies, like Fergus freely hands out gingerbread teacups and Fiona makes mini bath bombs solely to give away to her friends. I've already resolved to make everyone a wreath before Christmas. Everyone is helpful and friendly here, and the whole atmosphere is laidback in a way I've never known before.

I love this market and I don't want anything to happen to it. Elffield will have nothing without it. If Noel is right about the bus interchange, the whole place simply won't exist. And that's unthinkable.

The Christmas tree competition has helped, I know that. The rental fees that local businesses have paid for their trees to be here until January has given the market a much-needed cash boost. There's been an increase in customers, and there's a buzz around the place. The trees have been gradually decorated over the past few weeks, and excited children have been following their parents around and ooh-ing and ahh-ing over them. The incentives to shop at other stalls in the market have paid off too, people have been gladly handing in their coupons. I heard a customer say to Fiona the other day that she'd bought a candle and a bath bomb giftbox through the partnership with the candlemaker, and how pleased she was that her whole gift was sorted so easily and that she was going to tell all her colleagues to come here for their Secret Santa gifts. Sales are up for everybody. Stalls that were quiet and half empty of goods last month are full and bustling with customers again. A tourist bus came last week and dropped off a hundred tourists and picked them up two hours later, laden down with bags, and Fergus assured me that this is a bi-weekly occurrence as it gets closer to Christmas.

I slice a Christmas tree shape out of each pumpkin in turn,

pop in an electric tealight and arrange them so they form a path up to the Christmas tree. Noel's always saying he needs a way to make pumpkin season last longer, and if this takes off, the whole town could be lighting their roads and driveways with pumpkins to illuminate the way for Santa. But he needs more than a slight extension to pumpkin popularity. Everyone on this market needs more than a good Christmas season – we need a good year.

When I get back to the stall, Noel is exchanging money for one of the Christmas trees, having already sold a few from the stacks, and some wreaths. 'You didn't have to do that.'

'*You* didn't have to do *that*.' I nod to the retreating figure of a man carrying one of the small Christmas trees. 'I couldn't have done any of this without you, Noel. I'd probably still be sitting outside the house crying in the car. You *deserve* to win this competition because I want someone other than me to appreciate how creative and talented you are, and before you shrug that off, just shut up and take a compliment.'

He bends down and whispers in my ear. 'Do you have any idea how much you're making me want to kiss you?' He presses his mouth closer so his lips brush my earlobe. 'And I can't because Fergus is watching, but I think it's only fair that you know how much I want to.'

My knees definitely feel weaker than they should. 'You pretend to be all sweet and charming but you know exactly what you're doing, don't you?'

He pulls back and grins at me. 'If you look over at the biscuit stall now, Fergus is desperate to tell Fiona about this. He's fizzing so much that it looks like he's just *eaten* a bath bomb. If I did what I *want* to do right now, we'd be calling an ambulance for the pair of them.'

Thankfully someone else comes over to ask if we've got any smaller versions of the tree in the entrance, and Noel slips smoothly into his well-practised chatter about Peppermint firs and the benefits of them, showing off our three-foot and four-foot tall specimens, but the man doesn't need any persuasion as he hands over the money and walks away with a three-footer.

***

By the time of the judging, the supply of trees is seriously diminished and so is my pile of business cards because I've been handing them out all morning due to the amount of enquiries we've had about when we open. Noel's been in and out all morning, carrying the purchased trees to cars, taking addresses for delivery later, and generally being charming and so knowledgeable when talking about Christmas trees that customers start to glaze over and agree to buy anything he suggests. Every inch of me wants to throw my arms around him and smother his gorgeous face in kisses because he makes every aspect of my life seem brighter. I still can't believe how many Christmas trees we've sold. Noel suggested bringing more and I said no, envisioning piles of unwanted trees dying where they stand because it's barely the last week of November and I thought it might still be too early, and now I'm wishing I'd taken his advice. The Peppermint firs have already sold out, there's one lonely-looking Blue spruce and a couple of Nordmann firs left, and that's it. The mistletoe bunches are long gone and the wreaths sold out within the first hour. People have even asked if they can buy the decorated display trees as they are, to which Noel has smoothly responded by handing them a business card and telling them we might have some leftover peppermint-themed tinsel at the farm and to pop by when it opens next weekend.

It's lunchtime when a majority of the schoolchildren in Aberdeenshire are herded into some form of order by their teachers at the front of the market, ballot papers and pencils clutched in little hands as every child marks their favourite tree and posts their paper into a red postbox usually reserved for letters to Santa. Their laughter and chatter reaches every corner of the market, and the exhilaration is clear to see on their faces.

It's weird to be involved but not involved at all. There was no point in me doing a Christmas-tree-themed Christmas tree, but I want Noel to win so badly that I'm as invested as anyone else with a tree in the race, and we're surrounded by other market traders who have rented their own trees and representatives from the businesses who have got involved, staying to watch the progress of the judging.

A local car dealership who have decorated their tree with silver tinsel, hanging car air fresheners, and keyrings bearing the logos of well-known car brands. A takeaway delivery company whose tree is adorned with metallic baubles of pizza, fries, and hot dogs. A DIY shop whose decorations are samples of custom-mixed paint cards in a rainbow of colours. A second-hand furniture shop from one of the nearby industrial estates have made chairs, tables, and sofas out of miniature clothes pegs and strung their tree with bunting bearing the shop's logo. A seafood restaurant from the nearest big town who have gone for a lobster and crab theme, and a pet supplies shop whose tree is laden with garlands of plaited dog leads and their branches are hung with metallic collar ID discs, engraved with the names of people's own pets that they asked locals to put forward in the store. The bookseller's tree is covered in free bookmarks with a sign up saying 'help yourself' and strung with paperchains of well-known book quotes, the flower seller has tied poinsettias on to every branch of his tree, and the Scottish souvenir seller has hung up lots of flags and mini nutcrackers wearing kilts and playing bagpipes.

All the stalls are temporarily shut while the votes are counted. An audience of customers stand around waiting. Children, teachers, parents who have accompanied the schools, parents who have popped down anyway to watch their children having the festive equivalent of a day in parliament, making a decision that you'd think was equally vital. Teachers have obviously played up the importance of having an input into their festive surroundings, and each child acts like a Westminster politician, but more civilised, as they wait for the town mayor to count each vote. The news crew wander around filming everything, photographers are snapping pictures, and there are reporters walking around with notebooks and Dictaphones, asking the children how they decided on their favourite and trying to get them to reveal their top-secret votes. Fellow stallholders come over to wish Noel luck, and even Glenna has ventured down with Gizmo for moral support.

We wait with bated breath.

After what seems like hours, the local mayor is ready to announce the winner. He taps his microphone to make sure all eyes are on him. 'By a clear margin, the winner is . . . Roscoe Farm's Cinderella pumpkin tree.'

Noel cheers and I shriek and jump on him without thinking, so excited that I don't know what to do with myself. He catches me easily and my legs encircle his waist and my arms wrap around his shoulders. 'You did it!'

He pulls me tight to him and spins us around. '*We* did it.' His voice is muffled against my shoulder, but I can hear the unsteadiness in it. He genuinely didn't expect to win. It makes my arms tighten around him because I'm so proud, I could burst.

By the time he puts me down, the mayor has announced that Fiona's tree has come second and the pet supply shop is in third place, and is looking at us, saying, 'If Mr Roscoe is quite ready . . .'

My lips are throbbing where they were pressed against the skin of his neck, and I have to grip onto one of the tables for support as he goes up to shake the mayor's hand and thank all the kids for their votes. He gives a speech about loving this community, thanking everyone for their help in pulling the competition together, and finishes by saying how much he hopes everyone will continue supporting the market even when Christmas is over. He points me out and mentions that I supplied the trees and invites everyone to visit Peppermint Branches and starts talking about the hot chocolate and roasted nuts, and Santa and the sleigh. Despite the fact that Fiona, Fergus, and Glenna are all watching me like a bird of prey might watch a mouse before they swoop down and carry it away in their claws, I can't help thinking how sweet it is that he's using *his* win as another way to push *my* business.

The mayor steps back up onto the makeshift platform and promises the council will have the bare tree at the other end of Elffield decorated in a replica of the winning tree before next weekend. Noel thanks everyone again and jumps down, and he's enveloped by a crowd of well-wishers. He meets my eyes over the swarm of people between us and gives me a wink as another little old lady pulls him down and pinches his cheek.

I'm totally distracted as the crowd starts to disperse and people come over and quickly snap up the last of my trees. I'm brimming with pride as I watch the polite and patient way he talks to everyone who stops him as he makes his way back over. Everyone here loves him. Every customer, every trader, all the teachers who gather round to congratulate him and the children who nervously come up to shake his hand and ask him questions about pumpkins. Everyone is so happy for him, and I feel it bubbling over in me too. He deserves this so much. A win, a boost that someone other than me thinks he's amazing at every aspect of his job, some recognition of all the effort he's put into trying to save this market.

He's done so much for me. I have no idea what I would've done without him. Even when I thought he was a twat – on that first day, he gave me the courage to try to prove him wrong, and then on that first night, he gave me the confidence to stay and really make something of Peppermint Branches. What would I have done if he hadn't been there? Would I have chickened out because it was too difficult? I wouldn't have known where to begin without his advice, and now it feels like the start of something special – with the farm and with Noel, and I'm not sure which one I'm more excited about.

***

Noel packs our display trees away and loads the back of the truck with empty crates, even more now than when we started because Iain arrived mid-afternoon with more trees and pumpkins, and another crate of Glenna's goodies, and they all sold out too.

There's one bunch of mistletoe left from the second batch and I hang it over Fiona's stall on my way to the winning tree to turn off the fairylights and the tealights in the pumpkins. I kneel down and crawl underneath the tree and feel around until I can reach the battery pack disguised at the back, trying to avoid taking my eye out with the scented needles, and nearly scream in surprise and bang my head on a branch when I emerge to find Fergus and Fiona behind me. The tree must get a fright too because it chooses that moment to drop a load of needles, most of them into my hair.

'Oh, sorry, lass, we didn't mean to make you jump.' Fergus thrusts a gingerbread wheelbarrow at me to make up for the scare.

'So there *is* something going on between you.' Fiona folds her arms across her chest. She's trying to look serious but there's a smile playing on her face. 'I knew I wasn't imagining it, stubble rash or no stubble rash.'

'I don't know what you're talking about.' I open the gingerbread biscuit and nibble a wheel off, trying to keep a straight face and not give anything away, because just the thought of Noel makes me grin uncontrollably.

'I was having a lovely chat with Glenna earlier,' Fiona says. 'She happened to mention that he didn't come in until *very* late last night, and that she heard him talking to someone – a female someone – when the snow started falling, *and* that he was singing to himself as he got ready this morning.'

If gingerbread and bath bombs fail, they can definitely turn to a career in surveillance. 'We were both up late working. He was telling me to make sure I set my alarm because we needed to be on time this morning, and he knew I'd have brained him with a pumpkin if he'd honked his blasted truck horn outside my window one more time.'

'I suppose that's why neither of you can get the smiles off your faces, no matter how hard you try,' Fiona says.

'That's just because he's won the competition.' I bite another gingerbread wheel off to stop myself smiling.

'You look happy in a way that you didn't when you first got here.' Fergus shares a glance with Fiona. 'And he seems happy in a way that he never has before. He's been protecting himself so hard since his last relationship that I didn't think he'd ever trust anyone again, but I've never seen him as relaxed around someone as he is with you. We were just trying to say that we think those two things are probably related. And we're really happy for you both. It's so nice that you get on so well after everything that's happened between you.'

I cock my head to the side in confusion. What exactly does he think has happened between us? Fergus must've eaten too many gingerbread Hoovers today because he's not making any sense.

'After all what?' As I say the words, a stone of dread immediately settles in my stomach. Things never go right for me, and so far, everything has been wonderful with Peppermint Branches, and meeting Noel has been a gorgeous, sexy bonus. Something *has* to go wrong at some point, and I suddenly have a crushing and irrevocable feeling that I'm about to find out what.

'After losing Peppermint Branches, of course,' Fiona says. 'He put on a brave face and said he wasn't bothered, of course, but he was devastated. You could see it in his whole demeanour. I don't think he smiled again until he brought you along to the market.

We were so pleased that you two liked each other and were able to put it all behind you or it would've been so awkward.'

'Losing it?' I ask as the confusion builds. Maybe he was supposed to inherit it or something . . . He speaks about Evergreene like a beloved grandfather, but there's obviously a history between him and the son, so maybe something happened there and *that's* the vague feeling I keep getting that there's something he isn't telling me.

Fergus gives me a look like *I'm* the one not making sense here.

'In the auction, obviously,' Fiona says with a giggle. 'You'd expect someone who works with their hands to have much nimbler fingers, but you won fair and square, and he knows that. I think it says a lot about his character that he's been so gracious about it. You must've been worried that he'd be a bit funny with you when you first met him.'

The gingerbread turns to stone in my mouth. R-five-hyphens-81. I can't believe I didn't see it before. Those hyphens hide the letters 'oscoe'. Everything that didn't quite make sense suddenly adds up perfectly. 'I must've been worried because I was moving in next door to the other bidder?'

They nod along, unaware that they've confirmed my greatest fear. They have absolutely no idea that I didn't know. I sink back on my knees and look up at the unlit tree, and I feel like the whole market is falling down around my ears. Tears form in my eyes and I blink them furiously, trying to stop myself crying. I can't let Fergus and Fiona know that they've just revealed a secret that Noel's obviously been trying very hard to keep.

'Nooo.' I do an overexaggerated handwave and force the tightest smile in the history of the universe. 'I wasn't worried. He's . . . well, he's Noel, isn't he? The friendly pumpkin farmer with a heart of gold. I knew he'd be a gentleman about it.'

'Well, it doesn't matter now you're together, does it? What a lovely story to tell your grandkids one day.'

I almost laugh at the absurdity of that statement. Never mind grandkids because we are most definitely *not* together now I know that. Now it all makes sense.

No wonder he was so grouchy when I first arrived. No wonder he was irritated and incredulous and wanted to know how I'd won the auction with mere seconds left on the clock. And I was stupid enough to believe he was just making conversation.

He must have hated me. Peppermint Branches means the world to him, and this clueless girl turns up having snatched it literally from underneath his fingers. I swan in and nonchalantly tell him I was drunk and didn't have a clue about Christmas tree farming and I'd won the auction without even trying. I know Noel. I know how seriously he would've taken that auction. How much he would have got his hopes up when there were no other bids until the last few minutes. He would've pinned everything on winning that.

And then I ripped his dream away from him. He must've been heartbroken. Devastated.

He must have wanted it back.

He even told me that his father wanted to buy Evergreene out one day and run both farms together and I still didn't fall in. Those two farms are his life, his love. His heart. It's not me who's given his heart back to him – it's working on Peppermint Branches again. Helping me, supposedly. But why would anyone do that? Why would he help me so much, teach me so much, when he must hate me for stealing the farm he wanted? I thought he was doing it out of kindness because he could see I was out of my depth. But if it's that simple, why didn't he tell me about the auction?

Fiona clicks her fingers in front of my face like she's waiting for a response to a question she's asked several times.

'Oh, er, yes,' I mumble, hoping it was the right answer. I feel like I'm floating above the market, looking down on everything through a fog. In the few weeks I've been here, I've grown to trust Noel *completely*, and now I feel like the metaphorical rug has been physically pulled out from underneath me.

'We definitely need you to share a stall next year,' Fiona is saying. 'Magical things happen when you two work together. He's never sold as many pumpkins as he has this year and look at how many Christmas trees you've sold today. It's simply wonderful.'

The gingerbread biscuit hangs limp in my fingers. 'It's great,' I croak out. My voice is raspy and my throat is dry. I can barely get my words out, and I'm not sure if I want to cry or scream or both.

They share another glance like they're not sure what's wrong with me. 'Do you want a hand with those pumpkins? You didn't bring a bag to carry them back in.'

I look down at myself like I might accidentally have a carrier bag attached to my person. 'No, it's fine. They can stay until tomorrow.'

'Noel usually clears them up. They start to go off.'

'Let them rot.'

Fergus's eyebrows shoot up so fast that they nearly meet his rapidly decreasing hairline.

'I mean, until tomorrow,' I say quickly. I can't let them know I'm upset or give them any reason to think they've said the wrong thing or go and tell Noel that I know. 'First thing, when I come to replace them. It's been a long day, I just want to get home to bed, and it'll be quieter tomorrow, there'll be plenty of time.'

'I bet there are plenty of *reasons* to get home to your bed tonight, hmm?' Fiona puts such a clear emphasis on what she thinks will be going on in bed tonight that even Fergus blushes.

'And on that note, we're going to go for a cuppa before Fergus gets overexcited and *we* end up spending the evening in the A&E department. Have a good night!' She slips her arm through Fergus's as they walk off towards the hot drinks counter and I watch as he tucks her arm in against his side and tugs her closer.

I should be excited to rush back and tell Noel about that adorable display of affection, but everything's different now. This changes it all. I sink back onto my knees as I watch them disappear around the corner and the tears come without my permission. My hair has fallen down again and I pull it forwards to hide my face and concentrate on picking the dropped needles out of it.

The stall. His kindness in allowing me to share his stall. The way he even used his winner's speech today to push Peppermint Branches. I thought he was being nice to talk about *my* business. Isn't he just making sure that he's got plenty of customers for when he inevitably takes over?

I always used to think that people are only nice to you if they want something, and Noel's the one who's been changing that, who's made me have a bit of faith in people again. How can I have come to trust him so much in such a short amount of time? Why was I so hypnotised by his piercing and his hair that I didn't stop to question his motives?

Everything he's done must've had a purpose behind it. Gorgeous, funny, warm guys like him don't fall for plain emotional wrecks like me – they see a weakness and they exploit it. Like Steve did. Noel certainly saw my weakness in the car on that first night, and he grabbed his opportunity. He didn't win the auction, but he saw a chance to wrestle the farm back from my grasp. That's why he changed so much. Not because we had a connection or because he liked me, but because he saw an opportunity to gain my trust, to 'help' me, because I was so clueless and grateful for his advice that I never stopped to question *why* he was helping me or if the advice he gave was sound.

And now I know he's been lying all along.

It's a genius plan, really. Keep your enemies closer and all that. He's shown me everything, from what trees to cut to how to propagate seedlings for future years, and I've trusted him blindly. But how do I know if anything he's said is true? How do I know if he's told me the opposite of what I should be doing, so he can swoop in and takeover like a hero when it all inevitably falls apart? What if the only thing he's been helping me to do is run the farm into the ground so I'll have no choice but to give up and sell it on to him?

Chapter 15

'Where's the "Hot Scot Pumpkin Farmer Who Looks Like Luke Evans" you keep texting me about then?' Chelsea asks through the phone.

'I don't *keep* texting you about him,' I say. 'I've barely mentioned him.'

'You've barely mentioned him *today*. Is he there? Can you put him on and make him say "mu*rrr*de*rrr*" a few times for me?'

No matter how much I don't feel like laughing, a giggle escapes at the idea. Noel would laugh. And be all too happy to oblige. 'He's not here.'

She makes a noise of disappointment. 'Where is he, then? Sawing down trees topless? Toplessly dragging stumps out of the earth with his bare hands?'

'Why does he have to be topless?'

'Because you keep texting me about his arms and his chest. If you mention those mystical forearms one more time, I'm liable to drive up there to see for myself.' She sighs reflectively. 'Ooh, ruggedly tearing the branches from Christmas trees with his teeth? Topless, of course. Sawing wood back and forth, gentle but firm at the same time? No shirt, the breeze blowing his hair . . .'

'It's snowing! No one's going shirtless in that.' I'm in the kitchen, still the only room with a window, and the wind outside is blowing up the already fallen snow and hurling it around. 'It's a bit of a blizzard actually.'

'Men can still go topless in the snow. You'd have an excuse to *warm him up* then. Seriously, Leah, hasn't anything happened between you yet?'

'Oh, something's happened all right.' I tell her about what I found out on Friday.

It's Monday afternoon now and I haven't seen Noel since. After Fergus and Fiona left, I told him I needed air and walked home, and when he phoned that night, I told him I was tired and going to bed.

Since Friday, the stall at the market has been invaluable now that it's Christmas tree season, and every tree I've sent there has been sold, along with the wreaths, but I've made Iain go in my place with the excuse that I need to get the farm ready to open to the public this weekend. This Saturday will be the last day of November and it's officially opening day, so it's not exactly an excuse. There *is* tons to do. There are final checks of the caravan's food preparation area, and still plenty of trees left to shear. If the snow keeps up, then I'll have to grit every inch of the path around the farm. The Santa I hired has had to be shown around and it's taken a while for the background check paperwork to come through. Apparently Noel's been painting the finished sleigh a beautiful metallic red with gold edges and sparkly silver stars – or so one of the farmhands has reported back to me because I don't want to run the risk of seeing him – and I've sprinkled glitter all over the freshly cut grass in the empty field opposite the house, ready for where it will stand for children to meet Santa.

'What does it matter if he was the other bidder?' Chelsea sounds confused. 'You won and he didn't, end of story. I lost out on a fabulous handbag the other day because Lewis distracted me. Another bidder got it for an absolute steal, but fair's fair. I'm not going to track them down and claw it off their arm.'

I laugh at the thought and it makes me realise how much I miss seeing Chelsea every day. We text all the time, but it's not the same as meeting for lunch or a quick drink on the way home from work. 'This is a bit more complicated than a handbag, Chels. And the point is that he lied about it. It wouldn't be as bad if he'd just told me, believe me there's been *plenty* of opportunities, but he didn't.'

'Probably because he knew you'd react like this.'

'On the first day I arrived, I *mentioned* the other bidder to him. Why didn't he say, "Oh yeah, by the way, that was me"? He didn't know how I'd react then. If he was anything like the straight-to-the-point, honest, stand-up guy I've thought he was, he wouldn't have kept it hidden.'

'He probably knew how it would look. If you'd have known, you'd have been sleeping with one eye open waiting for him to poison you in the night.'

'Which is exactly what I'm doing now, except he's been killing me with kindness. He's given me so much advice, Chels, and I've trusted everything he's said. He even told me not to worry about studying books on Christmas tree farming because I could ask him. He obviously said that because the books might give me good advice that goes against the rubbish he's been telling me to make sure everything goes horrifically wrong and the only way out will be to give it up and sell it to him.'

There's a crash outside as something blows over in the wind, and Chelsea sighs. 'Are you sure he didn't say that because he wanted an excuse to spend time with you? All men like to feel needed.'

I walk to the door and pull it open, entering a battle of wills with the wind that does its best to pull it back again. A flurry of snow hits me in the face as I stand in the open doorway. I look out across the fields in front of me as I shake it out of my hair. The novelty has already worn off. It's barely stopped snowing since Thursday night. The roads are impassable now and we're so far out in the countryside that no gritting lorries come past. The white stuff has settled up to mid-calf level, with drifts along the roadside and around the house that are much deeper. I just hope it melts by Saturday because, although the trees look pretty covered in snow, the reality is that the whole farm is obscured by the blizzard, the fields look bleak and empty, it's freezing, and the wind is galeforce. No one is going to come to pick their own Christmas tree in this. Not many people would be daft enough to risk leaving their houses.

I can't help thinking about Noel and wondering where he is, though I'm annoyed at myself for still caring. All his pumpkins are gone from the fields now, only the ones he's stored in the barn for winter remain, and the view from my backdoor is white and bare. Even his farmhouse in the distance is concealed by the fog. I kick a chunk of snow off the top step and think about him feeling needed. Chelsea's kind of got a point there. He's said as much in one of his unguarded moments. But if it was that simple, why didn't he tell me that he wanted Peppermint Branches too?

'I cried in front of him on the first night, Chels. I told him about Mum and Dad. He knew I was vulnerable. He—'

'I know Steve took advantage, and I know catching him like that hurt you much more than you'll admit, but not all men are like that. Noel could be a genuine good person who wanted to help someone who needed it.'

I pick up the doormat and jiggle it around to shake off the snow that's blown in, then I close the door and wander back towards the kitchen with the phone to my ear. 'No one is *that* kind. He's invested in Peppermint Branches being a success this year because he wants a strong customer base ready for next year after the trees have all been cut badly and the saplings have all died because I planted them wrongly and I've run out of money to fix the problems, and he can swoop in to buy me out. He knows exactly how tight my budget is – I told him on the first night.'

'Just because Steve was a git . . .'

'At least Steve was honest about what he wanted. Noel wanted Peppermint Branches – he just conveniently didn't mention it.' I lean my elbows on the kitchen unit and look out at the blanket of white outside, the huge white flakes fizzing around in the air. 'He let me share his market stall at no cost.'

'I thought you said he didn't need the space once pumpkin season was over.'

I ignore the little pang. He did say that, and Fergus and Fiona did tell me it was nice to see his stall in action after October because usually it goes quiet. 'And what about the trees? The Peppermint firs, Chels. He's been taking care of this certain type of tree that Evergreene grew. He said it was because they were a special, scientifically perfect variety, but how can I ever tell now? How can I trust anything he's said?' My voice wobbles and I have to stop myself and take a few deep breaths, because I did trust him. I trusted him so much, and now I keep going over everything he's ever said and questioning his hidden motives. I wish I could go back to before I knew and carry on thinking how lucky I was to have moved in next door to the most generous and thoughtful neighbour in existence.

'If you didn't care about him, you wouldn't be so upset,' she ventures. I can tell from her tone of voice that she's half-expecting me to hang up on her.

I did care about him – that's the problem. I've never felt the way Noel makes me feel before. And now to find out that he's hidden something that changes everything . . .

The wind howls, making such a screaming noise outside that it echoes how I feel on the inside. Half the roof of an outbuilding sails past, crashing into the skeletal trees and lodging itself on the wire fence on the opposite side of the road.

'I don't need him.' I watch the fence slowly sag under the weight of the roof. 'I bought this place because *I* wanted to run a Christmas tree farm, not because I had a sexy neighbour to help me. Nothing has changed from when I got here. I've already learnt loads – enough to get me through the first Christmas season, and then I'll have plenty of time in January to learn what to do in the spring. I've got farmhands working for me now. I can put a trailer on my car and deliver trees to customers and transport them to the market. Stall leases will open up in the new year, and Fergus and Fiona are bound to have their ears to the ground about that one, so if I can get in quick enough then I'll have my own stall. I *don't* need him.' I say it again for emphasis but I'm not sure which one of us I'm trying to convince. I was out of my depth six weeks ago, but I'm not now. I don't need him, but it's been nice to have him, and not just because he's full of advice and he's not entirely disagreeable to look at. It's because he makes me laugh. He makes me feel special. He catches my eyes across the busy market and it makes me feel like we're the only two people there. It's because his kisses are so gentle but so full of passion and need and desire, and his hugs are something that should be sold as a cure for all the world's ills, the way his arms wrap around me and squeeze just a little bit too tight and linger for just a little bit too long – just long enough to make me feel like the most precious thing he's ever touched.

I don't realise I'm crying until tears drip onto the unit.

No wonder I swore off men before I got here. This sort of thing doesn't happen if you stay single.

Chelsea must hear me sniffle because she does that changing the subject thing when she isn't really sure whether I want to change the subject or whether she should let me cry for a bit. We've had many conversations like this since my parents died. 'I wish I was closer. I'd buy a tree for every room and proudly tell everyone that my best friend grew them.'

I half-snort and half-laugh at the idea of Chelsea having a tree in each of her miniscule rooms. 'At this stage, the trees are anything from five to ten years old. I didn't have anything to do with growing them this time around. I've got my predecessor, Mr Evergreene, to thank for that.'

'Probably just as well because we can barely fit a tree into the living room as it is, Lewis would lose the plot if I came home with one for each room. Unless they're really tiny. Have you got any tiny ones that would survive a journey in the post? It seems wrong that my best friend's got a Christmas tree farm and I'm getting a dusty plastic one out of the attic.'

I stand up straighter. 'That's actually an amazing idea. How many people would be thrilled to have a tiny tree? Loads of people must be without the space for a big one but would still like a real Christmas tree, and there are loads here. The years without shearing have allowed the mature trees to produce cones and their winged seeds have spread on the wind and sown themselves. Little trees are springing up everywhere. Noel said they need digging up and putting through the shredder because they're not evenly spaced and they could've cross-pollinated with an unknown wild tree and grow up without the characteristics that customers want in their perfect Christmas trees. Why aren't I selling them? I could slash them into the traditional shape, plant them into pots and sell them as little tabletop trees. Most of them are only about a foot tall. They'd be easy enough to pack and send in the post. I could have a website and sell them online.'

'Are they going to grow big though? I'd love one but you've seen the size of my garden, I couldn't plant it afterwards, and we've already had leaflets through the door saying the council are going to charge us thirty quid if we leave the Christmas tree out with the recycling. It's a shame you can't rent them out for Christmas and then take them back.'

'Oh my god. Chelsea, that's brilliant!' I yelp in excitement as my mind is flooded with plans. Renting Christmas trees is a fabulous idea. There must be so many people in the same position as Chelsea who would love a real tree but stick to a plastic one because it goes neatly back into its box in January. A real tree is a big thing to have to find something to do with afterwards. If you can't plant it in your own garden, you've either got the responsibility of taking it to the tip or paying the council to get rid of it for you. What if it could come back here? What if I could deliver it at the beginning of December and pick it up in January? People could rent the same tree every Christmas. They could watch it grow every year. My dad would've loved that idea. He was always so sentimental about his Christmas trees. They were planted in the garden every January until we ran out of space. When I was young, I remember him getting the arborists in to cut down the oldest ones which had shot up to thirteen feet tall. In more recent years, the tree would stay up until Mum shouted at him about it being bad luck to leave it up after Twelfth Night on the fifth of January, and then he'd carefully lay it in the back of the car and take it to the tip. He would have been delighted at the prospect of having one for Christmas, sending it back to the farm and having it tagged with our family name, and then having the same tree back again the following year, a little bigger and a little fuller – the family Christmas tree. 'I'm going to look into this idea. I could block out a whole field for returning trees so they're all in one place and not confused with the trees that are for sale. It's too late for this year, but I've got ten months ahead where I've got to work out the best way to make this a successful business. I need to find out if this is financially viable and what kind of area I could cover. This is such a brilliant idea. Thanks, Chels.'

'See?' She says. 'Girl power, circa the Spice Girls, 1996. You've got this. You don't need some sexy Scottish pumpkin farmer to help you.'

The wind slams against the house again, hitting it so hard that the building shakes, and I watch in dismay as one of the dormant trees in the distance suddenly lists to one side and slowly crashes down onto a bed of silent snow, sending up a storm of mud and snowflakes as the huge rootball at its base lifts from the ground and covers the now horizontal tree with a shower of earth.

'How can the weather be so bad there that I can *hear* it through the phone?'

Thunder cracks behind a far-off mountain even though it's still too light to see any lightning, as if trying to answer Chelsea's question for me. 'It's awful. We don't have storms like this down in London. Apparently it's a blizzard coming in from Scandinavia that's hitting land right at the corner of Aberdeenshire, only about twenty miles from here. People at the market have been talking about it for days but I didn't think it was going to be this bad.'

'It sounds awful.'

'I'm going to go and have a look around. I've already lost at least one tree, probably more judging by the amount of creaking wood I can hear, and whatever's in the shed where that roof came from needs to be protected from the elements. I'll talk to you later, okay?'

'Leah, be careful,' she calls after me as I hang up.

I shove my arms into a hoodie and shrug a waterproof coat over the top of it, pulling it tight around me. I yank my welly boots on and brace myself to go outside.

The blizzard slams into me from all sides as I spit out a mouthful of snow and pull my hood back up from where it's flapping behind me, trying to make a break for freedom from the rest of the coat.

The wind tears the gate out of my hands as I go to open it, and I have to chase it until it clatters against the fence on the opposite side of the lane and drag it back to secure the latch. I pull my hood tight and shove my hands into my pockets as I trudge down the lane, the depth of the snow making it hard to walk. I told Iain and the other two workers not to come in today, even though there's still so much to do and we really need all hands on deck. According to the news, there's transport disruption across the whole east side of Scotland, there are trees down across roads and railways, and it seemed too dangerous to work amongst trees when the wind is this strong.

I tell myself it'll be better tomorrow while I peer into the Nordmann fir field, the wind banging the heavy wooden gate against the post like it weighs nothing, clattering with every gust. Two trees are down and one of the tallest ones is leaning precariously against its neighbour. It'll be extra work to remove the fallen and damaged ones before Saturday and make sure it's safe again, but there aren't as many casualties as I expected given how bad it sounds out here.

Further around the track, the Peppermint fir field looks pretty much unscathed, and as I turn away from the gate and start traipsing towards the bridge, I hear a shout.

'Leah!'

Bollocks. Bollocks, bollocks, bollocks. Noel's through the hedge and dashing between the Peppermint firs before I have a chance to turn and run. I should have known he'd be out checking things on his farm too and been more careful to avoid him. I've seen him in the distance a few times since Friday and managed to sneak away before he's caught sight of me, but there's nowhere to hide this time. I'm going to have to face him.

My heart is hammering in my chest at the thought of seeing him again, and not in the same way it was last week.

He puts a foot on the gate and vaults over it rather than pushing it open, landing with a thud in the deep snow. At least he's dressed for the weather in snow boots up to his knees and a thick padded coat down to his thighs, a red scarf is wrapped across his face, under the hood of the dark coat which is curled around his face like an Eskimo.

He pulls the scarf down so he can speak. 'At the end of this, we're going to wake up in Oz with a witch's legs sticking out from under the house.'

'I'm sure we are.' I give him a tight smile.

I see the hurt cross his face. He's not stupid. He knows I'm not pleased to see him and it makes something ache inside of me. 'What are you doing out in this?'

'Making sure everything's battened down. Did you see half the shed roof go flying off just now? Have you got any damage?'

I wave my hand vaguely towards the Nordmann firs. 'A few trees down. Nothing I can't handle.' The cold air bites my fingers and they're tingling within seconds. I quickly pull my hand back inside my sleeve as he turns around to survey the area.

'I did a circle of my land this morning to check for damage, I couldn't help noticing you've lost a few in the lower fields too, and that was only the parts I could see. There'll probably be more before this blizzard ends.'

I shrug and look down. 'Oh well, these things happen.'

When I look up, he's turned back and is watching me with a raised eyebrow. He knows there's something wrong, and I try to hold his gaze, to challenge him, because he has no right to act like I'm the one who's done something wrong here.

'Things are going well at the market. Visitors are up, and the whole of Elffield is busier than it has been in years because of the news coverage, the tourists are loving it all, and the main Christmas shopping season hasn't even started yet. No one's going to knock down something this profitable. They've already taken Elffield off the list of contenders for the bus interchange. It's not the answer to all our problems, but we've saved ourselves for now, and the council have agreed to a meeting with the stallholders in the new year to make a plan going forward.'

'That's good.' That's not just good, that's brilliant. We did it – the one thing we set out to achieve, even if it's only for a year and next Christmas we'll have to do something bigger and better. I want to jump on him and cheer and celebrate, but what I actually do is burrow the toe of my welly boot down into the snow until I can press it against a stone.

'The Cinderella tree went viral on Twitter, and the council sent workmen out to decorate the big tree near the motorway. My phone's been ringing off the hook with enquiries for next year. I've already signed contracts with two more shops to stock my pumpkins next October.'

'Good. You work hard. You deserve it.' It sounds disingenuous even though I mean it. He *does* work hard and he deserves success.

He looks frozen as he hovers there, and I know he's trying to figure out what to say. There have never been awkward silences between us before. I'm being off with him, but I can't bring myself to come out and tell him I know. He knows I'm being cold and clipped, and any other day, I'd have thrown my arms around his neck and squealed in excitement at the good news, but I don't know what to say to him, and I was hoping to avoid him for a bit longer while I figured it out.

He looks around like he's desperately searching for words to fill the silence, his eyes eventually settling on the bridge I was about to walk across. He takes a few steps towards it. 'The river's frozen solid. It's been a long time since I saw that happen.' He brushes snow off the bridge railings with glove-covered hands and gestures for me to come closer. 'It's a picture-perfect winter postcard.'

I shuffle towards him, knowing he can tell how reluctant I am. He turns to give me a soft smile, and his hood blows down which is nearly my undoing. His hair is up in a ponytail but more bits of it have blown out than remain in and the wind tangles them around his face. His ears are red from the cold, and the snow lands in flakes on his hair, and it's so cold that they don't even start to melt from body heat like snow usually does when it lands on you. He doesn't bother to put the hood back up, and every part of me is screaming to wrap my arms around his neck and pull him down to me. He looks completely dejected as he lingers, waiting for me to clue him in on what's changed between us.

'Do you want to give the hot chocolate machine a final test run to warm up?' I offer against my better judgement.

'No, because I can see how much you don't want me to and I'm not about to push myself in where I'm not wanted. I just want you to tell me what I've done wrong.'

'Noth . . .' I go to tell him it's nothing but I cut myself off because being the other bidder in the auction *isn't* nothing, but I can't find the words to tell him what it is, and I don't want to hear his excuses. I hate seeing him looking so hurt. I want to hug him so badly that I'll believe anything he tells me, and I can't fall for it again.

He shakes his head when I don't answer. 'I had to mess it up sooner or later. I suppose I should be grateful that it was sooner. I must've saved us both a lot of heartache down the road.'

'Noel . . .' I look out at the frozen river, snaking its way across the farm until it disappears under a hedge and through the empty land next door. It's an impressive sight and looking at it is easier than trying to think of what to say to Noel.

'Is it because I kissed you? I thought you were into it, but if I overstepped a mark or something . . . I'm so sorry.'

Oh god, Noel, don't apologise for kissing me. I swallow around the lump that springs to my throat at how sincere he looks. He genuinely thinks I'm annoyed with him because of that breathtaking kiss the other night. If only it was that simple.

'I know you're avoiding me.'

'I'm not avoiding you.' My voice comes out hoarse and unstable. 'Just busy. Preparing *my* Christmas trees, for *my* business, which *I* bought, for *me*.'

I can see the cogs turning in his head as he tries to figure out what I mean. 'Every time I catch a glimpse of you out in the fields, by the time I've climbed across the hedge and come over, you've disappeared. I know better than anyone how easy it is to hide in these trees. I just didn't expect you to be hiding from me.'

'I'm not hiding from you, I'm shearing trees. There's a matter of days until the farm opens and there's a lot of work to be done. You taught me that.'

He nods and kicks at a drift of snow piling up around the bridge railings, his nose red in the freezing air, snowflakes settling in his dark eyebrows when he looks down. I want to tell him about potting up the tiny trees and selling them online, that I'm going to send one to Chelsea to make sure they can survive a journey, and I'm bubbling to tell him about the idea of renting

Christmas trees and see if he thinks it's something to be excited about too, and if he thinks it could be financially viable, but how can I trust anything he says?

'Tell me what I've done?' His voice breaks and I hate the way he swallows before he speaks again. 'How can I fix it if you won't even talk to me? Please, Lee. I thought we had something wonderful here, and something's obviously gone horribly wrong. Don't I even deserve to know what?'

I bristle at the words because I don't know if he hasn't realised what I've found out, or if he genuinely doesn't comprehend that acting the way he has when he was the other bidder is not okay. 'I don't owe you anything,' I snap. 'No one asked you to do the things you've done for this farm. I'm sorry you won't get any return on it now but you should've thought of that when you started your little scheme.'

'What?'

We stare at each other for a few long moments, and then I jam my hands back into my pockets. 'I have to go.' My voice quivers as I brush past him and concentrate on getting as far away as possible, my thighs burning from the effort of pushing through the snow as I clomp further round the track, praying he doesn't follow me.

I can't talk to him at the moment. I've been constantly on the verge of tears since Friday, and I'm not strong enough to *not* believe his excuses. After I caught Steve and realised that he'd clocked how isolated I was and used it to his own benefit, I vowed I'd never let a man see my vulnerability again, that I'd never give anyone a chance to use my weakness against me, and mere weeks later, Noel caught me crying in the car and it started all over again.

'Leah! What are you talking about?' he calls after me. 'I don't understand!'

'Of course you don't,' I mutter to myself. The only thing he doesn't understand is that I'm onto him.

I know he's still there without turning around. I open the gate of the Norway spruce field, pushing it against the huge blockade of snow it dredges up as it opens, and go in, ducking behind the hedge and crouching down so I'm out of sight. After a few minutes, the crunch of his boots echoes through the empty farm as he walks away.

I let out a sob and the tears fall as I sink to my knees in the snow. How did it ever come to this?

I want to run after him and brush the snow out of his hair. I want to go back with him, snuggle up in front of his fire with Gizmo and put everything back the way it was before Friday afternoon. He made everything about this place better, and without him, it feels as empty and desolate as the fields look lost under the snow.

Chapter 16

It's Wednesday when it starts to rain, but it's not just regular rain. These are huge pounding drops that beat against the roof and hammer on the boards blocking the windows, making me feel that the house is going to cave in under its force.

The main road is running like a river as the snow turns to water, and the drifts around the house that had reached an impressive size have melted and are surrounding me like a moat. If it wasn't for the steps, I'd have to swim out.

It's a weird day, everything feels bleak and miserable. There's so much to do before the farm opens to the public on Saturday, but it's too wet and too cold to get out and do anything. I told Iain and the two seasonal workers not to come in again today. It's not safe. The Met Office has issued a red 'risk to life' warning and advised people to stay inside, and the wind is making the rain slam against the house in sheets, sounding like rounds of gunfire when it hits.

There's been an emptiness since I walked away from Noel on Monday. I can't stop thinking about him. I can't believe that anything he said was untrue. He was so genuine, so raw and open with me . . . how can any of it have been a ploy to get my trust? And what did he think he was going to gain out of it anyway? I've pored over the books I bought about growing Christmas trees and nothing in them contradicts any of the advice he gave me. In fact, most of the things he said are actually more sensible than what's written in the books, and I keep thinking that I should swallow my pride and go over there and talk it through. I definitely miss him enough to believe him, especially when I think about the look of bewilderment and rejection on his face at the bridge the other day, which is stuck in my mind like a screensaver – it pops up whenever I'm inactive for a few moments.

Thinking about the bridge makes me think of the river and what Noel said about it flooding. It was frozen solid a couple of days ago, but with all this snow and rain . . . I've pulled my boots on before I've finished the thought. There's no way that river can cope with this deluge of water. I shrug my coat on again, open the door, and immediately regret it. I have to hold the door with both hands to stop the wind crashing it shut again.

Outside, the weather is *worse* than it sounds from inside. The coat proves completely useless in rain this heavy because I'm soaked through before I've even reached the gate. The trees are obscured by a wet haze as I follow the track, which is running with so much water that it flops over the tops of my wellies within a few steps.

I know something's severely wrong from the sound of rushing water. It's so different from the usual gentle trickle of the stream. This is a thundering, pounding gush that reverberates through the earth itself, and I stop in horror as I round the corner and get to the bridge.

The stream is no longer a stream. It's a crashing, swirling river, and the banks have burst.

I remember what Noel said on that day we crossed the trickling little stream on the way to the apple tree, about how it has never flooded, but it would be a disaster if it did. About how it would drown the Balsams and the Blue spruces. About how I'd lose them all.

The grass surrounding it is completely flooded. There's so much water that it's lying on the surface because everything is already too wet for it to drain away, and more water is pulsing out with every second, spreading further. It's nearly reached the first row of Balsam firs and is edging towards the Blue spruces.

My first instinct is to call Noel for help. He'll know what to do. But I can't do that. That's the point – I have to rely on myself, no one else.

I can't just stand here watching the trees drown, their roots glugging as they gradually sink in floodwater. Come on, Leah, think.

A river ran through the village I grew up in, and it flooded all the time in winter. I remember seeing the council workers down there in the pouring rain, digging spillways to divert the water. That's it! I turn around and splash back through the mud towards the barn.

There are loads of different shovels with different purposes, but I don't know what they're all for, so I grab as many as I can carry and try to map it out in my head as I race back. If I dig a channel across the top of the Balsam fir field, it would give the water somewhere to spill into before it reaches the trees.

It might already be too late to save them. I splosh through the puddled water and run to the other bridge and through the Blue spruce field until I reach the Balsam firs again from the opposite bank.

I start halfway along the riverside where the bank is at its lowest point and the most water is flooding out. I ram the shovel into the ground and shove my foot down, pushing it in deep and heaving up a huge clump of saturated earth and chucking it to the side. Water floods into the hole instantly, but I carry on, digging the same spot until I can't get the shovel down any further and water from the river has pooled into it. I move on, overlapping the dig sites until they meet, moving slowly along the path of the river. The ground is so wet that the shovelfuls of earth are too heavy to pick up, but it doesn't matter. None of it matters. There must be at least two thousand trees directly below the river – the only thing that matters is saving them.

I pile the earth I take out onto the edges to create a barrier and start following a roughly parallel line with the river towards the border of my land. After that, it can flood anywhere it wants, I've just got to get it past the trees.

'Why didn't you call me?'

I jump so much that I nearly fall over. I ram the shovel into the ground and use it as a pole to keep myself upright, slip-sliding in the mud as I turn around to look at Noel. 'What are you doing here?'

'Came to make sure the river wasn't flooding. Now I see I should've come earlier.' He has to shout to be heard from the opposite side of the rushing water.

'I don't need your help, I can manage.' I try to concentrate on digging and not look at him again, but the temptation is too much.

He takes his coat off and throws it aside, picks up one of the spades I'd dropped and starts towards the river.

Within minutes, there isn't a centimetre of him that's dry. He's wearing jeans and only a long-sleeved undershirt with the sleeves rolled up, although I can't tell what colour either of them started off as because they're now dark with rainwater. His hair is loose around his shoulders, looking longer than usual with the weight of the water, and he's covered in mud from the waist down, splashes of it covering his top too, being quickly washed away by the rain that's still pummelling down.

'What are you doing?' I shout again.

'You're going to lose all of the Balsams and most of the Blue spruces if we don't do something *now*. I don't care how much you hate me, I'm not letting you lose these trees. You don't have to handle things like this on your own.'

The passion in his voice makes me realise we can't avoid the soaking wet elephant standing between us any longer. 'For you or for me?' I say before I can chicken out.

He stops and looks up. 'What?'

'You want to save them for you or for me?'

His dripping eyebrows furrow. 'What are you talking ab—'

'I know who you are, Noel. R-five-hyphens-81. I know you were the other bidder.'

'*That's* what all this has been about? That's why you won't talk to me?' He makes a noise of realisation and smacks his forehead. 'This is exactly why I didn't tell you.'

'Everything you've done—'

'—will be irrelevant if we don't drain some of this water away *now*. It's flooding further with every second we waste here. *We* are going to save these trees – not for me, not for you, but for Peppermint Branches because this *place* is special, no matter who owns it.'

I know from the frantic tone in his voice and the panic on his face that this is more serious than I thought.

He jumps into the river and starts shovelling sloppy wet mud from underneath the water, waist-deep and flowing fast.

'You shouldn't be in there,' I yell. The wind is so strong that it's difficult to stay upright. 'What are you trying to do?'

'Raise the banks and straighten the channel. Water flows faster along a straight course, and the quicker we can move it away from the trees, the more chance they'll have of not drowning.'

'What about you? You look like you're in with a pretty good chance of drowning!'

He looks over his shoulder and shoots me a grin. 'Nah. Hypothermia, on the other hand . . .'

'It's not funny.'

'Why, because you care? You think I'm some kind of underhanded con-artist who's befriended you solely for the purpose of stealing your farm, so don't pretend to give a toss when you obviously think so little of me.' He goes back to shovelling mud out and throwing it up onto the edges.

I hate the way it makes me feel because I care about him so

much that I want to wade into the river and drag him out. I'm pretty sure that when rivers are flooded, the general advice is *not* to stand in them. 'I do care about you, Noel. Why do you think I'm so hurt?'

'What about me? How do you think I feel?' He's shouting to be heard over the howling of the wind and the battering of rain. 'I let my guard down with you, I told you things I've never told anyone before. I thought we meant something to each other, and one bloody rumour is enough to change all that.'

'*Is* it just a rumour?' I say, hope suddenly lighting up inside me. Maybe I've got this all wrong.

He doesn't reply. That's answer enough. I let out a sigh and go back to digging, and Noel moves along the river carefully, scraping silt from the bottom and earth from the sides of each bank to make them steeper, and piling it along the top to make the sides higher and try to contain the water.

Everywhere is slippery and the rain is still beating down, turning the already sodden earth into pure sludge. My wellies sink into it and I slip every time I move. I can feel his eyes on me. 'Will you concentrate on not drowning, please?'

'Only if you concentrate on not falling over.'

'In case I fall in a puddle and get wet?' I shake a dripping sleeve at him.

He throws another shovel of silt over his shoulder, seeming to have perfect depth perception as it lands exactly on top of the pile without him even looking. 'I'm sorry I told you not to worry about the river flooding. You had instincts and I told you to ignore them. I wish you hadn't trusted me.'

Me too. But I don't mean about the river. 'I thought this river never flooded.'

'There's a first time for everything. Weather like this has never happened before – not in conjunction with this much snow anyway. The biblical rain is bad enough, but coupled with the six-ish foot of snow that had settled all liquefying at once as the rain melted it . . . no watercourses could cope with this torrent. Put the news on when you get back – everyone will be in the same position as us.'

My coat is so heavy that it's weighing me down and I understand why Noel got rid of his. I shrug it off and throw it out of the way, and keep digging, trying not to make it obvious how worried I am about him. If he loses his footing, he'll be swept away.

I'm trying to dig the trench as fast as I can, slicing through the grass, the water following along with every shovel of earth I remove, cutting a line across the top of the Balsam fir field. We work in silence. The wind is still screaming past my ears, dragging my hair out of its tie and flapping it around, and the rain turns to hailstones that sting everywhere they touch. It's too loud and the few words we do say have to be shouted to be heard, but I want to talk to him. I want him to explain. I want to say that the trees don't matter as much as getting him out of that sodding river before he drowns.

I drive the shovel into the ground and watch as the overflowing water follows, each shovelful of earth taking it further away from the Balsam firs. Noel overtakes me in the river, moving slowly, using the shovel as a walking pole to stay upright against the flow of water. His face tightens in concentration every time he stops and scrapes the shovel up the left side of the bank, again and again. He gets to the edge of my land where the river disappears underneath a bridge of wire fence and earth, worn away naturally by the flow of the water, and uses his shovel to hammer at that and widen it too. When he's satisfied, he turns around and trudges back, heaving earth from the right side of the riverbank now, and I can tell that what he's doing is working. The water *is* flowing faster, and even though it's washing back in some of the mud he's piled at the edges, the extra height is slowing down the spill.

I wipe rainwater and sweat out of my eyes, only succeeding in spreading the mud from my hands further, and try to concentrate on the trench, the overflowed water now pooling so deeply in it that it's started to rise above the edges.

The rain turns to hailstones again, pinging everywhere they hit and bouncing off, and I keep my head down and try to just keep digging, repeating the words like a mantra in my head. When I get to the holly bushes that run along the edge of my land, I dig as far underneath as I can, until I can get my shovel under the wire fence that marks the border between Peppermint Branches and the unused grassland next door and dig a gap to give the water a place to run out.

I stand upright and put my hands on my lower back, unsure if I'll ever be able to straighten it out again, and well aware that *everything* is going to hurt tomorrow. I turn around, digging my way back along the trench as I go because it's already full of wet mud, pulled back in by the force of the water.

'I don't think there's much more I can do in here,' Noel says eventually. 'Which might give you a chance to concentrate on what you're doing and take your eyes off me for a second.'

I hate that I can't say something flirty to him like I would have before. Instead, I watch as he throws his spade over the heightened bank and it splashes into the water pooling on the grass. He starts to move, shuffling through the river, the force of the water rushing towards him making it a struggle.

And then he slips and crashes down into the water.

'Noel!' I throw my shovel and rush over, skidding onto my knees right at the uneven edge, nearly going headfirst into the water too.

He's splashing around on his back, trying to get back onto his feet.

'I'm fi—' Another rush of water hits him in the face, making him splutter.

I reach down to him. 'If you don't give me your hand right now, I'm going to kill you.'

He manages to get his feet back under him and struggles

upright, his hands on his knees, bracing himself against the flow of the water. 'That's counterproductive.'

'It's not funny! People drown in floodwater like this. You could've already caught an unthinkable amount of life-threatening diseases.'

'It's melted snow and mud, Lee. What do you think is going to happen to me? I'll start turning into a dirty snowman?'

I ignore his sarcasm. 'Can you climb up the bank now it's like this?'

'No, there's that wee beach by the bridge, I'll go up there.'

'You cannot stay on your feet and walk all the way back there! Give me your hands and I'll pull you out.'

He looks dubiously between me and the bridge. The shallow stone beach where we sat when he showed me around for the first time is around a curve in the river from here and you can barely see a hint of the bridge's railings peering through the rain and mist.

'Don't stand there thinking about it!' I shout at him. '*Now!*'

The bank is steep where he's dug the sides away, a far cry from the gentle slope he helped me up the other day, and I end up lying down in the mud to anchor myself and holding both hands out to him, wet skin slipping on wet skin when he takes them, inching backwards on my belly as he struggles to get purchase with his feet under the water.

Somehow I manage to pull him far enough until he can get his elbows on what's left of the grass and wriggle the rest of the way up until we're both lying in the puddled water, gasping for breath.

He instantly goes to get up, but thinks better of it because he sways before he gets as far as his hands and knees, and he stays in that position, his chest heaving as he pants, his arms shaking from the exertion of the digging and the effort of holding himself up, and probably from the cold too.

I push myself onto my knees and shuffle across until I'm near enough to reach over and brush his dripping hair off his face, unable to *not* touch him, even though nothing's right between us.

'Thank you.' His voice is wrecked and barely above a whisper, but he turns his head into my hand instead of pushing me off like I expected him to, so I keep tucking the same bit of hair back. He's breathing hard, and I want to throw a warm blanket over him and wrap him up. 'You're freezing.'

'I'm fine.'

'No, you're not. Sod the trees, Noel. You're more important. Trees can be replaced – *you* can't. Go home to dry off and get warm. I'll stay here and carry on.'

He yanks his head away from my hand and pushes himself up onto his feet. 'Trying to get rid of me? In case I was in any doubt about how unwanted I am on *your* farm, trying to save *your* trees?'

It stings me, probably just as much as it stung him when I said something similar the other day. 'The opposite, you prat! I bloody love you, Noel, I don't want to see you hurt.'

He looks down at me sitting in the mud and I look up at him and it takes a few seconds for me to realise what I've said and panic. I didn't even realise I felt that way until the words came out, I certainly didn't intend to say it to him. After all this, that's the last thing he was supposed to know and the last thing I was supposed to feel. I decide to carry on from the previous sentence, eschewing that one completely. 'I mean, these trees are my responsibility, not yours.'

He's quiet for a minute before he speaks. 'Sometimes people can help other people out. They can share their problems and their responsibilities because they're neighbours, friends, or . . . more. Not because they want anything out of it.'

'You can't blame me for thinking what I think. *You're* the one who didn't tell *me*. I've been honest since the day I met you – *you* haven't.'

Instead of responding, he walks around pushing at the grass with the toe of his boot, assessing the area. I take it for what it really means – he obviously isn't going to say anything more.

I try to ignore him, to not watch him or think about what

he's doing when he disappears into the trees. I get to my feet, retrieve my shovel, move further along the riverbank and start digging another channel.

'The ground's saturated,' he calls over when he comes back. 'Balsams are tolerant of wet soil, but I don't think the closest ones are going to survive this. The ones further back might be in with a chance if we can stop the river reaching them.'

I look up at the sky, letting the rain batter down on my skin and rinse away some of the mud.

Noel disappears into the trees again, and when he comes back this time, he's hauling a fallen Christmas tree. He drops it and runs back up the track, disappearing from sight and returning minutes later with a bow saw from the barn. I try not to watch as he starts sawing through the trunk of the fallen tree, separating it from the clump of roots and earth at its base. He looks between the ground, the trees, and the river, and seems to make a judgement before he rolls the trunk of the fallen tree into position.

I can't pretend I'm not looking. 'What are you doing?'

His wet hair flies around his shoulders as he turns to look at me like he genuinely didn't realise I was watching. 'Using the casualties to protect the others. These are already lost to the storm. The best thing we can do with them is build them up as a dam to save the rest.'

Once again, I think about how lost I'd be without him. From the moment I arrived until right now. How much of this would I have been able to learn on my own? Even now, after six weeks of absorbing his knowledge, I *still* wouldn't have thought of something like that. There's still a voice in my head saying that if he wants Peppermint Branches for himself, of course he's going to do everything in his power to save the trees, but there's another part, growing by the second, that trusts him.

When he comes back from another run into the Balsam firs, he's got another fallen tree, which he saws at the base and rolls alongside the previous one.

I can tell he's flagging when he goes to get the third one. His shoulders sag and even from this far away, I can see how rapidly his chest is rising and falling, how every time he bends over with his hands on his knees to catch his breath, it takes him longer to get back up.

By the time I've dug the second channel all the way out to the edge of the land and back to where Noel is, I'm knackered. My limbs are shaky from the exertion, my legs are burning, my arms are trembling from the frenzied digging, and my fingers are cramping after being wrapped so tightly around the handle of the shovel for so long. Noel's panting for breath but he doesn't stop working, pushing a third huge tree trunk into a formation between the river and the Balsams.

'I'm sorry,' he says without looking up.

The words hang in the air between us. No emphasis. No explanation. I'm not even certain that he's talking about the auction.

I push my shovel into the ground and lean on it, letting out a huge sigh. 'Why didn't you tell me?'

'Because of this. Because I knew what it would look like. Because I didn't intend to get involved. I certainly didn't intend to fall in love with you.' He sinks to his knees and leans over, his elbows on his thighs, his chest heaving. He looks so shattered he could collapse.

Every part of me is sodden and heavy with rain, but his words make me feel like the sun has just come out. Butterflies in my belly take flight under sunny skies and rainbows.

'You're wrong, you know,' he says. 'About everything you're thinking. I know what it looks like, and I *don't* blame you for thinking it, but it's not that at all.'

The rain is bouncing off his shoulders and all I want to do is wrap myself around him and give him a hug. I force myself to think sensibly and get to the bottom of this while he's talking. 'You've done so much for this place, spent so much time helping me and teaching me. You've let me use your land for the caravan *and* the space on your stall. You've grown trees for me. You've gone out of your way to make sure customers come back this year, and from day one, you've said I don't belong here. Why would you do any of that if you're not planning on being the next buyer? You've made it blazingly obvious that you don't think I'm going to stay.'

'I *thought* that. I don't still think it. You've surprised me every day. You've *impressed* me every day with your fresh ideas and positivity. You've made me feel excited about life again because of how much *you're* excited about this place. I was trying my hardest not to get close to you, because the last time I fell in love with someone . . .' His voice breaks and he stops.

'They took everything they could get out of you and then left?'

He looks away.

'How could you ever think that?' I ask, even though I already know the answer is because of how badly he's been hurt before. 'You're amazing, Noel. I don't know what I would've done without you. You've made me believe in myself. You've made me believe in magic. You've made me laugh when it was the last thing I felt like doing. You've made me feel capable of jumping headfirst into this huge life change and like I wasn't crazy for doing it. And you've made me feel like I'm home.'

'You've made me feel things too, Lee. You've reminded me of what it's like to *feel*, to connect to someone other than a Chihuahua. I was existing in a closed-off box until you got here, and you reminded me of what it's like to have someone to share your life with, to let someone be part of the good times and the bad. I never thought I'd want to let anyone in again, but I didn't have a choice with you. You were under my skin from the moment you walked off with my dog on the first day, and I've been falling for you every moment since then. You think I haven't been aware of this lie between us for every second of every day? I missed the opportunity to tell you when we first met, and it just got worse from there. I knew what it looked like. I knew what you'd think because I'd think exactly the same thing. And I was too head-over-heels to risk what I knew would happen when you found out.'

His words make my legs feel weaker than they do anyway. The urge to throw my arms around him doesn't dissipate, and I kind of hate myself for thinking the worst of him without even giving him a chance to explain. 'Why didn't you buy it yourself?'

'I tried, but Evergreene's son refused to sell it to me. He hated my guts because Evergreene was like a grandfather to me, but their relationship was strained and uncomfortable. He wasn't interested in this place. He ransacked it for valuables and handed it over to the estate agent, but no one wanted it. I remained the only offer, he still refused to sell to me, they got fed up with him, he got fed up with no one falling over themselves to throw money at him, and it ended up going for auction.'

'And you were going to win the bid.'

'I wasn't giving up without a fight. Even though he'd refused my offer, I had every right to bid on the auction, and the winning bid is a legally binding contract. He knew it and I knew it. That's why it took so long for him to give up and send it to auction – because he knew there was a good chance I'd win.'

'Why didn't Evergreene just leave it to you?'

'Because he had more faith in his son than he deserved. He thought that inheriting it would inspire some as-yet-undiscovered sentimental side and bring him back here to become a Christmas tree farmer. All he wanted was for this to stay a family business, for his son to take over from him like he'd taken over from his father and his father from the father before him. I'll always be second best to his real son, but I love this farm as much as he did, and he would've loved you. You've got the relentless enthusiasm a place like this needs. And buying a Christmas tree farm without even seeing it is exactly the sort of thing he'd have done.'

'You're not second best.' I sink down beside him and my knees splash droplets of mud over us both. I slide my hand down the side of his face and lift his head, forcing him to look at me. 'You're knackered, but you'll never be second best.'

He closes his eyes against the relentless rain and lets out a long breath, and I brush his hair back where I'm still holding his head up. 'I'm sorry. I should have told you when I found out and given you a chance to explain. I *knew* you weren't like that, Noel, but I shut down and pushed you away.'

'I should have told you. God, I know I *should* have, but I knew it would make you question my—'

I kiss him. I half-expect him not to respond, but I can't stop myself doing it anyway, and my hands tighten in his hair when he surges up and kisses me back, letting out a moan of desire that echoes how I'm feeling too.

His arms slide around my waist and he overbalances, pulling me down with him until I'm lying on top of him in the mud, our wet clothes dragging against each other's as his lips don't leave mine.

His hair is wet, tangled, muddy, and so is mine as his fingers stroke through it and pull it aside. His lips trail across my jaw and down my neck, his wet skin sliding against mine, my fingers curling into the sodden material of his long-sleeved T-shirt. Everything's wet and slippery and I'm pretty sure we're both covered in more mud than you would generally want from a kiss, but none of it matters, because he's here and he's the best thing that's ever happened to me.

Everything but his kiss has faded away. I've forgotten how cold I am, how wet I am, and how much water is still pooling around us. I haven't forgotten how shaky my limbs are but I'm not sure if that's from the digging or just a side-effect of kissing Noel. I vaguely register the rumble of cars on the road and the slamming of doors, but I don't think anything of it.

'And you tried to tell us there was nothing going on between you.' Fiona clears her throat and Fergus lets out a whoop.

‘See? I told you they were getting jiggy with it!’

I’m not sure whether to be horrified or impressed that a man as far into his seventies as Fergus knows the term ‘getting jiggy with it’ and isn’t afraid to use it in public.

Noel and I scramble apart and get to our feet, and I shout across the river to them. ‘What are you doing here?’

‘Glenna phoned. Said the farm was in trouble and you needed help. We’re the cavalry.’ Fiona glances behind her as Glenna, Iain and the other two farm workers, the baker, the bookseller, and the candle woman appear. ‘The mostly elderly cavalry who aren’t quite sure what they’re doing and need a bit of direction. And tea!’ She starts dispatching people towards the house for tea, coffee, and pumpkin bread duties, but I interrupt.

‘It’s dangerous. The ground is wet and muddy, you might fall.’ I envision these poor old people flailing around on their backs in the sludge, a tangle of limbs unable to get up with broken hips and dislocated shoulders and legs sticking out at all angles.

‘Oh, never mind that nonsense. Have you *seen* those two big, burly farmhands? If you think a bit of rain is going to put me off watching them work, you’ve got another thing coming. Opportunities to *appreciate* men like that don’t come along every day, you know.’

I giggle and the tears that have been threatening finally spill over. Noel drops an arm around my shoulder and tugs me into his side. ‘Why would they do this?’ I turn my face into his wet chest to hide. ‘It’s horrible out here. Why would they voluntarily come out in this?’

‘Because they like you, Lee,’ he says softly in my ear. ‘Because they care about you and this farm and how much work you’ve put into it. You’ve helped all of us at the market – why shouldn’t they help you when you need it too?’

‘Because—’

‘People can be kind without wanting anything in return. Let

them. Just because you were stung once doesn't mean you will be again.'

I slip my arm around his waist and squeeze tight, trying to reflect the same sentiment back at him.

The farm workers come across the bridge and Noel and I explain the situation and what we've done so far. Before I know it, there's a hive of activity all around. The two seasonal lads seem to know exactly what to do, and they start digging another trench to divert the water towards the back of the farm. Iain jumps the fence and starts digging from the empty land on the opposite side to give the water a bigger escape route.

Noel, the bookseller and the baker disappear into the trees and return with yet another casualty while Fergus leans on his walking stick and directs the positioning to build the tightest makeshift flood defence wall possible. Fiona's supervising the digging like she's judging a wet T-shirt competition, and Glenna's at the house with Gizmo, getting the fire roaring and keeping an endless supply of tea, biscuits, and pumpkin muffins coming out.

The rushing of the water is replaced by the chatter of friends and shouts of direction from Fergus, whose skill at building gingerbread houses makes him an expert at building makeshift tree walls.

Glenna puts a hand on my shoulder and pushes a cup of tea into one hand and a pumpkin cupcake into the other, making me jump because I was so lost in thought that I hadn't seen her coming over.

'You didn't have to do that,' I say, meaning both the tea and calling the others.

'Of course I did, flower. I came out to check on things when Noel didn't come back and saw what was happening. If you can't rely on your friends when you're up to your neck in water and struggling, when can you? All I did was give Fergus a quick ring, knowing Iain would know what to do. They did the rest.' The hand on my shoulder squeezes again. 'We help our own round here, Leah. You're one of us now whether you like it or not.'

'Oh, I like it. I like it a lot.' It should be impossible to cry while holding a cupcake, but my eyes sting again and I have to blink furiously to try to hold back the tears.

These new friends who turned up at exactly the moment that Noel and I couldn't do any more on our own, expecting nothing in return. None of them are paying any mind to the rain. They're just getting on with the task at hand.

'I think you're just what Elffield needed, and maybe it's exactly what you needed too.' She looks me directly in the eyes. 'And not just Elffield.'

I follow her pointed gaze towards Noel, who's currently sawing through a tree trunk to fit into the flood defence wall. Like he can sense me watching, he looks up and meets my eyes, and his whole face lights up with a smile.

The kiss that was interrupted is definitely going to be resumed later.

Glenna goes back towards the house, and I pick up my shovel again and start trying to deepen the channels I've already dug. There's so much sodden earth that they're gradually filling with sloppy mud rather than the water, but I can already see the difference it's making. It was too frantic earlier with just me and Noel, but with so many hands on board, it's easy to take a step back and realise that the level of the river is dropping and it isn't as forceful. The surface water has started to drain into the channels, and I lose track of time as we all work together to stop this being quite such a disaster after all.

A couple of hours later, everyone is cold and wet, but full of smiles, Christmas songs and bad cracker jokes that make us all laugh because of how bad they are. Everyone heads back towards the house to dry off in front of the fire, but I grab Noel's hand and hold him back.

'How bad do you think the damage is?'

He makes a face. 'It's impossible to tell at this stage, but I think you've lost a fair few Balsams and some Blue spruces. Judging by how wet the ground is, I'd guess at six or seven hundred trees, maybe more if the rest of it doesn't drain quickly.'

'That's pretty much all the Balsam firs.' There's a pang of dread in my stomach. It's a big chunk out of the six thousand trees that are here, and I'm well aware that stock is likely to be short in the next few years without this blow too.

'We can cut some of the Balsams from the far end and sell them at the market, but that's it. You'll have to close the whole Balsam field this season. You can't let the public wander around with these trenches threaded throughout the field in case someone slips.'

I groan, but I'd already planned on doing it anyway. The ground is too wet and dodgy to let people in.

'There are chains for the gate and "keep out" signs in the barn, and one of your first expenses needs to be getting a flood wall built. It won't be cheap, but it'll stop this ever happening again.'

I groan at that too. More money outgoing, and even less incoming.

'It sounds like a lot, but we can deal with it.' Now we've got a bit of privacy, he presses his lips against mine again. 'I promise. It's just a blip. One of many that we farmers get chucked at us by Mother Nature, but we overcome them as and when they crop up, and sometimes they lead to even greater things that we never expected.'

He waggles both eyebrows and I tangle my hands in his hair and pull him down, losing myself in the heat of his mouth against my cold skin as his piercing presses against my lips in a spine-tingling sexy way, and the shivers running through me have nothing to do with the wet clothes and hammering rain.

I don't even notice that the heavy drops of water have changed to light flakes until I register the iciness settling on my back.

'Snow!' I squeal against his mouth, and when we pull apart, his eyes are dancing with a lightness that was missing earlier.

'Snow is good.' He pulls me closer, wrapping his arms around me and squeezing tight as we stand there, ankle-deep in mud with water still pooling at our feet and gentle snowflakes landing on us. 'It'll freeze the ground and give the river a chance to drain, and it'll be amazing for people walking around. You're still opening on Saturday.'

'Even after this?'

'Even more so after this. We need to assess the storm damage and clear up any trees that have fallen before then, and grit the paths on Saturday morning, but you can't let this change anything. It's not great, but it could've been so much worse.'

The snowflakes come down thicker as we walk back hand in hand. It's already starting to settle and the ground starts to crunch underneath our feet before we've reached the house. The outside world is covered in a blanket of white again and the wind has eased from the howling gale of earlier, making perfect white snowflakes dance around us. Nothing has ever felt more magical than standing on this perfect farm, in this perfect place, with this beautiful man, surrounded by beautiful Christmas trees, with new friends and a community that I never thought I'd be part of, and I'm happier than I've ever been.

Chapter 17

I follow the track on foot, walking behind a family with three children excitedly carrying their chosen Christmas tree that I've just cut down. It's Saturday morning, the last day of November, and the farm is buzzing with people on opening day. The sun is bright in the sky after the storms of the week, and I'm surrounded by the sound of dripping as the snow starts to melt from branches all around me. The elf hats are pinned to intermittent Christmas trees, glittery footprints are spread between the trunks, and the silver bells hanging in the branches jingle with every wisp of the gentle breeze. I swing the saw by my legs as I walk, humming along to the strains of Frank Sinatra's version of 'Little Drummer Boy', which is playing from a speaker on the roof of the caravan. The track around the farm is frozen earth, surrounded by the snow that has settled again, and all around me are the excited screams and laughter of children as they dash around, playing hide and seek behind the Norway spruces, and their squeals of disappointment as the crunch of their shoes in the snow gives away their hiding places too easily, interspersed with the good-natured arguments of families who disagree on which type of tree to get and how high their living room ceiling is.

When we get back to the wide open driveway, the family drink hot chocolates and watch as I run their tree through the netting machine. I take it to their car, parked on the verge halfway along the main road because there are so many cars here that they couldn't get any closer. A huge thrill goes through me as they hand over the money and thank me profusely, promising to be back next year.

Noel's serving hot chocolates in the caravan and he leans forward and beckons me over when I get back. I stand up on tiptoes so I can hear him.

'Congratulations. That was your first sale on your own little Christmas tree farm. You're now officially a Christmas tree farmer.' He leans out of the window and presses his lips to my cheek, taking advantage of the brief lull between customers. The hot chocolate stand was definitely a good idea. But then again, when *isn't* hot chocolate a good idea?

Fiona and Fergus are chatting to customers, and Glenna and Gizmo are organising the queue to Santa's sleigh, although Gizmo is arguably more popular than Santa himself. It's the little elf outfit that does it – the stripy red and green jumper with fluffy white edges, complete with a tiny jingly hat, his own pointy ears sticking out through holes in the top, the hat moving every time his ears stand to attention. And while Noel's pouring hot chocolates, he keeps whistling the tune from *Gremlins* to get his attention, delighting everyone nearby as Gizmo cocks his head from one side to the other every time he hears it. He'll be viral before tonight given the amount of videos people have taken of him.

Iain and the two farmhands are spread out around the fields somewhere, cutting trees down and carrying them for customers. I stand in the driveway which is now lined with piles of netted trees and trees in pots arranged in size order from my tiny little thirty-centimetre tall ones to much larger six-foot ones. Some are flashing with fairylights and sparkling with tinsel for decorative purposes, but most are potted up for sale, and I'm watching the supply diminish fast. It's going to be hard work after everybody leaves tonight to restock the ready-to-buy ones for tomorrow. There are wreaths hung up along the fences, and bunches of freshly cut mistletoe tied with ribbon dangling all around, and Noel's made the most beautiful chalkboard signs and put them up at the junctions of the road on either end, and people just keep coming.

'Well, this is a bit better than the ugly plastic thing in our loft,' says a voice behind me.

'Chelsea!' I jump on her and Lewis catches us both. 'I thought you weren't coming unless it magically turned into a vineyard on the French Riviera.'

'Couldn't let my best friend's opening day go unnoticed, could I?' She hugs me back. 'You can still send me a little one to test its survival in the post, but we're not leaving without your finest Christmas tree. Lewis has even put the roof-rack on the car for it.' She pulls away and holds me at arm's length. 'Why do you look so different? Your skin's all glowing and you look so healthy and fit.'

'Lugging Christmas trees around will do that to you.'

'Or the healthy glow of love.' She scouts around for my hot Scot pumpkin farmer, and I catch Noel's eyes and beckon him over.

Fiona takes over making hot chocolates and manning the chestnut roaster, and Noel comes over carrying a cardboard tray of four hot chocolates for us.

'Oh my god, is this him?' Chelsea says loudly, fanning a hand in front of her face. 'You said Luke Evans, you didn't say *Dracula Untold*-style flaming gorgeous Luke Evans multiplied by a thousand degrees of hotness.' She turns to him before I can even introduce them all properly. 'Please say murder.'

Noel laughs enough to cover his blush and obliges, deliberately elongating the Rs, and Chelsea makes him teach Lewis how to say it properly.

'It's beautiful up here.' She sips her hot chocolate as she looks around. 'I'd be disappointed if it was a vineyard on the French Riviera now. This is much better.'

If that's not a cracking endorsement, I don't know what is.

'And now you know it must be special because no one's *ever* heard me saying I prefer *anything* over wine before.'

I hug her again before she and Lewis go off to wander around and meet Gizmo, Glenna, and everyone else.

Noel wraps his arms around me from behind, pulls me against his chest and we stand there watching the comings and goings of customers and Christmas trees.

'They'd be proud,' he whispers in my ear.

I know who he's talking about without him saying it. And for the first time since they died, I think they would. I can imagine Mum here, serving hot chocolate and dishing up roasted chestnuts from the oven, and Dad would be in his element stomping around amongst the Christmas trees, talking the ears off of anyone who'd listen about the pros and cons of different species. I never thought losing them would lead to something positive, but I *know* that this is what they'd have wanted in their absence.

Noel squeezes me as tight as he can without jogging the cups in both our hands, and I lean back and reach up to kiss his cheek.

'Thank you,' I whisper against his skin, warmed by the sun despite the chill in the air.

'Thank *you*, beautiful,' he murmurs back. 'You've changed my life too.'

He suddenly stops and turns us sharply towards the caravan, or more specifically, towards the two pensioners lurking at the edge of it. 'I *told* you we'd catch them snogging behind the bike sheds one day.'

Glenna's taken over from Fiona on the food and drink in the caravan, and Fergus has given up trying to foist mince pies onto unsuspecting customers when our backs are turned – and the two of them have stopped for a tea break, except there's not much drinking-of-tea going on, but there is quite a bit of kissing.

I turn into his chest to muffle the squeal and he's almost bouncing up and down with joy.

'It's taken them long enough,' he whispers.

'I know you put that mistletoe there. Actually, I *know* you made a huge show of putting it up this morning when you knew Fergus and Fiona were watching because I wondered what you were up to. And now I see.'

'All right, so I meddled a bit, but look at how happy they are. They've been in love for years, but the magic of Peppermint Branches is what's finally inspired them to take that final step. I keep telling you, there's something about this place.'

I watch as Fiona twirls a lock of her lilac hair and Fergus giggles like a child, both of them looking decades younger than their years. Maybe he's got a point. Everything does feel just that little bit special here.

Gizmo's obviously getting under Glenna's feet in the caravan because she appears in the doorway and sends him over to us, and he comes trotting across, his tail wagging as his lead trails behind him.

I bend down to pick him up and he greets me with a licky kiss as 'Oh, Christmas Tree' starts playing on the radio.

'That's pretty fitting, isn't it?' Noel's voice is low in my ear when I stand back up. One of his hands leaves my waist and slides upwards so he can stroke Gizmo as well and he squeezes the both of us tighter.

It really is. I snuggle back against him and hold the little dog tighter against my chest.

Nothing has ever been more perfect than this moment, and I can't wait for what the year ahead is going to bring because, whenever we're together, it's easy to believe in the magic of Christmas again.

Acknowledgements

Mum, this line is always the same because you're always there for me. Thank you for the constant patience, support, encouragement, and for always believing in me. I don't know what I'd do without you. Love you lots!

Bill, Toby, Cathie – thank you for always being supportive and enthusiastic!

An extra special thank you to Bev for always asking about my writing, and being so caring, kind, encouraging, and for so many lovely letters!

Special thanks to three talented authors, great friends, and supportive cheerleaders – Marie Landry, Charlotte McFall, and Elizabeth Clark, and an extra special thank you to Marie for a million inspirational gifs of Luke Evans!

The lovely and talented fellow HQ authors – I don't know what I'd do without all of you!

All the lovely authors and bloggers I know on Twitter. You've all been so supportive since the very first book, and I want to mention you all by name, but I know I'll forget someone and I don't want to leave anyone out, so to everyone I chat to on Twitter or Facebook – thank you.

The little writing group that doesn't have a name – Sharon Sant,

Sharon Atkinson, Dan Thompson, Jack Croxall, Holly Martin, Jane Yates. I can always turn to you guys!

Thank you to the team at HQ and especially my fabulous editor, Charlotte Mursell, for all the hard work and support, and for always knowing exactly how to make each book better!

And finally, a massive thank you to *you* for reading!

A Letter from the Author

Dear Reader,

Thank you so much for reading *Snowflakes at the Little Christmas Tree Farm*. I hope you loved reading about Leah and Noel, and their pumpkin and Christmas tree adventures as much as I loved writing about them, and enjoyed a festive trip around Elffield like I did!

This story came about when I saw a Christmas tree farm for sale – instant daydream! I couldn't make the move myself, but the beauty of being a writer is being able to explore the 'what ifs' of lives we'll never get to lead, and the characters of Leah and her grumpy, gorgeous new neighbour instantly popped into my head! I definitely enjoyed getting to know Noel and his crazy hair, and I think I've given myself a bit of a thing for Scottish men with lip piercings! I'd definitely like to own a Christmas tree farm in real life too!

One thing I didn't expect when I started writing this book was that Gizmo the Chihuahua would turn into a tribute to my own darling little Chihuahua, Bruiser, who died in February. It was therapeutic to write some of Bruiser's quirky characteristics into a fictional version, and I hope Gizmo made you smile as much as his real-life counterpart always made me smile!

If you enjoyed this story, please consider leaving a review on Amazon. It only has to be a line or two, and it makes such a difference to helping other readers decide whether to pick up the book or not, and it would mean so much to me to know what you think! Did it make you smile, laugh, or cry? Would you like a neighbour like Noel? Would you give one of Fergus's mince pies a try?!

Thank you again for reading. If you want to get in touch, you can find me on Twitter – usually when I should be writing – @be_the_spark. I would love to hear from you!

Hope to see you again soon in a future book!

Lots of love,
Jaimie

Turn the page for an exclusive extract from another enchanting novel from Jaimie Admans, *The Little Vintage Carousel by the Sea . . .*

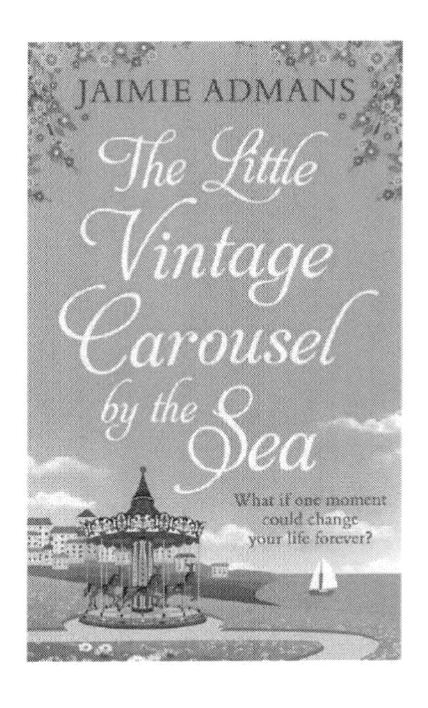

Chapter 1

Why does every man in London think that eight o'clock on a warm June morning is the ideal time to remove their shirt and get on the tube? I consider this as I peel myself away from a sweaty back and turn around to find myself face to face with someone's wet armpit. There's often a good time for shirtlessness, but the middle of rush hour on a crowded train is not it.

I sigh and stare at my feet. Every morning I get on this train and get off feeling like a floppy sardine that's just been let out of a tin and probably smelling worse. All to go to the soulless office block of the women's magazine where I work as a fact-checker, and then do the exact same thing at half past five with all the other sweaty, irritable commuters who would really love nothing more than to poke their boss in the eye and run away to a beach somewhere.

Someone stands on my toe and a handbag hits me in the thigh as someone else swings it over their arm. Ow. Only four more days to go until the weekend, and then I can have two whole days of not having to leave the flat and face the crowds of London. Two whole days of uninterrupted Netflix, apart from when Mum calls to update me on my ex-boyfriend's latest news, which she knows because they're still online friends even though I deleted him over two years ago.

I jump back as a briefcase threatens to take out my kneecaps. There's got to be more to life than this.

I look up and my eyes lock on to a man near me. Train Man is going somewhere today. Usually he only has a backpack with him, but today there's a huge suitcase leaning against his leg, rucksack straps over both shoulders, and a holdall bag hooked over one arm. He's standing up and holding on to a rail like I am, his attention on the phone in his hand, the lines around his eyes crinkled up as he looks down at it, and the sight of him makes something flutter inside me.

I see him quite often, but he's always already on the train when I get on, and we're usually much further apart. Up close, he's even more gorgeous than I'd always thought he was. He's got short brown hair, dimples denting his cheeks, and the kind of smile that makes you look twice, which I know because he's one of the rare London commuters who smiles at others.

The noisy tube train full of other people's body parts in places you don't want other people's body parts, the noise of people sniffing and coughing, an endless medley of beeps as people play with their phones, snippets of conversation that aren't meant for me . . . they all fade into the background and the world turns into slow motion as he lifts his head, almost like he can feel my eyes on him, and looks directly at me. If it was anyone else, I'd look away instantly. Staring at strangers on the tube is a quick way to get yourself punched or worse, but it's like a magnet is holding me, drawing my gaze to his, and his mouth curves up a tiny bit at each side, making it as impossible to look away now as it is every other time he smiles at me.

I feel that familiar nervous fluttering in the deepest part of my belly. It's not butterflies. My stomach must have disagreed with the cereal I shoved down my throat before rushing out of the flat this morning. Even though it's the same fluttery feeling I get every time I see him and he sees me. Maybe it's because I'm never usually this close to him. Maybe those dimples have magical powers at this distance. Maybe I'm just getting dizzy from looking up at him because I'm so short and he's the tallest person on the train, towering above every other passenger around us.

His smile grows as he looks at me, and I feel myself smiling back, unable not to return his wide and warm smile, the kind of smile you don't usually see from fellow commuters on public transport. Open. Inviting. His gaze is still holding mine, his smile making his dimples deepen, and the fluttery feeling intensifies.

I feel like I could lean across the carriage and say hello to him, start a conversation, ask him where he's off to. Although that might imply that I've studied him hard enough on previous journeys to work out that he doesn't usually have that much luggage. And talking to him would be ridiculous. I can't remember the last time I said hello to a stranger. It's considered weird here, not like in the little country village where I grew up. People just don't do that here.

He's wearing jeans and a black T-shirt, and he tilts his head almost like he's trying to hold my gaze, and I wonder why. Does he know that I spend most journeys trying to work out what he does, because there's no regularity to his routine? I'm on this train at eight o'clock every morning Monday to Friday, I look like I'm going into an office, but he's always in jeans and a T-shirt, a jacket in the winter, and sometimes he's on this train a couple of times a week, sometimes once a week, and other times weeks can pass without me seeing him. I don't even know why I notice him so much. Is it because he smiles when our eyes meet? Maybe it's because he's so tall that you can't help but notice him, or because London is such a big and crowded place that you rarely see the same faces more than once.

His dark eyes still haven't left mine, and he pushes himself off the rail he's leaning against, and for a split second I think he's going to make the move and talk to me, and I feel like I've just stepped into a scene from one of my best friend Daphne's favourite romcom movies. The leading couple's eyes meet across a crowded train carriage and—

'The next station is King's Cross St. Pancras.' An automated voice comes over the tannoy, making me jump because everything but his eyes has faded into the background.

I see him swear under his breath and a look of panic crosses his face. He checks his phone again, turns around and gathers up his suitcase, hoists the holdall bag higher up his arm, and readjusts the rucksack on his shoulders.

I feel ridiculously bereft at the loss of eye contact as the train slows, but I get swept along by the crowd as other people gather up their bags and make a mass exodus towards the doors. He glances back like he's looking for me again, but I'm easy to miss amongst tall people and I've moved from where I was with the crowd. He looks around like he's trying to locate me, and I want to call out or wave or something, but what am I supposed to say? 'Hello, gorgeous Train Man, the strange short girl who's spent the entire journey staring at you is still here staring at you?'

I'm not far behind him now, even though this isn't my stop and it's clearly his. I can see him in the throng of people, his hand wrapped around the handle of the huge wheeled suitcase he's pulling behind him as the train comes to a stop.

As if the world turns to slow motion again, I see him glance at his phone once more and then go to pocket it, but instead of pushing it into the pocket of his jeans, it slides straight past and lands on the carriage floor at the exact moment the doors open and he, along with everyone else, rushes through them.

He hasn't noticed.

Without thinking, I dart forward and grab the phone from the floor before someone treads on it. I stare at it for a moment. This is his phone and I have it. He doesn't know he dropped it. There's still time to catch up with him and give it back.

Zinnia will probably kill me for being late for work, and I'm still a few stops away from where I usually get off, but I don't have time to wait. I follow the swarm as seemingly every other person in our carriage floods out, and I pause in the middle of them, aware of the annoyed grunts of people pushing past me as I try to see where he is. I follow the crowd off the platform and up the steps, straining to see over people's heads and between shoulders.

I'm sure I see his hair in the distance as the crowd starts to thin out, but he's moving faster than a jet-powered Usain Bolt after an energy drink.

'Hey!' I shout. 'Wait up!'

He doesn't react. He wouldn't know who I was calling to, if the guy I'm following is even him.

'Hey! You dropped your—'

Another passenger glares at me for shouting in his ear and I stop myself. I'm already out of breath and Train Man is nothing more than a blur in the distance. I rush in the same direction, but those steps have knackered me, and the faraway blob that might still be the back of his head turns a corner under the sign towards the overground trains, and I lose sight of him.

I race . . . well, limp . . . to the corner where I saw him turn, but the station fans out into an array of escalators and glowing signs and ticket booths, and it's thronging with people. I walk around for a few minutes, looking for any hint of him, but he's nowhere to be seen. In the many minutes it's taken me to half-jog half-stumble from one end of the station to the other, he could be on another train halfway across London by now.

I pull my own phone out and glance at the time. I'm twenty minutes late for work, and still three tube stops and a ten-minute walk away. Zinnia is going to love me this morning. I put my phone back in my pocket and slide his in alongside it.

I'll have to find another way to get it back to him.

I could just hand it in at the desk in the station, but he'll probably never see it again if I do that. If I dropped my phone, I'd like to think that a stranger would be kind enough to pick it up and attempt to reunite it with me, rather than just steal it. Why shouldn't I do that for Train Man?

There's something about him, there has been since the first

time I saw him standing squashed against the door of a crowded train, right back in my first week at Maîtresse magazine. I know Daphne's going to say that this is the universe's way of saying I'm supposed to meet him after all the smiles we've exchanged, although she regularly says that when she's trying to set me up on dates, if she's not too busy reminding me of how long it's been since my last date.

But it doesn't mean anything. He isn't even going to know that I'm the girl he smiles at sometimes. I'm sure I can just get an address and pop the phone in the post to him.

Simple as that. It won't be a problem.

Dear Reader,

Thank you so much for taking the time to read this book – we hope you enjoyed it! If you did, we'd be so appreciative if you left a review.

Here at HQ Digital we are dedicated to publishing fiction that will keep you turning the pages into the early hours. We publish a variety of genres, from heartwarming romance, to thrilling crime and sweeping historical fiction.

To find out more about our books, enter competitions and discover exclusive content, please join our community of readers by following us at:

facebook.com/HQDigitalUK

Are you a budding writer? We're also looking for authors to join the HQ Digital family! Please submit your manuscript to:

HQDigital@harpercollins.co.uk.

Hope to hear from you soon!

If you enjoyed *Snowflakes at the Little Christmas Tree Farm*, then why not try another delightfully uplifting festive romance from HQ Digital?

Made in United States
Orlando, FL
30 March 2022

16302182R00193